HOLOCAUST
SPEAKS TO THE HEART

Holocaust is a novel of consuming passions. Of hatred, and love, too. It is the incredible story of how six million innocent human beings perished from the face of the earth. And how some few—with courage, dignity and the will to live—survived.

Holocaust is a saga of fire and blood and years of sadness beyond tears. If you believe in humankind, this novel will restore your faith, despite its chronicle of monstrous deeds unparalleled.

Holocaust is a mesmerizing novel about an event none of us should ever forget, lest it happen again.

D0034257

AN NBC-TV BIG EVENT

TITUS PRODUCTIONS

Presents

JOSEPH BOTTOMS	TOVAH FELDSHUH
ROSEMARY HARRIS	IAN HOLM
MICHAEL MORIARTY	GEORGE ROSE
ROBERT STEVENS	MERYL STREEP
SAM WANAMAKER	DAVID WARNER
FRITZ WEAVER	JAMES WOODS

In

HOLOCAUST

Teleplay by
GERALD GREEN

Directed by
MARVIN CHOMSKY

Produced by
HERBERT BRODKIN and ROBERT BERGER

HOLOCAUST

Gerald Green

BANTAM BOOKS · TORONTO · NEW YORK · LONDON

HOLOCAUST
A Bantam Book | April 1978

ISBN 0-553-11877-3

Published simultaneously in the United States and Canada

Bantam Books are published by Bantam Books, Inc. Its trade-
mark, consisting of the words "Bantam Books" and the por-
trayal of a bantam, is registered in the United States Patent
Office and in other countries. Marca Registrada. Bantam
Books, Inc., 666 Fifth Avenue, New York, New York 10019.

PRINTED IN THE UNITED STATES OF AMERICA

To the Memory of
The Six Million, the Survivors, and Those who
Fought Back.

Prologue

Below our tiny house, on the soccer field, my sons, Ari and Hanan, are kicking a ball. They aren't bad, especially Hanan, who is five. Ari is a year younger, thinner, shyer. He doesn't seem to like the body contact as much.

I'll have to work with them. Teach them the moves, how to pass off, to feint, how to "head" the ball.

Watching them, I'm reminded of the way my brother Karl and I used to play in the little park opposite our home in Berlin. Our home was also my father's medical office. Sometimes my father's patients would stop under the shade trees and watch us.

I can still hear their voices—maybe Mr. Lowy, who was his patient for as long as I can remember— talking about us. *Dr. Weiss' kids. See the little guy? Rudi Weiss? He'll be a professional someday.*

Karl was three years older than I. Thin, quiet, never an athlete. He'd get tired. Or he'd want to finish a painting or read. I guess we both disappointed our father, Dr. Josef Weiss. But he was a gentle and thoughtful man. And he loved us too much to ever let us know.

All ended. All over. Karl and my parents and all of my family died in what is now called the *holocaust*. A fancy name for mass murder. I survived. And today, seated in this cinderblock bungalow above the Galilee —I see its dark-blue waters in the distance beyond the fields and peach orchards—I finish this chronicle of

1

the family Weiss. In some ways, it is a chronicle of what happened to millions of the Jews of Europe— the six million victims, the handful who survived, those who fought back.

My wife, Tamar, an Israel-born sabra, helped me prepare this document. She is far better educated than I am. I barely finished high school in Berlin, being too busy playing soccer, or tennis, or roaming the streets with my friends.

Tamar attended the University of Michigan in the United States. She is a child psychologist and is fluent in five languages. I still have difficulty with Hebrew. But I am no longer a European. Israel is my country. I fought for her liberty in 1947, and I will fight again, and again, and whenever I am asked to. In my days as a partisan in the Ukraine, I learned that it is better to die with a gun in one's hand than to submit to the murderer. I have taught this to Ari and Hanan, and, young as they are, they understand. Why should they not? Several times a week Syrian artillery from across the Jordan drops shells on Kibbutz Agam, or on some of our neighbors. Fifty meters from our little house there is an underground shelter, complete with beds, water, food, toilets. At least once a month the bombardments become sufficiently strong so that we must spend the night there.

My sons, Tamar and I sometimes watch our soldiers moving our own guns across the dusty roads below, to pay the Syrians in kind. More than once, my own unit has been called up to assist in "neutralizing" the enemy artillery. I find no pleasure in these duties, but I do them willingly. Nor am I overjoyed at the necessity of teaching small children, infants, about the need to battle for one's life. But I have learned a great deal about survival and I would be less than a good father if I did not impart this knowledge to them early. Already they know not to yield, not to bow one's head.

The information I collected for this narrative about my family came from many sources. Twice during my summer vacations I visited Europe. (I'm employed as athletic director at the local high school, and like all members of the Agam community I am required to turn my entire salary over to the kibbutz; however, special grants of funds are sometimes made, and Tamar's parents helped me.) I corresponded with many people who knew my parents, my brother Karl, and my Uncle Moses. I have met scores of survivors of the camps here in Israel, people from the Warsaw ghetto. Tamar assisted me in translating most of the material, and with much of the writing.

A major source for information on my brother Karl came from his widow, a Christian woman named Inga Helms Weiss, who is now living in England.

Approximately a year ago, hearing about my search for the story of my family, a man named Kurt Dorf wrote to me. He was a German civilian engineer attached to the German army, and he had been a prominent witness for the prosecution at the Nuremberg trials. He had located the diaries of his nephew, an SS officer named Erik Dorf. Kurt Dorf was kind enough to send me a copy of his nephew's lengthy, detailed account. These diaries are of a fragmented and desultory nature. Oftentimes, Erik Dorf did not even date his entries, but fortunately he did mention enough places and dates in his rambling account so that I have been able to determine at least the month for each entry. There is a gap between the years 1935 and 1938. The material from this period has apparently been lost or destroyed.

I have interspersed sections of these diaries with the account of my family's destruction. It seems to me (and Tamar) that the motives of the murderers are of as great importance to us as the fate of the victims.

I never knew Major Erik Dorf, but in one of those crazy coincidences with which those dreadful years are filled, he and his wife had at one time been *my father's patients* in Berlin. Three years after my father had taken care of him and his family, this same Erik Dorf was signing orders and establishing procedures that would lead to the murder of Karl, my parents, my Uncle Moses—and six million other innocents.

It seems unbelievable that it is only seven years since

the nightmare ended, since we were delivered from the murky hell of Nazi Europe. Tamar says that actually we are never delivered from this tragedy. Our children, and our children's children, must be told about it. And so must the children of the world.

Forgive, Ben-Gurion once said, *but never forget.* I am not quite ready for forgiveness. Perhaps I never will be.

I

THE
FAMILY
WEISS

Rudi Weiss' Story

On August 8, 1935, my older brother Karl and a Catholic girl named Inga Helms were married. They were both twenty-one years old.

Clearly, I remember the hot summer sun over Berlin. Not a breeze stirred the leaves of the poplars and oaks in the beautiful garden of the Golden Hart restaurant. The restaurant was famous for its outdoor dining—white trellises heavy with grape vines, statues, fountains, and a thick lawn. Our wedding party had been given a private area, between high dark-green hedges.

I was then seventeen. My sister Anna was thirteen, the baby of the family. Vaguely, I recall her teasing me, and my chasing her, almost pushing her into the fountain. We came back to the long linen-covered table, with its bowls of fruit, champagne and ice cream, and with the wedding cake, and we were mildly reprimanded by my mother.

"A little decorum, children," she said. "Rudi, your tie? What did you do with it?"

"It's too hot, Mama."

"Please put it on. This is a formal occasion."

Of course I did, if a bit unwillingly. My mother had a commanding manner. She always got us to obey. When we were little, she sometimes spanked us. My father, on the other hand, Dr. Josef Weiss, was so gentle, easygoing, and preoccupied with his patients that he never, as far as I can recall, criticized us or bawled us out, let alone struck us.

There was an accordionist present, and I remember him playing Strauss waltzes, lively airs from *Rosenkavalier* and *Fledermaus*. But no one was dancing and I knew why.

7

We were Jews, already a marked people. Thousands of Jews had already left Germany, their businesses and properties stolen by the Nazis. There had been outbreaks of beatings on the street, humiliations, demonstrations. But we had stayed on. My mother always insisted that Hitler was "another politician," an upstart who would be put in his place soon enough. She was certain that things would get better. Her family had been in the country for centuries, and she felt more German than any flag-waving bully in the street.

Still, the uneasiness at the wedding table was for more reasons than our Jewishness. The two families, the Helmses and the Weisses, really did not know each other. The Helmses were rather plain people. Inga's father was a machinist, a flat-faced shy man. Not a bad sort, I suppose. His wife was a modest woman, rather pretty, in the same way Inga was—long-faced, blond, with clear blue eyes. Inga had a younger brother, who was about my age. His name was Hans Helms, and I knew him from soccer games. He was one of those athletes who puts up a great show when he's winning, but folds when he's pressed. We'd played opposite each other a few times, and I'd gotten the best of him. When I mentioned the games, he claimed he didn't recall them. He was a private in the German army and was wearing his uniform that day.

Inga suddenly kissed my brother on the lips—perhaps to break the dull silence around the table. My brother looked embarrassed. Karl was thin, tall, a dark young man with thoughtful eyes. He had met Inga at the Academy of Commercial Art. She was the secretary to the director of the school, Karl a prize student.

My mother felt Karl was marrying beneath him. The humble working-class family seated opposite us confirmed her views that hot August day.

But Berta Weiss did not reckon with Inga's unbreakable will. (My mother's was fairly strong, but Karl's love for Inga would not bend to it.) And they were truly, deeply in love. I think Karl saw in Inga strength, determination, a vigorous and vivacious girl, the kind of woman he needed. He was a worrying, pessimistic man, not at all like Anna and me.

"Kiss me once more," Inga said.

"I'm not used to it yet . . . in public," Karl said.

She seized him, kissed him, brushing back her veil. She was lovely in her lace and silk gown, the little crown of daisies on her head.

Anna and I began to applaud. I whistled through two fingers. This seemed to relax the Helms family. They smiled hesitantly. Hans Helms winked at me—man to man.

On our side of the table were my parents, my father's younger brother Moses, who had come from Warsaw for the wedding, and my mother's parents, my grandparents, Mr. and Mrs. Max Palitz. My grandfather was quite a man—white-haired, stiff-backed, decorated by the Kaiser for heroism in the war of 1914–1918. He ran a bookshop. He always said that he had no fear of the Nazis, that Germany was his country, too.

My mother was by far the most elegant person at the wedding party—slender, in a light-blue gown, white gloves, a big white hat. She touched my father's arm.

"Josef," my mother said. "It's traditional for the father to make a toast."

"Oh yes . . . of course."

Papa got to his feet slowly. His mind seemed elsewhere, as if he were worried about a patient's loss of weight, a hospital case, a woman who had died of cancer weeks ago. His practice had been reduced to the ill and the poor, Jews only, the ones who had not had the money or foresight to leave. He treated all of them with the same consideration he would have shown a Rothschild.

My father held up his champagne glass. People rose. Anna nudged me. "I'm going to get drunk, Rudi. The first time."

"You'll get sick first," I said.

"Children," my mother said softly. "Papa is about to make a toast."

"Yes, yes," my father said. "To the happy couple.

My new daughter, Inga Helms Weiss, and my son Karl. May God grant them long life and happiness."

I tried to lead a cheer, but the Helms family still didn't seem very cheerful. The accordionist struck up another tune. More champagne was poured. Inga forced Karl to kiss her again—lips apart, their eyes shut in passion.

My father toasted our new in-laws. Then he introduced my mother's parents, the Palitzes, greeted the Helms family by name, and introduced my Uncle Moses.

"Enough introductions, Josef, and more champagne," my grandfather said. "You make it sound like a medical lecture."

A few people laughed.

There was a burly man seated next to Mr. Helms who did not smile. I saw under his lapel a *hakenkreuz* pin—what the English and Americans call a swastika. His name was Heinz Muller, and he worked in the factory with Mr. Helms. And when my Uncle Moses, a shy, plain man, had been introduced, I heard this Muller whisper to Inga's father, "Hear that, Helms? *Moses*."

I made believe I was arguing with Anna and kept an ear tuned to what this fellow was saying. He asked Hans, "Anyone try to talk your sister out of this?"

"Sure," Hans Helms said. "But you know how she is when she makes her mind up about something."

Brother knew sister. Inga had set her sights on Karl, and now she had him. She had overcome the opposition of her own family and of my family, and the atmosphere of the times, and she had married Karl, in a civil wedding so as to offend no one's sensibilities. For all her strength, I sensed a tenderness and compassion in her. She was, for example, very close to Anna and me, interested in our schoolwork, our hobbies. She had begun to teach Anna needlepoint work; had watched me play soccer. And she treated my parents with the utmost respect. (My mother kept her at a distance, I might add, and continued to do so for a few years.)

It was now Mr. Helms' turn to propose toasts. He

got to his feet, a stubby man in a shapeless suit, and offered praise to all, ending with a tribute to his son
Hans, in the service of "the glorious Fatherland."

This intrigued my grandfather, Mr. Palitz, whose
eyes lit up. He smiled at Hans. "What branch, son?"

"Infantry."

"I was infantry myself. Captain in the Second
Machine-gun Regiment. Iron Cross, First Class." He
fingered the boutonnière he always wore. It was as if
he were saying to all of them, "Please notice. I am a
Jew, and a good German. and as patriotic as anyone
here."

I heard Muller mutter to Hans, "Wouldn't be allowed to clean an army latrine today."

Grandpa didn't hear him, but there was a moment
of strain. Inga suggested we dance to *Tales from the
Vienna Woods*. People got up to waltz.

Anna tugged at my elbow. "Come on, Rudi, dance."

"I can't stand your perfume."

"I don't use any. I am naturally sweet."

She stuck her tongue out at me, and turned to Uncle Moses. I'd gotten up to stretch, and I could hear
my father talking to his brother.

"I know what you're thinking, Moses," my father
was saying apologetically. "No religious ceremony. No
breaking of the glass. Don't think ill of us. The boys
were bar-mitzvah'd. Berta and I still attend synagogue
on the holidays."

"Josef, you need not apologize to me."

Anna was persistent. "Uncle Moses! Dance with me!"
She dragged him to the lawn under the summer trees. I
can remember the way the sunlight and the shade
formed checkered patterns on the dancers.

"Are you happy?" my father asked my mother.

"If Karl is happy, I am."

"You haven't answered me."

"I gave you as good an answer as I can."

"They are fine people," my father said. "And Karl
loves her so much. She'll be good for him. A strong
woman."

"So I have noticed, Josef."

I made believe I was a bit tipsy, wandered around the table, and caught scraps of conversation. Muller was holding forth again, talking in a low voice with Mr. Helms, Hans and some of their relatives.

"Too bad you couldn't have made Inga wait a few months," Muller was saying. "The party bigshots tell me new laws are in the works. No mixed marriages. Might have saved you a lot of heartache."

"Oh, they aren't like the *others*," Mr. Helms said. "You know . . . physician . . . old man a war hero . . ."

Suddenly Hans Helms was seized with a fit of coughing. He'd been smoking a cigar and he seemed to be strangling on it.

My father, who was waltzing with my mother, left her and came running to Hans. Quickly, he forced Hans to swallow a cup of tea. Amazingly, the seizure stopped.

"An old remedy," my father said. "Tea counteracts the nicotine. Something I learned when I was a medical student."

The Helms party looked at my father curiously. I could almost read their minds. *Jew. Doctor. Intelligent. Polite.*

"Exactly what kind of a doctor are you, Dr. Weiss?" Muller asked arrogantly.

"A good one," I shouted. I wanted to add, "None of your damned business."

"Rudi!" my mother said. "Manners!"

"I'm in general practice," my father replied. "A small private clinic on Groningstrasse."

Hans collapsed into a chair. His eyes were tearing, his collar open. His mother was patting his blond head. "Poor Hans. I hope they treat him well in the army."

My father tried a little joke. "If they don't, you have a physician in the family now. I make night calls, also."

Inga and Karl kept dancing, floating, joyful. So did a few other couples. My grandfather sat down opposite young Helms.

"Guess it's changed since my day," Grandpa Palitz said.

"I guess so," Hans said. "Were you in combat?"

"Combat? How did you think I got my Iron Cross?

Verdun, Chemins des Dames, Metz. I went through it all."

Mrs. Helms looked uneasy. "Let's pray there are no more wars."

"I'll drink to that, madame," my grandfather said.

Muller sat down next to Hans. There was a vague smile on his face as he studied my grandfather's white head.

"Understand your son-in-law was born in Warsaw," he said suddenly. "Still technically a Polish citizen."

"What of it?"

"Just wondering where your family loyalties are, considering the international situation."

"I don't give a damn about politics," Grandpa Palitz said.

My mother, overhearing him as she danced, came back to the table. The music stopped for a moment. Inga and Karl and my father also gathered around.

"We don't discuss politics," my mother said firmly. "My husband considers himself as German as I do. He went to medical school here and he's practiced here."

"No offense, madame," Muller said. Again, that flat, cold smile widened his mouth. It was a smile I was to encounter in so many of them over the years. Look at the photos of the end of the Warsaw ghetto. And you will see this smile on the faces of the conquerors, the murderers of women and children. Study the photographs of the naked women lined up outside the chambers at Auschwitz, then see the faces of the armed guards. *Smiling.* Always some strange humor moves them to smile. Why? Is it a smile of shame? Are they hiding their guilt with laughter? I doubt it. Perhaps it is nothing more than the essence of evil; a distillation of everything that is vile and destructive in man.

Tamar, my wife, who is a psychologist, shrugs her shoulders when I talk of this. "They smile because they smile," she says, with a sabra's cynicism. "It is funny to them when others suffer and die."

My father now supported my mother's reluctance to discuss politics with Muller or any of the Helms family.

In his polite way, he said he was an expert only on things like influenza, and setting fractures; politics were not his field.

But Grandpa Palitz was not the man to take a hint. He leaned across the table—summer wasps and bees now buzzed around the fruit and the melting ice cream—and leveled his pipe at Muller and Helms.

"Hindenberg, there was a man for you," Grandpa said.

"A patriot, yes," Muller said. "But old-fashioned. Behind the times."

"Bah!" my grandfather said. "We need a few like him today. Some honest generals. The army should run that gang right out of office."

Muller's eyes were almost closed. "What gang?"

"You know who I'm talking about. A few good army men could handle them in an afternoon."

Again, there was an embarrassed silence. My parents were shaking their heads. Mama touched her father's arm. "Not today, Papa, please."

Inga came to the rescue. In her lilting voice she said, "I can't believe it, Karl! The militarists are all on your side of the family!"

People laughed. My father made a joke about Grandpa reenlisting. Mr. and Mrs. Helms and their son were silent. Muller started to whisper something in Mr. Helms' ear, then stopped.

Inga tried to liven up the wedding party. "Why don't we all sing? What would anyone like to sing?"

She gestured to the accordion player to join us. Soon Inga was making people get to their feet, gather in a circle.

Inga had this power, this gift, of getting things done, of influencing people—not cruelly, or by playing the domineering female, but by the gayness and liveliness of her personality. She seemed to enjoy every moment of her life, and she had the gift of transferring this joy to others. Once she took Anna and me to the zoo for the day, and I cannot remember enjoying the animals so much, walking until my feet ached, but happy to be with her and with Karl. Yet oddly, she was not a well-educated girl—business school was the limit of her training—and she was not effusive, or loud, or boisterous. She was quite simply *alive,* loved life, and made one feel the same way.

"Do you know the *Lorelei?*" asked my mother.

The accordion player bowed his head. "I'm sorry, madame. But Heine . . ."

"Heine is forbidden?" my mother asked, incredulous.

"You see, the party's musical department says—"

"Please," my mother said.

"Go on," Inga said. She kissed the musician on his forehead. "You must play it for a bride. I love it."

He began to play. Karl put his arm around Inga, Inga put her arm around my father, and so on. But the Helms family, while joining in the song, seemed a bit apart from us. The old melody, the old words lingered in the hot, summery air.

> *I do not know why this confronts me,*
> *This sadness, this echo of pain,*
> *A curious legend still haunts me,*
> *Still haunts and obsesses my brain . . .*

Uncle Moses nudged me as I walked by. "I'd have preferred to have heard *Raisins and Almonds,*"

I had no idea what he was talking about. He was a kind and devoted man, but he was—*different.* Polish Jews, my mother often said (not in any critical way), were just *different.*

"Singing is boring," Anna said. "Look what I brought along."

She had a kid's soccer ball, and she bounced it off my head. Soon I was chasing her, and we were kicking the ball on the lawn in back of the restaurant. I teased her, pushing the ball past her, faking her out of position, every now and then letting her get the best of me. Once she slipped on the grass and went down.

"You did that on purpose," Anna cried.

"An accident!"

"I'll show you, you rat!"

And she kicked the ball over my head—and into a

group of men dining in a protected little area of the garden.

I ran after it. Then I stopped. One of the men had picked the ball up and was holding it out. "Yours, kid?"

"Yes," I said.

There were three of them. Youngish, sort of heavy. All wore the brown shirts, baggy brown trousers and black boots of the Storm Troopers. Each wore a swastika armband—the black spiked cross in a white circle, the rest of the band scarlet. I looked at their faces. Ordinary Berlin faces, men you might see in any beer garden on any Sunday, drinking beer, smoking. Except for the uniforms.

I knew who they were, and what they thought of us, and what they were doing to us. Just a year ago, I'd gotten into a street fight with some of them. I'd got my eye blackened, knocked one of them down, and then I'd run like the wind, over fences and into alleys to escape them.

"What are you looking at, kid?" the man who held the ball asked.

"Nothing."

Anna was several yards behind me. She saw them too, and she began to back away. I wanted to say to her, *Don't, don't show them you're afraid, they don't know we're Jews.* Her face was pale and she kept moving away. She seemed to understand, perhaps better than I did, that these were our enemies, that nothing we did, or said, or pretended to be, could save us from that blind, unreasoning hate. Yet the men now seemed indifferent to us.

The ball was booted at me. I hit it with my head, in a perfect arc, and when it came down, I kicked it toward Anna. I had the feeling of a narrow escape, although from what I was not sure.

Anna and I stopped under the shade of a laurel tree. We looked again at the three Storm Troopers.

"The wedding party's ruined," she said.

"No it isn't," I said. "They're nothing to us."

We could hear our family and the Helmses, singing on the other side of the hedges.

"Come on," I said. "I'll play goalie and you try to kick it past me."

"No. I don't want to play soccer, and I don't want to sing."

She ran off. I tossed the ball gently at her and hit her in the backside. Normally Anna, spunky, always ready to tease, would have turned and tried to get even with me. But she just kept running. I looked once more at the men in brown shirts, and I wondered to myself whether we should all be running.

Erik Dorf's Diary

Berlin
September 1935

Marta complained again today of fatigue. She has not been right since Laura's birth. I insisted she see a doctor.

Having just moved into this tiny flat in this quarter (where I lived years ago as a boy), I recalled a certain Dr. Josef Weiss on Groningstrasse. My parents had used him, and sure enough, his office is still there in a four-story limestone building. He and his family still live in the upper stories, and his clinic occupies the ground floor.

Dr. Weiss, a soft-spoken, rather weary-looking man, examined Marta thoroughly, and then, as gently as possible, said that he suspected she had a slight systolic murmur. Marta and I must have looked shocked, but he assured us it was of a minor nature, probably connected with her anemia. He prescribed something to strengthen her blood, and told her not to overexert herself.

As he chatted with her, I studied the dark paneled walls of his office. Diplomas. Certificates. Photographs of wife and children, including one of a young bridal couple. It makes no difference to me, but I remember my parents saying that Dr. Weiss was a Jew, but a very fine one.

The physician, learning that we had two small children at home, suggested a maid a few days a week, and Marta—without shame—told him we could not afford one. He replied that she need not be the perfect Berlin housewife, scrubbing and cleaning all day, although moderate exercise was good for her.

As we were about to leave, he halted me at the door to his waiting room, and remarked that he had once had patients named Dorf. Was I possibly related? I acknowledged that my father had indeed been his patient when I was a small boy, some twelve years ago.

Dr. Weiss seemed touched. He remembered my parents well. Mrs. Weiss used to buy bread and cake from the bakery of Klaus Dorf. How happy he was to see me again! Why hadn't I mentioned it at the start?

Marta lifted her chin, and with that peculiar North German pride of hers, remarked that her husband, Erik Dorf, lawyer, did not like to ask special favors—of anyone. She didn't say it cruelly, or to put the doctor in his place. She was merely setting the record straight.

In any event, Dr. Weiss was certainly not offended and he chatted on—how he had cured me of chicken pox when I was six, how he had seen my mother through a severe bout of pneumonia. And how, he asked, were they now? I told him my father was dead, that he had lost the store during the depression, and that my mother was living with relatives in Munich.

He was moved by this, I could see, and said how sad it was that so many good people were hurt during those years. Suddenly he said, "And those wonderful, crusty stollen. On Thursdays?"

I could not help smiling. "Wednesdays. I used to deliver them."

He seemed almost reluctant to let us leave, as if the memories of my parents' humble bakery, my youthful services as delivery boy, were pleasing recollections. Marta made a point of saying how far I'd come—a lawyer, paying my way through the university. The doctor agreed. Then we departed through the waiting room. I noticed that his patients seemed, for the most part, poor people.

Later, we sat in a small park and I read the help-wanted advertisements, as I had done for a long time. Night watchman. Warehouseman. Clerk. Hardly anything for a bright young attorney, especially with two young children and a wife to support. Marta has talked of taking a job, but I won't hear of it. We have no grandparents or other relatives to look after the children, and quite frankly, she isn't trained for anything. Her old-fashioned parents in Bremen thought it improper for women to go to work. She was raised to marry, bear children, cook and go to church.

I remarked that I might have trouble paying the doctor bills, and she responded that if Dr. Weiss was so happy to see me again, and even recalled my father's stollen, he'd certainly trust me until I found work. Marta is ever the optimist, the planner, the one who looks ahead and sees things getting better.

I'm not that way. Ever since I saw my father lose his business, his store, his self-confidence, and finally his life, I have tended to hide my native moroseness beneath a false cheerful facade. My appearance helps—slender, tall, fair. Marta and I make an attractive couple—she petite and blond, with excellent bearing and graceful hands.

Although it was an extravagance, what with our bills mounting, I bought vanilla ice cream cones for us, and we strolled through the small park. Marta, gently at first, then a bit more firmly, began to lecture me. I am too shy, too self-effacing. I don't brag to people that I graduated in the top tenth of my law-school class. Why?

How can I explain to her that in my shame over my father's failure, I find it hard to brag, to thrust myself forward?

She tossed her half-finished cone into a trash bin, and looked annoyed. "You reject my suggestions all the time," she said. "Erik, please . . ."

I knew what she wanted, what she wants. I have told her a dozen times I do not want to be a policeman. An uncle of hers has a connection with General Reinhard Heydrich, who is rumored to be one of the most powerful of all the rising new political leaders—heading up the Gestapo, SS and other security services. Marta has never hesitated to say that she thinks I should at least talk to this powerful man. Thousands of young Germans, university men, would give ten years of their life for such a chance. But I am not even a party member. Nor is Marta. We are rather nonpolitical people. Oh, we see every day how things are improving —more jobs, the currency stabilized, factories running. But politics are beyond me.

I have told her that my father may have even been a Socialist at one time. The Nazis would surely find out. What then?

But this time, in the park, she was adamant. She said I would hurt her poor heart, that I owed it to the children, that perhaps what was wrong with me was that I was not more wholeheartedly in step with the new Germany. I reminded her that for the past few years I have slaved over law books, worked part-time in an insurance firm, barely managed to keep my health and my sanity, and hence have small time for politicians, or parades, or rallies.

In the end she won. I agreed to ask her uncle to make an appointment for me with Heydrich. After all, I love and respect Marta, and perhaps she is sharper than I am in realizing that the new government offers new opportunities.

And so we put our arms around each other's backs, and like young lovers, walked down the tree-lined street. At a kiosk I glanced at the posters—Hitler in knight's armor, warnings not to buy from Jews, exhortations to all to work harder. Maybe he's right.

Today, September 20, I was ushered into Reinhard Heydrich's office for an interview.

He is a tall, handsome, impressive man. No man is

better suited to wear the black uniform of the SS. He holds several posts—chief of the Gestapo, chief of the Security Service. He reports directly to Reichsführer Himmler, the head of the SS, the "army within an army," that loyal legion of men sworn to uphold Nazi doctrine, racial purity, the security of Germany.

As Heydrich read my *curriculum vitae,* I studied him. He was a wonderful athlete, I've heard (he still is a superb physical specimen), and an accomplished violinist. In fact, a violin rested on a stand nearby. A Mozart cantata was open. I know a little about him— former naval officer, organizer for the party, a brilliant theoretician, a man with a deep belief in the need for security and order, and the limitless power of a police force.

His manner was polite. I saw nothing in him to explain the street rumors I've heard (from left-wing types who attended law school with me) that in the party he is known as "the evil young god of death." How wrong people can be! I saw a refined, intelligent man, thirty-one years old.

Abruptly, he looked up and asked me what made me think I was suited for work in the SS special branches he commanded, such as the Security Service or the Gestapo.

To be candid, I did not know what to say, so I took the easiest way out. I told him the truth. "Sir, I need a job," I said.

This amused him. At once he revealed the kind of insightful man he is—seeing through people clearly, aware of motives, prescient, a born psychologist. He replied that I had given him a frank and refreshing answer. All sorts of frauds and fakes came to him for jobs, and here was I, a bright young lawyer, making no long speeches about my love of Fatherland and Führer, but merely after a job.

Was he taunting me? No, he was sincere. Still, there was something mocking in his metallic blue eyes, and when he turned back my way, it was as if I were looking at a different person. The two sides of his face—

a handsome face—seemed disparate, mismatched. Was he enjoying some kind of inner joke, some cynical laughter, at my expense? I'm not certain.

Heydrich talked about the party, the new government, the end of the corrupt and inefficient parliament. He told me that police power, properly used, is the true power of the state. I suppose I should have argued. I learned other notions in law school. What about courts? The legal process? Human rights? But I was too awed by him to respond.

"Given modern technical knowledge, and the patriotism of the German people," he said, "there are no limits to what we can do, no enemies who can overcome us."

I must have looked confused, for he laughed, and asked me if I really knew the distinctions between the SS, the SD, the Gestapo, the RSHA. When I confessed I did not, he laughed out loud and slapped the table. "Splendid, Dorf. We have trouble keeping them apart ourselves sometimes. No matter. They all report to me, and of course to our beloved Reichsführer, Herr Himmler."

He then asked me how I felt about Jews, and I answered that I had never given them much thought. Again, he turned the hard, crooked side of his face toward me. Quickly, I added that I certainly agreed that they had an influence far out of proportion to their numbers in such fields as journalism, commerce, banking and the professions, and that perhaps this was bad for Germany and for the Jews themselves.

Heydrich nodded. He then launched on a major thesis of his—an expansion on the Führer's own words in *Mein Kampf*. Some of it was hard to follow, but it seemed to boil down to the fact that just as Bolshevism, to succeed in Russia, needed a *class* enemy, so the Nazi movement, to succeed in Germany, needs a *racial* enemy. Hence the Jews.

I said, "But surely, they *are* an enemy."

Heydrich had cleverly maneuvered me exactly into the position he wanted me to be in—indeed the attitude which he hopes eventually all Germans of all ranks and stations and beliefs will accept. The Jews are not only a tool toward domination, they are in fact, and by all historical evidence, *enemies*.

Now he warmed to his subject. He quoted *Mein Kampf*, the involvement of Jews in every form of human corruption, their betrayal of Germany in the World War, their control of the banks and foreign capital, their dominance in Bolshevism.

My head was swimming, but I have always had the knack of looking interested, of agreeing with a nod, an interjection, a smile. He was enjoying his lecture, and I did not dare to interrupt. At one point I was tempted to ask how Jews could be both Bolsheviks and capitalists. But I prudently held my tongue.

"Mark me, Dorf," he said. "We'll solve a multitude of problems—political, social, economic, military and above all racial—by coming down hard on the Chosen People."

I confessed this was new ground for me. But recalling Marta's admonition, I said I had an open mind.

This pleased him. Even when I confessed I was not a party member, had not worn a uniform since my scouting days, he seemed indifferent, responding that any fool could wear a uniform, but he needed good minds, good organizers around him. He said that the party and the SS had their fill of hoodlums, hacks, eccentrics. He was trying to build an efficient organization. "Then am I to assume, sir, that I'm hired?"

He nodded in affirmation, and I felt a sudden thrill, as if I had crossed a barrier, climbed a mountain.

Then he told me I'd be inducted, sworn in as soon as the usual security check was run on me. A steely tone entered his voice. For a second I feared him. Then he laughed, and said, "I must assume you wouldn't dare come in here unless you were lily-white."

"I suspect I am, sir," I said.

"Good. Go down to personnel and fill out the necessary forms."

As I was leaving, he called me back. "You know,

Dorf, I stick my neck out with you. Hitler once said he wouldn't rest until it was a disgrace for any German to be a lawyer."

He saw me flinch, and added, "I'm teasing. Heil Hitler, Dorf."

I found it very easy to respond. "Heil Hitler," I said.

Yesterday evening, September 26, I put on the black uniform of the SS for the first time. Later that night I took the blood oath:

> I swear by God this holy oath, that I will render to Adolf Hitler, Führer of the German Nation and People, Supreme Commander of the Armed Services, unconditional obedience, and I am ready as a brave soldier to risk my life at any time for this oath.

I have been given the rank of lieutenant, and assigned to a minor post in Heydrich's headquarters. The truth is, I am much more than a glorified clerk. a low-level aide to Reinhard Tristan Eugene Heydrich. A great deal of my time is spent untangling the relationships between the Gestapo, the SD, the RSHA, and other branches of the SS. Heydrich mockingly tells me that he prefers keeping it muddled, as long as everyone knows he is the boss.

Marta helped me put on my black tunic, black breeches and black boots. I jammed my Luger into my leather holster and felt like an idiot. Marta brought the children from the bedroom to admire their father. Peter is now five, Laura three. Marta, who has always favored Peter, lifted him up. One look at the high-crowned black cap and he burst into tears!

I had a sudden strange concern. Have I done the right thing? Of course, no importance can be attached to a child bawling at the sight of his father in a new costume. Perfectly natural. But Marta was annoyed with him when he howled again and retreated. He and little Laura tearfully watched me, peeking from behind the door.

I said to Marta I hoped I would not have to wear the rig all the time. We aren't at war. Why strut about eternally in jackboots?

"But you *must,*" she said. "People will respect you. The local merchants will know who you are. I'll get the best cuts of meat, the best fruits and vegetables. If you have power, use it."

I said nothing. It had never occurred to me that one of the benefits of wearing an SS uniform would be thicker veal chops, riper melons. But Marta has always been a farseeing woman. The weakness in her heart has never affected her sharpness nor her intelligence.

Once more I tried to reach for Peter to kiss him good night. But he ran from me. As I kissed Marta and left, for the induction ceremony at headquarters, I could not help but recall the scene in the *Iliad* where Hector puts on his burnished helmet with its plume. His wife, Andromache, holds up their son to admire him, and the child screams in terror. Screaming and frightened at the aspect of his own father.

Peter's reaction disturbs me. I do not conceive of myself as man whose own children run from him.

Rudi Weiss' Story

In the three years, between 1935 and 1938, the slow strangling of Jewish life in Germany continued. We did not leave. My mother kept insisting things would "get better"; my father gave in to her.

Anna had been forced to leave school, and now attended a private Jewish school. She was a superb student, much smarter (I felt) than either Karl or myself. Karl kept painting, struggling to make a living, shut out from almost all commercial work. Inga, ever devoted to him, worked as a secretary and was the main support of their marriage. Myself? I helped around the house, played soccer in a semi-pro league. We barely managed to get by.

My father's patients, it was now evident, were those who, like us, had not had the foresight to leave.

Erik Dorf's Diary

Berlin
November 1938

Some routine files, reports from neighborhood informants, came across my desk today and I saw a familiar name—Dr. Josef Weiss.

Frankly, it was a break in the rather boring jobs I've been given. I do get to attend meetings with Heydrich now and then, but I'm rarely privy to top-level decisions. I try not to complain, though, I'm efficient, well-organized, and Heydrich knows he can depend on me to follow up on his orders. "Give it to Dorf," he often says when he wants a memorandum simplified, or made readable, or properly worded.

I really have no complaints. Marta's heart condition seems to have stabilized. The children are healthy. We eat well.

The sight of Dr. Weiss' name today, November 6, was what made me think of Marta's improved health, and that visit we made to his office three years ago. I read the notation, a report from a minor official who lived across the street from the Weiss clinic.

Dr. Josef Weiss, a Jew practicing medicine at Groningstrasse, 19, has been treating at least one Aryan patient. This is a violation of the Nuremberg Laws and should be looked into. The woman in question is a Fraulein Gutmann, who has been observed going into his office.

This is trivial stuff. Normally I would have bucked it to a local official of the RSHA, the department that deals with the Jewish question.

I mulled over the report for a while. Was it any of

my business? Oh, I am committed to our program, and I accept Heydrich's views on the Jewish problem. I have reread *Mein Kampf* and digested it again, accepting in the main its arguments against the Jews' eternal threat to Germany, and I suppose I should not have let an old loyalty to a doctor interfere. So I'm not sure why I did what I did today. Perhaps, I told myself, as I changed from my uniform to a plain gray suit, I owe Dr. Weiss a favor.

His waiting room looked dingier than I remembered. Paint flaked from the ceiling and walls. An old Orthodox Jew was sitting there, and a young couple. I knocked on the frosted glass door. Dr. Weiss opened it. He had on his white coat. He looked older, his face lined, and he had turned quite gray. He asked me to wait a moment. He was examining someone.

Then he recognized me. "My goodness," he said. "It's Mr. Dorf. Do come in." He told the patient to wait outside.

Again I glanced at the photographs on the wall—his wife, his children, the wedding picture. I studied the younger children. The boy looked rugged, tough. He wore a soccer shirt.

"My younger boy, Rudi," the physician said. "Played center for Tempelhof. A great athlete. Maybe you've heard of him."

I shook my head, and tried to suppress a certain sorrow. The doctor was bragging about his son, his ruggedness, his athletic skills, something we Germans respect—almost as if pleading to be accepted for something other than what he is.

He asked how Marta was, if I had come to talk about her, and I had to cut him short. I could not let past associations intrude. I showed him my badge, identifying me as a lieutenant in the SS, Berlin headquarters.

His face turned grayish, his smile left, and he asked if he had done anything wrong. A momentary guilt washed over me. Why should anyone persecute this man? As far as I know, he is the essence of decency. (Heydrich would answer that one can never tell with

Jews; they hide their evil plans behind a facade of good works and charity.)

I told him of the report that he was treating an Aryan woman. He admitted it. She was a former maid, Fraulein Gutmann, and he treated her *gratis*. It made no difference, I said, he had to stop. Dr. Weiss said he would. Then, trying to disarm me, he reminded me that he had once treated many Christians, including my family.

I realized at that moment what Heydrich means by steeling oneself to certain deeds. Times have changed, I said. Old customs are gone. For his good as much as ours. I impressed on him that I didn't normally run such errands, warning Jews, that I was an administrator.

He forced a smile. "I see. You're a specialist. You don't make house calls."

I got up. "Don't treat the woman again. Restrict your practice to Jews."

He followed me to the glass doors. Before opening it, he said, "All this is beyond my comprehension. I was your family doctor. I was concerned about your wife's health."

I stopped him. "Why haven't you left Germany? You're no pauper. Get out."

He opened the door slightly, and I could see the people in his waiting room. "Jews get ill and need medical care," he said. "If all the doctors left, what then? It's the poor and the old who have lingered here."

"Things will not get easier for you."

"How much worse can they get? We are no longer citizens. We have no legal rights. Our property is confiscated. We are at the mercy of street bullies. I can't belong to a hospital. I can't get drugs. In the name of humanity, what else can you do to us?"

Heydrich is right about the dangers of getting too close to Jews. They have that habit of appealing, whining, ingratiating themselves. Although I must admit that Dr. Weiss bore himself with dignity.

"You must not come to me for help," I said.

"Not even on the basis of an old doctor-patient relationship? I considered your parents decent people. I have reason to believe they respected me."

I shook my head. "I bear you no personal malice. Take my advice and get out."

As I left I heard a piano playing somewhere in the house. I think my father once mentioned that the doctor's wife is an accomplished pianist. She was playing Mozart.

Rudi Weiss' Story

November 1938, and we were still in Berlin. Looking back, I find it hard to blame my mother. Or anyone in our family. We stayed. We suffered for it. Who—except a few—understood the horrors that awaited us?

I remember the endless discussions. Stay. Leave. It will get better. We have a friend here. Some influence there.

My mother and my sister Anna were playing a Mozart duet one day when my father came trudging upstairs. I knew his tread. Not a big man, but a strong one. He let my mother and Anna finish the piece on the Bechstein, then applauded. Anna made believe she was angry. The piece was a new one they'd learned; it was supposed to be a surprise for my father's birthday.

I was sitting in the corner of the living room reading the sports pages. Ever since my childhood it had been the only part of the paper that interested me. My parents, annoyed with my poor schoolwork, often said I had learned to read only so I could know the soccer scores, who won the prize fights.

"It was beautiful," my father said. He kissed Anna. "I will love it even more on my birthday. Anna, you'll be a better pianist than Mama some day." He patted her hair. "Sweetheart, Mama and I must talk. Can you leave us, please?"

Anna pouted. "I bet I know what about." In a sing-song, she said, "Are we leaving or are we staying?"

Somehow I was allowed to remain. Perhaps they felt I was old enough to listen. My father stoked his pipe, sat down across from the Bechstein. "Remember the Dorf family?" he asked my mother.

"The baker. The ones who owed you all that money, then moved without ever paying their bills."

"Their son was just here."

"To pay old debts?"

"Hardly. Young Dorf is an officer in the Security Service. He warned me not to treat Aryans, and said I should get out of the country."

I made believe I was riveted to the sports page, but I listened. My father seemed perplexed, more worried than I had ever seen him.

"We should have left three years ago," he said. "Right after Karl was married. When we had a chance."

My mother brushed back her hair. "Are you saying that we stayed because of me, Josef?"

"No, my dear. We . . . both made the decision."

"I convinced you. Didn't I? I said it was my country as much as theirs. I still believe it. We'll outlast these barbarians."

My father tried to shoulder some of the blame. The Jews who had stayed behind needed medical care; he had a job to do. But Mama—and I—knew he was acting, and not very well. It was her iron will that had kept us there.

"Maybe there's time," my father said. "Inga says there's that chap in the railway department who might arrange something."

My mother smiled. "Yes, perhaps we can ask again. But last time he wanted a fortune in a bribe."

"If not us, then the children—Karl, Rudi, Anna. Let them get a fresh start somewhere. That Dorf fellow upset me."

My mother rose from the piano bench. She stroked the polished surface of the Bechstein. Hers. Her family's. "We'll survive, Josef," she said. "After all, this is the country of Beethoven, Mozart and Schiller."

My father sighed. "Unfortunately none of them are in office now."

I left, saying nothing. My father was right. I had the feeling we had waited too long.

That afternoon I was sure of it.

I had put on my green-and-white soccer uniform and my cleats and had gone out to the local soccer field for a game against a team from another neighborhood, the Wanderers. We were called the Vikings. I was one of the youngest players on our team, and one of the best. I played inside left or center and I had led the league in scoring the year before. There had been a few other Jewish players in the league, but they'd quit. I'd been allowed to stay on, I guess, because I was too good to let go. Besides, I never took any crap from anyone. They only called me "kike" or "Jewboy" once. Not only could I move a ball the length of the field, through half the defense, but I could use my fists when I had to. And my teammates would stick up for me. Most of the time.

That day some big guy on the Wanderers, a back named Ulrich, deliberately tripped me while I was passing off. I had jolted him a few times, and he didn't like the idea. When I got to my feet, he punched me. Soon they had to pull us apart, but I had belted him hard in the stomach, and I'd hurt him.

My sister-in-law Inga's younger brother, Hans Helms, was playing for the Wanderers, an outside right. He tried to tell Ulrich to lay off and play ball. But I could see there'd be more trouble.

There was a throw-in. Ulrich and Helms started kicking the ball downfield. I stole the ball, and started the other way, when Ulrich hit me from behind. This time I got up swinging and we had to be separated again.

"He tripped me," I shouted at the referee. "Why didn't you call it?"

Ulrich's nose was bleeding. I'd landed a right this time before they separated us. "Lousy kike," he sneered. "Leave it to a kike to fight dirty."

I tried to tear away from them. Hans Helms was one of the gang holding me back.

"Weiss, maybe you better get out of the game," the referee said.

I looked at my teammates, waiting for one of them —at least *one!*—to stick up for me. But they were silent. Our captain kicked at the dirt. He couldn't look me in the eye.

"I've started every game this year," I said. "Why should I quit?"

"We don't need Jews," Ulrich said. "We don't play against them."

"Come in the alley and say that," I said. "Just the two of us, Ulrich." I was raging inside, furious. Why didn't my own team stick up for me? Why was I being left alone?

The referee stepped in front of me. I was struggling to break loose. "Weiss, you're suspended for fighting. Go on home."

Once more I tried to appeal to my teammates, fellows I had played with for two seasons. They respected me. They knew I was a good player, one of the best. A sportswriter had once said I'd be a professional someday. But not a word.

Hans Helms tried to be kind, but he made it worse. "Rudi, the league wanted them to dump you last year—they made an exception."

"To hell with them," I said. I walked away.

I heard the whistle blow, the shouts, the bodies thudding, as the game resumed without me. I knew I'd never play again.

There was a bruise under my right eye, a cut under my right ear, from the fight I'd just had.

"What happened?" my father asked. He was washing up in his office. The last patient had left. He smelled of medical alcohol.

"Some guy started a fight with me," I said. I didn't tell him about being kicked off the team, how I had bloodied Ulrich's nose. I certainly didn't tell him that his daughter-in-law's brother was on the opposing team. There was a blind rage in me. My father, everyone else in my family, was incapable of it. Strangely, I was almost as angry with them for bowing, bending, refusing to fight.

"You know your mother doesn't like you fighting," he said.

"I know she doesn't. But if anyone swings at me, I'll swing back."

He shook his head. Papa had always been a handsome man—tall, straight-featured. Now he seemed to bend a little every day, his face growing lines. "Well, you'd better wash up. Inga and Karl are coming for dinner."

"I can bet what we'll talk about."

He took my arm. The medical odor was stronger. When I was injured, he'd tape my ankle, patch my wounds. We used to joke that if he ever failed as a doctor he'd make a great trainer for a soccer team. "Do you want me to put some iodine on that?" He pointed to the cut.

"No. I've had enough of them so I know how. Thanks, Papa."

Dinner that night was one of the saddest I remember.

The same talk, the same discussions. Why hadn't we left in 1933? Or at least after Karl was married? My poor father. He was in awe of my mother. She was beautiful, a born lady. *Hoch-deutsch,* he used to call her. A family whose ancestors had been "court Jews" —friends of princes and cardinals. And Josef Weiss of Warsaw? His father owned a little pharmacy that my Uncle Moses now ran. They'd saved every penny, and borrowed, to send my father to medical school. It was my mother's parents, the Palitzes, who, in spite of their objections to their daughter marrying a Polish Jew, had helped him open his practice.

Inga and Karl had come to dinner. They were talking about this man with the railways who might get us out.

Karl, always a bit gloomy—he'd gotten thinner, quieter—shook his head. "But there's no place left to go," he said.

"France, perhaps," my father said. "Switzerland."

"Turning Jews away," Karl said.

"Nobody wants us," I said.

Karl smiled bitterly. "Fellow at the United States consulate the other day told me that the Americans won't even fill their quota for German Jews. They can let some more in, but they won't."

Anna spoke up. As always, she was courageous, spunky. "Who cares? We have each other, don't we, Mama? And that's what matters."

My mother nodded. "Absolutely."

"That group that was taking children to England," my father said. "Perhaps if we asked . . ." His voice dwindled into silence.

"Closed down," Karl said. "Inga and I asked."

"We could run into the woods and hide," Anna said.

My mother told Anna and me to clear the table. We got up and began removing dishes. No one had eaten very much.

"I'm not sure of anything any more," my father said. "Poland, perhaps. Technically I am still a Polish citizen."

"I won't hear of it," my mother said. "Things are not much better there."

In the kitchen I said to Anna, "Mama always has her way."

"Maybe 'cause she's always right."

When we got back, my mother had taken command of the situation. She was convinced that Hitler would let up on us. He had Austria, he had Czechoslovakia. What more did he need? He was a politician, like any other politician, and he had used the Jews to unite the country. Now he could forget us.

Karl was shaking his head, but he did not argue with her. My father tried to put up a brave front. He never, as long as I knew him, wanted to hurt Mama's feelings. The kindness he showed his patients, the poorest and meanest of them, was always reflected in the way he treated his family. I can never remember him striking any of his children. And God knows I, at least, deserved it more than a few times.

My mother asked me to turn on the radio.

A newscaster was describing an outrage of some kind that had taken place in Paris. Vom Rath, a German diplomat, had been shot by a Jew. We froze in our places as the voice droned on. A seventeen-year-old named Grynszpan had fired the shots. He was the son of Polish Jews recently expelled from Germany.

"This vicious, bloodthirsty act of the international Jewish conspiracy will be avenged," the newscaster was saying. "The Jews will be made to pay for this cowardly attack on a German patriot, an act which illustrates the murderous plotting of international Jewry against Germany, indeed against the civilized world."

"Louder, Rudi," my father said.

I turned up the volume. No one spoke.

"Already, spontaneous acts of reprisal by the German people are taking place against the Jewish plotters."

"Turn it off," my mother said.

Karl grimaced. "For God's sake, Mama, stop closing your eyes and ears to the truth." Inga took his hand.

"I said, turn it off."

The announcer went on. "Herr vom Rath is in critical condition. Whether he survives or not, the government states, the Jews will be made to pay for this vicious act."

"Good for you, Greenspan, or Grinspan, or whoever you are," I shouted. "You should have killed the son-of-a-bitch."

"Rudi!" my mother cried. "I said turn it off!"

"Do as your mother says," my father ordered.

As I turned off the radio, there was a loud noise of shattering glass. It came from downstairs, from my father's waiting room, which looked out on Groningstrasse. I flew downstairs. Anna was a step behind me.

The living room was a mass of broken glass. A

brick lay in the middle of the carpet. I ran to the window and shouted through the jagged hole: "Cowards! Lousy cowards! Show us your faces!"

But they were gone.

Behind me stood my family—frightened, pale, silent.

Erik Dorf's Diary

Berlin
November 1938

Vom Rath died last night. Heydrich's office called me in the middle of the night, and at once I dressed in my uniform and called for a taxi.

As we waited, the children woke up and came into the kitchen, where Marta had made fresh coffee for me. They were rubbing their eyes and seemed frightened. There were shouts in the street, sounds of glass breaking.

I tried to explain to Peter, who is only eight, that some bad people had killed a good German man in France.

"Why did they kill him, Papa?" asked Peter.

"Oh . . . they were evil. Crazy."

Marta took Peter close to her, pressed his blond head against her bosom. "They were Jews, Peter. Bad people, who want to hurt us."

I added, "But they will be punished."

Laura asked, "Are all Jews bad, Papa?"

"Most of them."

"Papa's going to punish bad people," Peter said. "That's why he's got a gun."

Laura began to weep. The child is only six. "I'm scared, Mama. I don't want Papa to go away."

Marta, equal to any crisis, calmed the children and put them back to bed. Then she helped me into my tunic, my boots, my belt.

"What will happen now?" she asked.

"It's begun already. Reprisals. We can't let any crazy Jew who gets an idea into his head kill a German diplomat."

"They won't expect you to—"

"Me? Marta, Lieutenant Dorf is a memo writer for Heydrich. Besides, this sounds like Goebbels' show. He's jealous of the Security Police."

There were street noises filtering into the room now—marching sounds, a band, men singing the Horst Wessel. Distantly, I heard glass shattering. Marta cocked her head and listened. "What will all this mean for you? Your career?"

I told her I had no intention of throwing bricks through the windows of Jewish shopkeepers to advance my career. I am not a brawler, a hoodlum. But what am I, then? she asked. A clerk, I replied. An argument was about to begin, and I could not stomach one before going to work. But Marta persisted. She admonished me to speak up, to make suggestions, to give Heydrich ideas. If I were not a street brawler, I had a mind. He'd hired me for my mind and here was a chance to use it, she said firmly.

She was right. I suspected some major moves against the Jews were in the works and that I would be involved. The usual programs were too trivial, I knew. Boycotts. Expulsions. Expropriations. I've signed papers, issued orders, but I've never been up close to the action. The nearest I've gotten to it was my brief visit with Dr. Weiss. It does not appeal to me. Although I understand Heydrich's concern over the Jewish problem, I am confused, uncertain. Yes, actions have to be taken. But what kind? By who? These were the jumbled thoughts that were running through my mind as I left for work before the sun was up.

All day Heydrich kept calling junior officers in and out, raging at the way Goebbels' thugs had jumped the gun on the reprisals. His SA gangs had been breaking Jewish store windows, beating Jews, burning synagogues. All this without informing Himmler or Heydrich.

I often take my lunch at my desk, and it is only rarely that I attend the elaborate meals served in Heydrich's private dining room. This day, he was out of sorts, and seeing me eating alone, sipping my coffee, he seemed to take an interest in me. It was as if his immediate subordinates had disappointed him, and he was looking for someone to talk to.

"Dorf, when you've finished your lunch, come in," the chief said.

Rarely do I get invited into his office alone. I somehow knew this was the chance Marta had told me to look for. I gulped my coffee and entered Heydrich's office. At once he began to berate Goebbels. He had nothing but contempt for the man he called "that damned cripple."

I commented that some kind of reprisals were necessary after the Vom Rath outrage. He seemed surprised that I offered an opinion.

"Yes. But *we* should be doing it," Heydrich said. "And doing it as the police arm. No foreigners, including foreign Jews, should be molested. No non-Jewish property should be burned. We should be holding rich Jews hostage for reparations. Taking them into protective custody, that sort of thing."

What a brilliant man he is! Goebbels, for all his noisy chatter, his bombast, is a failed screenwriter. Heydrich is a genuine intellect.

"Suppose," I said, "we let our men take over."

"In SS uniforms? That's all we need, Dorf."

"No, sir. As civilians. No banners. No insignia. No marching bands and songs. Punish the Jews, arrest those under suspicion, but make clear that this is the righteous anger of the German people rising spontaneously against the Jewish Bolshevik plot." The words tumbled out of my mouth.

"Not a bad idea, Dorf. Go on."

I explained that we should teletype orders to local police forces to stay out of the action. They could discreetly stand by and watch. Tell them to act *accordingly* —which, of course, means they are to keep hands off the demonstrators, our own SS men.

Heydrich was smiling at me. "That's the kind of legal mind I can appreciate, Dorf. Put the order out. We'll get away with it, and we'll beat Goebbels at his own game."

"Thank you, sir."

"Business suits and topcoats. I like that. The enraged citizenry. And why not? We've got the whole country behind us. Germans understand police power. They like the authority we impose on them."

As our meeting concluded he told me that my papers for promotion from first lieutenant to captain would go through immediately.

This day is imprinted in my memory—November 10, 1938. It is the day I finally came out of my shell, as Marta has wanted. Heydrich has just been waiting for me to "open up," as it were. Now, in a crisis, he has made use of my intelligence.

And as if in celebration of my new importance and the manner in which as man and wife we have revived my career, Marta and I made passionate love tonight. Marta has always been a little tentative, hesitant in her lovemaking. More of that proper North German upbringing; a strict father, a timid mother. (She confessed to me tonight that she was sixteen before she really understood the sexual process, where babies came from.)

But my new boldness, the manner in which I had, through the use of my brain, strengthened my position with one of the most feared and powerful men in Germany, gave us both a kind of sexual arousal; we hid nothing, forbade nothing, explored our bodies in a new relationship, which seemed of a piece with my new status.

Rudi Weiss' Story

The world now knows it as *Kristallnacht*—the night of broken glass. It marked the true beginning of the destruction of our people. I saw it; was in the midst of it. And if ever I lacked sufficient understanding of the aims and methods of the Nazis, I had the evidence now.

The cowardly bastards came down the street on which Grandpa had his bookstore. Smashed windows. Burned merchandise. Beat up any Jew they could lay their hands on. Two men who tried to fight back were beaten to death on the spot—Mr. Cohen, the furrier, and Mr. Seligman, who ran a dry-goods shop.

They broke the window with the gold lettering: H. PALITZ BOOKSTORE. Grampa was a tough old bird. Like my mother, he was convinced—even at this late date!—that he was a better German than they were, that his Iron Cross would protect him, that some miracle from Heaven would make them go away.

So he came out of the store waving his cane, after the first brick had shattered the glass, and shouted at them to go away. The mob answered by throwing his books into the street—rare editions, old maps, everything—and setting them afire. They called him an old kike, knocked him down, beat his back with canes.

He kept protesting that he was Captain Heinrich Palitz, formerly of the Second Berlin Machine Gun Regiment. It made them angrier. My grandmother looked from the window, screaming for the police. Three Berlin policemen stood on the far corner and watched as the gang, seven or eight, knocked Grandpa down again and again, turned his head into a bloody pulp, ripped his jacket off.

One of them made him get on all fours and rode him, as if he were a horse.

Then he saw Heinz Muller, the friend of the Helms family. Factory worker, union man, he was some kind of minor official in the local Nazi Party now. He was in civilian clothing, leading a singing gang. As usual, the Horst Wessel song. They wanted Jewish blood.

They dragged Grandpa to his feet—the police were still watching, smiling those flat, cold smiles—and Muller handed my grandfather a toy drum.

"You're such a fucking war hero, Palitz," Muller said.

"Lead the parade. Beat the drum, you old Jew liar."

Behind grandfather were a half-dozen other Jewish store owners. Their shops had been smashed, looted, burned. The street was ablaze.

That bastard Muller! My grandmother watched, weeping, terrified, as Grandpa began to beat the drum, and the Jewish merchants, with signs reading JUDE hanging on their necks, were paraded down the street.

And no one lifted a finger.

My grandmother called our house and told us what was happening. We knew. We could hear glass shattering all over our neighborhood.

My parents stood frozen in the living room.

"I shall call the police," my father said. "This is intolerable. Yes, there are laws against us, but this kind of violence . . ."

My father's pathetic belief that there still was some kind of justice in Germany almost made me cry. Being a just man, he could not believe otherwise.

"We must wait . . . wait and pray," my mother said. "It can't last forever. What good can it do them?"

"You can wait," I said. "I'm going out to get Grandpa."

My mother grabbed my sleeve and tried to hold me back. She was used to having her way, forcing her children to bend to her will.

"I forbid it, Rudi! You can't fight them all!"

"Yes," my father said. "They are looking for excuses to kill us! We mustn't fight back!"

"They've got all the excuses they need."

I pulled away from my mother and ran down the stairs. As I was putting on my sweater, Anna came running after me.

The street was a wreck. Every store had been smashed. Most were on fire. Mr. Goldbaum, a jeweler, was playing a fire hose against the remains of his shop. Everything he owned had been stolen. Those patriotic Germans, those aroused citizens, eager to avenge Vom Rath's death, were ordinary crooks and murderers.

A truck came rumbling by. I grabbed Anna and we

hid in an alley. It was an open truck. Some men were carrying photographs of Hitler, swastika banners. There were men parading up and down with signs denouncing the Jews. Mr. Seligman, from whom my mother used to buy draperies and bed linen, was lying face down in a pool of blood and broken glass.

The truck stopped and the hoodlums jumped off.

"Look who's with them," I said to Anna. "That rat Hans."

"Rotten pig. I always hated him."

"Yeah, Inga's brother. I wonder about *her* sometimes. Boy, I'd like to get him alone for five minutes."

Then we saw the parade. Grandpa, his head bloodied, one eye closed, was being forced to lead it, beating on the toy drum. Every few steps, he and the other storekeepers would be beaten with clubs and chains. Hans Helms was talking to Muller. Hans was a weak sister, a yellowbelly. He was stupid and lazy. Someone like Muller could lead him around.

I stepped out of the alley. Beyond the street the sky was turning orange with fires. I could hear women wailing. And more glass breaking, as if they meant to break every Jewish-owned window in Berlin.

The mob seemed to be getting weary of its game. Muller's gang began wandering off. Grandpa was still standing erect, refusing to cry, or beg, or plead.

I walked up to him and took his hands. "Grandpa. It's me. Rudi."

Anna came running out and took his arm.

At the rear of the column of Jews, a drunken young man was rifling pockets—stealing wallets, pens, watches. Muller shouted at him. "Hey. The party says none of that. This is a patriotic demonstration, not a fucking robbery."

"That's what you think, Muller," the man said.

"You obey orders," Muller shouted. Then he looked at me in the dim light and walked toward me. There was a moment of recognition, almost human, in his eyes, and I wonder now, could there have been something decent in this man, something that was crushed? After all, he was not, like some of the SS, a gangster or a tramp, a rootless troublemaker; he had a trade, he knew respectable people. What had impelled him to become a brute? I'm not sure I know yet; nor am I sure that it matters any more. An honorable man who turns criminal, especially if he moralizes about it, is perhaps more to be hated than a habitual burglar or murderer.

Tamar scoffs at my philosophizing. "They had two thousand years of preparation for what they did," she says. "And they all took part, or almost all. The men who ran the gas chambers and the ovens went to church, loved their children, and were kind to animals."

Muller asked if he knew me, and Grandpa replied that I was his grandson, Rudi Weiss. In response, Muller slapped my grandfather's face and said, "Shut up, you old kike."

"He's an old man," I said. "You want to fight someone, fight me. Not a mob. Just you and me, Muller."

Five or six of them gathered around us. Anna hugged Grandpa. Hans Helms was with them. He saw me. Of course he knew me well by now. I could see him whispering in Muller's ear. "Weiss . . . Inga's Jew relative . . ."

Muller rubbed his chin, glared at me through the haze of smoke. People were coughing, doubled over.

"Okay, Weiss. Beat it. Take the old shit with you. Get off the street."

I suppose I should have been grateful to him, and to Hans. But something was building up in me. I knew what. Revenge. Some day I wanted the sheer joy of smashing their faces, shaming them, letting them know they could not do this to us.

We helped Grandpa to his house. He and my grandmother lived in an apartment over the bookstore. Once he stopped and picked up a burned first edition of Johnson's dictionary, then an early edition of *Faust*. He turned the charred pages sadly.

"Heinrich, Heinrich," my grandmother wept. "How could they do this to an old man?"

He wiped blood from his forehead, stiffened his back. "I'll survive." He looked at the burned books again. "But my books . . ."

"Anna and I will clean up," I said. But I saw it was useless. He would never sell a book or a print or a map again.

Erik Dorf's Diary

Berlin
November 1938

Two days have passed since what the press is now calling *Kristallnacht*—the night of broken glass.

I took it upon myself, now that I'm a Captain and have risen in Heydrich's esteem, to assemble data on the events of that historic night.

The chief was relaxed, sipping cognac, listening to *Siegfried*.

"Wagner is a wizard," he said. "A magician. There, Dorf, is what a pure Aryan soul can produce."

I listened a moment, hating to interrupt his reverie.

"What chords," he said. "What sublime chords."

"The reports on the action, sir. On *Kristallnacht*."

Wagner's haunting music—I believe it was the Rhine journey—seemed an accompaniment to my rather grave report. There had been thirty-six deaths. Usually when Jews resisted. The foreign press could hardly raise a fuss over that. Seventy synagogues had been burned, and over eight hundred Jewish shops and businesses destroyed. Where our people seemed to have gone overboard was in the matter of arrests. More than thirty thousand Jews were imprisoned.

Heydrich looked up. "Thirty thousand? My God, those fools. They'll fill Buchenwald overnight." He turned off the record player. "No matter. We'll fill it eventually. And we'll need many more Buchenwalds. Our enemies—all of them—Jews, Communists, Socialists, Freemasons, Slavs—they'll all have to be contained if they resist."

"There may be protests, General. Boycotts. Retaliatory actions."

Heydrich laughed. What a controlled man! There is a rumor that in a drunken rage one night he fired his Luger at his own reflection in a mirror (but I refuse to believe the story).

"Retaliation?" he asked. "Because a few Jews have been beaten? Dorf, Jews are always in season as game."

"I suppose so. Almost as if we had a moral precedent for punishing them. After two thousand years . . ."

"Moral precedent!" Heydrich laughed again. "That's marvelous."

"I'm sorry if I said something stupid."

"Not at all, Captain. Of course a moral precedent. And a religious one. And a racial one. And above all, the practical values. How else unite our people?"

He put on another record. I left my reports on *Kristallnacht* on his desk and started to leave.

"Still neutral on Jews, Dorf?"

"No. I quite understand their importance to us," I said.

"And the threat they pose. You know the Führer's creed. Jews are subhuman, created by some other God. His intention—it's all spelled out—is to set Aryan against Jew until the Jew is destroyed."

I listened, nodding.

"And if someday—the Führer told me this personally—millions of Germans must die in another war to fulfill our destiny, he will not hesitate to annihilate millions of Jews and other vermin."

It was an odd sensation listening to his calm voice, hearing Wagner's celestial music rise in the lofty room. He made it sound logical, inevitable, a fulfillment of some historical imperative.

Rudi Weiss' Story

On November 14, 1938, a few days after the night of broken glass, my brother Karl was arrested.

Many Jews had gone into hiding, made last-minute efforts to leave, bribe their way out. It was almost impossible now.

Karl's arrest was a tribute to the thoroughness of the SS operation. He lived with Inga in a Christian neighborhood, in a small studio next to her parents' apartment. But the Nazis had informers everywhere. Inga was sure someone in the building had talked.

Karl was a commercial artist, and a good one. But by now he was barely able to eke out a living. Christian publishers and advertising people would have nothing to do with him. For a while Inga tried passing his work off as her own; but most of them knew. Karl did not like the idea, in any case. He had ideals—the integrity of the artist, the truth inherent in art. (Beautiful notions, but of small help against brutes armed with clubs and guns.)

The day they came for Karl, he was painting Inga's portrait. He kept teasing her, calling her his "Saskia." She had no idea what he meant. Karl explained that Saskia was Rembrandt's wife and the artist, being too poor to hire models, had painted her over and over— just as he had done hundreds of self-portraits.

"But I am no Rembrandt," Karl said. "Just an unemployed commercial artist."

He stopped painting, went to the couch. They lived very simply—almost no furniture, a few plants, some Picasso drawings tacked to the wall.

"You're a splendid artist," Inga said. "You'll get your chance someday."

"God, I love you," he said suddenly. And kissed her.

"No more than I love you."

"I'll hurt you. I'm marked, Inga. I don't want you to

46

be hurt because of me. They have a name for you, Inga. You're a race defiler."

"I don't give a damn what they call me." She took his shoulders. "Look at me. We're getting out. Somehow. That proper, corseted, perfumed mother of yours. Always having her way. She took the fight out of you. I said, look at me."

"I see the most beautiful girl in Berlin."

"And a stubborn one. We'll buy forged identity papers. We'll go to Bremen or Hamburg. They'll never know you're a—"

"You're dreaming, Inga. It's the end for me."

He stopped painting, seemed to lose all interest in his work that day. He kept reading and rereading the newspaper accounts of *Kristallnacht*. Outraged German citizens, furious at "Jewish domination" of banks, the press, business, were still roaming the streets. She tore the paper from his hand and tried to rouse him.

"Kiss me," Inga said.

"It won't change the world."

"It may help."

They clung to each other. At that moment, Ingrid's mother, nervously wiping her hands on her apron, entered without knocking. She stood there as if about to cry, yet angry with her daughter. "Police," Mrs. Helms said. "They want your husband."

Karl turned white, did not move.

"Police? For Karl?" Inga got up and ran to the door. "Who . . . Why didn't you warn us!"

Mrs. Helms made a helpless gesture with her hands.

"No!" Inga shrieked. "He's done nothing! Tell them anything . . . tell them he's gone . . ."

"It's no use. They're all over the block, arresting Jews."

Inga's eyes were blazing. "And you are rejoicing, I suppose. You could have lied for us. What in God's name are you? You are my mother, and you . . ."

Inga, in her rage and sorrow, grabbed her mother and started shaking her shoulders. "I am your child, and you let this happen!"

Karl had to pull her away. Inga was weeping now, tears more of anger than fear. It had never occurred to her that Karl, sequestered in the studio, forgotten by his former patrons, would be found.

Two men in civilian clothing entered. They showed their badges: Gestapo. They were polite, offhand. Karl had five minutes to pack a bag and leave.

"No," Inga said. "You must have a reason . . . papers . . ."

"Routine questioning," one of them said.

"What is he suspected of?" Inga cried.

"He'll be back in a few hours," the other detective said. "It's nothing important."

Dutifully, Karl threw toilet articles into a bag, some clothing. He knew what was in store, but Inga would not accept it.

"I'll go with him," she said. "I will get an attorney."

"Good luck, lady," the Gestapo man said. "Hurry it up, Weiss."

Suddenly Inga threw herself between the two men and Karl, hugged him, and with strong arms, tried to keep him from leaving. "No. No. They have to have a reason. You've done nothing. They can't take you." She turned to them. "He isn't political. He's an artist."

"It's all right, Inga," Karl said. "I'll be back."

Both knew he was lying. There had been too many stories in the past six months—sudden arrests, people vanishing into the night.

The men had a hard time disengaging her arms.

"I'm going with him," she said.

Inga's mother was trembling. "No, no. You make it worse for us."

"Be quiet," Inga shouted. "If I find out who informed on him . . ."

"Inga, your mother is right. You must stay." Karl kissed her.

Stubborn, strong-willed, knowing that she was Karl's shield and protector, she had to be torn from him.

"Don't follow us," one of the men said.

"That friend of Papa's, Muller," Inga cried. "He told them!"

"Muller has not been here for months," her mother said.

"No, but he drinks beer with Papa, and when Hans is on furlough." She threw herself at Karl again. "My darling! I'll get you free! They won't hurt you, I promise. Tell me where you are, I'll come to see you!"

Again, she had to be torn from my brother.

They escorted Karl out the door—and into the gates of hell.

The very day on which Karl was arrested, my grandparents, whose apartment had been burned, moved into our house on Groningstrasse.

I recall that on that same day, a man who had been my father's patient for as long as I could remember, a printer by the name of Max Lowy, was being examined.

My father was changing the dressings on the wounds and bruises that Max Lowy had suffered during the terrors of *Kristallnacht*. Lowy was a sparrowlike, chirpy man, full of Berlin street slang. He was a skilled artisan, although uneducated. An ordinary man, and utterly devoted to my father, as were so many of his patients.

"Easy there, doc," Lowy said.

"They did quite a job on you, Lowy."

"Six big bums. Chains, clubs. Bastards wrecked my print shop, too. Ruined all the typefaces. What the hell do they care about words? Except to poison the air with them."

"A familiar story. My father-in-law's place is a wreck also."

Lowy was irrepressible. Even in the dread final moments he would remain an optimist, a man who could not be crushed. "I hear the worst is over, doc," the printer said. "Goering's sore at Goebbels over the riots. Didn't want him rocking the boat after Munich. You believe that, doc?"

"I'm not sure what to believe any longer."

"I mean, look at it this way. What's the point of picking on Jews forever? That business of killing Christ was a long time ago. Why keep after us?"

"We are of value, my friend. We unite the people. I'm afraid the Nazis care very little about Christ or religious dogma."

"Yeah. Except when they can use it."

My father finished the bandaging—he did it like an artist—and said, "Good as new, Lowy."

My mother knocked at the door. She summoned my father into the hallway.

I'd just arrived, shepherding my grandparents from their ruined apartment. Anna—no fear in her, or at least she never showed it—had come along to help carry the bags.

"This will be your home," my father said to the old people.

Grandpa pointed to their few bags. "All we have left. They stole everything. The books . . . gone . . ."

My mother patted his hand. "You'll be safe here. And there's plenty of room. Mama and Papa, you'll stay in Karl's old room."

Grandpa Palitz was shaking his head. "We have no right to make life harder for you."

My father said, "Don't be silly. We are honored to have you live with us. I've got some good news. One of my patients, fellow with his ear to the ground, he says it's going to end. The fever has run its course."

Anna and I picked up the bags and started up the stairs. How blind they all were! Or am I, through the lens of fourteen years, here in my home in Israel, being cruel to them, unkind to their memory? They were not the only ones fooled, lulled, made to feel secure one day, destroyed the next.

"Yes, I'm inclined to agree," my grandfather was saying. He still wore his Iron Cross! "Economically it makes no sense. Schacht must realize that. To destroy businesses, drive us out of the economy? No sense at all."

I came downstairs, full of despair at their ability to deceive themselves. "They'll never learn," I said. And to my mother, surprised by my own freshness, "Nor will you."

My father was on the telephone and he looked pale, shaken. "Inga, yes, yes, I hear you . . . but why . . . what reason? Karl. I understand. But what did they say? Do you want someone to come over? Yes, yes. We'll try to make some calls."

He hung up. I can remember him trying to keep the bad news from my mother. His tall figure was almost bending with the effort of containing his emotions.

"They've arrested Karl. They gave no reason. He's at the main police station. With thousands of others."

My mother began to weep. Not hysterics, mind you, but discreet tears. "Oh, my son, my Karl."

"Inga is at the police station. She won't leave until she gets more information. She'll call again soon."

As Anna and I watched, frightened, my mother lost her self-control—that quality she most prided. She began to sob freely, and fell into my father's arms.

"Karl'll be okay, Mama," I said. "He never did anything. He can't be charged with anything." I lied to cheer her up; they didn't need reasons any longer. They hadn't for years.

"Rudi's right," my father said. "You'll see. He'll be released. They can't keep filling the jails with innocent people."

My mother looked into my father's hurt eyes. "We are being punished. For my pride. For my stubbornness. Oh, Josef, we should have run away, years ago."

"No, no, not at all. It isn't your fault, no one's."

She was amazing. In a moment, she was in control of her emotions again, brushing the tears away, straightening her dress. "I must go to make my parents comfortable. Rudi, you will do the shopping for dinner."

"If there's a store open."

My father patted me on the back. "You're resourceful, son. You'll find one."

She started up the stairs, staggered. My father ran to her and took her arm.

"I am all right, Josef," she said.

"You must rest, I'll give you a sedative."

"No, no, I am fine. You left a patient waiting. I shall be fine."

"So I did," my father said. He walked to the glass doors, ashen-faced, trying to hide his fears from her, from all of us.

Anna and I watched, said nothing. I cursed myself for being so young, so inexperienced, and worst of all, so unable to help them.

Outside, shopping bag under my arm, I stopped on our steps.

Two louts, grinning bastards in brown uniforms, were painting the word JUDE on the low brick wall in front of our house. They ignored me. I clenched my fists, started down the steps.

They carried short wooden clubs in their belts, sheathed knives. What good would a fight do? Oh, how I wanted to wade into them.

"What are you staring at, kid?" one asked.

I said nothing.

"Your old man's a Jew isn't he?" the other asked. "Why not advertise it?"

And they went on painting. The six-pointed star next to the four letters.

Erik Dorf's Diary

Berlin
November 1938

Marta is amazed at my rapid rise. I've become one of Heydrich's favorites. He likes what he calls my "agile legal mind."

As she sat in my lap earlier tonight, more beautiful than ever, happier than she had been in years, I told her that Heydrich wants us to go to the opera with him some night. We are climbing the ladder. We will have to socialize more, entertain.

"Erik, all those rich women. I'll be embarrassed."

"You'll be the most beautiful one there."

Marta blushed. "Oh, you know me. I'm content to look after the house and the children."

"A much better house. I've got my eye on a new apartment. In a better neighborhood."

Marta kissed me, threw her arms around me. "Oh, Erik. I'm so happy for us. And you once sneered at —what did you call it? Police work! Look how you've succeeded!"

Sitting here with my cognac (it was a long, tiring day at work), I know it is not in my nature to be boastful, but I am finding it easier to talk about myself. And of course, Marta delights in this new version of *Captain* Erik Dorf. I told her, as she listened, smiling, how I solved a tricky problem growing out of recent events.

Many German insurance companies were on the verge of bankruptcy because of claims by Jewish shopkeepers for damages. After mulling the problem, I advised Heydrich that we should let the companies pay the damages, but before the Jews could collect, the government will *confiscate* the payments on the grounds that the Jews incited the rioting and hence are not entitled to reimbursement. The money can then be returned to any Aryan firm that requests it. (Jewish insurance firms are exempted from such repayments.)

Marta confessed she had trouble following my legal reasoning, but she agreed that it is a just solution. The Jews, as she said, brought all this on themselves.

My attitudes toward Jews are unquestionably changed since my naive days three years ago. Now, I see clearly how they have insinuated themselves into our life, spreading their tentacles, preventing Germany from realizing its destiny. I understand what the Führer means by a "Jew-free" Europe. It can only be for the good of all concerned, including the Jews. Every now and then some old concept of law troubles me, but it is not hard to dismiss it under Heydrich's benign leadership. He was right, of course, at that first meeting. I have to put aside old-fashioned notions of justice. There are times and cases where they simply do not apply.

When Peter and Laura finished their baths, they came in wearing their new bathrobes. I kissed them.

"Children," I said, "you smell like spring flowers."

Peter sulked. "I'm no flower. Maybe she is." He is almost nine—tall, sturdy, with his mother's fine features and strong will.

Laura, who tends to be thoughtful, moody—much like me as a child—leaned heavily on my knee, the way children will do when they want attention. Her innocent eyes found mine, and she asked, "Papa, why does everyone hate Jews?"

Peter answered before I could. " 'Cause they killed Christ. Didn't you learn that in Sunday school?"

"Oh, there are other reasons," Marta said. "Something you will understand when you are older." She began to shepherd them off to bed.

I pondered Peter's ingenuous yet truthful response to Laura's question. Yes, they killed Christ. And although the party, our movement, the Führer's writings on the subject make little of this, we are certainly beneficiaries of a long tradition. My historical knowledge is not sufficient, nor am I a philosopher, but it seems to me there is an almost unbroken chain from the denunciation of Jews for the greatest crime against God ever committed to what we are planning for them. After all, we have not invented anti-Semitism.

My ruminations were halted by the door buzzer. Marta looked startled, but I cautioned her to stay with the children, that I would answer it.

It was Dr. Josef Weiss, standing in the hallway, looking older, stooped. "Captain Dorf," he said. "I am sorry to intrude at this hour, but I was afraid if I called you would refuse to see me."

I was annoyed with him. He should have known better. "I told you not to come to me."

"I have nowhere to turn. My son Karl—he's a bit younger than you, you may remember him from the old neighborhood—has been arrested. Not a word sent to us, nothing. No reasons given. He's never had a political thought in his life. He's an artist. He . . ."

His voice dwindled away.

I couldn't help him and told him so.

"What crime have we committed? What have we ever done to you? My father-in-law was a hero of the German army. His shop and his home were pillaged by ruffians. My sons . . . they have always felt as German as you—"

"These actions are not directed at you personally, or your family," I said.

"That makes it no easier for us."

"Doctor, these are long-range policies. For your benefit as well as Germany's."

"But lives are wrecked. People destroyed. Why?"

He was getting on my nerves. He had no right to come to me. "I can't discuss this with you."

"Captain Dorf, please. You have influence. You are an officer in the SS. Help my son."

As he stood there pleading with me, Marta appeared in the hallway. "Erik? Is anything wrong?"

"No, my dear."

Weiss bowed to Marta. "Mrs. Dorf, maybe you'll understand. Put yourself in my place. Suppose it was your son taken away, as mine was. You both once entrusted your health to me . . . I ask only—"

Marta's voice was firm. She ignored him. "Erik. The children."

Dr. Weiss would not leave. I walked away from him, to Marta.

She whispered to me, "Make him leave. He'll endanger your career. Explain to him you can't do anything for him. You didn't arrest his son."

"I've told him so."

"Tell him again. Be polite, but tell him there is absolutely nothing you can do."

I returned to the door. "Dr. Weiss, I'm afraid I cannot help you. These matters are out of my jurisdiction."

"But a word to your superiors . . . at least to let us

know where my son is . . . what charges he faces . . ."

"I can't. I'm sorry."

His face dropped. "I understand. Good night, Captain."

The door closed.

I was briefly troubled by his visit. He has always seemed to me a rather decent fellow, and for all I know, his son is also. But I have crossed some bridge, forded some river, and I cannot go back. Heydrich and Himmler have often warned us to be wary of the "good Jew," the one, as a compassionate German, you want to save. Our program is a long-range one, a complex one, and deals with whole peoples, vast changes. We cannot let sentiment, false sympathies stand in our way.

Only we, the SS, the elite of the SS, Heydrich says, have the steel to get this job done. I know now, after hearing the physician's slow tread in the hallway, what he means.

Rudi Weiss' Story

A few days after Papa's visit to Erik Dorf—I had no idea who he was, how important he was, just that he had refused to help us—my father was ordered deported to Poland.

My father, always seeing the best in people, or refusing to think the worst, was convinced Dorf had nothing to do with it. Possibly he was right. It was general policy at the time. All alien Jews resident in Germany —and there were thousands of Polish Jews—were forced to leave.

In fact, when the fellow with the briefcase entered the office, while my father was fixing some kid's sprained ankle, he was even hopeful that it was good news from Dorf, maybe about Karl.

But the man was from the immigration office and he said to my father, "You are Dr. Josef Weiss, born in Warsaw, Poland, and you are here illegally under the new laws. You are ordered deported to Poland. Be at the Anhalter railroad station tomorrow at six a.m. with food for one day and one bag."

I listened outside the office door, weeping for my father, wanting desperately to help him. How I hated those men who had come for him! How I longed to hit them, make them feel pain!

"But my wife and children . . . the people I take care of . . ."

"The order applies only to you. Give these documents to the transport officer tomorrow."

What I remember most clearly is that instead of going upstairs to tell my mother, or being so stunned that he could not continue his work, my father returned to the boy on the examining table and resumed treating his ankle.

My brother Karl had been sent to a prison camp, Buchenwald. The account of his internment there I learned from a man named Hirsch Weinberg, who had been arrested a few days before Karl. Weinberg was a tailor by trade, a native of Bremen. He remembered Karl Weiss the artist well.

Buchenwald is near Weimar. The Germans had built a huge camp there for anyone considered an enemy of the Reich. After *Kristallnacht,* it became a hellhole, packed, unsanitary, a place where hundreds died daily of beatings and disease, or were executed for whatever reason pleased the guards.

The torment began from the moment the prisoners walked through the gate with the legend ARBEIT MACHT FREI—work makes you free.

Karl and a batch of other prisoners were ordered into a receiving room filled with typists, guards, office managers—all SS personnel. The usual opening questions, after name and address and profession, were on the order of:

"Name of the whore that shit you?"

"What pimp screwed her to make you?"

"What crime were you arrested for?"

As Karl waited his turn, shivering, fearful, a burly

young Jew with the look of a truck driver refused to answer these insults. He protested; his mother was no whore, his father no pimp, and he had committed no crime. At once he was dragged into an adjoining room. There were screams, thudding noises.

A few minutes later, beaten and cowed, he was dragged back in, his head a bloody pulp, one eye closed, and whimpering, he answered all the questions.

Karl was next.

He gave his name, his address, and his occupation: artist.

An SS sergeant carrying a short whip walked up to Karl and shoved the butt end into his side. "One of those Jew Bolsheviks, Weiss? Drawing lying cartoons for some Communist rag?"

"I'm a commercial artist," Karl said. "I don't belong to any party. I—"

The whip cracked across Karl's face.

When Weinberg told me this, all I could think of was Karl, always skinny, a kid who was naturally picked on, chased. I was four years younger, but I was always strong, fast, and my creed was, if you hit me, I'll hit back. I wanted to weep when I spoke to Weinberg, but my wife Tamar was present, and she does not believe in tears.

"The whore who shit you?"

"No . . . my mother . . ."

Crack. The whip landed again.

"Berta Palitz Weiss," Karl said.

"The pimp who raped her?"

"Josef Weiss. Dr. Josef Weiss."

"What crime did you commit to be sent to Buchenwald?"

"I . . . I did nothing."

"Try again, Jewboy. What crime did you commit?"

"Nothing. Honestly. I was at home, painting. These men came for me. There are no charges filed."

"You're a Jew. That's reason enough."

"But . . . but that's not a crime."

They laughed at this. The sergeant and two other louts dragged Karl into the adjacent room and beat him senseless. He awakened in a dark barracks, where he met Hirsch Weinberg, who tried to teach him some tricks of survival.

Still unaware of where Karl was, or what was happening to him, we all went to see my father off for Poland. It was the last day of November, 1938.

I remember the scene at the bleak railroad station. About a thousand Jews, most of them older and poorer than my father, with their miserable bundles and packages of food. There were rumors the Poles were turning them away. The Jews would be left in a no man's land, floating between Germany and Poland.

But my father tried to be cheerful. "If you cry, Berta," he said to my mother, "you'll make me angry."

She dabbed at her eyes. No, she would control herself. Around her, other families made no secret of their sorrows. They wept, they begged, they tried to keep their loved ones from boarding the train for the Polish border.

"Why, this may be the best thing that's happened to us," my father said. He was a terrible actor. Yet who could tell? Maybe he was right.

"My brother Moses said he'd meet me. We'll head right for Warsaw. Moses has connections. I'm sure I can get work at the Jewish Hospital."

We listened to him—silent, attentive, concerned. As yet, the shock of his leaving had not sunken in. Karl gone, my father forced to leave. The blows were falling one after another.

"I'll go with you," my mother said. "They'll let me. I'll get my papers tomorrow."

"No, no," my father said. "The children need you. I'm told the Poles are being difficult about even letting Polish Jews back in, let alone Germans." He took Inga's hand. "And we must be optimistic. Inga will find Karl, she'll get him freed, and you'll all be together again."

As I write this, I am again appalled at how so many of us, my parents included, could have deceived themselves for so long. Tamar claims it was a form of mass hysteria; a self-deception that spread among Jews. I argue that many were helpless, without money, with no place to go. Few countries would take them. Fighting back was unknown to them. We had been a people who accommodated, gave in, bent, tried to make arrangements, hoped that tomorrow would be better. Now, to the east of our kibbutz, Syrian guns are firing again. But this time we fire back. Morality is a marvelous, admirable thing; but I have yet to hear of a moral stance, a righteous position, that ever deflected a bomb or a bullet.

Anna began to sob. She threw her arms around my father, crying, "Papa, Papa, don't leave us. I'll be afraid without you. Please, Papa, stay with us."

Inga took Anna aside, brushed her hair, kissed her. "Papa will be all right, Anna darling. He will come back."

Anna was truly bawling. "Shut up," I said. "You make it worse."

My mother asked, "Josef, how did this happen to us?"

"It wasn't our doing, Berta. We had no control over events." Then he smiled. "But you must believe me. I'm feeling optimistic. This will open our eyes. I have a feeling we'll be reunited in Poland. Or somewhere else. England, perhaps."

"I made you stay," my mother whispered.

"Now, no more of that," Papa said. He was brisk, businesslike. (And no worse a businessman ever practiced medicine.) "Berta, you should sell the clinic. Find a smaller apartment."

She wiped her nose, managed a smile. "And you must not go running out on night calls. Wear your rubbers in the rain. Poland is a very damp place."

"I will, if you promise not to sell the piano. Anna must continue her piano lessons, no matter what."

Two Berlin policemen approached. People were being herded toward the train. "Move it along. We're boarding in five minutes."

Mama turned to us. "Children. Rudi, Anna, Inga. Say goodbye to Papa."

Anna was uncontrollable now. "Papa, Papa . . . we'll come to live with you! Uncle Moses can find us a place!"

"Of course, Anna, my darling. But meanwhile, you must look after Grandpa and Grandma, and we must find Karl. Work at your music, Anna."

He hugged me, looked into my eyes. "Rudi. Maybe you should go back to school."

"If I can, Papa."

"The world doesn't begin and end with a soccer game, you know. You must prepare yourself for a career."

What could I say to him? *Career!* But I played his game. "I'll try, Papa. Maybe I can be a physical-education teacher—as you once said I should be."

"Splendid idea."

People surged forward. Among them, I noticed Max Lowy, the printer. He was a Polish Jew also; he was being deported. He seemed undismayed, ready to accept fate's blows.

"Hey, Doc!" Lowy shouted. "You too? I thought they were just kicking out guys like me? You know the wife, doc."

A tiny dark woman nodded at my father. He tipped his hat, always the gentleman. In fact, on seeing the Lowys, he turned to my mother, who was still crying, and said cheerfully, "You see, Berta? I'm the only physician deported with his own supply of patients."

They hugged for the last time. I heard him say, "They cannot defeat us. So long as we love one another."

"Josef . . ."

"Remember your Latin, my dear, *Amor vincit omnia.* Love conquers all."

The crowd shoved him away, and they were separated. At a barrier, a policeman and an SS guard examined my father's papers. A loudspeaker was bellowing instructions: "Follow the guards to the train. This is the special train for the border only. . . ."

My mother ran to the iron railings, and we followed her. She was waving to him, calling, "Goodbye, Josef, goodbye. Let us know where you are. We'll come . . ."

I turned my face away to hide my tears. What I really wanted to do was to hit somebody—one of the Berlin policemen, the guards directing people to the trains. What right had they to do this to us? What had we ever done to them? There was a suppressed fury in me. I could have killed them—the grinning party members, all of them in boots and uniforms, braggarts, bullies, liars . . .

"Oh, you're so brave," Anna taunted. "You're crying also." Her eyes were wet, her cheeks soaked.

"I am not. I don't cry."

She grabbed me, and held me, and we both wept. But I forced myself to stop. "They'll never do that to me," I said. "Never."

"Won't they?"

"No. I won't go the way Papa and Karl did, and Mr. Lowy, just giving in."

I was boasting to buoy my courage. But as I look back at the moment, I realized I had made a vow to myself. They would not humiliate me, force me to do their bidding, the way they had forced so many others. Jews were supposed to agree, be polite, obey, listen, accept. But I had never understood this. I did not look for fights in the street, but I never ran away. And when I played soccer I played to *win*. And if the other fellow played dirty, I could trip and shove, and if need be, throw a punch.

"What will you do?" Anna asked, still weeping.

"I'll fight."

We watched my father climb aboard the train and wave to us a last time. My mother put her arms around us. Inga stood just behind us, shaking her head in sorrow. I could see there was shame in her face—shame for her own people.

"Let us go home, children," Mama said. Her voice was calm again.

All prisoners in Buchenwald had to work. Karl was an artist, so it was assumed he was accomplished with his fingers. He was assigned—through Weinberg's influence—to the tailoring shop.

Weinberg explained to him how much better off he was working inside. At least it was reasonably warm, and the work was not exhausting. Outside, prisoners died daily in the quarries, the road-building teams, the so-called "garden" detail, which consisted of ditch-digging.

The older man—he'd been a tailor by trade—explained that deaths by beating and torture for any infraction were the order of the day. Late for roll call, answering back, talking out of turn—all these resulted in severe beatings. And anything considered more grave —an attack on a guard, theft—meant a quick death, usually in a special room where the prisoner was made to stand in a corner. Through a hole behind his head, an unseen executioner killed him with a single shot.

"Does anyone ever get out?" Karl asked.

"Heard stories of some rich guys buying their way out. *Goyim* mostly. Maybe even a few Jews. The SS runs this like a racket. They keep the valuables, the gold, divide it up. So it might even be the bastards take a bribe from some rich Jew and let him go."

The kapo—the prisoner-guard or trusty—came by and warned Weinberg to shut up. Weinberg made some excuse—he was just explaining the ropes to Karl. (This kapo's name was Melnik, a big fellow, a pickpocket on the outside. The Nazis often took common criminals—Jew and Gentile—and put them in positions of authority. It helped terrify the other prisoners.)

When Melnik was out of hearing, Weinberg took a box of cloth patches and started to explain them to Karl.

"So you'll know your fellow inmates," he said. He began to hold up triangles of varying colors. "Red means a political prisoner. Anything from a Trotskyite to a monarchist. Green, a common criminal. Purple, Jehovah's Witness. Black, what they call shiftless elements—beggars, tramps, so on. Pink is for homosexuals. Brown is for gypsies."

"Gypsies?"

"Buchenwald's full of them. They give the guards fits because they won't work. The SS ordered two of them buried alive yesterday. When they dug them out their tongues were sticking out like salamis."

Weinberg then showed Karl the six-pointed yellow star.

"I know what that is," my brother said. "But what's this?" He picked up a cloth patch with the four letters BLOD on it.

"Idiots, morons, feeble-minded," Weinberg explained.

"But . . . what crime can they have committed?"

"Considered useless by the state. You should see the way the guards have a field day with them—teasing, dressing them up. Some of the guards take the feeble-minded women and do things . . ."

"I can't believe this."

"Can't you? Listen. I've heard stories. There's a house not far from here where they take the crazies. Half-wits, cretins, cripples. They gas them to death."

"Gas?"

"Some guy on a truck detail swears it's true."

The kapo came by and shut them up again, threatening Karl with his truncheon. The kapos wore dark caps and dark jackets, in contrast to the striped suits of the prisoners. Everyone hated them.

Suddenly music was piped over the loudspeaker. Not recorded music, but real music, from the Buchenwald orchestra.

Weinberg winked at Karl. "Half the Berlin Philharmonic is in here. The guards like good music. Germany will go to hell listening to *Das Rheingold*."

One morning, in March 1939, my mother and I heard voices downstairs. My father's office had been closed for months, of course. We couldn't imagine who it could be.

I followed Mama down to the old office—my mother still dusted it every day, kept it clean, in the vain hope that some day Dr. Josef Weiss would practice again—and we opened the doors.

A tall shaven-headed man wearing rimless eyeglasses, along with two workmen, was taking inventory and moving things about.

The bald man clicked his heels and bowed. "Ah, Mrs. Weiss. I am Dr. Heinzen. I have been assigned to take over your husband's office. You'll recall my telephone call? The keys, please."

Mama sent me for them. I could hear Heinzen checking out my father's equipment. "X-ray . . . basal metabolism . . . diathermy . . . autoclave . . ."

I returned with the ring of keys and gave them to my mother, who handed them to Dr. Heinzen. "These are all of them, doctor. Office, rear and front entrance, garage, basement."

"You are most kind."

"I am unable to say the same for your people."

"I apologize for the abrupt manner . . . still, it was a pity to let this office, this equipment go to waste. I knew your husband professionally, and I am personally sorry."

"You knew him before he was fired from Central Berlin Hospital."

"Other times, other customs, madame. I am a party member, and the party has ordered me to take over the clinic and the house."

My mother's eyes were on fire. "And our reimbursement?"

"The party medical board is reviewing your case."

Mama gave him a slip of paper with an address and phone number on it. It was Karl's old studio, Inga's apartment. "If you have any word for us, Dr. Heinzen."

He bowed. "You shall be the first to hear, madame."

I couldn't take any more. "They're stealing everything, Mama. Crooks. That's all they are." I moved a step toward Heinzen. He stared at me as if I were crazy. The two workmen stopped moving my father's desk and looked up.

"Rudi, please," my mother said. "Take your father's diploma."

I walked past Heinzen, removed Papa's diploma from the wall and left.

They were still checking out everything that had

been my father's, preparatory to stealing it. I could hear Heinzen's voice: "Fluoroscope . . . centrifuge . . . ultraviolet lamp . . ."

We spent all day packing. There was little space in Inga's apartment, and we took only essentials. Anna and Mama and I sat in the darkened parlor. I knew we would never live in this house on Groningstrasse again. It seemed to me I could hear my brother Karl's voice, when I had once played a trick on him, a rotten trick. *Hey, Rudi, you hide my paints? I need them.* . . .

"Can't we take the piano, Mama?" Anna asked.

"Maybe later, Anna. Inga has so little room."

"Well, let's play one last piece together."

My mother and my sister sat at the piano and began to play the *Lorelei.* I could hear Anna saying, "Oh, Mama, remember how we all sang this at Karl's wedding?"

The piano music sounded louder, filling the house. For some reason I now hated it. In a sense the Bechstein, and all it symbolized, had kept us glued to Berlin. We were prosperous, secure, people with pianos. Who would hurt us? (Now, a *kibbutznik,* a man who owns virtually nothing and gives his meager salary to the commune, I realize how little people need to get by, how destructive these material things can be. I don't mean that starvation or poverty are ennobling; far from it. But to be a slave to *things?* To define one's life in terms of pianos and fur coats? Perhaps it explained—in part, only—why we had blinded ourselves.)

We had told our grandparents to be dressed and packed and ready to leave by four that afternoon. I knew grandpa—the old military man. He would be ready.

I knocked at the door, but there was no answer.

I went into the room. It was dark, the shades drawn.

"Grandpa, time to go," I said.

For a moment I thought they were sleeping. But

they were fully clothed. Grandpa was wearing his dark suit, his wing collar shirt, a black tie. Grandma was wearing a black velvet dress. They were lying peacefully on the bed, their arms about one another.

I walked to the night table and saw an opened dark-brown bottle. I smelled it. A strange sweetish odor, like rotten peaches. Then I took a mirror from the dresser and held it to their mouths. No fogging. They were dead.

I cursed the damned music, the damned piano, and I even wanted to hate my mother, hate my father for having deceived themselves so long. I bent over my grandparents and kissed them on their cheeks, wondering how I would be able to tell this to my mother. Perhaps, I reasoned, the old people had chosen the only way out. And they had not been alone. That winter, after *Kristallnacht,* thousands of Jews chose suicide. For them, all hope had vanished.

Erik Dorf's Diary

Vienna
July 1939

Marvelous day. Heydrich has sent me to Vienna to confer with Adolf Eichmann, who heads up the Jewish "resettlement" program in Austria and in the new territories of Bohemia and Moravia—the so-called "protectorate" of what was once Czechoslovakia.

A charming man. Slender, dark, casual and polite in his manner, but with rather intense eyes. He claims to know a great deal about the Jewish problem. He told me he spent time as an agent of some kind in Palestine, and that he speaks some Yiddish and Hebrew.

"I understand them," he said to me. "They have been conditioned to obey, to accommodate, to bend. Well, we will bend them."

He explained, not without a touch of humor, that he handled Austria's Jews (and would now proceed to handle the Czech Jews) as if running a factory.

"Imagine this large factory building, Dorf," Eichmann said. "A Jew enters at one end, with all his valuables, his properties, his birthright. We process him, the way one would a pig or a chicken, and he comes out plucked, denuded, with nothing but an order to get out of Austria, or accept a ticket to one of our camps."

This conversation took place in the lovely Prater, that vast, beautiful, flowery park. Heydrich was kind enough to let me take Marta and the children here for a summer holiday, and we are all enjoying the fairyland atmosphere. (Eichmann, always the cautious fellow, made no comments about the Jewish problem in the presence of my family.)

"More ice cream?" he asked Peter and Laura.

Marta ordered the children to say "No, thank you" to Major Eichmann. They did. She was firm about good manners.

Laura, her little face flushed with excitement, asked, "Mama, can we ride the carousel now?"

Around us, balloon peddlers, men selling pinwheels and toy flutes, flower vendors, nannies pushing prams, formed a colorful crowd. It was indescribably lovely. I could understand why the Führer had wanted Austria. It is German. It belongs to us.

"Laura, I'm afraid that pastry and ice cream will go around and around in your tummy," Marta said.

At which point both Peter and Laura began to cry for a carousel ride. Usually, we were strict with them, but today was a special day.

"Go on," I said. "This is a day for children."

Eichmann smiled. "And if they get ill, Mrs. Dorf, I'll provide free medical care."

When Marta and the children had left—Marta complaining that she would need a rest after the youngsters had their fill of rides—Eichmann looked at me with kind, understanding eyes.

"Your wife is ill?"

"A slight heart murmur. She tires easily, but she's fine otherwise."

I wondered how he knew she was ill.

"Charming woman," he went on. "I'm delighted Heydrich sent you here. Berlin appreciates my operation. Train scheduling, warehousing, processing. You'll have to see our stockpile of fine old china, silver, antiques. A room full of Steinways and Bechsteins. All the property of the state, of course."

"I had no idea . . ."

"Oh, Himmler is very strict about looting, private gain. Except for a few of us who enjoy the privileges of rank."

A rather enigmatic fellow, Eichmann. Does he really feel that the seizure of Jewish property is the privilege of those of us in the upper echelons of the SS? I cannot be sure. He has intense, glittering eyes, and it is difficult for me to gauge if he is being sarcastic and mocking at times, or if the intensity of those eyes convey fervor and devotion.

Flattery, I have learned, is always a useful tool with my superiors, so I complimented him repeatedly on the reports in Berlin. His handling of Jews was exemplary. Now, with Czechoslovakia absorbed, he will be responsible for another quarter of a million Jews. Eichmann is as susceptible to flattery as Heydrich. He spoke freely of his clever methods for attracting Jews, registering them. They were not threatened; they were promised relocation, fair treatment. Honey, not garlic, Eichmann said, is what draws both flies and Jews.

But how, I asked, did he explain the expropriation of their valuables? He laughed. Oh, that was simple. The possessions were being held "in trust" for them until the international situation quieted down. But did they believe this? I asked. Again that jewel-like glitter illuminated his eyes. They believe it because they have no choice, he said. They have no arms, no powers to resist, no press, no advocates in government. But then, I was about to say, it really gets down to a matter of *force*. For all Eichmann's "psychology" and alleged knowledge of Hebrew, Yiddish and Jewish mores, the rock-bottom fact was that we had the power of life and death over them. But I did not tell him this.

"And for my part," he said, "I simply obey orders. *Un bon soldat*. You understand French, Dorf."

"How do you know?"

"I've seen your file. I try to get a look at everyone's records. It helps."

For a fleeting instant I was ill at ease. Why should he look at my file? He noted the discomfiture on my face.

"Father, Klaus Dorf," Eichmann said. "A baker in Berlin. Killed himself with his World War Luger in 1933 after his business failed. He was apparently a Socialist at one time."

"I'll be damned."

"You worked your way through law school. Excellent student, but a bit self-effacing. Wife, the former Marta Schaum, from a Bremen family. Church people."

I must have turned pale, begun to sweat a bit. He knew a great deal about me, perhaps more than he was letting on. Not that I had anything to hide. But it was a little unnerving to know that Eichmann, my genial, generous host, had learned so much about me. To tell the truth, I was vaguely frightened. The happy day in the Prater had an edge of nightmare about it.

Eichmann must have noticed the change in my expression. He slapped my boot and assured me he meant no harm, none at all. The SS, being a police and security operation, obviously has to know its own members well. Gestapo, SS, SD, RSHA, all the specialized branches—they all keep an eye on one another.

"It's how we survive, Dorf," he said.

I told him it was not my intention to survive in that manner, but rather by being utterly obedient to Heydrich, the most brilliant man I had ever met.

At this point, Eichmann leaned back and yawned,

and that mocking look passed over his lean features again. "Of course, Dorf, of course. Brilliant, inventive, fearless. But like all of us, Heydrich has an Achilles' heel."

I must have looked as if I'd been struck with a brick.

"You mean you haven't heard the rumors? Heydrich is supposed to have a Jew in his family tree."

"I don't believe it."

"Went to court years ago to sue. Paid people off. Had records burned. It drives him crazy. That's why he's so intent on following the Führer's racial policies. To kill the Jew in himself. At least that's what they say."

It took me a few seconds to absorb this shocking information—false though it may have been. "And what do they say about me?" I asked.

"Oh, that you're a hard-working, loyal aide to the chief of the Gestapo and the Security Service. A sort of house intellectual. I must tell you, Dorf, Heydrich's memoranda are infinitely more readable since you took over."

"You're baiting me, Major."

"Not at all. I love the substitute words you've developed for us. Code words, as it were." He seemed to savor the sound as he spoke. " 'Resettlement,' 'relocation,' 'special handling.' Marvelous synonyms for getting rid of Jews."

"I'm pleased to have supplied amusement for a brother officer."

Eichmann snapped his fingers, ordered more wine. The waiters fairly sprained their ankles racing to serve him. People know him well. They understood the power of the black uniform and the jack boots.

"You needn't be upset," Eichmann said. "Reports on you are good. Besides, Heydrich has the goods on everyone. It's his insurance if this Jew business ever surfaces again. He's got dossiers on Himmler, Goering, Goebbels. Sometimes I think he even keeps a file on the Führer."

I sat there, too disturbed to think clearly.

Marta returned with our children. "Too much excitement," she said. "For them and for me."

I suggested we go to the Sacher Hotel—Eichmann had gotten us a prized suite of rooms at party expense —and rest.

Peter would not hear of it. He wanted to ride the Ferris wheel. So did Laura. They set up the kind of wailing that can only come from the throats of over-stimulated children.

"All right," I said. "I'll take them. Marta, you keep Major Eichmann company."

Marta sat. Eichmann bowed to her, complimented her again on her beauty and charm. They talked about our children, how much they meant to the future of Germany, the new revitalized Germany that was re-making Europe.

I watched them touching wine glasses, drinking to family, home and honor. As I lifted the children into the Ferris wheel, I was able to dismiss Eichmann's rather startling revelations (if that was what they were) about our organization being a nest of internal spies.

It has been, truly, a happy, fruitful day. Perhaps I have not advanced my career by acting a bit naive in front of Eichmann. But Marta, with her simple charm, more than makes up for it.

Later tonight in the Sacher Hotel, we loved one another with a fervor, an abandonment of hesitation about new—what shall I say?—approaches, methods, that astonished both of us and left us gasping, wilted. In some way, the new powers I feel in my work, the fearlessness of being a member of the organization, are having an effect on our sexual engagements.

Rudi Weiss' Story

My father was in one of the last groups of Jews to be allowed into Poland. He and the people with whom he was deported spent a week being shuttled back and

forth on cramped, filthy trains before the Poles reluc-
tantly agreed to accept them. A woman died of heart
failure aboard the train, and my father attended her
to the very end.

A survivor told me how it worked.

First, the Jews were lined up on the German side of
the frontier, after they had disembarked from the train.

They were marched through muddy roads for several miles to the actual barrier. Some old people collapsed. Those who protested were beaten and clubbed.

My father, luckily, was in fairly good condition. He
walked with Max Lowy, the printer, and Lowy's wife,
Chana.

When the red-and-white-striped barrier was visible,
the SS guards halted the column. Everyone had to
empty his pockets. They were allowed to take only
ten marks with them.

"You stole this money from the German people, and
now you will give it back. We reclaim the money in
the name of the German people."

Watches and jewelry were snatched from the Jews.
My father was forced to surrender his fountain pen,
his watch, his wallet. The SS guard stared at the ca-
duceus in my father's lapel—the serpent-and-staff of
the physician. "What the hell is that?" he asked.

"I am a physician. It was a gift from my wife
when I graduated from medical school."

The SS man plucked it from his lapel. "The Polacks
don't care about doctors. They're animals, almost as
low as kikes."

Somehow my father assumed the role of leader.
Most of these Polish Jews were poor, uneducated people. They turned to him naturally in their ordeal. He
led them through the snowy fields—it was a bitter-cold
day—and across the barrier, as the Polish immigration
guards and army officers in their oddly peaked caps
inspected papers.

"Papers ready, proof of citizenship," a captain
shouted. "As if we need any more damned Jews."

I look back on this incident—the contempt, the
hatred of the Poles—and on later incidents, far more

brutal, and I am left with a numb inability to comprehend it. The Poles were hated by the Germans almost as much as we were hated. Hitler made no secret of his plans for them. They were to be *slaves,* a notch above Jews in the Nazi table of organization. One might imagine a community of interest in the face of oppression. But no. No pity. No understanding.

When finally the full weight of the German army, the SS, the official murderers and torturers descended on Poland, the Poles still found the time and energy to hate Jews, to betray us, and to stand by idly, indifferent, as we were systematically destroyed. I cannot fathom it to this date. It was as if in the midst of a tough soccer game, some players on the losing side were to turn on their most weary teammates and begin to beat them.

After hours of waiting, inspections, questionings, the last group of Jews was allowed to walk on to Polish soil. At a road junction, relatives and friends of the expelled people had been waiting for days, shivering, terrified, uncertain if their loved ones would ever arrive.

Lowy and his wife tagged after my father. "You got family here, doc? Me and Chana—nobody."

"A brother," my father said. ·

And Moses was waiting for my father. He was a bachelor, my father's brother, a quiet, contemplative man who once thought of studying for the rabbinate, but was forced by economic circumstances to take over my grandfather's pharmacy in the Jewish quarter of Warsaw.

The brothers looked at one another, but would not cry. My father had learned some of my mother's reserve, her absolute calm and dignity. So the two men, who had not seen each other since Karl's wedding in 1935, merely studied each other. Their breath formed clouds in the frigid air. Around them, people wept, embraced, gave thanks, cursed our enemies.

"So . . . you are here," Moses said.

"Yes. Back to the homeland, as it were."

"A pleasant journey, Josef?"

"Not quite the Orient Express. They kept shuttling us back and forth for eight days. I understand we are the last the Poles will let in."

Suddenly the casual banter ended, and the two men embraced, weeping in each other's arms. Moses, embarrassed—he carried timidity to the point of nonexistence, my mother used to say—dabbed at his eyes. "Dust. The curse of Poland."

"In January, Moses?" my father joked. "Don't be ashamed to cry."

"I'm not ashamed. But tears serve no purpose. I suppose we must get moving. The Polish army refused to let us bring any transport here. Not even a wagon. It's a mile walk to the rail station."

The column of people picked up their bundles and bags and began to follow my father and my uncle. My father told him of our tragedies. Karl in prison. The office closed. He asked if his wife had been able to get a phone call through to Warsaw. When he saw my uncle hesitate, he knew that he had bad news of some kind.

"What is it, Moses?"

"Josef, the Palitzes are dead. The old people. They took their own lives."

My father staggered, halted, gasped. Those decent old people. A man of enduring patience, always full of sympathy for the old, the ill, the poor, he found it impossible to comprehend such limitless brutality. He worried about my mother, about Anna and me, he told Moses later. And within him, a worm of doubt began to gnaw: perhaps things much worse were in store for the family he had left in Berlin. The suicide of the Palitzes was perhaps a portent, an omen.

They plodded on, through snowy fields, ice-packed roads. A few Polish peasants came out to stare at them. Once, an old man collapsed. My father attended him, pleaded with a Polish farmer to let him spend the night in the warm hut. The farmer refused. The man had to be carried to the station.

Moses tried to be optimistic. Things would get better. In Warsaw, he had arranged for my father to work on the staff of the Jewish Hospital. There was even a small apartment he could share, if my father didn't mind living over a drugstore.

"I lived over one until I was nineteen, Moses."

Moses had brought bread, sausage, cheese. They munched as they walked to the station, sharing what little they had with Lowy and his wife.

When my father introduced the Lowys to Moses, Lowy joked, "Some way for Jews to meet, on a dirt road in Poland. They don't mark the way with kilometers, but with anti-Semites."

Then he asked if he could come to Warsaw with them. He and his wife had no one. They were originally from Krakow, but their families were long gone.

"Look," Lowy said. "No charity, not a cent. I'm a skilled workman. A printer. Look at my nails. Forty years of printer's ink under them. But it would be nice if, at least, I could be with some folks I knew."

"Warsaw is no paradise," Moses said.

"I gave up on paradise long ago," Lowy said. "I'll settle for a bed and a cup of tea. And maybe some type to set, a press to run."

Moses liked him at once. "Of course, Mr. Lowy. You will come with me and my brother."

And so they trudged along, weary, bone-cold, unwanted, to the train for Warsaw.

By August 1939, my mother, Anna and I had been living in Karl's studio for some months. Inga, forever generous and caring, had moved into her parents' apartment, adjacent to us. She slept in Hans' bed. He was off on maneuvers somewhere in the east.

In the studio, we had moved aside Karl's easel and his paint table, and stacked his drawings and canvases behind the closet. My mother and Anna shared the couch. I had located an old bedroll I had used on camping trips and I slept on the floor.

From the house on Groningstrasse, my mother had salvaged more than enough kitchen equipment, hardware and such things as lamps and rugs to make it reasonably comfortable if crowded. She had also, wisely, been withdrawing money from the various bank accounts for several years, and before my father left, he had revealed to her that he had been keeping a great deal of his income in cash. So for the time being we could support ourselves.

The neighborhood was a Christian working-class section, and we tried to be seen as little as possible. Inga volunteered to shop for us. The worst thing was the terrible boredom.

Sometimes I would kick a soccer ball by myself in the nearby park, or run a few miles to keep in shape, but I was restless, impatient, and to be truthful, a bit frightened. I did a lot of the cooking and cleaning up in the small studio. There'd been a girl I'd dated in high school. Once I tried to find her; her family had disappeared. No one would tell me where they had gone.

It was not an easy life, but we knew that many Jews had it much worse—including my brother Karl. There seemed no future for us, no way out. That is what frightened me, although my mother maintained her usual calm. I can see her clearly, tying her apron, pushing back a strand of graying hair as she started to chop vegetables for our evening meal—soup made with a few neck bones. We'd traveled a long way down since those fine dinners at the old house.

If my mother was terrified, or brimming with sorrow, she managed to conceal it most of the time. She was no wailer, no breast beater. But I did see a change in Anna. Once a spry, vivacious and aggressive girl, she now lapsed into silences, sulked, and would not respond to my teasing. "I hate it here," she said to me—almost every morning, when we rose to take our turns in the small bathroom, and look for ways to use up another day.

One day Heinz Muller called on the Helms family. He was now a sergeant in the SS, what branch I was not certain. Inga had told us that he had once hoped to marry her and had asked her father for her hand.

She detested him. Muller was delighted that my brother—his rival—was now in prison, but he had to tread carefully in Inga's presence.

It was a hot summer's day, and the door to the Helmses' apartment was open, as was ours. Voices drifted in, as I lay on the couch reading the sports pages for the eleventh time.

Inga was pleading with Muller to find out for her where Karl had been taken. We knew that many of the Jews arrested after *Kristallnacht* had simply vanished. Some had been murdered, executed on fake charges.

"I'm only a sergeant," Muller said. "I can't poke my nose into the files."

"But to find out where he is—"

Her father broke in. "Inga, Muller can't stick his neck out for—"

"Say it, Papa. My Jewish husband."

Muller hemmed and hawed, then said, "I suspect he's in Buchenwald, a civilian prison. They sent most of them from Berlin there."

"Can I write to him? Can I see him?"

"I'm not sure. They're tough about it. A letter, maybe. But my advice is . . . forget about it. Leave him alone. Your father is right, you do yourself no good."

"Sound advice," Helms said.

Then her mother: "Muller's right, darling. Maybe it was for the best."

"When I think of that fancy mother of his, with her airs, and that doctor—a lousy Polish Jew is all he was," Helms added.

"Stop!" Inga cried. "You have no shame! I won't let you talk this way about my husband!"

They were silent for a while, just some low-voiced grumbling from her father and her mother's whine.

There was an abiding quality of strength and justice in Inga. That combined with her love of Karl, made her a formidable woman. A word about how they met may explain this better. Karl was a student at the art school, as I have mentioned, where Inga, a pretty, very "Aryan" girl, worked as secretary to the director. When the employees of the school—clerks and teachers —asked for salary raises and were refused, it was Inga Helms who led the petition-signing, the meetings, the plans for a strike.

Karl remembered seeing her getting up at such a meeting and demanding that they be prepared to close down the school if necessary. No, she said, she was no Red, no Socialist, had little interest in politics. But she knew what was *right*. The teachers—all sensitive party people—listened to her. (The strike was forbidden, but their salaries were raised.)

She had this rare quality one finds in some people —a built-in, almost biologically fixed sense of justice. After the strike meeting, Karl, shy, often tongue-tied, saw her leaving by herself. He decided she had no boyfriend and invited her to have coffee with him. They fell in love almost at once. Karl told me that for all her humble background, she had an intense understanding of people, of motives, and spoke well.

She protested she was only a secretary, and knew nothing about art, could not discuss Picasso or Renoir with him. Karl had laughed. He was emboldened to take her hand when he walked her home. "You need remember only one thing," he said. "A critic named Berenson said it. 'The purpose of art is to enhance life.'" Impulsively, she kissed him. There was no doubt that they would marry someday.

I recalled those traits in Inga, as I heard her father's loud voice. "It's we who have the right to be angry! You married one, and then you take their goddam family in! Living next door to us!"

"Be silent!" Inga cried.

Muller sounded calm, like a family counselor. "Bad business hiding Jews. You can get hurt."

"Muller, I beg of you," Inga persisted. "Can I send him a letter? Can he buy his way out? What can you do for me?"

"Buy? I've heard of rich Jews doing it now and then—for a king's ransom. But a poor artist like your husband, never."

"Help me. Please, help me."

And her father: "Muller, don't go sticking your neck out for her, or for that Jew she married. It's bad enough we got them living next door."

"I am disgusted with all of you!" Inga cried.

Now her father was raging. Like all weaklings, he lost his temper, enjoyed shouting at his children. "I want that Jew bitch out! And her brats also!"

"No! They are my family! And sometimes I think they are closer to me than any of you!"

I heard a door slam.

Muller was trying to pacify Inga's father. "Well, can't say she wasn't warned. Beautiful Aryan girl, mixed up with them. Damn, if only you'd forced her to postpone the wedding. The Nuremberg Laws would have been passed, and the whole thing would have been illegal."

"Muller . . . as an old friend," Inga's mother was saying, "you'll say nothing about . . ."

"Your Hebrew in-laws? Not a word."

In the studio, I was listening to the radio. Anna was doing homework. Now that she could not attend any public school, and all Jewish schools had been closed, my mother acted as a private tutor, giving her books to read, assignments to complete. I could have used some education myself; but I was too angry, too upset to learn. Besides, I'd never been much of a student.

On the radio, the announcer was quoting Hitler's latest speech. The Führer's patience was exhausted with the Poles. The Poles were being arrogant, quarrelsome, and they would have to answer to him. He warned England and France to stay out of it.

"Poland, you're next," Anna said.

I agreed. "It's crazy. Nobody believes him when he says he's going to do these things. I looked at some stuff in *Mein Kampf* once. Why didn't anyone take it seriously? What he said about Jews, and Slavs?"

My mother was writing a letter, hopeful it would reach my father in Warsaw. It was a warm day, but she wore a shawl. She seemed to have turned gray, pale. "People deceive themselves when they're frightened, Rudi."

"Like us," Anna said. "We're as bad as those dumb politicians who give in to him all the time."

Inga appeared at the door and motioned to me. I got up from the window seat and stood in the vestibule with her.

"That pig Muller thinks Karl is in Buchenwald. I'm going there."

"They won't let you near him."

"I'll try. He is my husband, Rudi. He needs me."

"Did Muller say he had any chance of being freed?"

"No. But I'm going anyway."

I looked at her long, pretty face. I had to admire her. She could have divorced Karl, ignored him, fallen back on her Aryan status to save herself all this heartache.

"I'm going to go away also," I said.

"With me?"

No, I told her. I could do my mother and Anna no good hiding in the flat. Or could I? I was the man of the family now. But I told Inga that I was convinced we would all be arrested, deported. There was still a Jewish Council of sorts in Berlin, but it was quieter and quieter every day; we were isolated, under siege. I said I would never let anyone take me. At least they would not take me alive.

Her eyes looked into mine, as if to say, "The way Karl went?" But she did not utter the words, and I was sorry for my foolish bravado. How did I know what I would do? I was no one to be bragging to her of my unproved courage. She had defied her family, married a Jew, stood by him. I asked her why.

"I loved him," she said.

"It had to be more than that."

"Respect, affection. Karl is gentle, he cannot hurt anyone. I saw too much bloody fighting in the streets —right in this neighborhood. Reds, Nazis, all of them. And my father coming home bloodied, tenants in this building screaming, battling. Karl was a revelation to me. I did not know there were people who did not understand cruelty, violence. So what if he was a Jew? I have always been my own master." She smiled. "Rudi, I am an old hand at running away. I ran away twice when I was a child—to get away from this awful place. But I didn't get very far."

I asked her if she would think I were a coward if I left my mother and Anna. She thought a moment and said no. She would look after them; a better protector than me. I'd be marked, picked up sooner or later.

I recall this conversation now, and I wonder whether I should have stayed. Tamar says it was the wisest decision I ever made. I could not have saved Mama and Anna from what happened to them. I would have become nothing more than another victim.

Inga and I walked into the studio.

"What were you two talking about?" asked my mother. "Did I hear you mention Karl?"

"No, Mama," Inga said.

Anna looked up from her book. "I wish Karl were here. And Papa. It wouldn't be so bad if we were all together."

"Papa is fine," my mother said. "His last letter said things were not that bad in Warsaw." I barely concealed my anger with her blindness. Things were dreadful in Poland. "Papa is busy at the hospital. He's the associate chief of medicine, and widely respected in the Jewish community."

"Rudi, test me on dates," Anna asked.

I sat down opposite her, with her workbook, where, in her small neat handwriting, she had written her homework.

As I read the dates off, I thought to myself: Here are Jews for you, worrying about history, learning, words, lessons, books—when their world is going up in smoke. Again maybe I was being too harsh with my own people. What else did we know but to learn, to mind our business, to make deals, to pray and hope that bad times would end?

As I began to read, the radio announcer was list-ing new rules governing Jews. The yellow star was to be worn. We could not use public transport. No Jew could receive social security or any other government benefit. Synagogues were to be closed.

I shouted at the radio, "Go to hell, you lousy bas-tard."

With infuriating calm, my mother said: "That won't help, Rudi."

"It'll help me."

"You going to test me or not?" asked Anna.

How I pitied my sister, my mother. They thought life could go on—school, growing up, family.

"Okay, okay. Fifteen twenty-one."

"Diet of Worms."

And the radio voice intervening: "All Jewish docu-ments and passports must be stamped with a J . . ."

"Sixteen eighteen," I said.

"Start of the Thirty Years' War," Anna shouted.

Yes, we knew about history all right. But we didn't understand the history being made at that moment.

The radio droned on. "Possession of any weapon by Jews will be deemed a capital crime and can be . . ."

"Seventeen seventy-six."

"American Revolution!"

"Regarding the yellow star," the voice said, "it will be worn at all times, and failure to wear it will mean an offense against the state . . ."

"Eighteen fourteen," I said. And I wanted to kill the voice coming from the radio.

"Defeat of Napoleon!"

"Stores owned by Jews must be registered and own-ers must . . ."

I jumped from the table and turned the radio off.

My mother seemed oblivious. Or was this her way of trying to give us courage, to maintain this act, this little drama of hers—that all would work out if we remained calm, and let the storm blow over?

She looked up from her letter. Her face, once fresh and unlined, was gaunt. She ate little. There were hol-lows beneath her eyes. I knew that she saved the best food for Anna and me, bribed local merchants, watched our small savings, worried about our health.

"Anna," she said, "it's important you keep up with your lessons. We'll work on algebra tomorrow. In spite of everything, you must prepare yourself for your life ahead. And I assure you, you will have a good life. Rudi, it wouldn't hurt for you to read a book now and then."

I saw tears rimming Anna's eyes. I patted her hand, but said nothing.

That night, when they were asleep, I filled a knapsack with toilet articles, some underwear, a few other things. As a kid, I'd done a lot of camping, outdoor living. Karl had never enjoyed it; he was always the one who got bit by mosquitoes, or got poison ivy. I had an old woodsman's knife my grandfather had given me, and I packed that also.

Of course I hadn't told my mother or Anna a word of this, but a week earlier, I'd been to see a man who had worked with Lowy, the printer. He was an engraver, a fellow named Steinmann, and he had concocted a fake identity card for me. The photograph was me, but everything else was false, and I was identified as a student exempt from military service because of ulcers.

It was two in the morning when I kissed my mother and Anna as they slept, slung the knapsack over one shoulder, and as softly as I could in my hiking boots, walked into the hallway.

Inga knew I was leaving. She came out of the apartment in her bathrobe. "So. You've made your mind up."

"I can't stay. I can't help them. Maybe I can save my own neck, come back for them . . . I don't know."

"Where will you go?"

"Anywhere they can't find me."

"How will you live, Rudi?"

"Steal. Lie. Fight."

She gave me a roll of marks. "Take this. At least —for a few days."

I thanked her. We hesitated a moment, studying each other's faces. We were a great deal alike, I now realize. Stubborn, resentful of being shoved around, ready to resist, to refuse to accept meekly what others forced on us. My parents never quite understood me. "A mutant," my father used to say, "an intruder of some kind in this family of readers and artists." (He said it jokingly, and his affection for me was never any less than it was for Karl and Anna.) In the same manner, Inga, having seen brutality and bloodshed as a child—her quarter was one of the worst for the terrible street fights of the twenties and thirties—had developed a dread, a hatred of violence, and of those who commit it.

And none of this had lessened her capacity for compassion, for kindness. I wondered, with a dread, wasting feeling, how Karl would manage in prison without her strength to sustain him.

"Rudi, you must write to us," she said. "It will be a shock to your mother, but I will try to explain why you have left. And to Anna."

"I won't write for a while. Tell Mama not to worry about me, ever. Take care of her. Be good to Anna. She's a fresh kid sometimes, but she loves you. As much as we all do."

We kissed as brother and sister.

"If you see Karl, tell him I'm okay. Tell him the Weiss brothers will be together again . . . soon. Maybe Mama's right. Maybe it'll end. They'll decide they've beaten us up enough, stolen all we have, and they'll quit. Goodbye."

She kissed me again, and I could hear her voice: "Goodbye, little brother."

I walked down the tenement steps, through the courtyard and into the dark street. I had a whole set of lies ready if I were stopped. My plan was to ride the rails of a freight train, sneak on and off trains, and make my way south. Anywhere but Germany.

II

THE GATHERING DARKNESS

Erik Dorf's Diary

In twenty days, Poland has fallen.

But military success is not all we seek. The security of the conquered lands, the racial purity of that part of Poland which will be incorporated into Germany, the policies against Jews, Slavs and others in the "Government-General"—all these remain in a rather muddled state.

Our office keeps getting annoying reports about the actions against Jews in Poland.

It is not that the actions are against policy—Heydrich says we are fighting a double war, one against foreign armies, another against the Jewish conspiracy —but that they are haphazard, disorganized, piecemeal.

The beards and earlocks of these strange Orthodox eastern Jews seem to arouse our men. They cut them off, tear them off, burn them.

Jews are herded into synagogues and the buildings are set afire.

In Bielsko, Jews were strung up in the yard of a Jewish school, rubber hoses were shoved into their mouths, and the water turned on until their stomachs burst.

Rape is frequent, although the soldier who indulges his passion in this manner runs the risk of a charge of race defilement.

Jewish women are stripped and made to dance naked in the streets—to the amusement of the Poles as well as our SS men.

In one town, Jews were driven naked from a communal bath to a slaughterhouse, and burned alive.

One report says—I am asking someone to verify it, but I see no reason to disbelieve it—that in a Polish village, three rabbis were beheaded, and their heads displayed in the window of the local department store, owned, of course, by a Jew.

And so on. All disorganized, planless, at the whim of some local SS commandant.

"The army is somewhat annoyed," I said to Heydrich, after reading the morning reports from Poland.

"Why should they be? Keitel himself, that whore, issued an order to his glorious army telling them that Jews are poisonous parasites, that they're a plague to the world. I remember the field marshal's precise words: 'The fight against Jewry is a moral fight for the purity and health of God-created humanity.'"

"Don't misunderstand me, sir," I said quickly. "It's not the acts against Jews that bothers the army. It's the undermining of army authority in occupied areas. Our men take precedence, commandeer equipment, give orders."

"Well, the army will have to live with it. Let them conquer and occupy. We'll handle the Jews and the other vermin."

But he was disturbed, I could see.

In the next few hours, Heydrich, with that blazing, inventive mind of his, drew up a new formula for handling the Jews of Poland. They will be shoved out of the territories we take over, into places like Lublin and Warsaw, there to fester, as he put it, in their own communities. And the Jews themselves will handle the movement, the organization of these vast ghettoes. Jewish councils, consisting of the oldest and most influential members of the Jewish community, will do the work for us.

"If they refuse?"

"Jews don't refuse. They cooperate. They are terrified, unarmed, without allies."

Poland, it develops in Heydrich's plan, will be a

vast dumping ground for the Jews of Europe—not just Polish Jews, but those remaining in Germany, Austria and Czechoslovakia.

He asked me to summon all his aides to an important meeting tomorrow—September 21—to formulate precise plans for handling the Jewish question. Random shootings and hangings are no way of solving a mass campaign against a subtle enemy.

I have gotten to know the chief's mind reasonably well, and every now and then I try to pierce it. "General, perhaps our problem is that very few of us have a clear idea of the ultimate goal regarding the Jews."

"You tell me, Dorf."

"Oh . . . elimination of their influence from Europe. From the world, for that matter."

"And what does elimination mean? Sterilization? Banishment? Impoverishment?" He paused. "Extermination?"

"I don't know. The last notion, that is. It's only been hinted at."

"Go back to the Führer's works, Dorf. Read between the lines."

"Yes, but the annihilation of what—eight million people or more—seems a rather large task, a bit impractical."

My insides were shivering.

"One might argue that," Heydrich said. "But for the purposes of tomorrow's meeting, keep it in the back of your mind. I will talk about something called 'planned overall measures' leading to a final goal, as opposed to *stages* that will lead to this goal."

Heydrich, for all his mastery of organization, of propaganda, of a complex police operation, can sometimes make me dizzy with his circuitous verbiage (although I have the feeling he's learned some of it from me).

"How clear . . . how precise will you make all of this at tomorrow's meeting?" I asked. "You may be misunderstood."

Heydrich laughed loudly. "Oh, Dorf. Sometimes

you act as though you're still a law student. Make sure Eichmann is present tomorrow. *He* won't misunderstand me."

I nodded, trying to digest all of this. "Maybe some form of quarantine, of containment, would be a good way to start."

Heydrich sat down, threw his long legs up on the desk, crossed his booted legs and leveled one of his elegant fingers at me. "Tell me, Dorf, do the Jews serve a purpose?"

"Purpose?"

"How much of what we do to them is out of conviction, and how much is opportunism?"

"I'm not certain. Conviction, yes. The Führer, Himmler, yourself—you've made no secret of your views."

"But to go to all this trouble to . . . eliminate them?"

He paused on the word "eliminate." All of us are learning quickly to use code words, to dance around some ultimate truth. I wonder why? If what we plan are moral acts (as Keitel has put it), if Christianity has condoned the hatred of Jews for centuries, why are we so reluctant to brag about our true plans? After all, we are fighting a plague, a world enemy, a conspiracy. Or so Hitler contends.

Heydrich went on. An excellent speaker, extremely articulate, he now expanded on his thesis. Anti-Semitism not only binds the German people together, it will serve as a cement to hold all of Europe in one piece under our rule, he says. Most European countries abound with anti-Jewish movements, who will cheer us on. The Croix-de-Feu in France, the Arrow Cross in Romania, various native Fascist parties in Hungary, Slovakia, Croatia. Places like the Ukraine and the Baltic states, under the Bolshevik heel, will be swarming with pro-German sentiments, and these sentiments will be all the stronger if we show them our feelings about the Jews who have been oppressing them.

He winked. "A great deal of what we peddle to them will be lies, Dorf, but useful ones. Once we rouse their anti-Semitic passions to help us resolve the Jewish problem, they'll be next in line."

Heydrich went on. The groundwork is already laid for us—two thousand years of Christian doctrine, supported by eminent Church fathers and doctors, proving the Chosen People to be Christ-killers, deicides, well-poisoners, the devil's spawn, the spillers of the blood of Christian children for their Passover feasts. An endless list of old ideologies, much of it nonsense, but extremely useful.

We then discussed more immediate problems. The random killings and burnings will have to cease. The SS will be in charge of a vast eastward movement of Jews. Only Bolsheviks, criminals, resisters and potential leaders—rabbis, professionals and so on—will be executed. The mass of Jews will be quarantined in Polish cities like Lublin and Warsaw. In effect, he said, "the germ carriers will be isolated."

I suggested we call these areas "Autonomous Jewish Territories," and Heydrich approved the term, complimenting me.

"It will sound as if they're permanent communities," I said, "But of course, as you say, they'll merely be a stage toward . . ."

He laughed again. "Regulation of the Jewish problem! By God, Dorf, I'm getting like you."

"Sir?"

"Using language to say what I don't mean. Remind me at tomorrow's meeting. Emphasize the point. No one is ever to talk about annihilation or extermination."

Berlin
November 1939

There was a lavish ball tonight at the chief's headquarters.

We have a great deal to celebrate. Poland is finished. Russia occupies eastern Poland, and Stalin, in sheer terror, has negotiated a peace pact with us. The

French and English sit on their guns in the west, too frightened to move.

You could not tell that we are engaged in a war. I have never seen so many elegant uniforms, women more dazzling, bejeweled, healthily beautiful, in that best of all German ways.

Marta is radiant, ravishing. A few years ago, she was a dutiful housewife, content with cooking, children, wifely work. But the social demands made upon us have endowed her with a new elegance, a style that I find hard to believe. She wears high-fashion clothing with great flair, waltzes or foxtrots to perfection, can even flirt a bit.

I watched her dancing with Heydrich, and thought of the modest Marta Schaum I'd married. But I should have known she was a woman of enormous potential. The way she practically marched me off into my new career! She has, to be truthful, *made* me. From a jobless lawyer, full of self-pity, and excuses, I have become confident, influential, and engaged in extremely important work regarding Germany's future. There's no doubt that the war will soon end. England and France will come to their senses, Russia will be content to take over part of Poland, and we can live in peace once more, reshaping Europe.

And so, while admiring Marta in her pale-green dress—how wonderfully it set off her golden hair, piled high on her small delicate head—dancing with Reinhard Heydrich, I heard a voice behind me.

"Leave it to Heydrich to find the most beautiful woman," the voice said.

I frowned, but did not turn. Obviously, the speaker did not know he was talking about my wife.

"Quite a beauty," the voice persisted. "Her husband should know Heydrich was cashiered from the navy for compromising a superior's wife."

Angrily, I spun around. "That woman dancing with him happens to be my wife, and I'll thank you—"

"Calm down, Erik," the speaker said.

I was staring at a tall, weathered-looking man in a

civilian tuxedo, and when he smiled at me, I could not help laughing at the trick he'd played on me. It was Kurt Dorf, my Uncle Kurt, whom I haven't seen in four or five years.

"What a wonderful surprise," I cried. "I had no idea you were back in Berlin."

He explained in his quiet voice that he was now working for the army in Poland—as a road builder and general civil engineer. He seemed impressed with me.

"My goodness," Kurt said. "My brother Klaus' little boy. An SS officer. A captain. And at Heydrich's elbow, I'm told."

"Oh, that's an exaggeration. But why are you here?"

"The generals regard these affairs as a bonus for my meeting their timetables."

We studied each other. He resembles my father, but is taller and tougher-looking. My father settled for a life as an impecunious baker, and failed. Kurt has always been driven, worked hard, held jobs that helped him get his degree in civil engineering. He is a bachelor, something of a loner, a man with few friends.

"I wish Papa were alive to see us meeting like this," I said.

"I'm sure he'd be proud." He nodded at Marta. "And Marta. She's beautiful, Erik."

"I love her more every day. More than love, Uncle Kurt—respect, admiration."

"She seems to have earned the respect and admiration of your boss. He hardly looks like the Blond Beast people talk about."

This drew me up short. Kurt should have watched his language, but he was always an outspoken, rather unsophisticated man. "Blond . . . ?" I asked.

"A street expression. You look shocked."

I stared at him. Heydrich escorted Marta back to me. She bowed to him, told him what a great honor it had been. He kissed her hand. He said we would have to arrange another opera party some evening.

Marta then recognized Uncle Kurt, threw her arms

around him and kissed him. Heydrich watched.

I made the introductions. "General, my uncle, Kurt Dorf."

Kurt said it was an honor to meet the head of the SS and that he had encountered many of his field commanders in Poland.

Heydrich studied Kurt's strong face, the civilian tuxedo for a moment, then said, "Dorf, Kurt, engineer and road-building expert. Assigned to General von Brauchitsch. In charge of roads and termini in the occupied territories. Correct?"

"Totally. I had no idea your office was so well informed about humble road builders."

"We're well informed about everyone."

Heydrich moved away. The music resumed. Marta suggested I dance with Eichmann's wife. It would not hurt my career, she hinted.

Uncle Kurt escorted Marta to the bar. They drank champagne. What followed was a most curious conversation, a bit disturbing to her. Kurt, not especially diplomatically, said in a rather low voice that Heydrich did not at all seem to him what some people called him—the party's "evil young god of death."

Marta was shocked and said so. Who would dare say such a thing? Oh, the usual political enemies. Marta informed my uncle that we both worshipped Heydrich. He was the shining example of the Germany of the future—fearless, sensitive, intelligent, noble. Kurt tried to apologize; he was an engineer, not a politician, a mere road builder. That's why he had remained outside party politics, a civilian. He changed the subject, and praised Marta for being so beautiful, for having a successful husband and a lovely family.

"It was simple," my wife said. "We became part of the new Germany, with all our hearts and souls."

"So you did."

"You could sound a bit more cheerful about it," Marta said.

"Oh, I'm part of it too. I know what a good job the regime's done. People back at work—even though it's mostly at wartime jobs. No strikes. A stable cur-

rency. And once France and England ask for peace—
the future is ours."

"Then you and Erik are in agreement. The only
difference is, he wears a uniform and you don't."

"Oh, dear Marta. How wonderfully you simplify
things. Still, you may be right."

He asked her to dance, apologizing for his age, his
stiffness from hiking up and down the bad roads of
Poland. She obliged. It was a marvelous evening—
seeing Kurt again, Marta making such an impression
on the chief. There really is nothing standing in our
way.

Rudi Weiss' Story

As I have mentioned, my father and my Uncle
Moses were members of one of the first Jewish councils organized in Warsaw, in December 1939.

Much has been written about them—good, bad,
neutral. What could they do? They were helpless,
without arms, without friends. The Poles were only too
delighted to see the wrath of the Nazis descend on
Jews, not realizing that the day of reckoning would
come for them also—slaves to the New Order.

So my father and my uncle served the council, tried
to make life a little better for the hundreds of thousands now being crammed into Warsaw. The same
thing was happening in Lublin, Krakow, Vilna, and
other cities in Poland. We know now what it meant—
a step toward Hitler's final solution.

Trains arrived almost daily, cattle cars packed with
poor, hungry, frightened Jews. People died en route.
Children smothered. The passengers wallowed in their
own filth. There was no water, only the parcel of food
they were allowed to bring along. And always the
clubs and whips of the guards. Not only Germans,
but many Poles, who joined the SS as auxiliaries.

They were lied to, these Jews, as they would be
for years to come, and they believed the lies. Resettle-

ment. Your own community. Your own cities. Away from the Poles . . .

A man who lived through such a transport recalls my father and my Uncle Moses meeting such a train on a wintry day. There were frozen bodies on board. Two babies had suffocated.

They tried to make the people welcome. Lowy worked with my father, assigning people to quarters. The Jews lived eight and nine to a room. Sanitary facilities broke down. Roofs leaked. There was no fuel to heat the buildings. Each day, more beggars appeared on the street.

One woman on the train refused to give up her dead child. A rabbi had to convince her that the child had to be properly buried, returned to earth.

My father hated his work on the council, but he stayed with it. He much preferred working at the Jewish Hospital, as overcrowded, understaffed and miserable as it was. But he had gotten into a bitter argument with a German army doctor, and he had been temporarily suspended. The German physician had been treating typhus patients with a drug called uliron. It did not cure them. It killed them, under conditions of dreadful pain. My father protested, argued with the German. They threatened my father with punishment, beating, imprisonment, but he refused to back down. Temporarily, the use of uliron was suspended. (Later, far more fiendish experiments were performed on Jews; we were their guinea pigs, their laboratory animals.) But for the time being, my father was limited in the hours he could spend at the hospital, at his first love, medicine.

Returning from the train that cold day, with the new shivering arrivals from western Poland, my father told Uncle Moses he hated the business of deciding who got what house, how food should be distributed, and so on.

"People respect you, Josef," Moses said.

"Do they?"

"Oh, yes. Just as I do. Ever since we were kids

here, hitching rides on those same trains. You were the smart brother, and I was the slow one. I remember the day you won the chemistry prize—how proud Papa was."

My father smiled. "Yes. And that principal wouldn't let me accept it in the auditorium, because, as he put it, I was of the Hebrew persuasion."

"Right. And I stole it from his office. A certificate and fifty zlotys. Where did I find the nerve? It was the last brave thing I ever did."

"God, how you remember."

The brothers walked into the ghetto. As yet the wall had not been erected. They passed from the so-called Aryan side into the old Jewish neighborhood.

"And that run-down drugstore," Moses went on. "That was my reward for not being as smart as you."

My father took Moses' arm. "I hurt you. I didn't mean to. There was money only for me to go to the university."

"No, no . . ."

"The pampered son. And how often did I call you, or write to you? I wonder. Subconsciously, was I ashamed that my family were poor Polish Jews?"

"Of course not. You were a busy man. A career, wife, children."

My father stopped. Around them walked the hungry, beaten, eternal victims—the Jews of Eastern Europe. "I'm sorry, Moses."

"No apologies are needed. We're joined together again, in a kind of fraternal misery. Let's do the best we can for these people."

There was a reunion at the Helmses' apartment on New Year's Eve, 1939. Karl had not been released from Buchenwald. But Hans, Inga's brother, was home from the Polish front. And Muller, in the uniform of an SS sergeant, was present.

My mother and Anna still shared the old studio next door. They, of course, did not attend. My mother had her pride. And Anna, guest though she was in

Inga's (and Karl's) old home, made no secret of her resentment of the Helmses' attitude toward her.

Although the German armies had been victorious in Poland, and the French and English seemed reluctant to fight, sitting in their bunkers in the Maginot Line, a wartime economy was in effect. Oddly, the Germans did not seem to be suffering. They were looting Poland and Czechoslovakia systematically. Shortages could be made up simply by taking food from the occupied countries.

But for Jews, life had grown unbearable. The wearing of the yellow star was mandated. Jews were easy targets on the street. My mother, too proud to submit, became a recluse. Anna occasionally ventured out to visit a friend unlucky enough to have been left behind. They could not attend the cinemas or the theater, ride public transport, shop in Christian stores. Inga still supplied them with food—a dull diet of starches, a bit of meat, ersatz coffee. Inga had taken a secretarial job at a factory. She had had difficulty in getting employment locally whenever it was learned she had a Jewish husband in prison.

But for the Helms family, it was a time of celebration. Poland, gone. The Allies, trembling with fear. Hans Helms, drunk, talkative, was bragging about the way their tanks and 88s had cut through Poland.

Muller chuckled. "Like a hot knife through butter, eh, Hans? Gave the Polacks a run for the money." He drained his beer stein, eyed Inga. "Me, I'm too old for combat. I'm a damned prison guard. Buchenwald."

Inga, who had been silent and full of sorrow most of the evening, sat up. "Buchenwald? Have you seen my husband?"

"Is he there?"

"You said so yourself . . . that he was probably sent there."

"Did I?"

Muller played cat-and-mouse with her, as she pleaded for help. He agreed to look Karl up in the camp records. It was a huge place, she realized. But

Muller would try. Once he touched her knee and she recoiled. He wanted to assure her that Buchenwald was not too bad a fate for Jews. Her brother, Hans, could tell her stories of what was done to them in Poland!

Drunk, but aware of what he was saying, Muller talked about how much worse things would get. Why had France and England gone to war? Jewish bankers, of course. Inga's father joined in. He hated the idea of their hiding two Jews next door—in-laws or not.

Inga was furious, shouting that she barely recognized them as her family. When Hans taunted her as a kike-lover, one who had brought shame to them, she hurled a stein of beer in his face. Muller and Hans roared with laughter. Inga ran out of the room, to spend the night with my mother and sister.

They had become virtual prisoners in the studio. My mother's last bank accounts had been confiscated, although she had managed to hide some cash in the lining of a coat. It was impossible to get medical care any longer, even from Christian doctors who had known my father. No one would lift a finger to help Jews.

Inga recalls that as she entered the studio, the radio was celebrating the New Year with a Bach chorale.

"Sebastian Bach, Inga," my mother said. She was writing to my father again. Most of the letters never reached him. The Nazi authorities in what was called the "Government-General" of Poland intercepted mail to the ghettoes.

"I wonder if anyone plays our piano these days," Anna said softly.

My mother looked up. "The old Bechstein? Goodness, I can't imagine. That dreadful doctor who took over Papa's clinic did not seem very musical to me."

"He *stole* Papa's clinic," Anna said. "I hope they break their fingers if they try to play it."

Looking back, I see that damned piano as symbolizing an anchor, a deadweight that kept us in Germany, gave us a false sense of security. Some years ago, here at Kibbutz Agam, a Czech professor of languages confessed to me that he too had owned a fine piano in Prague—a Weber. He and his wife had always had the feeling that no possible harm could come to people who owned grand pianos.

My mother sealed the envelope. Inga saw the address to Dr. Josef Weiss, care of the Jewish Hospital in Warsaw. She kissed Mama.

"There is no harm in trying," my mother said. "Perhaps 1940 will be a better year."

"That's right, Mama," Inga said. "We mustn't stop hoping."

She sat opposite my mother in the darkened room and took her hands, saying, "You're cold, Mama."

"I'm always cold. Josef used to say it was my blue blood."

Anna looked up from her book. "What was your family yelling about in there?"

"Nothing important. Hans is drunk."

"They want to throw us out," Anna said.

My mother said, "Perhaps . . . perhaps we could find one of Josef's old patients who would take us in."

"Mama," Anna said angrily, "Papa's patients are gone—in prison, or escaped, or just gone."

"Anna, my child, we could try."

Anna's voice rose. She was seventeen then, tall and fine-featured, like my mother, and with the same strong spirit. But my mother's will was breaking, and Anna was young enough to show anger. "There's no hope, Mama, none. Karl is in prison. Papa is in Poland . . . and the Nazis are there now too, almost as if they came after him. And Rudi ran away. We'll never see any of them again."

My mother said nothing.

"Mama, you act as if this were a play, as if nothing bad has happened to us. Writing letters, talking about Papa's patients, as if any of them were left."

Inga tried to calm her. "It does no harm, Anna."

Anna was not listening. "You always had the notion you were someone special. So fine, so educated. And you taught us to feel that way. Oh, the Nazis would never hurt you or your children—and look what happened to us!"

"Anna, your mother is not to blame!" Inga said. She came to my sister and hugged her, tried to stop her from crying.

"New Year's Eve!" Anna wept. "None of us will be alive next New Year's Eve!"

Inga talked to her gently. My mother shut her eyes, rested her forehead on her clasped hands.

"Don't you understand how much your mother loves you, Anna?" Inga asked. "And how much she loves your father, and the boys? She writes letters, and talks about them, and stays hopeful to keep you happy."

"No! I won't listen! It's all a bunch of lies."

Inga said, "But people sometimes need lies to get from day to day."

"I don't! I want my father and Karl and Rudi . . ."

"Don't cry, child," Mama said. "Please don't cry. Rudi wouldn't like it, if he knew. And he was your favorite." The memory of me seemed to rouse her. She put on her eyeglasses again and began thumbing through old letters—letters from years back, reminders of the life we once had.

"I know we will hear from Rudi," she said. "I know he'll find a way for us to get out."

Anna leaped from the sofa-bed and knocked the letters from the table. "No! More lies! I won't listen any more! I'm running away also!"

It was a bitter-cold night. Anna grabbed her coat from the hook on the door.

"Inga, stop her," my mother cried.

"Anna," my sister-in-law said, "you have no money . . . no place to go. Rudi is strong and tough."

"Oh, let me alone. I know I can't run away. I just have to get out of here."

Worried. my mother got up. "Anna, please . . ."

But Anna raced past them, into the dark corridor, and down the winding stairs to the courtyard. Normally there was a guard on duty outside the apartment building. But it was the New Year and everyone was drunk, eating, celebrating.

Anna ran into the street. As if denying what had happened to us, she ripped the yellow stars from her coat.

Anna had always had this rebellious, independent streak in her. My father had spoiled her terribly. The baby of the family, the only girl. Instead of making her soft and timid, it had the reverse effect—she was aggressive, perky, almost impudent at times. My mother was always admonishing her—"Anna, ladies don't use such language," or "Anna, dear child, can't you be less noisy when your friends come over to play?"

Moreover, she was extremely bright, a much better student than Karl or me. Things came easily to her—studies, music, perceptions that eluded older people. There was a kind of life force in her, young as she was, a desire to experience a great many things, to plunge into whatever her passion of the moment was —collecting butterflies, American jazz music, needlepoint.

The suppression of her talents, her very freedom, the denial of her natural desires to mature, to have boy friends, must have been painful in the extreme to her. She told me once, before I ran off, that any of the eligible boy friends she had scoffed at, now gone, would be welcomed back with a kiss. Quite an admission, for the daughter of Dr. Josef Weiss.

And so, heedless, foolishly rebellious, she walked the darkened streets. Wartime security measures were in effect. Berliners being the law-abiding folk they were, the streets were empty.

Apparently Anna walked unseen and unmolested for several blocks. She wanted to look at our old home on Groningstrasse. She stood in front of it for a few minutes, thinking about the warm, close family life we had enjoyed there. The music. The games in the back yard. The park across the street where we had played soccer and tennis. Papa's patients waiting, thanking him; the comings and goings.

As nearly as Inga could reconstruct what happened, from Anna's hysterical account told before she lapsed into silence, three men approached as she stood shivering under the street light.

Two were civilians. One was in the uniform of the local Storm Troopers, an older man assigned to nighttime duty as a street warden. At first they assumed she was a prostitute, disobeying the curfew for a little business on New Year's Eve.

But a look at her young, fresh face told them she was not a whore. Then one of them saw the dark patch on the woolen coat, where she had ripped away the star. They were drunk, celebrating. One of them— Inga was never sure which one—even recognized her as the daughter of Dr. Weiss. He must have been a local man; perhaps even someone who had once been a patient.

She tried to run away. They held her back. She pleaded that she had just come out for some fresh air. She explained she lived some distance away, and that if they wished, they could escort her home, to make certain she was not up to any unlawful business.

One of the men then suggested they "talk it over" in the little park across from our house. It was deserted, the ground frozen, light snow covering the packed earth. At first she believed them, but when they began clutching at her clothing, tearing at her coat, violating her body with drunken hands, she realized what their intentions were. She screamed.

It did no good. People did not respond to screams in the night. They were heard too frequently. There was a small bandstand in the park, and the men dragged her there. When she screamed again, she was punched.

One man clapped a hand over her mouth to stifle her shouts. She struggled, broke free once, almost escaped. But they caught her, dragged her back, and while two held her arms down, stuffing her muffler into her mouth, the other ripped her clothing off and raped her.

They took turns.

When they had subjected her to several forms of sexual violence, sodomized her, made her perform acts that I cannot make myself write about, they thrust her aside and lurched off, leaving her weeping, bruised, bleeding, on the steps of the bandstand.

Anna, leaving a trail of blood in the snow, somehow found her way back to the studio. The church towers around Berlin had tolled midnight, the New Year.

My mother lost her composure when she saw her standing in the doorway. Her face was a mass of welts and bruises. Her lip was cut. She had bitten it herself to bear the pain and humiliation. Under the winter coat, her skirt and undergarments were in shreds. One shoe was missing.

Inga took her in her arms and tried to console her. My mother at last gained control of herself. She put Anna on the bed. They undressed her and bathed her, applied liniments and antiseptics to her wounds, and spent the night trying to find out what happened.

She could respond only in choked suffocating sobs.

So began 1940 for my family.

Wandering, hiding, I found myself in Prague, on a gray damp day in February. Of my family, I knew nothing. I was on the run—lying, using my faked ID papers, walking cross-country, sleeping in barns and haystacks.

I had developed a sixth sense where uniforms were concerned—any kind of uniform, police, army, SS men, local cops. I could almost smell them, hear them before they saw my ragged figure and my knapsack.

Once I spent three weeks as a farm laborer in Bavaria, digging potatoes and carrots, blending into the remote farming village, silent, pretending to be a half-wit rejected from military service. When an army unit encamped nearby, I vanished the next day.

I used back roads, climbed a thousand fences and stiles, ate whatever I could steal or beg. From discarded newspapers I learned of the awesome successes of the German army, the phony war in the west, the bombing of England. And day by day, I realized that the Jews were doomed, and resolved that if I was to die, I would die fighting. I kept my old camping knife hidden in my belt. I swore that if they came for me, if I were discovered, I'd kill at least one of them before they killed me.

Not far from Munich, in a town called Starnberg—I kept to small towns as much as possible, and secondary roads—I stole a pair of wire cutters from a hardware store. I'd become an adept thief. Brought up as a proper middle-class boy, full of the old Jewish rules forbidding stealing, cheating, or lying, I was learning that survival sometimes dictated something less than adherence to decorum. Many a shopkeeper noticed after my departure that he was missing a loaf of bread, a box of crackers, a pair of socks.

Moreover, I'd learned to travel cross-country—using my sense of direction, and local signposts. At the slightest sign of police or authorities, I'd duck into a field, or the woods, or cross a farm. Many a farmer's dog came for me, and once I outran a bull. I had learned to be cautious, how to hide, when best to travel. Oddly, midday was always a good time. Cops and SS men, all the security forces, seemed to enjoy long, heavy meals and naps.

It was on February 10, 1940, that I slipped across the Czech border at a point about twenty-five kilometers south of Dresden, as nearly as I can place it. Czechoslovakia was occupied, but there were still barriers. I waited until nightfall, hiding in a tool shed at an abandoned construction site. Then I headed south. I made sure to avoid the sentry posts along the road, and slipped under the barbed-wire barrier on my back, using my wire cutters to sever the strands. It was that easy.

Although Czechoslovakia was under Nazi rule—they called it the "Protectorate"—I had heard that the Czechs were less than cooperative with the Germans, and that the Czech police were inclined to take it easy on Jews. I would soon find out.

Prague had a large middle-class Jewish community. Perhaps the Germans would have some reason to ignore these Jews, at least for a while. I hoped to find my way south, if Prague was too dangerous, and make my way to Yugoslavia, and then perhaps to a coastal town on the Adriatic, where I might sneak aboard a ship.

It was a lonely and bitter life, but I found that the challenge of surviving from day to day, the game of wits I had to play, gave me the strength to go on. It was like a soccer game, those tense moments when everything depends on the right move at the right time—a feint, a kick, a pass, hurling oneself at an opponent, or evading his feet.

On a street in the old Jewish quarter of Prague, I stood in a doorway and looked at the Jews of the city. They reminded me of our Berlin neighbors—educated, middle-class, timid, worried, utterly unaware of the sledgehammer blows that would soon descend upon them.

Two Czech policemen were posting regulations on the doors of a synagogue. They did so—it seemed to me—almost apologetically. The Czechs had never been violent anti-Semites, at least in Prague. They were, my father had said, an easygoing and genial people.

But these regulations, forced upon them by the Nazis, were in no way easygoing or genial. It was Germany all over again.

An old man, to the annoyance of the rest of the crowd, was reading the regulations.

"No more clothing vouchers will be issued to Jews," he read. "All Jews failing to register with the Jewish Council of Elders will do so at once, or face serious punishment. It is forbidden to sell luggage, knapsacks, valises or leather to Jews."

The old man turned around. "Hah! Luggage! Where am I going? To America, maybe?"

Someone else resumed reading. "No Jew may carry a valise, trunk or knapsack without prior permission from the police, and a special permit." And so on. The usual preliminaries. Before arrests, detention, and God knows what else.

The policemen turned. I was a bit slow retreating into the doorway. One of them noticed my knapsack. I started to walk away, acting unconcerned, and they came after me.

"Hey," one of them said. "You saw the orders. What are you doing with that knapsack?"

I mumbled something about not knowing of the order. To show them my faked ID papers would be a risk. What was a German farm laborer doing in Prague?

I tried to look stupid, gestured with my hands. They backed me against a small store. It was a leather and luggage shop, a rather dingy, run-down place, and one of them took out a pad, while the other squinted at me.

"Give us the knapsack," one said.

I hesitated. Perhaps I had made a mistake coming to a strange city. Thus far I had survived by hiding in the countryside, blending with trees and forests, meadows, barns.

A young girl was standing behind the glass door of the shop. She looked at me, saw my distress and came out.

"No, he won't give you the knapsack," she said. "He'll give it to *me*."

"You, Miss Slomova?" the cop asked.

"I sold it to him, and he never paid for it. Come on, give it to me. You take it from him, or arrest him, and I'll never get my money."

She was very pretty. A small girl, fine features, dark-brown hair. And the darkest brown eyes I had ever seen. She lied very well, too, which I had found was a useful trait.

"You sold him that piece of junk?" the policeman asked.

"It was new when I sold it. I'm furious with him." She glared at me. "Don't try to get away with anything. You know that's mine, and you owe me for it. Things are bad enough here."

The Czech officers looked at each other. They were evidently local cops, and they knew the pretty girl.

"What do you think?" one asked the other.

"She's too pretty to argue with. If she says so, I'll believe her." He pointed a finger at me. "But you, watch your step. The Germans catch you breaking the rules, you won't last long around here."

The girl opened the door and I walked in. Her effrontery, her nerve, impressed me. And she had saved my neck. She watched until the cops were some distance down the street, then practically shoved me through the shop. Here was a girl I could admire, take to my heart. I was deeply grateful to her, this girl with courage, nerve.

"Quick," she said. "The back room."

Once more she looked into the darkening cold street. More people had gathered around the list of rules. They were muttering, some of the women crying.

In the rear of the shop, behind a curtain, was a table, some old chairs, and a gas ring, on which tea was brewing. I could smell it, and I craved it. My diet of stolen carrots and stale bread had left me weak. I got dizzy easily.

"Sit," she said.

"Why did you do that?" I asked.

"You were in trouble. You aren't a Czech. I'm not sure what."

"I'm a German." I paused. Like hell I was. That was behind me. "I'm a Jew."

"In Prague?"

"I'm on the run. Have been for a long time."

I looked at the wall. There was an old calendar, with a picture of a seacoast, sandy beach. "Palestine," she said. "I wish I was there."

"You're Jewish also," I said.

She nodded. "Who isn't around here? This is the famous Prague ghetto. What is left of it. The rich have left, the poor have vanished."

My head began to sway and I thought I would faint from hunger, weakness. She knelt in front of me and took my hands.

"My name is Helena Slomova. I'm alone. My parents were arrested two months ago. They said Papa was a Zionist agent. I don't know where they are."

"I am Rudi Weiss." It was the first time I had used my real name in a year, it seemed.

"Oh, God, you're faint. Here, some tea."

She gave me a hot mug of tea, apologizing because she had neither sugar nor milk, and I let its warmth creep into my hands, my arms. She stared at me with those luminous dark eyes, and I wondered how people could torment such a girl, subject her to pain and suffering.

Then she took the cup from me and rubbed my hands.

"I haven't held a woman's hands for a long time," I said. "Too busy hiding, running."

"What will you do now?"

I shook my head. I was exhausted. Maybe there was no place to hide, maybe the Jews were doomed, unwanted anywhere, unsafe anywhere.

Suddenly, as I looked at her small, perfect face, I leaned forward and kissed her. She opened her mouth, and we joined our lips for a long time. Then she stroked my forehead.

"I'm sorry," I muttered. "I shouldn't have. But you're a marvelous girl. So pretty, so brave."

"It's all right. I liked it. I'm lonely also. I cry every night, wondering about my mother and father."

"Maybe they're all right. I heard they're shipping Jews to Poland to live in their own cities. My father's there—he's a doctor in Warsaw."

She showed me photographs of her parents—plain shopkeepers, but the mother with the same delicate face and dark eyes that Helena had. "They were ready to go to Palestine, to find passage. But they waited too long."

We sat and talked, and I found it hard to keep my hands from touching her gently—her arms, her face. I tried not to. We barely knew each other. But she did not object. She was a small girl, but she had a certain sturdiness, a strength in her. And she was beautiful—even in an old white shopkeeper's smock.

I told her a little about my family, how I had run away, about my wanderings. And I suppose I even bragged a little about my skills as an athlete. Then, sensing that she was receptive, pleased to have saved me, I drew her to me. She sat on my lap—so small that she was almost weightless. But the softness of her arms, her hips, filled me with passion. Passion that I ill concealed.

"You trust me too easily," I said. "I've been learning to trust no one."

"You sound honest, Rudi. I believe what you're telling me."

"I don't mean that. I could . . . I might . . ."

She put her fingers to my lips.

What was wrong with me? I was breathing as heavily as if I had just run the 200-meter dash. It had been so long since I had been close to a woman; the truth was, I was a bit backward in this respect. She seemed more at ease than I was.

As her hand stroked the back of my neck, and she rested her face against mine, she told me about her parents' dream of a home in Palestine, of the man named Herzl who started it all, of the slow migration of Jews to the dry country on the edge of Asia. It all sounded terribly foreign and strange to me, and I must have looked dubious, or smiled, as if indulging her.

"What's so funny?" Helena asked.

"I don't know. When I think of Zionists, I think of those old guys in beards—kids rattling cans for pennies on the street corners. Not of beautiful young girls like you."

"Oh, you are a German. Very German."

"No longer."

We kissed again, held each other for a moment. The front door bell sounded, and Helena got up and walked through the curtain.

I could hear a man's voice. He was another shopkeeper, telling her to lock up. The Gestapo, dissatisfied with the policemen's laxness, was running its own investigation to make sure that the new regulations were obeyed.

I could hear her locking the front door, putting out the lights. In the back room, she took my hand. "You'll come home with me," she said.

I told her more about my family, people who now seemed like strangers to me. Once I had written to my mother, but had never dared give her an address. I told her about my kind, overworked father, a man who never lost his temper, and about Karl and Inga. And Anna. And my mother, so pretty, so talented, and so much the boss of our home. I even told her about the Bechstein piano. And I said I would go back only if I could save them, that I was determined to fight back, to keep running.

We talked, and ate a bit, and soon, as naturally as if we had known each other for years, we made love.

I had had some fumbling experiences before—lovemaking of a rapid, pointless kind. And Helena was a virgin. She was only nineteen. But we brought our bodies together that night as if we were meant to be man and wife, as if God had thrust us upon each other. She rested in the crook of my arm, a small, soft girl, with very white skin and dark-brown hair. My own flesh was hard and muscled, and my hands were coarse from work.

"Rudi . . . hold me . . . don't take your arms away."

"My hands will scratch you."

"I don't care."

"All because of that damned knapsack," I said. "I'll never get rid of it."

She sat up in bed and smiled at me. "And you will never get rid of me."

I asked if she had a boy friend, relatives, who might find us. She shook her head: no one.

"I wouldn't care if they did," she said. "I used to be a proper little schoolgirl. Blouse and skirt, lessons. Now, I just try to live from day to day."

I kissed her hair, her forehead, her eyes. "Helena Slomova. My savior in a luggage store."

"We were just lucky the Czech police are so lazy," she said. "And I flirted a bit with them. They knew me, they knew my family."

I got out of bed, worried. Where to? What now? I knew it would get worse. I'd seen whole Jewish communities vanish in German towns. It was only a matter of time before the Germans started emptying Czechoslovakia.

"What will you do now?" I asked.

"I don't know. I'm scared. I'm less scared now that you're with me, but . . ."

"Helena, I'll stay with you. But not here."

She sat up, pulled the sheet and blanket to her neck. It was freezing in the small bedroom. "There are ways of getting out . . . through Hungary, Yugoslavia. There are boats that will take you to Palestine, if you can pay."

We both laughed—we were penniless, without even the hope of buying passage. And frontiers to cross, guards to avoid, the SS and local Fascists on the lookout for people like us.

"You will come with me," I said.

"With no money? No papers?"

"I got this far."

"But you traveled alone. I'll be a hindrance to you."

I took her in my arms again. "You'll get healthy on a diet of raw turnips." Then I buried my head in her breasts, kissed her again and again. "The worst thing in the world is to be alone. I try to act tough, but I'm scared also. I have no family any more. I have the feeling I'll never see them. I need someone to be near me in the night. Someone warm, to hold me when I touch her. When it's dark and cold."

"Oh, Rudi. I need someone too."

"You'll sleep in haystacks. Steal from farmers."

She smiled. "Not really a honeymoon."

"It will be much worse to stay here and let them take us. They give no hope. They just lie. They have no mercy, no pity, and they want to get rid of all of us. No matter how."

We held one another closely, and then we made love again, and we were happy.

"Do you know the story of Ruth in the Bible?" she asked.

"I'm not sure I remember. I was a great one for cutting Hebrew school."

"All you have to remember is one part." She kissed my cheek. " 'Whither thou goest I will go.' "

Karl remained in Buchenwald.

It was not an extermination camp, but hundreds died there daily—beatings, torture, starvation. He survived by doing his work in the tailoring shop, and listening to old hands like his friend Weinberg, who knew their way around.

You could not survive alone. You needed to be part of a group—Communists, Zionists, whatever. The men in the tailoring shop had their own cadre, and they tried to share extra food, protect one another. But life was always in danger. They lived on thin soup and black bread. Sanitation was dreadful. The worst details were the quarry and the so-called "garden," where men were beaten to death for the slightest infraction. Burying rebellious prisoners alive was a favorite device of the guards.

A former Austrian army officer, a Jew, went to the camp commandant one day and complained of these barbaric practices. He was told that as an old army man, his advice would be carefully considered. Then he was taken out, made to kneel in the central square in front of the other prisoners and killed with a shot in the back of his neck.

One night in the crowded, foul barracks, the loudspeaker broadcast the surrender of France. Karl, Weinberg and the others in his "block" listened with heavy hearts as the news came over the speaker.

"France thus joins Holland, Belgium, Norway, Denmark, Austria and Czechoslovakia and greater Poland as parts of the New Order in Europe. The Führer has renounced all territorial claims and wants only peace and security for Europe. To this end, England will be asked to submit to . . .

"Christ," Weinberg said. "He's got it all, except Switzerland and Russia. Sure he has no more claims."

The loudspeaker went on: "Once again the Führer has emphasized his cordial and fraternal relations with the Soviet Union and sent his warm wishes to Comrade Stalin . . ."

"Just wait, Stalin," Weinberg said. He was sewing a lace-trimmed pink slip. "It'll come your turn."

"When will ours come?" Karl asked.

"Don't ask me, Weiss." Weinberg leaned over his upper bunk and whispered, "I hear some guy bought his way out. Fifty thousand Swiss francs to the SS commandant. His wife sneaked the money in."

"Wife," Karl said. "I haven't seen mine in two years . . . and no letters, not a sign."

"They've written us off, kid. But don't let it get you down." Weinberg hopped off the bunk and showed Karl the garment he'd been sewing, holding it up like a salesgirl. "Like that? For SS Sergeant Kampfer, for his whore."

Karl smiled. "Don't tease me, Weinberg."

"Who's teasing? Just to show you it's all business. I make fancy underwear for Kampfer, I get extras."

"You amaze me, Weinberg. Maybe you've got the right idea. Survive, laugh, act as if nothing's changed."

"Don't sneer, kid. I made a pair of lace drawers for Kampfer last week—sometimes I wonder maybe he's queer and wears them himself, but he says its for this Polish whore—and look what he gave me."

The tailor furtively took a half loaf of rye bread— real, fresh bread—from inside his striped prison tunic. He offered it to Karl. "Take half."

"I can't, Weinberg. You did the work. All I do is complain."

"Don't be silly. Be my guest. Rye bread like I used to buy in Bremen."

Karl thanked him and broke off a piece, and they sat there, chewing thoughtfully. As they did, Melnik, the kapo, came wandering through.

"Swallow fast," Weinberg said. "Hide the bread."

But during his detention in Buchenwald, Karl had been changing. It happened to many prisoners. They entered frightened, full of concepts of honor and decorum—and they became tough, bent on self-preservation. Karl was no fool; he never had been. And he was slowly learning that one stood up for oneself, in various ways, or perished. For example, in the tailoring shop, with Weinberg's support, he had battled for a seat near the only stove in the room—an important advantage—and won. Sad to say, the Nazis saw the value of pitting Jew against Jew. It explained the sadism of the kapos. And it explained how a passive man like my brother could develop a tough hide, a cunning, an ability to resist.

Karl glared at Melnik. "To hell with him," he said loudly to Weinberg.

"Weiss," the kapo warned. "Eating in barracks is forbidden."

Weinberg pleaded with Melnik to look the other way. But the kapo was a victim no less than they were. If the SS found out, he'd lose his soft job.

"You're a Jew like us, Melnik," Karl said. "Give us a break. We're not eating. We're just sampling it."

"Shut up. Give me the goddam bread. Every crumb."

"No," Karl said. "Weinberg earned it. This is for the tailors, not for a lousy cop and informer like you."

Melnik yanked the hard rubber truncheon from his belt and walked toward the bunk. "Fancy doctor's son from Berlin, eh, Weiss? Too good for us other prisoners. Give me that fucking bread."

"Give it to him, Karl," Weinberg said. He shoved his chunk of the loaf at Melnik. But Karl refused. He was starving, and the taste of the good bread had reminded him of all that he had lost, his life of freedom, wife, family, his skills.

When Melnik tried to snatch the bread from him, Karl went for him. They wrestled about, and the kapo began to beat Karl with his short hard-rubber club. Karl had become a demon—screaming, kicking, biting, trying to wrest the club from Melnik's hands.

Weinberg tried to intercede, and he, too, began to get clubbed. The other prisoners watched, cheering Karl on, but refusing to take part. The penalty for fighting in barracks could be death—a single quick shot in the neck, or public hanging.

"Weiss, Melnik," Weinberg cried, "for God's sake cut it out, Jews fighting Jews!"

"The little bastard attacked me," the kapo roared. "Guards! Guards!"

Another kapo came running in, and he too, a former criminal like Melnik, waded into the melee, smashing his club at Karl's clinging arms, then against the side of his head.

In seconds, both my brother and Weinberg were subdued, beaten almost senseless.

Punishment was meted out at once. The SS sergeant in charge ordered them to the "trees."

The trees were wooden T-shaped structures in the courtyard, on which a modified form of crucifixion was practiced.

Karl and Weinberg were tied with coarse ropes, their arms secured behind them, on the wooden crossbar. Their feet were left dangling about two feet above the ground. Circulation in both arms and legs was thus impeded, and their breathing became labored. Men were known to die after a day of this torment.

Weinberg remembers that Karl became incoherent after several hours. He kept repeating his wife's name, "Inga . . . Inga . . ."

"Easy, kid," Weinberg said. "Save your breath."

"I've quit, Weinberg. I want to tell them, they win, they've beaten me. Let them kill me."

"No, no, Weiss. It's always better to live. There's always a chance. Each of us who lives sanctifies God. I think I have that right. I'm not a religious man, but the rabbis tell us that."

"I don't want to live."

"Sure you do. Groan, if it'll help."

Weinberg assured Karl they'd be cut down in another day. Water would revive them. In fact, Weinberg had a friend in the Buchenwald dispensary who would fix them up. And the useful sergeant, who craved fancy underwear, would not let Weinberg, the best tailor on the post, or Weinberg's friend, die.

Since the assault on her on New Year's Eve, my sister Anna's health had begun to fail. She who had been so lively and happy refused to eat, to bathe herself, and finally, by July, to my mother's horror, she refused to speak.

There is a medical term for this state, Tamar tells me. Anna would sit hunched in the corner of the studio, her head against the wall, her body oddly contracted, arms bent and held tight against her chest, her legs drawn up. She would not take food, and my mother and Inga tried to force nourishment down her throat. Once the cleanest and sweetest of girls, she now turned away from soap and water, would not change her clothing, made no sounds except small whimpering noises.

Despite the fact that it was wartime, and that special medical services for civilians—let alone Jews!—were scarce, my mother and Inga thought they could appeal to a certain Dr. Haefer who had known my father, and was considered a rather liberal man. As far as they knew, he was not a party member, and still had a large practice in neurology.

My mother did not have the heart to go with Inga and Anna. Besides, it was best she remain in hiding. Inga did her shopping, advising her to stay in the studio as much as possible.

Dr. Haefer looked at Anna's hunched, withdrawn, motionless figure and seemed genuinely sympathetic. In private, Inga had told him what had happened to Anna and how she had gone into a decline since then —nightmares, hysterics, irrational behavior, and now this withdrawal from the world, this inability to take care of herself.

"And what is it you wish, Mrs. Weiss?" he asked.

"Perhaps some therapy. A sanitarium that will take her. I know I may be presuming. Considering she is a . . ."

Dr. Haefer nodded his head. He was being diplomatic. "Perhaps I can be of some help. There is an institution at Hadamar to which I have sent similar cases."

"We would be grateful, doctor."

At that moment, Inga had no idea if she was doing the proper thing. But the sight of Anna, huddled in the corner, her eyes blank, unfocused, her arms locked over her chest, convinced her that she had no options. It tormented Inga. The brutal, senseless incident. Anna's treatment at the hands of three of her countrymen—they might have been men she knew—filled her with a numb disgust. She could not conceive of a world so blind, so cruel, so bent on inflicting pain and humiliation.

To destroy someone as lively and as good as her young sister-in-law? For what purpose? To whose benefit? Inga was not a well-educated woman, but she had decent instincts. And now she saw a sweet young girl ruined, turned into a vegetable, unable to take care of herself. Inga had reported the crime to the police. When the sergeant learned that the girl involved was a Jew, he had dismissed Inga with a smirk. "A whore, surely, Mrs. Weiss, even if she kept it a secret from the family."

Inga spared my mother this story. She lied to her that the police would try to find the rapists.

"And what good will that do?" my mother asked. She was beginning to feel defeated, unable to go on. "It will not bring back my child's mind or restore her health. Oh, we are doomed, Inga."

As Inga thought of my mother, alone, at last breaking down, her iron will melting under the series of blows to her family, she heard Dr. Haefer telling his nurse to phone the sanitarium in Hadamar and see if they had space available for a patient. Apparently there was an efficient system of transporting people there at government expense.

"Will she be treated well?" asked Inga. "You know what I mean."

She meant, of course, that Anna was a Jew.

Haefer ignored the thrust of her query. "Within the limits of a wartime economy."

"You say she will leave today?"

"In a few hours. She can remain in my office until the bus comes."

A foreboding of terror overcame my sister-in-law. She had never heard of Hadamar. Anna was now rocking back and forth slowly, her arms locked around her chest. It was as if she were trying to contain demons in her, suppress an intractable pain, Inga thought. All the love that she and my mother had lavished on Anna after the ordeal had not liberated her from this private hell.

The doctor assured Inga that trained attendants would look after Anna at the sanitarium. Therapy would be administered. Certain new drugs might prove effective.

The nurse entered to escort Anna to a waiting room.

Inga put her arms around her and kissed her cheeks. But my sister did not respond. "Anna, Anna, my child, I'm Inga, Karl's wife. You must know me. Don't you remember Rudi? A wedding in the garden? The house on Groningstrasse?"

Anna's eyes were filmed, removed from the world.

"When you are better, I'll come for you. Mother and I will bring you home."

And still no response from my sister. Inga kissed her again.

"Doctor, I cannot believe what has happened," she said. She was crying. "She was the bravest and liveliest of girls. And now . . ."

"These cases are puzzling, Mrs. Weiss."

"Am I doing the right thing? Please tell me. Perhaps she should remain with her mother and with me. But she seems to get worse, less functional."

"The girl is deeply disturbed, almost autistic. The peculiar rocking motion—we call it perseveration. A certain sign of deep psychoses. You do well to surrender her to professional care."

The word *surrender* chilled Inga momentarily.

"You'll be advised of her progress," the physician

said. "And do give my regards to your mother-in-law. An accomplished pianist, as I remember."

He could not, Inga thought, be a bad man, or a man who would hurt Anna. Polite, sympathetic, he even remembered my mother. After all, he had known my father years ago.

"Goodbye, Anna," Inga said.

For a moment Anna raised her eyes—as if somewhere in her mangled mind a connection had been made, that someone who loved her was departing from her life. But the eyes remained vague, the mouth slack.

With a few comforting words, the nurse led her out of the room.

Erik Dorf's Diary

Warsaw
August 1940

Hans Frank is governor-general of that part of Poland we have not formally annexed to the Reich. A dark intense man with sensual lips, he tries to be tough, hard, but I see in him a certain defensiveness, a weakness. As if he were the intellectual boy in the class who tries to outdo the bullies with fake bombast.

Heydrich has sent me to Poland to see how our resettlement plan is working. We are moving hundreds of thousands of Jews east, concentrating them in places like Lublin and Warsaw.

Frank got off on the wrong foot with me, by mocking me as "Heydrich's new boy." I resented the word *boy* and told him so.

"Don't take offense, Major Dorf. His eyes and ears, so to speak. I imagine he sent you to Warsaw to check up on me. See how I'm administering the new regions."

"As a matter of fact, he did. First, your complaint that you need forty thousand more civil servants to administer the influx of Jews and the Polish labor force, and second, your statement that in Poland, you represent a greater force than the SS."

Frank's eyes narrowed. "So that's it. I know what they call me. 'The vassal king of Poland.' Looter, schemer."

"Let's get to the point," I said. I saw at once he was not a man to fear. "Forty thousand civil servants are out of the question. Let the Jews and Poles run their own population. We want the Polish nobility, intelligentsia and influential clerics destroyed. The mass of Poles will be used for forced labor, as will the ghetto Jews."

"You're pretty cocky for a twenty-eight-year-old kid," Frank said. "You really must have Heydrich fooled."

"Fooled?"

"I know you're a lawyer, like me. The party hates us. The Führer would like to shoot every lawyer in Germany. They remind him of Jews. What saves me is I bailed the big wheels out of jail in the twenties, when you were just a fart in the wind."

"I know about your early legal work for the party."

"And I know how you kiss ass with Heydrich. All I can say is, he's hiring a better class of clerks."

My face turned scarlet, hot, as the blood rose up my neck, ears, cheeks. But I found, to my satisfaction, that I do not fear Hans Frank. He is saddled with a huge job, but he is an outsider. I have learned from Heydrich that force is the ultimate truth. If you can hold a threat over a man, imply you have support from higher authority, suggest to a man, no matter how high-ranking, that not only do you not fear him, but you may possess the power to ruin him, you will in the long run get the best of him.

I certainly do not intend to be a mirror of Heydrich. He is a general, a true leader, and in a sense, Frank was right in mocking me as a "clerk." But I saw the self-pity in Frank's eyes, the weakness in his mouth.

Indeed, he made me think of myself, five years earlier, before the party and the SS stiffened my spine, taught me the usages of power.

I lay my briefcase on his desk, and we stared at each other in the enormous office, hung with red, white and black party banners, giant portraits of the Führer.

I could have baited him further, but I did not. The truth is that the inner circles of the party do not fully trust Hans Frank. He is always spouting off about the need for law, for legal procedures. I recalled too well Heydrich's admonition to me to forget the concepts I'd learned in law school. At the same time, Frank is without equal in ambition, bloodthirstiness, lack of principle, cunning. He is a bad mixture. The SS knows it and intends to bend him to its will.

"I'm sick of Jews being dumped on me," he complained, as I started reading from Heydrich's memoranda. "You shove the lousy disease-carrying kikes into Poland, and what am I supposed to do with them? Christ, we were better off when the SS was shooting them on sight during the invasion last year."

"Undesirables can still be eliminated. Communists. Criminals. Troublemakers. For the time being Jews who are productive, especially in the manufacture of army goods, can be left alone. And for God's sake, let them administer their own ghettoes. Our SS men should be used only to enforce discipline, to keep records, to get the job done."

Frank's erratic character makes it hard for me to conduct a coherent conversation with him. He may have been a lawyer, but his mind is a jumble. He began to rant about our "Autonomous Jewish Territories"—Warsaw, Lublin, Lodz. Sewers, he called them, stink-holes that would have to be destroyed.

Just as abruptly, he led me to the window and showed me the giant wall the Jews are being forced to build around the Warsaw ghetto. It will ruin Warsaw's economy, he whined. The Jews hold key jobs outside the ghetto. Now they'll be locked in. How could he keep the factories going outside? I replied that the wall, that mass of brick, rubble, concrete and stones, is being built on Himmler's direct order.

When he was about to explode again, I said firmly that the isolation of Jews is more important than the economy. He will have to find ways of keeping factories and businesses operating, if necessary, *without* Jews. He paced his huge office, his heels clacking on the polished floor. He lives well, envisioning himself a Teutonic knight, a medieval baron served by armies of Polish slaves.

After letting him rant a few minutes, I repeated the order: Wall in the ghetto.

At this point he leveled a finger at me, called me an errand boy and shouted that he knew damned well what the wall meant.

"Enlighten me, Herr Frank."

"You know fucking well what I mean, and what you mean, and what everyone from Hitler down means. The Jews are going to have to disappear."

I suggested he inform me precisely what he meant.

His face was an inch from mine. His breath was foul. His eyes were blazing. "Disappear. What the hell does a Jew-free Europe mean, Dorf? Where are we sending them? To the moon?"

This time I did not bait him. He was closer to an ultimate truth than I care to admit to myself, or at least to articulate—even to the vassal king of Poland.

"Maybe I have a stronger stomach than you," Frank bellowed. "Maybe I don't pussyfoot the way Heydrich does. But I told my men not long ago, it might be a problem to shoot or poison the three and a half million Jews in Poland, but we'll sooner or later take measures that will lead to their annihilation."

"I know you did. It was against orders."

"Orders, shit."

But he had given me a start. We use code words so often, walk around ultimate solutions, suggest things to one another without spelling them out, that Hans Frank's blunt words staggered me. To fortify myself, I fell back on something Eichmann has taught me—if in doubt, *obey*. Mass murder is not a pleasant prospect.

But what if it is not truly murder, but a protective measure, a prophylactic against contamination? I kept these rationalizing thoughts to myself. Such subtleties would be lost on a Hans Frank.

He was complaining now—collapsed in his great carved throne of a chair—that he'd be forced to do our dirty work, and he didn't like the idea. When the time came, he said, he'd "rub our noses in it."

I could not resist taunting him about his bloody boasting—and his curious insistence on "justice, legal methods." Like a patient schoolteacher, I quoted Heydrich to him. Old notions of justice are finished in the Third Reich. We, the police arm, decide what is just, what is unjust.

"The face is the face of Dorf, but the voice is the voice of Heydrich," he said.

I let him think I took this as a compliment. We drank cognac, and he tried to be conciliatory. I'd thrown some fear into him. He was to keep his mouth shut about "annihilations," wall in the ghetto, get the Jews to do the work, the registering of their own people, and work out arrangements to accept hundreds of thousands more Jews.

He grunted his agreement, and invited me to ride around the ghetto in his staff car.

The Warsaw ghetto is a depressing, filthy place, evidence that the Jews are incapable of keeping their own house in order. The streets are rubble-strewn, littered with garbage. To my astonishment, I even saw two corpses, lying in the gutter, unattended. Beggars, or homeless wanderers, Frank explained. Perhaps the feebleminded. The Jews, allegedly famous for their close family ties, their charitable interest in their own poor, are falling apart as a community, he said disgustedly.

And yet, I am forced to admit that a curious vitality survives in the gloomy surroundings. Peddlers hawk wares from pushcarts. Draymen drive wagons through the cobbled streets. Old men enter synagogues, deep in conversation, their hands waving. Women push baby carriages. Stores, while dingy and ill-stocked, seem to be doing business. Against my better judgment, I have to conclude there is a life force in these people. Perhaps it is why they are so dangerous.

"The damned fools go on as if nothing's happening," Frank sneered. "They'll learn."

Then a curious incident occurred.

As the staff car turned a corner, impeded for a moment by a wagonload of lumber, I saw a tallish man in a dark suit and a battered black Homburg cross the street in front of us. He carried what looked like a physician's satchel.

For a moment I thought it was Dr. Weiss, the man who had treated my family, and later taken care of Marta. I last saw him but two years ago, when he came to plead for his son.

The man did not notice me. He was accompanied by another man, more humbly clothed, and they were conversing animatedly. They entered a building with a sign on it reading *Judenrat*—the Jewish Council of Warsaw—and I lost sight of them.

An amazing coincidence—if the man actually was Dr. Weiss. Of course, I have no business with him any more. He means nothing to me. He is part of the past. A rather decent man, as I recall, but a naive one, with a stubborn wife who refused to get out of Germany when she could have.

I asked Frank if he knew the man with the satchel.

He shrugged. "I don't keep track of every kike in Warsaw. He looks like one of the council members in that fancy hat. Damned lazy bunch. They'd better get organized, or we'll have a few shootings to move them along. Dorf, I've shot more than my share of council members in the small towns, when they drag their heels. That's what this whole thing is about, isn't it? No old concepts of justice. Just the noose and the gun, right?"

I didn't answer. For a while I could not shake the image of the tall man. Probably it was not Dr. Weiss. And if it was, what does that matter to me? He does not seem to be suffering unduly.

Rudi Weiss' Story

A handful of Jews survived the horror of Warsaw. Some live here in Israel, and in fact, a woman who lives near Kibbutz Agam, Eva Lubin, knew my father and my Uncle Moses. She was a resistance fighter, participated in meetings of the council, before it lost all credibility with the Jews and was replaced by the fighting units. Eva told me a great deal of what happened.

A man named Dr. Menahem Kohn was the council leader. He was, according to Eva, a conciliator, a man who would do precisely what the Nazis told him.

My father, after his defiant argument with the German doctor over the use of toxic drugs to treat typhus—remedies that killed the ill in awful pain—had something of the reputation of a resister. Nothing, at that time, could have been farther from the truth. He remained a cautious man, interested in maintaining some level of medical service, despite terrible crowding, lack of sanitation, shortages of food, heat and medicines. People succumbed daily in the hospital and around it. He and his brother Moses and the nurses watched helplessly. The children were the worst—dozens of them crammed onto lice-ridden wards, huddled, fearful, their eyes growing large, their bodies gaunt, forever crying for food.

That particular day, Eva remembers, there was a great deal of discussion about smuggling, which Dr. Kohn and most of the other elders regarded as a high crime.

A man named Zalman, a plain workman, representing the Jewish trade unions, had begun the discussion by commenting about the wall. "Eleven miles of it," he said. "To keep us in, and the Poles out. It's a prison, that's all."

My father agreed. "Warsaw will be the supreme ghetto of all time, I am afraid. It will get worse."

128

There was some argument about the work on the wall, Kohn insisting that Zalman's workers deliver more labor, more manpower.

Zalman tugged at his cap. "Not so easy, doctor. A lot of them know once that wall goes up, we're locked in. No trade, no jobs outside."

Kohn leveled a finger at him. "My friend, in Reszow, a Jewish council exactly like this one failed to deliver the workers quota of men. The council members were hanged publicly. We must cooperate with the Germans. We have no choice. We are what we have always been—victims."

"I can't tell that to my union brothers," Zalman said.

"You had better," Dr. Kohn said.

My father and my uncle were silent for a while. A ponderous gloom descended over the meeting of the Judenrat.

"We must stop moaning and groaning about this ghetto concept," Dr. Kohn continued. "At least it is something we understand, something we have lived with for centuries. We will be allowed our schools, our hospitals, our communal associations. The SS commandant himself has promised me. You see, gentlemen, they *need* us—skilled labor, trade, the Polish economy."

Again silence.

Then my father asked, "For how long will they need us?"

"I beg your pardon, Dr. Weiss?"

"Dr. Kohn, I ask how long will they need us? How long will several million poor Jews mean anything to them? In the long run we may prove a burden. Then . . ."

Dr. Kohn shook his head. "We have no choice but to cooperate in every way possible. Provide work details. Clean up the city. Keep the factories running."

Moses interrupted. "I hear these work details are not quite what they sound like. Men are beaten to death, shot, for mild infractions."

Zalman nodded. "It's true. I've been on some of them. We aren't treated like workmen, but like slaves."

"But we have absolutely no choice but to obey orders," Dr. Kohn said solemnly. "We cannot resist. We must not resist. There will be no smuggling, no black-market operations, no attempts at sabotage. We can only pray for things to get better."

Eva Lubin, who was at the meeting, remembers my Uncle Moses whispering to my father, "From his mouth and to God's ears."

In October, three months after Anna was sent to the mental hospital at Hadamar, my mother received a form letter from the hospital. It was brief, and it was signed by a "Director of Services."

A strange letter. It was headed "Charitable Foundation for Mental Care, Hadamar, Germany."

It stated that Anna Weiss, aged eighteen, had died of "pneumonia and complications." No date was given. They had taken the liberty of cremating her body to prevent the spread of infection. At some later date, Mrs. Weiss would be informed of the location of her daughter's grave.

Mama became hysterical. She wept for days. She was inconsolable. Anna had been the family baby, the brightest of us, the child with the greatest love of life. It was inconceivable to my mother that she could die this way—with no loved one near her, with her mind shattered, her hopes destroyed. She had been able to bear Karl's imprisonment—after all, he was alive. Even my vanishing had been understandable. But Anna's death was like a knife wound in her side that would never stop bleeding.

"It is my fault," she wept to Inga. "I asked that she be sent away."

"No, Mama," Inga said. "We felt it best for her . . . she could not live a normal life."

The women blamed themselves. From the Helms family, next door, there were clucks of sympathy, but no more. Inga heard them muttering that Anna had brought it on herself—running into the streets on New Year's Eve.

In the weeks following Anna's death, my mother

often seemed to be on the verge of losing her sanity. But whenever her hysteria would be at its worse, and Inga would grow concerned about her, that strength she held in reserve would surface, and she would force herself to maintain her balance by recalling Anna, Karl, me, my father.

"We will be together again," she would say. "I know it. We will remember Anna. When Karl and Rudi have children, they will name a child for her. Inga, do you remember what a tease she was? How she used to play with Rudi? The games they invented?"

"I remember. We won't forget our Anna."

I did not learn of precisely how my sister died until several years later, when Inga unearthed the evidence.

Anna was one of 50,000 victims—Jew and Gentile—of the Nazi "euthanasia" program.

It was not a sanitarium she had been taken to at Hadamar, but one of the first gassing installations, a model for the structures later used to kill millions of Jews.

There were twelve of these places like Hadamar, and the state made the decision as to who should enter the gas chambers—without consulting the families of the doomed.

In this manner, cripples, the feebleminded, the retarded, paralytics, and so on were driven to these murder mills, stripped, dressed in paper wrappers, and gassed to death with the exhaust from huge internal-combustion engines.

These early gassings began sometime in 1938 and continued for a few years. A great deal of secrecy surrounded them, but word seeped out. In a sense, they were rehearsals for what was to become the pattern for the extermination of the Jews, and many others, a few years later.

In my research, I learned that when comfirmation of the killing of these "useless" people reached the Vatican, strong protests were made to Berlin. Protestant churchmen also raised their voices. Idiots, Mongoloids, cretins, the crippled, were also children of God, the clergymen insisted. And so the "euthanasia" program was quietly phased out. But the plans were never set aside.

When the Jews were gassed by the millions there were no protests from the honorable clergy. Not a word. Except from a few brave men. One might count them on the fingers of one hand.

I find now that I must write about these matters as blandly and coldly as possible. Perhaps to keep myself from a lifetime of weeping over the murder of my beloved sister.

Erik Dorf's Diary

Berlin
November 1940

An anonymous caller informed my office yesterday, November 15, that a certain priest is delivering sermons aimed at subverting our racial policies.

The man's name is Bernard Lichtenberg, and he is provost of St. Hedwig's Cathedral. He is a plain, gray-haired fellow, in his middle sixties. I know little about his background, but what has impelled him to this rash course, I cannot imagine. The vast majority of churches, Catholic and Protestant, have either supported us or have been discreetly neutral.

Accordingly, I attended an evening service at St. Hedwig's. (I am not a Catholic, nor have I been a practicing Christian of any kind since my childhood. My parents were Lutheran, but my father had small use for organized religions.)

The church was less than a third filled. Perhaps word had gotten around about Lichtenberg's anti-state commentaries. Indeed, as his sermon progressed, following the mass, at least a half-dozen people got up and left.

The elderly priest was treading on dangerous

ground. I have nothing personal against the man, but anyone undermining our policies has to be stopped. Those are the orders from the top.

"Let us pray in silence," Father Lichtenberg said, "for the children of Abraham."

It was at this point that four or five people left. Others, quite obviously, held their heads up, and did not pray at all.

"Outside," the priest went on, "the synagogue is burning, and that, too, is a house of God. In many of your homes, an inflammatory newspaper is circulated, warning Germans that if they exhibit false sentimentality to Jews, they commit treason. This church and this priest will pray for the Jews, for they suffer."

More people got up and left.

"Do not let yourself be led astray by such unchristian thoughts, but act according to the clear command of Christ: 'Thou shalt love thy neighbor as thyself.'"

I waited until the service had ended, and then walked down the nave and into the sacristy. I was in civilian dress, feeling it a bit inappropriate to come to the mass in uniform. (Although many of our men are good Catholics or devout Protestants, and attend services in uniform all the time.)

Father Lichtenberg was having his vestments removed by an aged sacristan. I approached him and showed him my identity card and badge.

"Captain Erik Dorf," he read. "How can I help you, my son?"

"I listened to your sermon with much interest."

"And did you learn anything from it?"

"I learned that you are a kind-hearted man, but you are gravely misinformed."

He looked at me with tired, sensitive eyes. I wished that I did not have to confront him. "I know what is happening to the Jews. And so do you, Captain."

Rather than argue with him, I walked around the sacristy table, weighing my words. "Father, Pope Pius some years ago concluded a concordat with the Führer. The Vatican has said many times that it regards Germany as Christian Europe's last bastion against Bolshevism."

"That does not justify the torture and murder of innocents, Captain."

"No one is being tortured. I know of no murder of innocents."

"I have seen the Jews beaten and defiled in the streets. I have seen them sent off to prison for no reason—"

"They are enemies of the Reich. We are engaged in a war, Father."

"Against armies? Or against defenseless Jews?"

"I must appeal to you to be more temperate in your remarks, Father. Other churchmen have found no problem in reconciling their faith with us. In Bremen, last week, a new church was dedicated in the Führer's name."

He would not be sidetracked. "I have heard stories from our soldiers returned from Poland," the priest said. "They go beyond the mere transportation of so-called alien races."

"Confessions from battle-weary young men? You must take those stories lightly."

"But as a priest I must listen, and give absolution. I will follow my conscience in these matters."

He was a stubborn old fellow, decent enough, but blind to our aims, our goals. I bowed politely and told him not to let his conscience get him in trouble.

He thanked me and turned away. Then I heard him say to the sacristan, "Such an intelligent and charming young man. Our gift to the new age."

I caught the sarcasm in his voice, and I made a mental note to put him under surveillance.

Rudi Weiss' Story

Eventually my mother was arrested and sent to Warsaw.

I think she was almost glad to have the ax fall. Although she might have remained some months longer in Karl's old studio, she was deteriorating under the loss of Anna, the absence of her sons and her husband. Perhaps she was "denounced" by someone in the Helms family. Inga swears her parents said nothing, although they made no secret of their hatred of my mother.

In any case, she was arrested in a general sweep of that quarter of the city, put on a freezing cattle car with hundreds of other Berlin Jews, most of them women and children, and sent to Warsaw.

My father was working in the children's ward of the Jewish Hospital when he learned that a Berta Weiss, claiming to be his wife, had arrived at the Umschlagplatz, near the main rail station in the ghetto.

Max Lowy, the printer, my father's old patient, came running in with the news. My father and a woman named Sarah Olenick, a nurse, were trying to find food and medicine for the sick children. They died every day, huddled around a cold stove, moaning, unable to resist the diseases that ravaged the ghetto.

Lowy insisted he had seen my mother. At once my father left the hospital and practically ran all the way to the registration office at the station.

And so they were reunited, more than a year after my father's deportation.

Letters that my mother wrote to Karl (apparently never mailed, or returned, and saved by Inga) reveal the true depths of her emotions for my father. In front of the children, she was always restrained, very much the daughter of an old infantry officer.

But the letters were a different story. In one, she wrote:

It is perhaps my fault, dear Karl, that you are as shy and what shall I say—suppressed—as you are. I never made an outward show of deep love or emotion towards your dear father, indeed to my children. This does not mean I did not love you or him. How could I not? Your father is simply that kind of good man whose goodness is taken for granted. He treats the meanest of his patients, the worst beggars, scoundrels and complainers, with the dignity he would afford a prince. And as for unpaid bills! And his talent for not getting after them!

He confounds me at times, and I know he is a better person than I am. My love for him is mingled with a kind of wonder, an awe at his everlasting goodness. You have this in you also, Karl. . . .

My mother had always lacked the ability to show deep emotion, warmth, outwardly. An only child, raised in a hothouse atmosphere by strict parents, she was wary of kissing, hugging, let alone sexual suggestions in public.

But now she and my father kissed shamelessly, like young lovers. He joked about her insistence on standing on line to register, saying she was still the law-abiding Berliner. He assured her that even in the pitiful Warsaw ghetto, the bureaucracy was inept and she could wait a while to register, while they sat in what passed for a cafe, pretending they were at the Adlon Hotel.

"Where there are Jews, there must be places for people to sit, and hold hands, and talk," my father said. "Even if it is a coffee house with no coffee."

They looked at each other for a few moments. They had aged. The suffering had hurt them, etched lines in their faces.

"You are hiding something from me," my father said. He knew her moods, her reactions.

"Josef . . . Anna is dead."

She told him about the strange letter, about Anna's death from pneumonia in the sanitarium. Inga had tried to learn more, find the grave, and had been rebuffed.

My father cried freely, unable to control his sorrow. My mother lied to him about the events that led to her death. He was told nothing of how she was raped and abused by drunken hoodlums, how this had caused her mental decline.

"It was painless," my mother said. "The hospital people said the drugs dulled the pain, and that she died peacefully."

"I can't believe it," he sobbed. "My child, my Anna. What in God's name do they want of us? What tribute are they demanding? Our children's lives?"

For a long time, he said nothing, bending his head, pressing his hands to his eyes, while my mother lied about Anna. He was too good a physician to accept the story that she had simply gone into a decline. Such mental collapses, he argued, trying to temper his bottomless sorrow with medical analysis, were usually set off by a trauma of some kind. Had something happened to Anna? No, my mother said—just a gradual depression.

"The life in her, the life in her," he wept. "They killed it."

He understood now that no indignity, no humiliation, no torture was to be spared us—the family Weiss, and the Jews of Europe. For the rest of his life, he would not be able to dispel the vision of his lost daughter.

My mother tried to divert him. She asked about conditions in the Warsaw ghetto. Was there work for him? Where would they live? With her infinite capacity for optimism, for seeing the bright side, she said she would volunteer to teach school. She had heard that the schools in the ghetto, for all the deprivation, were active, full of eager students. She would be happy to teach a music class, perhaps literature also.

My father agreed, but he could not let the subject of Anna alone. "I can't believe she's gone. You haven't told me all. Where was this hospital? Who was the physician?"

She took his hand. "Josef, cry if you think it will help. But it will not bring our daughter back. Perhaps . . . perhaps . . . it is better."

"Better? Life is always better than death."

"I am not so sure. Don't ask me anything else."

"The boys?"

"Karl is still in prison. Yes, he's alive, getting by. Inga says she is still trying to see him, to pull strings and get him freed."

"Rudi?"

"Gone. Our wild one. Our street fighter. He vanished in the night, left me a note, and said we must not worry about him, but that he would not stay and let them arrest him."

My father shook his head. "How I miss them. I never talked to them enough, spent enough time with them. How I wish they were with us, so I could make things up. I once disappointed Rudi so terribly. The first time he started at center in a big game. Sixteen years old, the youngest player on the team. And I ran off to some medical meeting. He said he didn't care, but I knew he did."

"We'll make it up to them when this ends."

"Yes, yes, of course we will. And we must not dwell on our misfortunes. There are hundreds of thousands worse off. We at least will have work, and enough to eat, and a place to live."

They got up from the cafe, held hands like young lovers.

"Josef," my mother said. "I have never loved you more."

"Nor I you. Dear God, I look at you and I see Anna."

"But you must not cry again." She took his arm firmly. "Now you may take me to that elegant apartment."

"I'm afraid it's one room—over the old drugstore."

"And no piano? No Bechstein? I may leave you if there isn't."

"No piano," my father said. "But memories of one."

Some time before Christmas, Inga received a letter from Sergeant Heinz Muller, telling her to come to Buchenwald. He was vague, but he hinted that he might be able to arrange for her to see Karl. He could promise nothing, but he would at least try. And he ordered her to burn the letter.

My sister-in-law was a courageous and tenacious woman. She pretended to be a hiker, with boots, rucksack and staff, and approached the outer fences of the prison camp fearlessly. There is much to be said for a working-class background, for women who are independent and resourceful. Inga was ahead of her time.

Of course she was stopped by armed sentries. She could see double strands of barbed wire, a high fence, watchtowers, and a moat surrounding the place.

Distantly on the frozen earth of the internment camp, she could see men in striped suits moving slowly, flailing at the ground with picks and shovels.

An SS private came running forward to chase her off, but she insisted on seeing sergeant Heinz Muller, an old friend. The soldier, intimidated by her manner, rang up Muller on a field telephone, warning Inga to wait outside the outer barriers of the camp.

Muller came out of the guardhouse, buckling on his uniform belt, slicking his hair back. He was smiling, his manner cordial, almost oily.

Muller dismissed the curious sentry and extended his arms in welcome. She drew away.

"So. You got my letter."

"Yes," Inga said.

"How have you been, dear girl? The esteemed and honorable Mrs. Weiss."

"I'm well enough. I'm here to see Karl. You said in the letter you would arrange it."

Muller looked into the distance, at the men laboring out of doors under the lash of a wintry wind. There was, Inga remembers, a sniff of wet snow in the air.

"Regulations have gotten stricter," he said. "I don't have direct jurisdiction over inmates."

"Then why did you deceive me?"

His eyes had trouble meeting hers. "I felt as a favor to your family. Old friends, and so forth."

"I want to see Karl."

Muller grabbed her arm. "Are you afraid of me?"

"No. I know too much about you. And others like you. One must not show fear to you people. My brother-in-law Rudi understood that."

"Hah! That dumb soccer player. They'll catch him and take care of him also."

"Take me to Karl."

"Come. We'll discuss it in the guardhouse. We have a visitor's room there."

He led her to the barracks-like building, through a side door. At once she saw it was not a "visitor's room" at all, but his private quarters—bed, desk, chairs, photographs on the wall.

"This is your room," she said.

"Please, please. Guests are always welcome here. Sit down."

Inga did.

"Cigarette?" Muller asked. "Perhaps some cognac? Nothing is too good for our brave soldiers guarding the enemies of the Reich. We do as well here as they do on the front."

"I came here for one reason. To see my husband."

"Perhaps some coffee. Not ersatz, mind you. The real thing."

She shook her head.

"Ah, that Helms singlemindedness." He put a hand on her shoulder, then began stroking the back of her neck.

She endured it for a moment, before removing his hand. "How is he?"

"Not too well, I'm afraid. He got into some trouble in the barracks. Fighting, stealing food. I'm not sure. They took him off that cushy job with the tailoring shop and he's out in the quarry now. In fact, he and a friend of his, some kike named Weinberg, were strung up for a while."

"Oh, my God. Oh, my poor Karl."

"Yes, it's no party out there with pick and shovel. The guards don't allow any goldbricking. They work until they drop sometimes. And with winter coming on . . ."

Inga got up, raging, but controlled herself. "You lied to me. What a friend of my father's! You summoned me here falsely. I can't see him. And I learn he is being worked to death. I have heard stories of what goes on here."

"Nonsense. You work, you get by. You don't work, you get in trouble."

Inga loved my brother deeply, and the thought of him suffering, that frail man out in the snowy fields hacking at rocks, beaten, under the threat of death, broke her iron will. She held her head in her hands and wept softly.

Muller sat opposite her on his bed and put a gentle hand on her knee. "Don't cry. I'll help you."

She looked up, ashamed of her tears. "How? Can you appeal to let him be freed?"

"I am only a sergeant. But . . . I'll take him a letter from you."

"You will?"

"And bring his letter out, and post it to Berlin."

"I will be grateful to you."

"For you, Inga Helms, it will be an honor." He lifted her chin with one hand. Inga remembers to this day that for a big man, a former factory worker, he had an oddly soft hand—as if the easy life of the last few years had changed him. He also smelled of some scent, a male lotion.

Then he knelt in front of her. She recoiled.

"Don't, please," he said. "I am no monster. I'm doing a job, that's all."

"It's more than a job, what you people do."

"*You* people. Will you condemn a whole nation fighting for its rights, its very life? Someone's got to take care of internal enemies."

"Good God, Muller, spare me those party-line speeches."

"All right. We'll put it on a personal basis. You've known me a long time. I'm an old friend of your father's, your brother's. I was at your wedding. I watched while you married that Jew from a fancy family. And me, what about me? A mechanic all my life, no education. Was I to be sneered at, snubbed because of that? Inga, I loved you more than that . . . that . . ."

"Don't say it, Muller."

"It is the truth. I was dying in my guts when you exchanged rings with him. You should have been my wife."

"Please, don't talk about it. I brought a letter with me. Take it to him for me." She opened the rucksack, took out the letter and gave it to the SS man.

Muller eyed it as if it were poisoned, or might detonate in his hand. "Done. Risky business, Inga. But for you . . . your family . . . Heinz Muller will take the chance."

At this point he unbuttoned his tunic and draped it on a chair. Inga got up to leave. He stood in the doorway, barring her from going. Then he forced her to the edge of the bed.

"Your man Karl," he said. "I saw him yesterday. He looks awful. Another few days in the quarry may kill him."

"You said he was managing."

"Didn't want to upset you. But I'm telling you the truth now. They die every day out there."

"Help him, I beg you."

Muller began to unbutton his shirt. "I have a bit more influence than I let on. If we come to some kind of agreement, I'll get him out of the quarry and into an even softer job than the tailor's shop. They have an artist's studio here. He'd be perfect for it."

"What sort of agreement?"

"I think you understand." He took off his belt.

"You pig."

"Another week of hacking at rocks out there in the cold and he'll be one more dead Jew."

He came to her, freshly shaved, reeking of cheap men's cologne, and began to smear her face with wet, sucking lips. She fell under the weight of his body, let him raise her dress. He tried to be gentle, but his hot, trembling hands betrayed his crude passion.

In disgust, revulsion, she found a way of combatting her hatred of him and what he was forcing her to do. She stared at the barracks ceiling, listening to his grunts, his moans, accepting the clumsy thrusts, detesting him. It was a mechanical experience, she told herself—like minor surgery, or being fitted for an orthopedic device.

Oddly, he spent himself in seconds. He gasped, whimpered, fell away. Yes, she told herself, pure mechanics, something devoid of human qualities, detached from even the lower forms of physiology.

"I love you, dammit," Muller whispered. He was stumbling to the small bathroom. "I love you. You will come back. And you will love me."

She did not answer him, but thought: Perhaps I will kill you first.

I have lost any sense of how long Helena and I tried to cross into some country not occupied by the Nazis. We wandered again. Her skill with languages was an invaluable aid—Czech, German and later her excellent Russian. I posed as a stupid farmhand, talking as little as possible.

One day, sometime in January 1941, after spending a night in a deserted barn, I questioned an old farmer, and he told me that there was a thinly guarded stretch of border just to the south. He said the road forked, and the right fork led to a thick woods, where one might see eastern Hungary at one end, and even a bend in the Tisza River. It was a flat wooded area, he said, and one could find the barbed-wire barrier without too much trouble.

When night came, I led Helena to the place he had described. I had developed cat's eyes. I could see at night, almost smell my way to water, to farms, to human habitation. The human stink was a pronounced one in the wilderness.

We crawled on all fours through thickets of scrubby bushes to a four-stranded barrier. The wire cutters went to work. Within minutes Helena and I, on our backs, shoving with our feet, pressing our spines against the earth, scratched by iron barbs and thorns, passed into Hungary. We had no idea what village we were near, what our story would be.

I led. She followed. My nose sensed the odor—too

late. A man had stepped from behind a tree and was jamming the barrel of a short rifle into my belly. He was a short, fat man in a gray-green uniform, boots, peaked cap.

"Against the tree," he said.

Helena gasped. The man spoke German, but I was certain he was not a German. A Hungarian border guard. German was in common use in frontier areas.

"Papers," the guard said.

"We lost them," I said.

"Put your hands over your heads," he said. He cradled the rifle in one hand, leveled a flashlight at us with the other. "What are you doing here?"

"Please," Helena said. "We're trying to get to Yugoslavia. To the coast. Give us a chance."

"We can pay," I lied. We had not a penny between us.

"Fucking Jews," the Hungarian said. "You fucking Jews are all alike. You think you can buy the world."

I measured him. About thirty-five. Paunch. Small feet. He looked soft. A few good kicks, if I could take him unawares.

"Give us a break," I said. "We don't want to hurt anyone. In a few days we can be in Yugoslavia."

The guard gestured with his rifle. "Move. You first, the woman behind. If you try anything smart, I'll shoot her. To the path."

"Where are you taking us?" asked Helena.

"Border jail. The Gestapo sends a truck around every few days to pick up Jews, Communists, other strays from Czechoslovakia."

"Gestapo?" she asked.

"Sure. We got no argument with them. We're happy to send back a few Jews."

He marched us off. We must have walked about a hundred feet down a footpath. The barren tree limbs were thick on either side of us, the ground damp. There were evergreens—pine, spruce—and we must have been higher than I had calculated. In the distance I saw the outlines of a striped sentry box. Another light flashed. Someone called.

"Lajos? Are you all right?"

"Yes," our guardian answered. "Got two more."

I shoved Helena out of my way—so hard that her hip and leg remained bruised for a month—and leaped at the man behind her. I hit him with all my strength—arms, head, chest—and he went down with a soft blowing-out of air. I grabbed the gun and the flashlight, but not before kicking him in the chest twice, once more in the head.

The other sentry—the man at the box—began to shout. But he did not fire. Our guard started to get to his feet, and I gave it to him once more, a violent kick under the chin that knocked him out.

"Lajos? What happened?" the other called.

We heard his boots, the breaking of tree limbs.

In a rage, I leveled the rifle at Lajos' head, pulled the bolt. I would blast the bastard's head off. Partial payment to the Jew-haters of the world. Then I would take care of the one running toward us.

"No, no!" Helena screamed.

I did not shoot. But I grabbed her arm. The two of us raced for the barbed-wire barrier we had just crossed. We ran forever, it seemed. I dragged her, as wicked branches scratched her face and grabbed at her clothing, and roots tripped our feet.

"Run, dammit, run," I shouted.

"Can't . . . can't . . ."

"You'll run or you'll die."

The other sentry had apparently stopped to examine his comrade—the one whose head I'd kicked as if it were a soccer ball.

"Stupid goddam Jews!" he shouted. "You can't get away."

Shots pinged around us, breaking branches, whistling and whining. But he was shooting blindly. I forced Helena to bend low. The shots ceased. He had no stomach to follow us. Not after he had seen what I had done to his buddy. And knowing I was armed. Bullies and brutes have this common trait, I had learned as a kid—they hesitate when they think they will be in a fair fight, or at a disadvantage.

"No more . . . no more . . ." Helena wept. "Rudi . . . stop . . . my chest is burning . . ."

We rested a moment against a pine. The sweet smell of its branches reminded me of winter vacations when I was little—Mama and Papa, and the three of us, Karl, Anna and me, in an Austrian hotel learning to ski, skating.

"That's enough," I said angrily. "We must keep running."

"No . . . no . . . no more . . ." She was becoming hysterical. "We're finished, Rudi."

"No. They'll have to kill us before I give up."

I looked at the rifle. It was like a carbine, with a large clip for the bullets.

I grabbed Helena's arm and we veered off the path again. Soon I noticed that the barbed-wire barrier seemed to have been cut in several places, as if others had tried the same route we had. We followed it, then had to do no more than step across a fallen section.

"What a joke," I said. "I think we're back in Czechoslovakia."

"Does it matter, Rudi?" she cried.

"I'm not sure." I took her arms, held her gently, kissed her forehead, tried to make her stop crying. "We'll try again, Helena. I'm not ready to die for them yet. And you must not be either."

Erik Dorf's Diary

Berlin
April 1941

The talk everywhere—in government circles, at least —is of the Führer's so-called "Commissar Order" of last month. It will involve our people deeply.

I wasn't present at the meeting, since it was largely for the benefit of some two hundred senior army officers. It is no secret that a vast invasion of Russia "from the Baltic to the Black Sea" is imminent.

Hitler made these points among others: the war with the Soviet Union will be unlike any war in the past, and cannot be conducted in "knightly fashion" (his exact words). The Bolshevist-Jewish intelligentsia must be eliminated. (A junior officer who pointed out that many of the Bolshevik hierarchy and commissars were Great Russians, Ukrainians, Armenians, and God knows what else was quickly silenced.)

This job of "eliminating" on a grand scale all enemies of the Reich—Jews, Bolsheviks, clergy, commissars, intelligentsia—is so grave that it cannot be entrusted to the army. Heydrich, telling me this with a grin on his face, said that the army leaders, Jodl, Keitel, all those haughty types, swallowed this like children taking castor oil. On the one hand they hate the idea of losing jurisdiction, but on the other, they are relieved not to have to undertake tasks that only our SS, our fearless "Black Crows," will be courageous enough to undertake.

Not a single voice was raised at that meeting to protest what amounts to a blueprint for the mass killing of civilians, prisoners and anyone who remotely fits the Führer's all-inclusive categories. Keitel, that supreme prostitute, elaborated on the order by specifying that the Reichsführer SS (Himmler) and his men would be responsible for "tasks entailed by the final struggle that will have to be carried out between two opposing political systems." This rather elaborate phraseology simply means that the SS will be entrusted with the killing of Jews. (I use these words only in the secrecy of this diary; I would not dare use such terms in aide-memoires, or even conversation.)

To implement this "Commissar Order," Heydrich, ever the brilliant organizer, drew up a plan for four Einsatzgruppen, Action Commandos, who will divide the Soviet Union into four jurisdictions. The commander of each such team—they are designated A, B, C and D—will have full responsibility for cleansing these areas.

We are now, in effect, mobile killing teams, equipped to do away with vast numbers of racial and political enemies of Germany. We soon learned that the gallant Wehrmacht, so proud of its chivalrous traditions, not only is keeping out of our way, but is aiding us generously, and sometimes joining in the bloody business of eliminating these subhuman foes of civilization.

What went through my mind as these plans were delineated?

First, Eichmann's dictum—*obey*. But even obedience requires some understanding of precisely what orders one is obeying. And today, April 21, 1941, I realize that our mandate is part of an encompassing plan. An overview, if one wishes. I must blot from my mind notions of individual Jews. They are not important. Instead I must think of the Führer's grand plan for a new Europe, indeed a new world—ruled by the finest of men, we Aryans, and governed not by mushy antiquated concepts, but by the New Order of strength, will, pure racial strains and unlimited power.

The words sound a bit alien to me as I write them. But I see the profound historical validity of these concepts now. After all, American colonists decimated their Red Indians to form a new, potent nation. The British Empire was not built with kind words and soup kitchens. Zulus and Hindus were blown to bits, the innocent as well as the malcontents, to create a vast commercial system.

And the Führer's goal is far more honorable, more glorious than a mere empire of factories and farms. It involves the highest aspirations of the human spirit. The Jews stand in our way. All sentiment, all handwringing, all the rusty, useless Christian notions of charity and pity must be laid aside. I understand this a great deal better today than I ever did. Certainly better than that day I walked into Heydrich's office and acted like a *naif*.

To announce the Einsatzgruppen, Heydrich hosted a buffet at his headquarters. The atmosphere was informal, unbuttoned. No orders were read or distributed. The talk was loose, friendly, general. We understood one another. There was a large map of the Soviet

Union on the wall, to which the chief referred now and then, showing how the USSR was to be carved into areas of operation for our teams. Only the map gave any hint that this was anything more than a social gathering.

As a junior member of the SS, I was astonished and delighted to see what a high caliber of German had been attracted to our ranks. Many of the new group commanders had been in the field a long time, and were known to me only as names on a file card, in a dossier. Heydrich was bragging about his underlings, the men who would be in charge of rendering Europe "Jew-free."

"Colonel Blobel, for example," Heydrich was saying. We all were drinking fine French champagne. He pointed with his glass. "An eminent architect."

Paul Blobel, a bit overweight, a rather noisy fellow, given to boozing, nodded. "With ingenious designs for the Jews of Russia," he said.

Heydrich went on, "Colonel Ohlendorf is a lawyer —like you, Dorf—and an economic expert. Weinmann is a physician. Klingelhoffer was an opera singer. And our prize—Colonel Biberstein, a former Lutheran minister."

I was truly impressed. The foreign press has tried to depict us as thugs and murderers. I wish they could see the high quality of officer in our ranks.

"Biberstein," Heydrich teased. "Tell us about that organization you formed when you left the pulpit. What was it called . . . ?"

Colonel Biberstein blushed. "The Brotherhood of Love."

Ohlendorf laughed. "What the devil was the Brotherhood of Love?"

Biberstein knew he was being ragged, but he was a good sport about it. We are truly a fraternity, a group united in the knowledge of the grave tasks ahead of us. "I felt the need for a civilian organization, something outside the church as it were, to encourage human love through Christian faith."

"How did it work out?" Blobel asked.

"Badly, I'm afraid. That's how I ended up in the SS. First as a chaplain, now in a new line of work."

"Spreading the gospel, eh, Biberstein?" Blobel taunted.

"Oh, no need to spread it here," the former churchman said. "Here we are all converts to a new faith."

Blobel roared at this, and even more serious men like Ohlendorf and Colonel Artur Nebe smiled. I saw nothing funny about it, although Heydrich did not seem perturbed.

"A new faith, yes," I said. "And we're the apostles."

"Listen to Captain Dorf!" Blobel bellowed. "If that's the case, which one is Peter?"

"I'll be Doubting Thomas," said Ohlendorf.

"So long as we have no Judas," I said.

Blobel looked at me with sly contempt. He was drunk. At the buffet, he had babbled on about French champagne, Polish ham, Belgian endive salad, Dutch cheeses. All that was needed was Russian caviar, Blobel said, and that would come soon enough.

"A Judas?" Blobel repeated. "In this group?"

"I'm quite certain there'll be no betrayals," Heydrich said pleasantly. "What Captain Dorf was referring to, I believe, was the need for secrecy."

"How do you keep jobs like this secret?" Blobel persisted.

"No written orders," I said quickly. "No references to the Führer. Full cooperation from the army. The resettlement program must take place quickly, surgically, with no traces left. Even in casual conversation, let alone written reports, we are not to use the precise words that describe what the Einsatzgruppen will be doing."

Colonel Ohlendorf—bespectacled, handsome, fair, the very model of a scholar-turned-officer—tapped the side of his glass. "It may not be easy," he said. (He is not only a lawyer and an economist, but a Doctor of Jurisprudence.)

"Nothing important is," I said.

Ohlendorf stared at me. He was a bit offended. After all I am not only a junior officer, but a fellow lawyer.

Suddenly Blobel took my elbow and steered me away from the group. Biberstein was being teased again about his clerical career. Ohlendorf was asking him a theoretical question about Christian sanction for anti-Bolshevik measures.

"I've heard about you, Dorf," Blobel said. There was a mean tone to his voice. It was a spongy voice. "Heydrich's monitor, his spy. I'm told you gave Hans Frank a bawling out that had his ears ringing."

I have learned a great deal since joining the service. One thing is never to show fear, even if you feel it. Blobel outranks me, and has a great deal of service in the field, but I am close to Heydrich.

"You heard incorrectly, Colonel," I said. "Governor Frank and I had a useful, constructive talk."

His loose mouth was forging into a sneer preparatory to a retort when Heydrich summoned us to the map of Russia.

"A big area," Heydrich said. "And an even bigger job. Efficiency and production will be demanded. You'll be watched. Captain Dorf here will be assigned to the Russian front, as a sort of traveling representative of my office."

"Selling what?" Blobel blurted out. "Extermination?"

There was some nervous laughter from the men. I did not join in it.

"Careful with your choice of words, Blobel," Heydrich said. "You will inform Captain Dorf of your actions, your campaigns, but you will put as little as possible in writing."

"And may I suggest, sir," I added, "that the Führer's name be kept out of this. The Führer himself hasn't put this down on paper—precisely what he has in mind—although he made himself quite clear to the generals."

I could see them, the various colonels and majors, the men who would head the mobile teams, looking at me with mixed respect, distrust and a bit of puzzlement. Some of them had heard about the bright young fellow in Heydrich's office, and some had met me, if briefly. They were measuring me, and they were not entirely pleased.

I could swear I heard Ohlendorf mutter to Blobel, "He will have to be handled."

Heydrich turned to the wall map. "More than a thousand miles of the Russian front to manage after we invade," he said. "The Baltic to the Black Sea."

"And our groups will total only three thousand men?" asked Blobel.

"That's part of the challenge, Colonel," I said. "The plan includes the recruiting of sympathetic local militia—Ukrainians, Lithuanians, Balts. They'll be glad to help in the resettlement of Jews."

Ohlendorf, legal man that he is, shook his head. "Permit me to say, General, that these contemplated actions are a lot more comprehensive than mere resettlements. Herding Jews into Warsaw or Lublin, or some camp, is one thing. This is quite another."

"But in a sense easier," Heydrich said. "They need not be fed, clothed, given medical attention."

"Yes, but think of the piles of ammunition cases," Blobel said, laughing. No one laughed with him.

Heydrich liked Ohlendorf. He was very much like me—serious, precise, analytic. "Colonel Ohlendorf has a point. Bear in mind that the key to our operations will be mobility. The instant an area is secured by the army, we must be a step behind, ready to round up Bolsheviks, commissars, Jews, gypsies, any undesirable elements. The army will cooperate. It took the Führer's Commissar Order and even improved on it. Dorf, read them that recent army order."

I went to my briefcase and found the document to which the chief had referred. " 'General instructions for dealing with political leaders and others, following the Führer's order of March 1941. Eleven categories of persons in the Soviet Union are listed as subject to our jurisdiction.' "

"*Jurisdiction!*" shouted Blobel, by now quite drunk. "A ditch and a machine gun!"

We ignored him. I read on. " 'The categories include criminal elements, gypsies, officials of the Soviet State and party, agitators, Communists, and all Jews.' "

"This is an *army* list?" Biberstein asked. "Not an SS list?"

"Quite," Heydrich said. "They've taken the Führer at his word. Of course, the only thing is, the jurisdiction over these groups will be *ours*. But it gives you an idea of Keitel and the others' sincere desire to cooperate."

"I'm curious," asked Ohlendorf. "Will there be exceptions?"

"Exceptions?" Heydrich asked.

"Yes. People useful to us . . . labor . . . collaborators . . ."

Heydrich nodded. "Of course. Certain anti-Bolshevik elements will be used, certainly Ukrainians. And the Russians themselves, the nonpolitical ones, will be used as slave labor, which is all they're good for."

Biberstein was kneading his fingers. "And . . . in the case of Jews? Any exceptions to the Führer's order?"

"None," said Heydrich.

Blobel belched loudly. "That's clear enough. I thought that's what this meeting was really about."

"Let no one have any doubts," Heydrich said. "Europe will be rid of Jews, one way or the other."

"Are we to assume this order comes from . . . ?" Ohlendorf left the query hanging.

Heydrich looked at me. "Dorf, from your bottomless file of excellent memoranda, find that notation concerning the Führer's conversation with the Italian ambassador."

I dug into my briefcase and found the paper in question.

"Yes," I said. "A few years back, Mussolini's ambassador complained that Il Duce was upset about our anti-Jewish campaign. Afraid it would offend the foreign press, and so on."

"Typically Italian," Ohlendorf said. We all laughed.

"The Führer informed the envoy that in five hundred years, if for nothing else, Adolf Hitler would be honored for one thing—as the man who wiped the Jews from the face of the earth."

Rudi Weiss' Story

Helena and I found our way to Russia—whether for better or worse I do not know—in June 1941.

In the extreme western corner of the Ukraine, at the point where Czechoslovakia, Hungary and the Soviet Union converge—I had stolen a map from a railroad station some weeks before—we simply walked through a wire fence, and gave ourselves up to a Russian soldier.

He was a farm boy in a baggy gray uniform, and he relieved me of the rifle I'd taken from the Hungarian some months back, and marched us off to a Red Army encampment.

The slovenliness and indifference of the Soviets astonished me. All through Czechoslovakia we had seen troop movements, tanks and trucks moving eastward. For what purpose? Helena and I had been hidden by some Slovak farmers for several months, working in the fields for a bed in a hayloft and our food. Some days the sky would be hazed over with a film of yellow dust, from the endless parade of mechanized equipment on the move. The Slovaks treated us rather decently. The village was so obscure, the SS never bothered to send an inspection team there.

But now we were in Russia, standing in front of a Red Army infantry captain, who sat with his soft boots on a field table, eyeing us with disfavor, indifference.

"Where'd you get the rifle?" he asked Helena. He saw that it was of Italian make, an old bolt-action weapon.

"I stole it," I said.

Helena, who spoke excellent Russian, cautioned me to be quiet. She'd do the talking. I'm not sure what she told the Russian officer, but he seemed unimpressed. She turned to me helplessly. "The same story," she said. "He says they have no argument with the Germans. Don't we know Stalin and Hitler signed a treaty, and that they're good friends?"

"Tell him about the German tanks and trucks."

Helena did. He seemed even less impressed. He got up, a gangly, red-faced man in a sloppy, stained uniform. Men lolled about, kicked a soccer ball. At a field kitchen, the odors of stew drifted toward us. They were absolutely certain the Germans meant them no harm.

Helena spoke some more—flirting, lying, touching his arm. She told him we were Czechs who feared the Germans. Why? he asked. Oh, we were good party members, she lied. Yes, we had gone to the Marx-Lenin Academy (no such school existed) in Prague, and there was a price on our heads.

Then I saw the captain wink at the soldier who had brought us in and say, "*Zhidn*."

I knew what that meant—Jews, kikes, Yids.

"Yes, Comrade Officer," Helena said. "We are Jews, but we are also devoted Marxists and we praise the peace-loving Soviet Union and its wonderful people."

A debate followed—some junior officer sticking his two kopecks in, demanding we be sent back across the border —and Helena's red-faced captain finally deciding we could stay, but not at his camp.

"We have no fight with the Germans," the junior officer said.

"You will," I blurted out. "Helena—tell him again." She did.

"Bah. Maneuvers." The captain was utterly indifferent. The last thing the Germans needed was a two-front war. He gave Helena a small lecture on foreign policy. England would surrender, and then Russia and Germany would divide up the world.

"Please, Comrade Captain, let us stay," Helena begged. "My father was a founder of the Communist Party in Prague." (A bald lie, but she carried it off; her father had been a Zionist for years.)

"Kiss the bastard if you have to," I said.

Helena threw her arms around him and kissed his cheek. Even though she was tanned, her skin coarsened, her hair undone, she was still a beautiful, vivacious girl. She simply could not be resisted—not by Czech police, nor by Red Army officers.

Finally, he agreed to send us on to the big Ukrainian city of Kiev. There was a refugee center of some kind there, and we would be duly registered, perhaps jailed, or interrogated, or given jobs, if we could prove our loyalty to the USSR. It was all terribly confused and uncertain. I gathered, from what Helena told me, that the officer wanted to be rid of us. It was less paperwork for him.

She kissed him again. "For Marx, and Lenin, and Stalin, and for you, Comrade Captain."

He patted her behind once and sent us off to a truck loaded with other odds and ends of people who had slipped into the Soviet Union—Hungarians, Slovaks, all claiming to be political refugees from the Germans.

Soon we were underway on a dusty road. The truck bounced unmercifully, and we were bruised and choked by clouds of dust. An old Jew, crouched next to me, kept praying, bending back and forward, muttering Hebrew prayers. I understood enough Yiddish to gather he'd been visiting relatives near the border and was now going home to Kiev.

"What kind of a city is it, Grandpa?" I asked.

"Beautiful. Big. Cinemas. And many Jews, with our own synagogues and stores."

I put an arm around Helena. The old man asked if she were my wife, and I said yes. But I was reluctant to talk too much.

A half-hour later, jouncing along the rutted road to Kiev, we heard guns booming. They sounded like big guns, heavy artillery.

A workman in filthy clothes cupped an ear, listened, and said something to Helena.

"What is it?" I asked.

"He says its the Red Army. There's an artillery range near here."

Muller had lied to Inga. He made no effort to get Karl off the quarry detail. How my brother survived those months I don't know.

Finally, Inga, sensing she was being lied to—she brought a letter every month and got one in return, paying Muller's price—demanded that Karl be given the artist's job he had been promised. Hints in Karl's letter told Inga he was still hacking at rocks, at the mercy of the SS guards with their whips and clubs and dogs.

In any event, Muller enjoyed taunting him. Weinberg, who was on the rockpile with him, recalled the day Karl was finally transferred. He remembered because it was the day the SS guards shot two gypsies.

The gypsies, Weinberg said, infuriated the SS. They would refuse to work, and when they grudgingly went out to the quarry or the "garden," they were ingenious at finding ways to goldbrick. Moreover, with what seemed either outrageous bravery or foolhardiness, they often pretended not to hear the guards. They suffered for this.

It was a hot day. Weinberg recalled, and two of the gypsies in Karl's detail had lit cigarette butts. When the guard ordered them to stop smoking, one gypsy insolently blew smoke in the guard's direction.

A kapo was sent to beat them, and he got the worst of the fight. Karl, Weinberg and the others in the quarry—half-starved, battered men, who barely survived each dreadful day—watched as the gypsies, with some miraculous hoard of strength, wrested the baton from the kapo, and laughing, resumed their smoking.

Without any warning, the SS guard opened fire with his machine pistol, and the two gypsies tumbled into the rock quarry, heaps of bloodied clothing. They seemed, Weinberg said, to have died almost joyfully.

"Poor bastards," Karl said. "Braver than a lot of us."

"But foolish," Weinberg said.

My brother and Weinberg were ordered by the SS to drag the corpses up the steep incline. "There'll be

the same for you two Yids if you don't move," the SS
man shouted.

Karl and his friend waded into the filthy waters in
the sump and retrieved one corpse.

"Get the other one," the SS guard said. "And take
them to the crematorium."

Muller, who had been watching—it was nothing unusual for prisoners to be shot dead for a slight infraction—halted Karl at the edge of the quarry. He
spoke to the guard who had killed the gypsies.

"I want Weiss," he said.

Another prisoner was ordered to get the second gypsy, and Muller took my brother aside. They halted at
the shed where the quarry tools were stored.

"Your wife is a faithful correspondent," Muller said.

"Was she here today?"

"On schedule. The monthly visit."

"For God's sake, Muller, let me see her. Once, at
least."

"Oh, she's gone already. It's dangerous having her
hang around. For all concerned."

"Will you take a letter out for me?"

"Of course. Here's yours. Go on, read it."

"Later. When I'm alone."

Muller was smiling at him—an odd, possessive
smile. "Miss her, don't you?"

Karl nodded. "Muller, can't you get me out? You
know Inga's family. Forget about me, but why must
Inga have to suffer?"

There was a pause. "Don't be so sure she's suffering."

"What do you mean?" Karl asked.

"Women manage."

"What . . . what the hell are you smiling about? Did
she tell you anything?"

Muller's smile was a grin. "This is a business, Weiss,
a *business*. Jews should understand business. You
think I risk my neck playing mailman without getting
paid?"

It dawned on Karl what Muller was telling him.
"You're lying."

"Why do you think she comes here herself, in the flesh? She could mail me the letters."

"Good God . . . you . . . you make her . . ."

"No money changes hands. And I don't force her to do anything. She's more than willing, Weiss."

Karl clenched his fist; he told Weinberg later he would die the way the gypsies did, defiant, fighting, protesting. But my brother was no fighter. He had never been. And he was convinced he would someday be free again.

Muller shook his head. "You people always want something for nothing. No wonder the whole world hates you."

"I don't want her letters. Don't bring them any more."

"Oh no, my boy. It can get tougher for you if you refuse."

"I don't give a damn."

"Of course you do. You won't be in jail forever. Someday the Führer will decide you Jews have paid your fines, and you'll get out." He leered at Karl. "You won't even notice the difference in her."

Karl tried to walk away, back to his work. Muller grabbed his arm. "Be smart, Weiss. Play along with me."

"Let me go."

"You'll write her a nice letter, telling her how she is to keep coming here. I'll read it to make sure."

"Goddam you, I don't want to write to her, or see her again."

"You want to end up like those gypsies?"

"Maybe I should."

Muller gestured at Engelmann, the guard who had murdered the gypsies. He was a fat, bullet-headed man, a notorious homosexual who took his pick of the younger prisoners. "Or maybe you'd like to end up one of Engelmann's little friends. On the other hand, you may be too old and stringy for his tastes."

"Enough, Muller."

"I'm about to do you a favor. Tomorrow, I'll put

through your transfer to the art studio. Easy job. Indoors. But you must keep writing to Inga."

"No."

"I think you'll change your mind after a night with Engelmann."

Karl saw Weinberg and the others sliding into the quarry for the other gypsy—his body seemed to have vanished in the slimy waters—and he caved in. But he did not respond to Muller.

Muller walked up to Engelmann. "Go easy on my friend Weiss. He's being requisitioned for the artist's studio. Sensitive fellow. Wasted out here on the rocks."

"That's tomorrow, Weiss," Engelmann said. "Today, you're still breaking rocks."

Muller winked at Engelmann. "And the Jew doesn't even thank me."

My parents, in typical fashion, were doing their best to make life bearable for the imprisoned Jews of the ghetto.

My mother volunteered to teach music and literature. Amazingly, amid the illness and hunger and degradation, Jews still insisted that their children attend school. There were both secular schools (in which my mother taught) and religious classes.

Parents made an effort to send their kids off to school neat and clean, although clothing was in short supply. Scholars argued over Biblical texts. There was actually a nightclub cafe, where variety acts were performed, a theater group, concerts. All of this in the face of appalling overcrowding, lack of sanitation, diets of bread and potatoes, and a kind of growing defeatism, a sense that they were doomed, now that the wall locked them in, away from the "Aryan" section of the city.

One of my mother's problem students was a boy named Aaron Feldman, a pale jug-eared kid of thirteen, who was regarded as the king of the boy smugglers. Smuggling kept the ghetto alive in many respects. Anyone who could find his way out of the wall, through a tunnel or a hole, or by some ruse, and had money or goods to trade (or was brave enough to steal), helped feed and supply the Jews.

Aaron often came flying in late, his voluminous, ragged coat hiding a few eggs, or a can of jam, or sometimes even a chicken. My mother knew of this, but she did not have the heart to reprimand him—even if he was late for the rehearsal of a medley of ghetto folk songs.

I mention Aaron here because he seems the kind of kid I would have admired. Later, when the ghetto rose to fight the Nazis, he was in the thick of it. His smuggling did more good for the Jews than any conference, concordat, parley.

My father, working long hours at the Jewish Hospital and serving with the Judenrat, even came to the school one day to warn Aaron he must stop. Ghetto policemen had seen Aaron emerging from holes in the pavement, vanishing into gaps in the wall. Thus far they had looked the other way, but, my father warned the boy, the next time he would be arrested.

"They won't arrest me," Aaron said. "I give them eggs."

"Eggs may satisfy them, but they won't satisfy the Germans when they crack down on smugglers. You are not afraid?"

"Sure. But I'll do it anyway. They won't make me starve."

My father laughed. Perhaps he saw some of me in this cocky kid, who refused to sit back and be treated like a slave.

Eva recalls seeing my father looking into the classroom to which he returned my mother's delinquent student, and tears rimming his eyes, as she sat at the piano and led them in song.

And in the corridors, Eva recalls, there were colorful drawings by the children showing what the "new ghetto after the war" would look like—trees, parks, playgrounds, mothers pushing prams, bicycles. My father and the others who visited the school would often stop to look at the children's drawings and wonder if they would ever see such a day, such a place.

Shortly after trying to convince Aaron to mend his ways, my father attended a meeting of the Warsaw Jewish Council. The shortages of food were now a serious immediate problem. Dr. Kohn, the council chairman, wanted to concentrate on the healthy and productive. Skeletal, half-dead people in rags roamed the streets, begging, or simply surrendering, lying down in the gutter or against a building, waiting to die.

"We must try to feed everyone," my father said.

Zalman, the union leader, was distressed. "The smugglers kept us going for a long time. But the Nazis are shooting smugglers."

"Yes," Kohn added. "And an additional twenty Jews every time they catch one."

My father, having just seen the courage in Aaron Feldman's eyes, lost his temper—a rarity for him. He pounded the desk. "Those boys who crawl through sewers may be our salvation."

"Nonsense," Kohn said. "They'll get us all killed."

At this point, a slender young man of unremarkable appearance but with a calm and strangely commanding manner rose in the rear of the room. Like Zalman, he appeared to be a workman of some kind, in plain clothing and a workman's cap.

This man looked calmly at Dr. Kohn and said, "We will all be killed anyway."

"I beg your pardon?"

"I said we will all be killed anyway."

"How do you know?"

"It has begun already. The Nazis are killing Jews in Russia. Not just ten or twenty or a hundred. But all of them. They are eliminating the ghettoes. There will be no more ghettoes like this or any other. Just mass graves."

He spoke so quietly, but forcefully, that total silence descended on the meeting room.

"Just what are you saying, young man?" my father asked. "And how do you know this?"

"I am speaking of mass murder. Their policies have changed. Those ghettoes are merely gathering points.

In Russia, thousands and thousands of Jews are being systematically shot by the Germans. They mean to kill every Jew in Europe. We have reports from these communities."

"Ridiculous. Rumors." Dr. Kohn leaned back in his chair, but he said no more.

"What is your name, young man?" asked my father.

"Anelevitz. Mordechai Anelevitz. I am a Zionist. But it doesn't matter who we are, or what we are, rich or poor, young or old, Communist, Socialist or bourgeoisie. They will kill us all."

"Who let this man in?" was all Dr. Kohn could say in response to the challenge from the man in the cap.

"I tell this council, all of you, we should not be smuggling food alone, but also guns and grenades."

This, from a plain workman in a dingy suit, enraged Dr. Kohn. "Silence!" he shouted. "I don't know who you are, but you are a fool to speak that way. Such talk will guarantee our deaths."

My Uncle Moses was at the meeting, along with my father. He appealed to Kohn to let Anelevitz have his say.

"Not another word!" Kohn cried. "I can see this city of half-starved, disease-ridden Jews, suddenly taking on the German army. Anelevitz, the Germans cleaned up all of Poland in twenty days. They are rolling through Russia right now, annihilating Stalin's best divisions. And we are the people who are to resist such power?"

"We must."

Kohn tried a different tack. "Young man, I know all about you Zionist militants and your secret meetings. You are dreamers. Fighting is not the Jewish way. We have survived over the millennia by accommodating. Give a little here, submit a little, strike a bargain. Find an ally, a friend, perhaps some prince, some cardinal, some politician—"

Anelevitz said, "You are not dealing with cardinals or politicians. The Nazis are mass murderers. Their primary aim in the conquest of Europe is the killing of Jews. No matter what we do, how submissive we are, what bargains we offer them, how hard we work for them, they will kill us."

Eva recalls that a terrible silence fell on the meeting. Few agreed with Anelevitz. He had seemingly come out of nowhere, off the street, a humble, plain-spoken man. But he had uttered thoughts that at least some of them had had themselves.

"That is quite enough," Dr. Kohn said. "We will listen to no more. Leave."

"If this council is too cowardly to give the order to arm and fight, then the Zionists will. We do not intend to die without a fight."

"I said, get out," Kohn shouted. "And watch your tongue. Don't spread such ideas."

"You will all die here, tipping your caps to the Germans, showing up for work details, assigning people to factories, attending classes, arguing over the Torah. You have no authority and you represent no one."

"Throw him out!" Kohn shouted.

But no one moved. Anelevitz had cast some kind of spell over the room. He looked in appeal to the members of the council, found no visible supporters, and left—a disturbing presence.

My father and my Uncle Moses immediately got up and followed him into the dim corridor.

"I am Dr. Josef Weiss," Papa said. "My brother Moses. We are at the hospital most of the time."

"I know who you are," said Anelevitz.

"I . . . don't quite know what to say. We are not Zionists. We aren't political. We're professional people trying to make things a bit easier for the community."

Anelevitz told them that their political beliefs, the beliefs of any Jews, were irrelevant to the Nazis. Calmly, sure of himself, he said that in the long run the Germans would kill all.

My father had never believed this. Nor had Moses. But they looked at each other with a new understanding. There was something so quietly persuasive, so profoundly sincere in the young man's manner, that they felt obliged to talk to him.

"May we . . . spend some time with you?" Papa asked.

"Of course. We need council members. We are mostly working people, students, the young."

And so my father and my uncle were drawn into the resistance. They wondered at the time why so few had resisted. Why did most of the ghetto Jews act as if life could go on—schools, theaters, religion, jobs —when what faced them was eventual massacre? I am not sure that either he or Moses understood it then; nor am I certain I understand it now. In a strange way, with the psychological power of demons, the Germans had broken their will to live, by making them cling to life.

And in fairness, Tamar says, the record of resistance among Europeans of far greater strength and numbers was a spotty one. The absolute totality of Nazi terror, the refinements of the police state, the unhesitant use of murder, torture, deceit, deprivation, humiliation, left people without defenses. If one is to be critical of the Jews for failing to fight back as much as they should have, what about entire nations, like France, where resistance was marginal? Not an easy question to resolve.

But in any case, Papa and Uncle Moses were now committed.

Erik Dorf's Diary

Ukraine
September 1941

I am shaking. Still, I must write dispassionately, now. Try to forget; no, to understand. I too, at last, have killed.

As Heydrich's "eyes and ears" I am now on the

outskirts of Kiev, overseeing the operation of Einsatz-gruppe C, under the command of Colonel Paul Blo-bel.

I detest Blobel. He drinks too much and runs a slov-enly operation. I wonder why Heydrich has let him advance this far. But he apparently enters his assign-ment with readiness to do the job, and do it quickly. It takes a special breed of German to carry out our mandate; and I imagine that Blobel, for all his failings, is of that breed.

We stopped first at an enlisted men's barracks where some new men were being inducted. There are roughly a thousand men in each of the four "Action Commando" teams, these men recruited from the SS, the SD, the Criminal Police, and so on. We also will be using a great many Ukrainians and Lithuanians and Balts, who have no compunction about special han-dling of Jews.

"We also drew a lot of fuck-ups and goldbricks," Blo-bel said, as we approached the barracks. Men lounged about in their undershirts—the Ukraine can be beastly hot in September—reading, writing letters, cleaning firearms. No one came to attention as Blobel and I and our party approached.

"They're tired," Blobel said. "And they don't give a shit after a while. Got to keep them going with schnapps."

A sergeant got to his feet and saluted lazily.

"It's all right, Foltz, rest," Blobel said.

"New men today, sir."

"Fine, fine, give them the drill."

I could hear Foltz welcoming one of the new men —his name was Hans Helms, and he had been in an infantry division—to Einsatzgruppe C.

"You'll like it here," Sergeant Foltz mocked. "No one shoots at you. Regular hours. And we divide up the loot. After the officers get theirs. Don't look so dumb, Helms."

"I'm a combat soldier," Helms said. "I didn't ask to join this shitty outfit."

"You'll learn to love it," Foltz said.

The new arrival walked off to the barracks. I did not like the tone of Sergeant Foltz's lecture and I told Blobel so. The man was mocking our mission.

"Bullshit, Dorf," Blobel said. "What's the difference what their attitude is, so long as they do the killing?"

"Language, Blobel. We do not refer to killings. You know the approved words."

His fat, ruddy face stared at me. "Yeah. Your goddam special vocabulary. Special handling. Special action. Resettlement. Executive action. Autonomous Jewish communities. Transport. Removal."

I ignored Blobel. I shouldn't have to explain to this unsubtle and thick-headed man that the code words serve many purposes. First of all, they hide from the Jews the realities facing them. They are quite willing to tell themselves they are being "resettled," almost more eager to believe than we are to dissemble. Moreover, it makes matters easier within our own ranks and within the ranks of our allies.

After all, we remain a Christian nation, and there is always a chance that well-meaning but misguided churchmen (like Lichtenberg) will raise a hue and cry. The Vatican is sympathetic to our crusade against Bolshevism in Russia. Why muddy this relationship by shouting that we intend to shoot several million Jews? Then, there is the matter of final judgments, once we rule Europe. We can always say that some Jews perished while being resettled, died of their own filthy habits, their tendency to spread contagion, or were executed for sabotage and spying.

Blobel led me across a meadow to a wooded area. In front of a grove of tall birches and elms, a wide ditch had been recently dug. The piled earth behind it still looked damp. I estimated this ditch to be about ten feet wide and four feet deep. It was quite long, fifty or sixty feet.

"We make them dig it themselves," Blobel said. "Right to the end they think it's a work detail."

In front of the trench were two wooden tables. On each was a light machine gun and ammunition belts. There were also bottles of cheap Russian cognac, glasses, boxes of cigarettes. Behind each weapon was a three-man team, members of Blobel's SS Einsatzgruppe.

They appeared to me rather slovenly—collars open, boots unpolished. Two men were smoking, and one was sipping cognac. Hardly a military-looking unit. I complained to Colonel Blobel about their appearance, and made an invidious comparison to the army, where soldiers were expected to be trim and neat, even when going into battle.

In typical crude fashion, Blobel made an insulting remark about the army, and reminded me I was an SS officer, and we made our own rules. He referred to a "chickenshit" army major who had complained about "un-German" activities by the SS; Blobel had put him off with a few choice curses.

In the distance I saw the Jews. A group had been halted at the edge of the ditch. Under the prodding of SS guards, they were being made to undress. Clothing was being neatly stacked. People were being searched for valuables—watches and the like.

The fascination some of the guards showed for the nude and semi-nude women was totally uncalled-for. Women stood about in undergarments—slips, bloomers, garters—and were stared at. I could hear lewd comments. When they were at last naked, the women tried vainly to cover their breasts and pudenda. Some of the women held children in their arms. There were ancient crones barely able to stand, and one old woman who had to be carried by two men.

These were Jews from a village near Kiev, I had been informed. Many were Orthodox, with long beards, curling earlocks, and a lost, soulful look on their fleshy faces. No wonder Himmler and my other superiors have concluded that these are a subhuman species. One has only to see them naked, exposed, their white soft flesh tormented by the hot Ukrainian sun, to know they are unlike other people.

It is odd. I feel no hatred for them, but my awareness that they are indeed alien from us, and that they are plotters and connivers who, from the time of Christ to the present, have been history's great betrayers, makes it easier for me to accept what I witnessed for the first time.

"Go on, Foltz," Blobel said and grinned at me. "March 'em in. Don't overload the trench."

Orders were shouted below. About fifty of the naked Jews were prodded and clubbed, made to walk into the trench and face the two tables on which stood the machine guns. To my amazement, there was no resistance, just some slowness on the part of the older people. The Orthodox among them seemed to be praying. A woman crooned to the child in her arms. A child kept asking when he could go home. I could swear a girl of about twelve was asking if she would be able to do her homework from school that night.

It was over in seconds.

At a signal from Sergeant Foltz the guns chattered, short bursts of orange flame. The acrid stench of powder clogged my nose.

Through the haze I saw the Jews fall in shapeless heaps. Their bodies were stitched with small red holes.

The little girl who had just asked if she could do her schoolwork was lying across her mother's body. In death, they were embracing.

I half-heard Blobel saying, "Two bullets per Jew, my ass. Let that bastard Von Reichenau come out here and count the holes in them if he wants."

Quickly I put a clear plastic shield over my eyes. I was crying. Not, I realized, out of sympathy for the Jews. They died so easily, so quickly, so uncomplainingly, that it is difficult to accept that it was death at all. But out of some vague, imperfectly understood perception of the awful dimensions of our job. Heydrich has convinced me, beyond any doubt, that we are forging a new civilization. Hard and cruel deeds are necessary. I have now seen one.

Sergeant Foltz was walking along the edge of the ditch, his Luger drawn. Three times he kneeled and fired shots at short range.

"Why is he doing that?" I asked Blobel.

"Sometimes they aren't dead," he answered. "Act of

mercy. Better than burying them alive. But that happens also on a busy day." He squinted at me, as if suspecting that I had been crying. But he said nothing.

His bluff obscene manner serves him well in his work. And I will have to cultivate a similar defense. I can be frank about it in these pages. Ohlendorf, I have been told, another Einsatzgruppe chief, is capable of *intellectualizing* his work. A professor, expert on trade, doctor of jurisprudence, he sees the elimination of Jews as a social and economic necessity. I am surely as bright and as brave as Ohlendorf; I will take a page from his book.

A thought occurred to me right after the shootings: there is no future for the Jews in Europe. They are universally despised, for whatever reasons. We are solving a problem of almost worldwide dimensions. Our means and our ends are identical. In denying them the earth, we do mankind a great service. "Armed Bohemians" a critic of our movement once called us. I am glad to be one.

I also learned at that first shooting—after I gained my composure—that by asserting my considerable authority, acting the part of "Heydrich's man," I can stifle feelings of pity that might surface. For example, I noticed that there were civilians watching the executions, and that at least two men, one a soldier, were taking still photos and motion pictures. A civilian in a dusty trenchcoat was writing notes in a small book.

At once, to divert my own mind from the corpses —swarms of flies settled on them swiftly—I began to bawl out Blobel for running a public show. The civilians, he said, were Ukrainian farmers who enjoyed watching their lifelong enemies being executed. The photographers were taking pictures for their own amusement. Nothing official. The fellow in the trenchcoat was an Italian journalist.

I ordered Blobel to chase them away. There would be no picture-taking, no journalists present. To my gratification, I found that by immersing myself in these niggling duties, I could overcome any residual feelings about the victims. They soon appeared to me as mere casualties, by-products of our campaign. The war, as Hitler said, will be unlike any other war in human history, "not fought in knightly fashion."

A second group of Jews were now marched in. This time, they were less compliant. Several women were screaming, tearing their hair out. One threw herself at an SS guard, embraced his boots and tried to kiss his hands, his feet. He had difficulty in kicking her away from him.

"Heydrich will get a full report on this sloppy operation," I said. By giving orders, making myself part of the chain of command, I could detach myself from the people in the ditch. Some old men, looking like bearded prophets, were intoning prayers in Hebrew. An alien, wailing noise arose. Jews have had a lot of practice in dying, in serving as sacrificial victims. They have a *routine* for it, some kind of Talmudical procedure. Eichmann has often expatiated on this. It makes it easier for them to die.

Blobel walked away from me. "Foltz!" he shouted. "Give the order!"

Once more the machine guns stuttered. They sounded to me like the cracking of the earth under the impact of a meteor.

The Jews fell again, on top of the bodies of those who had died a few minutes earlier. In the distance, a third group—naked, shiveringly quiet—were being marched toward the trench. And farther in the distance, army trucks were unloading more Jews.

By now, I was pretty much in control of myself. The sheer magnitude of the operation—and I know there are hundreds like it, from the Baltic to the Black Sea —made me overlook what might be conceived of as cruelty. These people have to be our enemies, our racial rivals, people whose progeny could destroy Germany, whose wiles and wealth and evil notions could doom Aryan civilization.

It took me some time to realize the absolute truth of Heydrich's convictions, derived from the Führer and from Himmler. But they *have* to be the truth. A talented, energetic, intelligent, artistic people like our Germans could not take part in such acts unless what they did was ordained, obligatory, healthful for the future of the nation.

Fortified by these realizations, I confronted Blobel. "I am submitting a critical report on you, Colonel," I said.

"You're *what?*"

"You will clear the area of civilians. There will be no pictures taken by SS men or anyone else. Understood?"

To one side of the machine guns, some SS men, including Foltz, were picking through the clothing. One man, guffawing, was holding up an oversized pair of women's bloomers, waving them in the air.

"And there will be no more of that," I said. "Any property left by the resettled Jews belongs to the state."

"Save that bullshit for your meetings."

"Your language will also be reported. Heydrich ordered me to check up on the Einsatzgruppen. Yours fails miserably to meet standards that were set."

His choleric fat face was turning scarlet. The piggish features were splotched with red. "I fail, do I? Let me tell you something, Dorf. Ohlendorf and Nebe and the rest of us have our eyes on you. We know a spy when we see one."

"Don't try to undercut me, Colonel. I talk to Heydrich every day."

He sputtered something, could find no words. Just as the Jews can be made to fear, to have their wills destroyed, their spines cored, so even a Colonel Blobel can be rendered fearful—if the threat of humiliation, exposure, even death, hangs over him. Our men in the field know what kind of a man Heydrich is. He fears no one, nothing. And I, as his emissary, bask in that power.

Sergeant Foltz had marched fifty more Jews into the ditch. Below, the gunners were sipping their cognac, smoking leisurely.

This time, my lecture had its effect. Blobel ordered

the sergeant to clear out the Ukrainians, to chase the journalist, to stop the picture-taking.

The guns fired again; the Jews fell. The pile was now rather high, and I imagined that after a few more groups had been added, tractors would be used to cover the remains, work parties of Jews with shovels would be forced to bury their own dead.

Blobel suddenly reached into my black leather holster and took out my Luger, which I had fired but once, on the SS indoor range in Berlin.

"What are you doing?" I protested.

"There's a few still moving down there," he said. He laughed. "Go on, finish them off yourself. You know the old street tradition. You aren't a man until you've killed your Jew."

I told him to put my gun back. Instead he slammed it into my right hand. "Desk soldier. Paper captain. Fucking office boy. Go down there and shoot a few."

"They all seem to be dead."

"Can't be too sure. Jews are like rubber balls. They bounce back. Go on, I see a few moving."

What else could I do? There was no personal danger to me. The Jews surely would not hurt me. They had died like sheep, like unprotesting kittens. Heydrich's words helped sustain me as I descended the sandy hillside toward the foul pit. *Judaism in the East is the source of Bolshevism and therefore must be wiped out in accordance with the Führer's aims.*

"It's like eating noodles," Blobel yelled at me. "Once you start you can't stop." His underlings sniggered. "Ask my men what it's like, Captain," he shouted. "You shoot ten Jews, the next hundred are easier, and the next thousand are even easier than that."

Sergeant Foltz preceded me into the pit. We threaded our way through the naked, bloodied bodies. They seemed stitched with red holes. It is astonishing how little is needed to kill a man. Dead, the Jews seemed, in a way, more natural to me than alive, standing, waiting, praying, accepting their doom.

"One there, sir," Foltz said.

He pointed to a young woman with long brown

hair. Her eyes were pleading. The bullets had entered her shoulders, leaving bloody gouges, but had apparently not touched any vital organs.

She held one arm up to me, a long, well-formed arm—and I had a sudden vision of Marta's smooth arms—and her half-open eyes stared at mine.

"It's an act of kindness to end the poor bastards' suffering, sir," Sergeant Foltz said. "She ain't more than twenty."

I hesitated. Again, I saw Marta, so clearly I almost called her name. My eyes were hazed, and I saw the entire scene—the party of SS executioners above me, the silent guns, the men sipping cognac, the verdant meadow, the groves of trees, the wide bloody ditch, now giving off the metallic odor of blood, the swarms of savage flies—I saw all of this as if underwater, as if I were on some other planet, living a life that was not mine.

"Shoot, Dorf," Blobel shouted.

The woman's eyes sought mine. She was almost dead. Yet some stirring of life must have remained in her. She could not raise her arm again. Her eyes were dark, slanted. The long brown hair reminded me of a girl I had once known in high school. Why these random thoughts? The conviction overpowered me. *The terribleness of our acts justifies them.* One cannot do these things unless they are, in and of themselves, worthy deeds, parts of a great plan, a world-shaking idea.

I squeezed the trigger as I had been taught in that brief session at SS school. The explosion was surprisingly soft, almost like a child's popgun. The side of her head came apart at such close range. Bone, blood and bits of brain spattered my boots. My stomach began to churn, and it was an effort to prevent my lunch from bursting through my throat.

"That's how, sir," Foltz said. "You get used to it, after the first few times. They don't seem to mind. Never seen people like them."

He had to be right. I told myself that we are almost in league with the Jews, to effect their destruction.

How else explain the ease with which we are eliminating them?

"I'll handle the others, sir," Foltz said. I heard him as if he were talking through a long-distance phone. I jammed my Luger back into its sheath. I did not look again at the young woman I had just killed. If the men beneath me could kill thousands, hundreds of thousands, I had the duty to kill at least *one*. In a sense Blobel was right—although I detest the man— in forcing me to act.

Applauding, grinning, Blobel was winking at his sycophants as I approached his party. "Nice work, Dorf," he said. "Von Reichenau says two bullets is enough for a Jew. You did it with one."

Conversation was blotted out for a moment by a burst from the guns. More Jews were dying. And I am now convinced, a believer in the correctness of it. They have no other purpose except to die.

Rudi Weiss' Story

The wall was slowly strangling life in the ghetto. Its excuse had been that it was built for health purposes, to contain the spread of typhus. Actually, it was a vast prison, where Jews were expected to die by attrition, until the final solution went into effect.

But still Jews would sneak into the "Aryan" side. Many were women seeking food for their children. One such was a nurse named Sarah Olenick, who worked for my father in the children's ward at the hospital. Sarah had been caught and jailed.

Angered, my father called on the ghetto police chief, a Jew named Karp, who had converted to Catholicism, and had thus gained some favor with the SS.

"I want Sarah Olenick released," my father said.

"She's a smuggler."

"You know better, Karp. She went outside the wall to get bread for her children."

"She knew the rules. No smuggling."

"Please release her. She's needed at the hospital."

"A bit of class snobbery, doctor? Would you be as eager to have her freed if she were a beggar, or a laborer's wife?"

"I would."

"Then you can appeal for all eight of them."

"Eight?"

He led my father to a window in his office and pointed to the prison courtyard below. There were eight women of varying ages there, among them Sarah Olenick.

"What do you think I am?" Karp whined. "A monster? I get orders, I obey them, or they'll hang me. That beggar girl—Rivka—she's sixteen."

"What was her crime?"

"The same. Smuggling. She went outside the wall and got milk for her bastard kid."

My father lowered his head and tried to pray. Useless. He felt bound, constricted, imprisoned himself. "Karp, you are a Jew. Appeal to your masters—"

"I *was* a Jew. That's how I've saved my neck."

"But you know the SS. Use your influence. You can't let them—"

Karp began to rage. "Who the hell are you to talk? You and your brother Moses, so high and mighty on that council? What do you do but take orders from the Germans? Nod your heads and do what they say? Lists of names, work details, offenders. Hollering against smugglers as much as the Nazis do. Don't lecture me. You want to be a hero and complain to the SS? Try it."

My father looked once more into the courtyard, tried to catch a glimpse of Sarah—she was a tall, dignified woman of great patience and kindness—then walked away.

The eight women accused of "smuggling" were shot dead a few days later. The Jewish police refused to perform the execution, so some Poles from outside were ordered to do it.

A crowd gathered outside the prison to pray, to protest.

It did little good—either the prayers or the protest.

My mother, in her old coat, once fashionable and very much in the Berlin mode, stood by my father and held his hand. He had told her she need not come, but she insisted. "I am one of them," my mother said.

Aaron Feldman, the boy who specialized in smuggling, climbed the prison wall and shouted down to the crowd as the women were led in one by one, blindfolded, and shot dead.

They killed Rivka the beggar first. Then Sarah was shot. Then the other six women. Their crime had been to look for food for hungry children.

"Oh, Josef," my mother wept. "Could we not have saved them?"

"Hopeless," he said.

My Uncle Moses, that mildest of men, was not crying, but cursing. "I want revenge. I want to see some of *them* dead and covered with blood."

Again my father tried to persuade my mother to leave, but she insisted on remaining until the last volley of shots.

A rabbi began to lead the Hebrew prayer for the dead, and my parents, who barely knew the words, tried to pray along with them. My Uncle Moses was silent, so angry he could not speak.

When the prayers had ended, the crowd, many of them weeping, some relatives of the victims clinging to the prison gate and banging at it, began to dissolve.

Eva Lubin, my informant of this period in my parents' lives, recalls that she and Zalman, approached Moses Weiss. Anelevitz was standing nearby. His face, as usual, was meditative, as if forever focused on some goal, some future action.

"Can you come with us?" Zalman asked.

"Of course," Moses said.

Some people were still praying at the gate. Their voices, wrenched with sorrow, hung in the cold November air.

"I'm embarrassed that I can't pray any more," Moses said.

Zalman shrugged. "Prayers are no help, Weiss."

They led him to the basement of a house on Leszno Street.

In a dark room, hidden behind a false wall, were a table, books, piles of paper and a printing press.

It was a small, hand-run affair, but it was working. The printer was my father's old friend Max Lowy, his patient from Berlin. He and Moses greeted each other.

"So," Moses said. "Here is where it comes from."

"You object to our newspaper?" Zalman asked.

"Not at all. I wish it were longer. More news, more protests. I read every word."

Anelevitz said, "We're running short of ink. You have access to the pharmacy."

"You can't run a printing press with iodine."

"No," Lowy said. "But we can make our own ink. Lampblack, charcoal, linseed oil. I'll give you a list."

Lowy ran off a sheet, studied it with a critic's eye, crumpled it and threw it away. "I'm still a craftsman, even in a basement."

In the corner of the room, a shortwave radio crackled. So here, Moses realized, was where the overseas news came from. He understood that every single activity in the room was punishable by death, that any person caught here would be tortured to disclose the whole underground operation.

"A resistance paper?" asked Moses. "Up to now, you've been pretty passive, I'd say."

"No more," Anelevitz said. "We are going to arouse the people. After today, there is no way passive resistance can work. They must be made aware of what awaits them."

Moses hesitated. "If . . . if I bring you stuff to make ink, I'll be involved."

"Better to be involved with us than the council," Eva said.

"The council members are alive. Lawbreakers get shot."

"You'll die anyway," Anelevitz said.

"And better to die fighting, with a protest," Zalman said.

Moses looked at little Lowy, busily inking his ancient machine, and at the plain, earnest faces of the people in the cramped room.

My uncle was beginning to have doubts. What kind of army were they? How could they possibly resist? Maybe he and my father had been too impulsive, throwing their lot in with these visionaries, brave and admirable as they were.

"Listen, Zalman," Uncle Moses said. "You're a working man, a labor leader. Don't the Nazis know what good workmen we are? How we keep factories going? What good is it to them if they have a bunch of dead Jews on their hands?"

Zalman rubbed his chin. "Weiss, they'll close down every factory in Poland, let the Poles and Russians run them, before they'll let a Jew live."

Moses tried to pursue the argument. What chance did they stand against the Waffen SS, the German army? My uncle agreed that they should think of fighting back. But how? What sense did it make? Jews spent most of their time arguing with each other—Orthodox against nonbelievers, Zionists against non-Zionists, Communists against Socialists. Name an internal dispute, and you'd find it.

Anelevitz nodded at the door. "He can go. We don't need him. Just be quiet about what you've seen, Weiss."

But Moses lingered. He was fascinated with Lowy. The little man was all business. He might have been running a giant automatic press for Ullstein. On his head was a paper printer's cap. A smear of black decorated his nose.

"Hah," Lowy said in Yiddish. "The master craftsman at work. They'd throw me out of the union in Berlin if they saw the junk I put out here." He winked at Zalman. "Not the copy, mind you, but the quality of the printing."

Moses appealed to Zalman and the others. "Don't misunderstand me, I'm on your side. But logic says we are not all necessarily marked for . . . for . . ."

"Logic proves nothing, Weiss," Lowy said.

Moses needed but a moment more to decide. He extended his hand to Anelevitz. "I am with you," he said.

The young man smiled. Zalman and Eva embraced Moses.

"We could use the doc also," Lowy said. "It would help having a man at the hospital, a man people respect."

"I will talk to my brother."

Lowy pulled another sheet from the flat press, waved it a second to dry it, then gave it to Moses. "Not bad. Wouldn't win any typography prizes, but it'll do. Read it."

Moses took the sheet and began to read.

"To the Jews of Warsaw," the proclamation said. "Let us have an end to apathy. No more submission to the enemy. Apathy can cause our moral collapse and root out our hearts, our hatred for the invader. It can destroy within us the will to fight, it can undermine our resolution. Because our position is so bitterly desperate, our will to give up our lives for a purpose more sublime than our daily existence must be reinforced. Our young people must walk with head erect."

So Moses was committed. He not only joined the resistance that day, he volunteered to tack up the first call for resistance, at key points in the ghetto. He and Eva and a few others went out and, making sure no police were in sight, attached the underground leaflets to doors, walls and telephone poles.

Eva remembers Moses nailing the proclamation to the door of an abandoned shop, and then pretending to be a mere passer-by, just as my mother and father turned the corner. My father halted to read the words of protest, having no idea Moses had just posted them.

" 'A purpose more sublime than our daily existence

must be reinforced,' " my father read aloud. "Noble words."

My mother read it also. "Whoever wrote those words and put them up," she said, "are braver people than we are, Josef. And perhaps better."

"Oh, I don't know," Moses said. "Maybe just young and foolhardy."

Papa laughed. "Makes me think of Rudi. It's the kind of thing he'd be doing if he were here."

"Yes, you are right," Mama said. "If he were here, he'd be in the thick of it. You know, Josef, I have the feeling Rudi is safe. That he got away."

He kissed her cheek. "So do I. And Karl. And Inga. And all of us will be together soon."

Erik Dorf's Diary

Berlin
November 1941

This morning, November 16, Heydrich and I screened the photographs and the movies from the Ukraine.

To my surprise, he did not share my indignation at the visual records that people had made without authorization from our office. But he did agree that we had to exercise control over such undertakings, and that all films and photographs must be filed in his headquarters.

"Any reason, sir?" I asked.

"To show the world we did not flinch."

He sat in the darkened screening room, immobile, reflective, smoking, his musician's fingers stroking his long nose now and then.

We watched, as in flickering black and white the Jews were marched to the collection point at the edge of the pit, made to undress, prodded into the ditch, turned to face the guns. And then fell under the smashing impact of the bullets. I confess that watching it on film was easier than seeing it with my own eyes.

"They die rather peacefully," Heydrich said. "And the lack of resistance is remarkable. You know, Dorf, we'll fulfill the Führer's goal with a lot less difficulty than I imagined."

I told him how Blobel complained that millions of Jews were fleeing east, ahead of our victorious armies.

He yawned. "Oh, we'll get them all eventually. Russia will collapse and they'll be ours."

I then made some useful suggestions about careful supervision of all documentation of the Einsatzgruppen—films, photos, records, papers. A special unit would have to be set up to keep lists. He agreed. Already I'd collected some information, which I read off to him.

"The various commanders try to do the actual shooting anywhere from ninety to a hundred and twenty miles from the towns from which the Jews came. On these trips, either on foot, or by truck, Jews sometimes escape, I'm sorry to report. We've had our best results in Lithuania, where trained volunteers from the local populace have helped immeasurably."

"Good for the Lithuanians."

Colonel Jager, head of one of our commandos, calls Kovno a "shooting paradise."

Such phrases should be kept out of the records, but it seems to be the case. Kovno is Jew-free. And some random statistics, which I'll organize for Heydrich, into table form later: 30,000 Jews have been shot in Lvov, 5,000 in Tarnopol, 4,000 in Brzezany. Lithuania remains a prime area, however. It's estimated that about 300,000 Jews have been eliminated in the Vilna and Kaunas areas.

As I read off these statistics, I watched Heydrich for any reaction. There was none on his handsome face. The job is getting done. He is carrying out the Führer's wishes. A plague, a curse is being erased from Europe. Moreover, we now perceive our operation as no more bloody, or unusual, or remarkable, than a saturation bombing from the air, or the encirclement and annihilation of a Soviet division, or the administration of an occupied area. The foremost thing is getting the job done.

In truth, the statistics, as astonishing as they are in terms of numbers—I confess that envisioning the mass shooting of 300,000 Jews takes a bit of stretching of one's mind—makes it easier to accept. It proves we are a functioning, efficient organization in which orders are given, and orders are obeyed. One has to conceive of these operations not in terms of a single girl raising her arm, or a child asking about her homework, but in terms of the essential evil, the persistent perniciousness of Jews.

We kept watching the pictures on the screen. The photos were being flashed now. Naked women covering their breasts and private parts, and running, in that awkward, stumbling way women have, toward the ditch. Old, white-bodied Jews with bearded faces. They kept their skullcaps on even while facing the guns. Young men, wide-eyed, terrified. In terms of our mission, whatever the reasons (and there are many) we are the perfect agents for these acts, and we have found our perfect victims. It is like an Olympian marriage, something conceived of by mythological gods.

"I think the pictorial aspect of our work should not be scanted," Heydrich said. "Dorf, see to it that it's done under our sanction, and that all films are developed and screened and stored here."

I hesitated. "Of course I'll look after it. But . . ."

"Doubts?"

"None, sir."

Heydrich seemed rather remote from the grisly photographs on the screen. He smoked, we chatted, he asked a pointed question now and then. Only once did he surprise me, when he stressed that I "read between the lines" in the Führer's work, look up old memoranda, as if to reinforce in himself (and in me) the absolute rightness of what we are doing.

The last photo flickered on the screen. Three naked Jewish boys, in their teens, children with those strange curling earlocks and shaven heads. Their hands were raised, their eyes were round with terror. In seconds they would be dead. Statistics.

The lights went on. He turned to me, and then he reaffirmed (if so potent a man has to reaffirm his deepest beliefs) the need for purging Europe of Jews. He told me of a record some early party member had kept of a conversation with Hitler back in 1922.

Hitler had boasted that once he came to power, he would hang every Jew in Munich, then in every other city, "until the bodies stank." He would systematically keep hanging Jews until Germany was rid of its last Jew. "It's in the record, Dorf," the chief said. "We are doing precisely what he has always wanted."

I asked again why we were so careful to keep the work secret. Heydrich dismissed my query. What with England isolated, with our war against the Russians going so well, Churchill might very well sue for peace. Why complicate matters by letting the world know of the Jewish question?

That seems logical enough to me.

Rudi Weiss' Story

Kiev fell in a few days.

The great Ukrainian city which was supposed to resist the Germans to the death was now occupied by them. The Red Army vanished, beaten, almost leaderless.

As soon as I saw the first German troops, I forced Helena to leave the refugee center where they had taken us. The guns we had heard on the way in were not Soviet guns—they were the opening barrage of the Germans, crossing into the Ukraine.

All was confusion for a few days. We looked like any other impoverished Russians, pretended to be farm laborers. Helena's perfect Russian helped us get by. I stole bread several times—once right from the bakery wagon backed up to the big Continental Hotel, which was the German Army headquarters.

Fighting was still going on in a few sectors of Kiev. Some Russian guerrillas had stayed behind, setting off mines and boobytraps. And vast parts of the city were in ruins.

Hearing a machine gun fire, noticing corpses of both Russians and Germans in the street, I dragged Helena into the rear of a ruined shop, where we could eat our bread.

She began to cry softly. "It's over, Rudi. We are finished."

"No, dammit. Eat your bread. Make believe it's a potato pancake."

There was a water tap in the rear of the shop. I filled my tin cup with water and we drank.

"It's awful," she whimpered.

"Some thanks. I get us dinner. Make believe it's wine. I won't stand for any complaining. Wait till we're married."

She began to giggle, and I silenced her. Outside the smashed glass of the shop I saw movement. There were three German soldiers in full battle kit. They stopped, looked around, waited.

"What is it?" Helena whispered.

"They looked like SS. Probably getting ready to round people up."

"Oh, my God. Rudi, what will we do?"

"Hide. Get behind the counter. If they come in, tell them the usual lies. We're farmers. Bombed out."

Suddenly there was an enormous explosion, as if all of Kiev were coming apart. Plaster and debris fell around us. Outside it was even worse. The street seemed to be lifted in the air by the force of the blast. A second explosion followed, then a third.

I could hear the echoing of falling plaster, bricks, and then an ear-splitting crash, as if an entire block had collapsed.

Our eyes were blinded with dust, but I could see outside the store that the three soldiers were rising from the gutter, hitching belts, pointing toward the Continental Hotel nearby, from whose bakery I had stolen our dinner.

There was a great deal of shouting in the street, much confusion. More troops came running by. A motorcycle driver, covered with dirt, drove up and I could hear him screaming at the others.

"Continental Hotel. The Russians blew it up. There's dead and wounded all over the place."

Even as he spoke, there were two more deafening blasts, and they ran for cover against the side of the shop we were in. One man was struck by a falling beam and collapsed into the very store in which we crouched behind the smashed counter.

His comrades started to come to his aid, but the motorcycle driver ordered them out. "Secure the area. Arrest any Russky you can get your hands on. Shoot to kill the bastards. Jesus, there goes another one."

"What about Helms?" one of the soldiers asked.

"He looks dead. Christ, let's get out."

Sirens wailed outside. Trucks rumbled by. The detonations seemed to have stopped, but in their wake was a low, rumbling noise, as if the earth itself were settling.

Helms. I thought it was impossible. It was a common name. But the street free of Germans, I crawled to the front of the store and looked at the soldier pinned down by the wooden beam.

I stared at his fair, familiar face. It was Hans Helms. I knew he had been in the army for years, but I had no idea he was in an SS unit. I saw the death's head and the jagged lines on his collar tabs.

"I'm hurt," he moaned. "Lift that thing off me."

"Son-of-a-bitch," I said. "I don't believe it."

As yet he had not recognized me.

"Helena," I said. "When I lift the beam, drag him out."

I put my back to the beam, braced myself and moved it upward. Gently—too gently as far as I was concerned—she pulled him out.

"Take his rifle," I said.

She did so.

I took off his helmet. His head was gashed and blood covered his eyes. I stared into them and said his name: "Hans Helms."

He focused his eyes, blinked as if awakening from a dream and said: "Weiss. Rudi Weiss. For Chrissake, what are you . . . here . . . how . . ."

I grabbed him by his collar and began to shake him. "Never mind, you bastard. I never liked you anyway."

"Take it easy. They forced me into this outfit. I was a plain infantry guy. Fouled up, and they made me a Black Crow."

"You shit. You liar."

Helena was utterly confused. "You know him?"

"A relative," I said.

"Not my fault, Rudi," he gasped. "I never had anything against you. Jesus, get me some water."

Helena took his helmet and went to the tap at the rear. She filled it, returned. Helms drank. He seemed unhurt, except for bruises. His legs moved and his arms handled the helmet. So I kept the rifle in my own hands.

"Listen, Helms, I've been wandering for three years because of bastards like you," I said. "Tell me about my family. You ever see your sister?"

"Six months ago. In Berlin."

"Did she say anything about my parents? Karl? My sister?"

He hesitated. I jabbed the rifle at his throat. "Talk, asshole."

"Your mother and father are okay, Inga said. They're in Poland. Warsaw, I guess. It isn't bad. The Jews got a whole part of the city. Inga hears from them."

How much he was lying I had no idea. But even lies were better than no information. "Karl?"

"He's in Buchenwald. He's okay too. Inga helped get him a soft job."

I gave the gun to Helena and began to shake him again. "You son-of-a-bitch, I think I'll blow your head off right here. Tell me the truth. One more dead Nazi won't bother me. You can die for the Führer."

He began to plead. "Christ, Weiss, what did I ever do to you? I got nothing against you. We played soccer a hundred times . . ."

I thought of the helpless, frightened, unarmed Jews his kind had killed and I wanted to kill him; but I could not. "What about Anna?"

Helms inched away from me. "She's dead. She got sick. Pneumonia, I don't know."

I went for his throat. His hands clutched at my sleeves. "Jesus, I had nothing to do with it. No one hurt her. She just . . . got sick . . . she died. I don't know anything else."

He denied that his parents had informed on her. He claimed he himself was in Russia at the time. My rage prevented me from crying. For the moment I just wanted to hurt him, make him pay for the crimes against my family and all the other outrages I'd seen.

Then I could no longer contain my tears. I wept, loudly, unashamedly. "She was sixteen, Helena," I sobbed. "Those bastards, I know they had something to do with it."

"Oh, Rudi, I am sorry. You loved her so."

I looked at Helms' bloodied head. His eyes were frightened. These sons-of-bitches could also be afraid. They could learn what it was like to die, unable to defend oneself. "Give me his rifle," I said.

"No, Rudi."

"I'm going to blow his head off."

"Rudi, give me a break." Hans pleaded. "We took you and your mother and sister in. We took a chance."

"Because Inga made you."

"So what? We did it. Look—your father and mother are okay. Karl's okay—"

"You killed Anna."

"Didn't lay a hand on her."

"That uniform makes you as guilty as anyone who did. I know you're lying, Helms. Something happened. Tell me."

"I swear I don't know."

He knew about her being raped and abused, of course; but it is likely he knew nothing about her murder at Hadamar.

Finally, with Helena pleading with me, and explosions rattling the sky and the earth again, I decided to let him go. I had not yet reached the stage where I could shoot a defenseless man. Not yet.

"Help me out of here. I'm hurt. To an aid station."

"Maybe I'll bury you alive. The way your people do it to old Jews. Shovel dirt on them while they're still breathing."

"I never did anything like that. Listen. I can get you work passes. It won't be safe for Jews in Kiev, believe me. I'll see to it they leave you alone."

Helena looked at his fair, open face, covered with clotting blood. "Rudi, I think we can believe him."

She was of a trusting, gentle nature; but I listened to her. It took me a few seconds to decide to follow her counsel. Helms was perhaps different. I'd known him a long time. And he was Inga's brother.

We helped Helms to his feet, set his helmet on his head, slung his rifle over his shoulder, and we walked out of the shop into the rubble-strewn street.

To our left was a squad of Germans, and beyond them some trucks and horse-drawn wagons.

We each held one of Helms' arms over our shoulders, and we walked toward the squad. A sergeant came forward. I could hear him talking to his men, turning his head. "Christ, they've blown up half of Kiev."

"I'm hurt," Helms said to him.

"Who are you?"

"Corporal Helms, Twenty-second SS Division."

The sergeant nodded at us. "Who are they?"

Helena was about to speak, then stopped.

"Jews," Helms said. "They tried to kill me."

"No," I said. "We're Ukrainian farm laborers. Tell him, Helena."

"Jews, kikes," Helms persisted.

"You lousy, lying bastard," I said to Helms. "We saved your life, we risked our necks for you, and now . . ."

Two soldiers came forward and sat Hans down on a pile of rocks. A medic began to clean the wound on his head and bandage it, from a first-aid kit.

The sergeant looked at us as indifferently as if we were sacks of potatoes. "You two, on that truck over there." He jerked his thumb to the truck and the wagons, which were being loaded with Russian civilians.

"Why?" I asked.

He cracked me across my face with his pistol. "Shut your mouth, kike. You're being moved out for your own good. Move!"

Helena shuddered. I wiped the blood away. The two of us walked down the street to the trucks. "What's going to happen to us, Rudi?" she muttered.

"I don't know. I just want to live long enough to get even with that bastard Helms."

As we were shoved aboard the last truck, there was another earth-shaking explosion. A mine, almost beneath the spot where Helms and the others were standing, had detonated. I looked back and saw that my craving for revenge would never be fulfilled. Hans Helms had been blown to bits, along with the medical aide.

Erik Dorf's Diary

Kiev
September 1941

The Continental Hotel, army headquarters, is a mass of rubble. More than two hundred of our top army officers and men are dead.

Luckily, Blobel's command post is in a different part of the city. The army doesn't care to have us too close to them. The Waffen SS, the fighting branch, is generally accepted. But the army officers, while never impeding us (indeed, often aiding us), prefer to keep some distance between Einsatzgruppen personnel and themselves. In this instance it worked to our advantage.

The carnage and destruction in central Kiev is appalling. Russian engineers apparently mined huge areas of the central city, notably the hotel, and when they had cleared out, they set off timed charges. Who would have thought these primitive Slavs that clever?

Blobel was beside himself, bellowing orders into phones, trying to get information. He will catch the very devil for this from Heydrich. After all, the shooting of Jews is just *one* of our functions. We are also expected to eliminate saboteurs, criminals, commissars and any elements who might prove troublesome. Surely the Red Army had left spies behind to wreak such destruction.

Blobel and I detest each other, especially since the scene a few days ago when he shamed me into shooting the woman. (The fact is, I've since found out, he himself never pulls a trigger, but merely gives orders.) In any case, the disaster that has struck us in Kiev gave me a chance to get back at him.

"Your intelligence left a lot to be desired," I said, as he raced from phone to phone, taking in reports of more deaths, more devastation in the Ukrainian capital.

"Sure," he snarled. "We're so busy shooting Jews, we have no one around to watch the Red Army."

"You are supposed to do both."

He slammed a phone down. "Yes, and I can see you snitching on me to Heydrich. To Himmler. That drunken bastard Blobel, with his sloppy operation. Well, why didn't you know the Red Army had mined the city? What the hell do they think we're doing all day? Drinking vodka and screwing ballerinas?"

The explosions had ended, but a miasma, a thick mist of pulverized dust, plaster, earth, hung over the ruined city. I looked out of the window. SS squads were rounding up people—anyone loose in the street. The Russian army had melted away. Those not taken prisoner have run to the east. I console myself that they have put up a poor fight for Kiev, have been outgunned and outmaneuvered at every turn. It is said that "Great Stalin" is in a terrified sulk, can barely get himself to read the bulletins from the front, and is ready to surrender.

A thought occurred to me. "Blobel, you think of me as an enemy, but I'm not," I said. "Maybe we can salvage something out of this mess."

"What? Collect the insurance on the Continental Hotel?"

Blobel's sarcasm annoyed me. It is now my conviction that my mentality is so superior to his that I can bend him, make him listen to me, accept my decisions, even though he outranks me. "Neither of us will look too good when this report is filed," I said. "Instead of dwelling on why we weren't aware of the Red Army's minefields, why don't we blame the whole thing on the Jews?"

Blobel belched, opened his collar. "Christ, Dorf. Those old guys in beards? Those kids with earlocks? Those filthy women? Such people could mine a city, goddam near destroy it?"

Patiently, I explained to him that lies in the service of a greater truth, extreme statements and extreme actions in the pursuit of a great goal, are perfectly acceptable. Jews are both a means and an end, I told him again. Berlin will find our story acceptable on all levels. We need no further excuses for killing them, but emotionally, strategically, placing the blame for the destruction of Kiev on Jews will sit well with everyone. It will gain us the unwavering support of large sections of the Ukrainian population, and it will deflect any possible criticism from the outside—if word ever leaks out about the Einsatzgruppen.

I reminded Blobel of his mocking comment to me —if you kill ten Jews, it is easier to kill a hundred, still easier to kill a thousand.

At once he got on the phone and ordered a new 1oundup.

Rudi Weiss' Story

A few kilometers outside Kiev—the day was September 29, 1941—we were ordered off the trucks and wagons and made to walk.

It was very hot. We choked on clouds of yellow dust. People who stumbled and fell were shot. The guards blew their heads off with pistols and shotguns. Helena began to tremble. I held her close to me, tried to keep her from becoming hysterical.

Helena began to talk to a man in front of us, in the line of march. He looked well educated, well dressed, and said he was a schoolteacher. I don't remember his name—Liberman, Liebowitz.

"They're taking us to a work camp, I heard the guards say," he said—almost cheerfully. "That can't be too bad. They'll feed us, anyway."

"Yes," a woman added. "They say we'll be protected, for our own good, from the Ukrainians."

"Where is this camp?" asked Helena. "How far?"

"Oh," the teacher said. "Not too far. Just beyond the Jewish cemetery. Place called Babi Yar."

Helena turned to me. "A funny name. Babi Yar. It means Grandma's Ravine."

I whispered to her, "This is no work camp we're going to. They want revenge for what happened in Kiev. I don't believe anything they say any longer. We're going to run away as soon as there's a chance."

"Rudi . . . no . . ."

"I'll drag you by your hair."

I looked at the poor Jews of Kiev—the old, the weak, the Orthodox, young couples, women with babies in their arms. They believed; something in them impelled them to believe. But had we in Germany, so proud of being German, so modern, so sophisticated, been any smarter?

A convoy of German army vehicles roared by—staff cars, trucks, motorcycles. They were going in our direction. In the back of each truck I could see machine guns, muzzles pointed out, stacks of ammunition boxes.

The convoy raised a cloud of dust, a poisonous, choking cloud. It was dry on the road, the earth beneath our feet a cindery yellow powder. As the billowing dust rose and obscured us, and made the SS guards in their goggles and scarves cough and spit, I grabbed Helena's arm and pulled her off the road. We rolled down the embankment into an irrigation ditch. I waited a moment. A second convoy roared by. Again the walking column was enveloped in a cloud of powdery earth. Taking advantage of this, I yanked at Helena's sleeve and we ran, crouching low, to a grove of maples and oaks. The wild grass in the field was high and thick, and helped hide us. Soon we were out of the sight of the column, which had grown in size until it seemed to stretch all the way back to Kiev.

Beneath a rocky ledge we rested. She huddled in my arms and cried softly. I kissed her tears, kissed her nose, her mouth. I told her we would not die, that I would not let them kill us.

It was the foolish bragging of youth, but I had no other course but to lie to her, or at least to project a hopeful future.

Soon she stopped crying. She was so small, so courageous, so much a part of me. I have often wondered how so young and frail a girl could be so strong in character, so loving, so full of desire. Her background was humble. The daughter of a shopkeeper, pathetic Zionists, ordinary Prague Jews. But bred in her—how I do not know—was a love and a depth of feeling that reminds me in many ways of Anna, my lost sister.

"I will marry you someday," I said.

"Rudi, don't tease me."

"I mean it. But now, on your feet, little one. Before marriage, we have to start hiding again."

Erik Dorf's Diary

Extraordinary how the Jews have cooperated with our orders to pack a bag, bring food for one day, assemble at certain street corners, and be prepared for transport to work camps.

With Colonel Blobel and his aides, we went out to Babi Yar early today to see how the operation is proceeding. Of course, the word has already been broadcast all over Kiev that the Jews blew up the city. Obviously, the Red Army is content to let this story stand. And the Ukrainian civilian population seems almost delighted. Entire squads of them have been enlisted as auxiliaries in the SS.

Through binoculars we looked down to the ravine below, the place called Babi Yar. He laughed: "Just beyond it is the Jewish cemetery of Kiev. Appropriate, don't you agree, Dorf?"

"I suppose so. Of course, all reports must refer to this as a resettlement."

"Precisely what they were told, and precisely what they believe. Work camps. For their own protection. Their rabbis and other leaders convinced them to obey."

"It is astonishing how they cooperate," I said.

"They're subhuman. Descendants of another branch of the human race. Himmler is proving it every day. You know that our beloved Reichsführer collects Jew skulls and spends hours measuring them, comparing them to Aryan skulls?"

"Astonishing."

As we spoke, we could see, beyond the sandy ravine, a vast sea of Jews assembling. They were very orderly.

"By God," Blobel said. "We expected six thousand or so, and thirty thousand showed up."

It was fantastic.

"Perhaps they realize," Blobel said with a grin, "that whatever fate we mete out is atonement. Kiev is still burning from those damned Jew explosions."

I shaded my eyes and saw thousands of people milling about, or standing quietly in ranks, unloaded from trucks and wagons. Quite literally a lake, an inland sea, of Jews. The undressing had begun. It was strange: in the fore areas, near the ravine, the bodies melded into a great blob of pink-white flesh, while to the rear, the Jews were black-brown, with only the pale faces standing out to afford them a semblance of humanity.

I have developed a crust, an armor around any pity or compassion that might have remained in me. It is no longer so great an effort to keep Heydrich's words in mind. These are the mortal enemies of Germany, in every way imaginable.

I asked Blobel about the foreign journalists.

"Kept away. They're being shown the bomb damage and the fires in Kiev."

"Good. And the Ukrainians?"

"Except for the ones helping us in this action, they've been warned off. Not that they give a shit what we do to Jews."

The first groups of naked Jews were marched in. They were made to kneel in the ravine. One man was holding his hands over his head, whether in prayer or beseechment, I could not tell. A new technique was being used here, perhaps to save ammunition. The Jews were being shot individually, in the back of the neck. SS men armed with pistols simply walked down the line and dispatched them.

"No mass firings?" I asked.

"I'm experimenting. We'll go back to the machine guns if this takes too long."

He slapped his riding crop against his boot. "It gets tiresome, Dorf. Let's leave. This will take several days. I'm going to order them to move the waiting Jews farther away to avoid panic. I also want to try something Ohlendorf's used. He calls it the sardine method."

"Sardine?"

"First batch of Jews lies down in the bottom of the pit, side by side. Boom-boom. Dead. Next group lies on top of them, heads facing the feet of the dead. Boom-boom. They're dead, too. And so on, until the ditch is filled."

We walked away from the ravine. The shots were more frequent now, as were the moans and shrieks. But still, the place was curiously silent. Guards stood at the nearest road, where our cars awaited.

At one such roadblock, a tall man in a civilian top-coat, evidently a German, was showing papers to an SS corporal and protesting that he wanted to enter the area.

"I'm under special orders from Field Marshal Von Brauchitsch," the man was saying irritably. "Here are my papers. Here's his letter."

"Sorry, sir, no one allowed past this point."

The civilian looked up, angry, frustrated, and I saw that it was my Uncle Kurt. "I'm in charge of the road-building teams in this area. The ravine was to be sur-veyed today."

"Sorry, sir. Security area."

I walked up to Kurt and said, "He's right, Uncle Kurt. The area's closed."

Kurt looked up, puzzled, then smiled. We hugged one another. I was genuinely glad to see him. One gets lonely for reminders of home and family; I see Kurt perhaps once a year, but he is a good and faithful relative, and was close to my poor father.

"Erik!" he cried. "I heard you were in the Ukraine! I spoke to Marta before leaving, but she said she had no idea exactly where. How good to see you!"

I introduced him to Blobel, who did not seem im-pressed, but did invite me to his office for a drink later when the "tally" came in.

"Tally?" asked Kurt.

"Oh, a military exercise," I said.

Blobel's staff car drove off.

Kurt was admiring my uniform. "My goodness. Brother Klaus' little boy. And look at you. One of the

Reich's fire-eaters. A major, no less, in the feared SS. Can't believe it, Erik."

"War changes us."

"I don't think you've changed. You still look like a handsome eighteen-year-old."

I have never been an especially vain person, I can honestly state, but my Uncle Kurt's comments pleased me. If I maintained the outward mien of a young innocent, so much the better. The steel that has been forged in my character is *internal*. The man who now can stoically observe mass shootings, can himself fire a bullet into the head of a young girl, shows no superficial changes. My wife will see no scar on me, sense none of the hardness I feel within.

Oh, I have changed a great deal. But Kurt could not see it. I am a soldier, a front-line warrior in Germany's march to conquest. But I am lucky enough (unlike the drunken Blobels and sycophantic Nebes) to keep up the appearance of a clean, intelligent, manly young officer, peaceful in intent, compassionate and just.

So we chatted about the campaign in Russia, how well the armies were doing, the expectation, that with virtually all Europe under our rule, England might sue for peace. There is rumored to be a strong faction in the British government that favors the destruction of Bolshevism, to be followed by an Anglo-German agreement.

I offered Kurt a ride back to Kiev in my car. When we had exchanged some more small talk—Marta, my children, Kurt's work for the army, he asked, "That place Babi Yar. What was going on?"

I paused a moment. I could tell him some of what was happening, without lying. "Executions," I said.

"Ah. That would be your responsibility. Behind-the-lines security. Who were the . . . victims?"

"Oh, a mixed bag. The usual scum. Spies, saboteurs, anyone involved in the bombings and fire in Kiev. Common criminals. Black marketeers."

"Jews?"

"Yes, some."

"Some?"

"We don't keep count. Anyone who resists us is done away with."

Kurt stroked his chin. "I've been in the Ukraine several weeks, and these Jews seem the least likely of resisters. The ones I've seen act as if they can't do enough to oblige us."

"They're tricky people, Uncle. Actually, we are re-settling many of them. Keeping them away from the rest of the population."

"Resettling?"

"Yes. A sanitary measure, so to speak. So the war can proceed."

"Of course." He looked at me with a new intensity. "You were once one of the shyest boys I ever saw. Now look at you. Giving orders. Running resettlement programs. Changing the face of Europe."

"You credit me with too much power, Uncle. I merely obey orders."

Kurt laughed. "Don't we all."

At this point my car was blocked by another end-less, snakelike column of Jews. More and more, they were answering our summons to Babi Yar. They moved slowly. In the front rank were several bearded men, possibly rabbis or teachers, chanting and rolling their eyes.

"My God," Kurt said. "More of them. Some more of your saboteurs. All headed to that ravine."

"And other places."

"Ah," Kurt said. He did not sound as if he believed me. "To be resettled?"

"Yes, some of them. There'll be a triage of some kind, a selection process. The criminals among them will be shot."

Our car found a way through the mass of Jews. They seemed to give off an odor of filth, fear, old unwashed bodies, feces.

"A cruel business," Kurt said.

"Any war is."

"But . . . so many civilians? Is it really neces-sary . . . ?"

I offered him a cigarette and we smoked. I did not

want to talk about Babi Yar or any other aspect of our work.

"Tell me again about Marta, Uncle Kurt," I said. "I can't wait to get back to Berlin to see her, to see the children. Believe me, without them to inspire me, I don't know if I could go on."

He said nothing, but his pale eyes looked at me with a profound, sad, questioning quality.

For a moment I was disconcerted. Kurt's eyes were at that moment the eyes of my father. The look in them was precisely the look he fixed upon me when I had lied, or done something dishonorable. I was such an obedient dutiful child that these occasions were rare indeed. Which made it so much the worse, for I would experience not only guilt over having stolen a pencil, or cheated on an examination, but also a wasting sadness for my father. He was bedeviled by his failing bakery and his poor health, and I found it painful to make him also suffer my small sins.

Kurt's eyes now revived all these boyhood memories. I was being reprimanded. But for what? Kurt probably suspected what many of my duties were. One could not hide all the evidence. But what right had he to censure me—if I read his eyes correctly?

I am committing no sins. I am being obedient, following the rules, laws and destiny of the nation, of our leaders. Someday I will have to explain it to Kurt. I do not look forward to meeting him again. Nor to having to justify any of my actions to him. Nor to seeing my father's doleful face in the face of his brother.

Rudi Weiss' Story

The guards did not follow us into the woods. We hid in the forest for some hours, then forded a shallow stream, always listening for the sound of trucks, wagons, or marching feet.

At length, on this hot, parched day—it was the 29th

of September, 1941—we climbed a mountain and found ourselves overlooking a vast ravine, the Babi Yar of which the man on the truck had spoken.

Jews were being shot to death by the hundreds.

I was glad we were far enough away so that we could not see their faces or hear their voices. The pistol and rifle shots (later, machine guns were used) sounded like children's toy popguns. The victims fell noiselessly, almost in slow motion, into the sandy earth.

"Rudi, Rudi, so many of them," Helena wept. "The children, the babies . . ."

I held her closely, wondering where we would go, how we could avoid the SS patrols. The cities meant doom, death. Our only hope was wandering across the countryside. Surely some Jews had escaped. Some of the native population would have pity on us.

"I want to die with them," she wept.

"No, no, dammit," I said. "You'll stay with me. We don't die standing up, naked, shamed. We'll kill some of them when we die."

She began to scream. "No more! No more!"

I pulled her to me and slammed my hand over her mouth. She would have to learn not to scream, not to shriek, not to risk giving us away. She would also have to learn to hate, to want revenge, to realize that there was no way out for us except to run, to hide, and to try to fight. I would have to tell her worse things, too. That we would have to be ready to die, but to die in a brave and resisting way. I was sick of people placidly lining up, making excuses to themselves, following orders, and going to their death.

All day long the shooting continued. Files of Jews kept being marched into the marshaling area behind the ravine. The earth turned dark with Jewish blood. The Nazis understood something that it took the world a long time to learn. The bigger the crime, the less will people believe it happened. But I saw it happening. I would never be the same; nor would Helena.

Erik Dorf's Diary

Berlin
October 1941

Today Heydrich and I looked at the *official* photographs of the operation at Babi Yar.

I told him that although Blobel is a problem, he did deliver. We resettled exactly 33,771 Jews in two days. And he's still at it. The way the Jews oblige us, we may resettle close to 100,000 before the Babi Yar program is concluded.

"The bodies?" Heydrich wanted to know.

"Blobel will cover them with earth. Bulldozers, tractors. He estimates that a mass-burial pit about sixty yards long and eight feet deep will be needed."

We discussed the success of the other Einsatzgruppen in dealing with our mission. There are varying degrees of efficiency. Ohlendorf, our distinguished Doctor of Jurisprudence, economist, lawyer, our "house intellectual," is proving particularly thorough. His group, designated D, in charge of the Crimea, is well on its way to dispatching its 90,000th Jew. I mentioned that I much preferred Ohlendorf's cool efficient manner to Blobel's drunken blustering, but Heydrich did not seem interested.

More photos of the Babi Yar action flashed on the screen. The photos of naked and semi-naked women always seem to linger a bit longer. Heydrich leans forward in his seat and studies them with what seems a bit more than professional interest. This is often the case at our screenings. Not only the chief, but quite a few of the men find stimulation in the sight of naked Jewesses about to die. An explanation, a generalization eludes me. Heydrich has a happy home life, a lovely wife, children. It is said he was cashiered from the navy early in his career for compromising an officer's wife, but this hardly is in the area of sexual depravity.

Still, I'm forced to wonder if there might be some relationship between the kind of men we attract—on all levels—and the complex sexual needs of the human psyche.

Finally, Heydrich said that Ohlendorf was an admirable fellow.

"Ohlendorf had a few problems at first," I said. "It was very odd, but the German colonists in the Crimea and even some of our Hungarian allies raised protests."

"Did they?" He was staring at a well-formed Jewess, big-breasted, wide-hipped. Odd, how in seconds she would be dead.

"Yes. They said the Jews among them were entirely innocent, and Ohlendorf backed down—temporarily, of course. It's rather strange. Whenever a local population or an allied unit protests, we seem to draw back —as if we were—I hate to say it—rather ashamed of our mission."

Heydrich cocked his head. "Any such failures must be reported. Our mandate is clear."

I told him how Ohlendorf, despite his tenacity in rounding up and resettling Jews, had actually spared the lives of some Jewish farmers in Bessarabia on economic grounds.

"Oh, I know about that," Heydrich said. "Himmler visited the Crimea shortly after that, and Ohlendorf's Jew farmers were included in the order. There are none left."

III

THE
FINAL
SOLUTION

Erik Dorf's Diary

Berlin
December 25, 1941

A marvelous Christmas!

How good to be back with the family in Berlin, to celebrate this holiest of days. After a final trip to the eastern front—shortened somewhat by the Red Army's tenacious defense of Moscow, which temporarily halted our advance—I was given home leave.

I am exhausted. My tour of Russia has drained me. But it was a rewarding tour. The work of the Einsatzgruppen has exceeded expectations. Heydrich is pleased, but feels the need for a more comprehensive program. Still, 32,000 Jews have been eliminated in Vilna, 27,000 in Riga, 10,000 in Simferopol, and so on.

The only sobering note is that the United States has entered the war, following the Japanese attack on Hawaii. But no one is concerned over this. America is far, far away. They are, our intelligence says, utterly unprepared for war, and Roosevelt, under the influence of Jews, has made a blunder. Popular opinion in the United States will force him to undo his error. Moreover, the Americans may very well drive him from office if he continues on his reckless course. It is said there is a great deal of sympathy for Germany in the United States; Roosevelt may be impeached.

But none of these political or military matters concerned us tonight. We stood around our newest acquisition, a superb Bechstein piano, as Marta played, and we sang carols.

Peter, Laura, Marta, Uncle Kurt and I joined voices

happily as we sang *Tannenbaum, The Holly and the Ivy,* and *Bethlehem.* It was a wonderful, warm, endearing occasion. How much we love and respect one another!

Laura asked, "Papa, can we open presents?" She is a beautiful child—blond and fair like her mother, with a heart-shaped face.

And Peter: "Yes! Presents!" He is old enough to be a Hitler Jugend now, and proudly wore his uniform. (And was a bit annoyed with me for choosing to spend Christmas Eve in a plaid sports coat, rather than my uniform.)

"After the singing, children," Marta said. "You know the rules—singing, cleaning up the table, cleaning the kitchen, then presents. Rewards only after duty."

"Just like the army," Kurt added. "Your father did his duties at the front, and now he is rewarded with a long vacation."

"Quite correct," I said. "Just as Mama got this present—this beautiful piano—for being so brave while I was away."

Kurt, who has always had an eye for design and quality, ran his hand over the burnished mahogany surface of the Bechstein. "It's magnificent. They say the tone of these Bechsteins improves with age."

Marta played a few chords, reveling in the sounds. "I was stunned when the movers came with it. I couldn't believe my eyes."

Peter blurted out, "And it didn't cost a penny!"

"Really?" asked Kurt.

"It was sitting, unplayed, in that clinic on Groningstrasse, in an upstairs room," I explained. "The physician who runs the place, Dr. Heinzen, knows of my interest in music, and so he offered it to me."

"Offered?" Kurt looked puzzled.

"In the interest of party unity. I was helpful in arranging for the good doctor to take the clinic over."

Marta frowned. "I think it could use a tuning."

"Oh," Kurt joked. "Tuning a piano is no problem. Getting one is."

My uncle seemed to have some fixation on the piano and kept asking questions about it. He is quite naive about the process by which the party rewards good workers, high-ranking officers. Peter suddenly blurted out—he must have overheard a conversation between me and Marta—that the piano once belonged to the Jewish doctor who lived over the clinic.

Kurt was about to ask another question, when Marta clapped her hands and said, "Intermission! Time to open presents!"

The children flew to the Christmas tree and began to tear their boxes apart, ripping paper, strewing ribbons on the floor. There was a pair of live white mice for Peter, in a huge wooden cage, something he had asked for, since he was very much interested in biology. Laura got some special gifts I had found in Russia —a Ukrainian rag doll, and one of those clever "Petrushka" dolls, a series of wooden figures each smaller than the one before, so they stack into a single form. They were both delighted.

For Marta, I purchased a magnificent silk robe edged with lace, from the special purchasing agent for the SS, who handles such things.

"Oh, Erik, it is so beautiful," she said. She put it over her shoulders. It is the palest blue, almost as pale as her eyes. "Where did you ever get it? No shop in Berlin has anything like this!"

I kissed her cheek. "You won't believe this, but they do this kind of elegant work in the camps."

"The camps?" she asked.

"Yes. The detention centers. It's a kind of therapy for offenders. Many of them are expert craftsmen, and it's a shame to let their skills go to waste."

Peter was playing with his mice. He had one in each hand. "I'll name them Siegfried and Wotan," he said.

"You'd better not," I said. "One's a female, the pet-store owner assured me. You'd better count on a Brunhilde."

"Boy and girl?" Peter asked. "And they'll have babies?"

"That's right," Marta said. "And you'd better keep your mouse family nice and clean, and inside the cage."

Laura wailed. "My dolls can't have babies! It's not fair!"

I patted Laura's silken hair. "Peter is a man, and older than you, Laura, and mother and I want him to learn about these things."

"That's right, darling," Marta said. "The miracle of life. The goodness in all living things. We must respect it, even in a mouse, for they are God's creatures."

Kurt stoked his pipe, and through a haze of smoke looked at all of us, from some distance. An aging bachelor, he was somewhat out of it. "What a lovely concept, Marta," Kurt said. "The miracle of life. What a beautiful thing to teach children."

"Babies," Peter said. "I can't wait." He shoved a mouse at Laura's face, taunting her. "If they're sick, I might give you one. Or I might kill the sick ones."

"Mama, make him stop!" Laura wailed.

Peter chased her around the room, and I had to intervene, grabbing my son's arm, cautioning him to be more gentle—and generous—with his sister.

Marta said, "The children are so tired, Erik. Why don't we sing *Silent Night,* and they can go to bed, and then you and I and Kurt can listen to midnight mass on the radio."

I turned to Kurt. "Uncle, you see how being married to an efficient administrator has made Marta equally efficient?"

"It may be the other way around, Erik," he said. "Some of Marta's efficiency has rubbed off on you."

Again we gathered around the piano. We began to sing, but after a few bars, Marta stopped.

"That's odd," she said. "It's making a funny sound on the lowest notes. As if the hammers or strings are broken. Something is muffling the tone."

Kurt and I raised the huge mahogany cover to its highest position. My uncle peered into the inner workings of the piano, and fetched something out—what appeared to be pieces of cardboard.

"Photographs," Kurt said. He dusted them off. There were three photos, all framed in the kind of heavy cardboard used by professional photographers.

"Oh! Pictures!" Peter cried. "Let's see!"

"They were blocking the strings," Marta said. "Throw them out."

Kurt and I looked at the old photographs.

"Who are they, Papa?" Laura asked.

"Stupid," said Peter. "The people who used to own the piano."

I studied the photographs a moment. One was of Dr. Josef Weiss and a woman who must have been his wife, an attractive slender woman, smiling. They were dressed as if at a summer's outing. There was a lake, possibly the ocean, in the background. There was also a photo of a young couple, obviously a wedding picture—a slender young man bearing a resemblance to the doctor, and a blond woman with a rather Aryan face. The third photo, smaller, and not at all professional-looking, was of a twelve-year-old girl in braids, with her arm around a rather rugged-looking boy of about sixteen. The boy wore a soccer shirt and seemed well-muscled.

"Yes, that looks like Dr. Weiss," I said.

"And his family," Kurt said.

"I'm scared. It's like ghosts in the piano." Laura looked at the photos, stuck her tongue out at them. "Ghosts!"

"Where are they all now, Erik?" asked Kurt.

"Oh, Weiss was deported years ago," I said. "Not a bad sort of fellow, and a rather good doctor. But he was here illegally, a Pole, and he was breaking the law."

"And the rest of his family?" my uncle asked.

"Not the faintest idea. They left Berlin years ago."

Marta struck a loud chord. "We did not finish *Silent Night*," she said. Then she asked for the photographs.

I thought for a moment she wanted to look at them also. But she gave them to Peter and said, "Burn them, Peter. In the fireplace, with the wrappings from the packages."

Rudi Weiss' Story

That winter my mother became ill. There was nothing specifically wrong with her, I learned from Eva and other survivors, but she weakened, as did many in the ghetto, from the poor diet and the lack of medication.

According to my informants, my parents remained as devoted to each other as ever. My mother complained very little, but more and more, she had to forego her teaching—the music and literature lessons she gave, gratis, to the ghetto children.

One day, while a meeting of some key members of the council was taking place in the apartment adjoining my parents' room, Eva heard my father taking my mother's pulse, listening to her heart with a stethoscope. He was, as with all his patients, gentle, considerate, hopeful.

"What do you hear in my old heart?" she asked.

"Mozart," Papa said.

And she laughed. "Full of your old tricks, the same old jokes."

"We old general practitioners have a limited repertory. I still draw pictures of rabbits on my prescription pad to distract a child about to get an injection."

They talked about her going back to the school. If she failed to come, many of the children ran off—to beg, to steal, to smuggle.

The talk of the schoolchildren reminded them of us —of me, of Karl, of Anna. My mother kept photographs of us tacked over her bed. Sometimes my father thought it was not a good idea for her to be constantly reminded of her lost family.

"Oh, but they give me hope, Josef," she would say.

And he would play the game with her. He argued that anyone who was "useful" survived. "I'm a doctor, so I manage. Karl is an artist, they'll use him. And Rudi . . ."

"Rudi will make his way, Josef. I have faith in him."

Eva interrupted them to say that Uncle Moses had just sneaked back into the ghetto with a man from Vilna who had important information.

At that moment, my mother was talking to my father about some money that she had sewn into her old coat from Berlin. It was a kind of emergency fund, for God knows what purpose. But my mother had decided —knowing of the terrible condition in the children's ward at the hospital—that my father should use the money to purchase food for the sick youngsters.

He nodded his agreement. With shears, she began to cut the lining of the coat.

"Someone wanting to sneak *into* our ghetto?" my father asked Eva.

"A courier named Kovel. With important information for us."

"Ah. A high-level conference." He kissed my mother and followed Eva Lubin into the next room.

Kovel was a starved-looking bearded man with haunted eyes. But he had a precise manner, and as he sat, hunched over, rubbing his eyes and sipping hot tea, he told the group his story.

"Don't believe anything the Germans tell you about work camps or special ghettoes," Kovel said.

"Oh, of course we take whatever they tell us with a grain of salt." It was Dr. Kohn, the eternal conciliator, who spoke.

Kovel looked up. His shadowed eyes took in all in the crowded cold room. "They mean to murder every Jew in Europe."

"Impossible," said Kohn.

"You must mean reprisals on a large scale," my father said. Sensible man that he was, even he could not believe the truth.

"Not reprisals," Kovel said. "Annihilation. It is their intention to kill every Jew. Why can none of you understand what I am saying?"

Eva recalls the silence. Zalman, Anelevitz and she —working people, humble people—seemed to have a better grasp of events than the educated, the professionals. Anelevitz had been trying to tell them of their fate for some months.

Kovel went on. "There were once eighty thousand Jews in the Vilna ghetto. There are today less than twenty thousand."

My Uncle Moses was the first to react. "Sixty thousand . . . ?"

"Shot by the SS."

Dr. Kohn threw his hands up. "Utter nonsense. No one, not even the Germans, can march sixty thousand people out and shoot them. The logistics, the arrangements . . . impossible . . ."

"I'm not sure I can believe it either," my father said.

Anelevitz sat down next to the man from Vilna and asked, "How was it done, Kovel?"

"First the SS rounded up all Jews for work and forced them to dig ditches about twenty miles from the city. Then the Lithuanian police threw a cordon around the ghetto. No one could get out or get in. If you tried to fight back, you were shot. They forced everyone out with clubs and whips. They have a technique. The Jews are forced to undress, wait, are marched into the ditches in groups and shot, either with single shots in the neck, or massed fire from machine guns. There are no exceptions. When there are delays, the Jewish Council is forced to draw up lists. Then they are shot themselves."

Dr. Kohn wet his lips. "Ah . . . Vilna . . . perhaps an exception, a special case, you know . . ."

"No," Kovel said. "Ghetto after ghetto is being wiped out. Riga. Kovno. Lodz."

My father shook his head. "I know they are cruel and they hate us. But the German army . . . the old sense of honor . . . they must object."

Kovel laughed bitterly. "Object? They look the other way, or they help the bloody SS."

More silence.

Kovel told of more massacres—Dvinsk, Rowno, ghettoes the length and breadth of Poland and Russia.

"Open your eyes," he said. "Warsaw has the biggest

concentration of Jews in Europe. Your time will come."

"We are close to half a million," Dr. Kohn said. "They won't be able to dig enough ditches, find enough ammunition."

Uncle Moses interrupted him. "They'll find a way."

Anelevitz looked at Kovel. "Tell us what we must do."

Kovel took a rumpled sheet from his jacket. "Start with this. Send it out as a warning to everyone here. Read it for all to hear."

Eva Lubin took it, and in her girlish voice read the Vilna proclamation. " 'Let us not go to our deaths like lambs to the slaughter. Young Jews, I appeal to you, do not believe those who wish to do you harm. It is Hitler's plan to annihilate the Jews. We are the first. It is true we are weak and alone, but the only answer worth giving to the enemy is resistance. Brothers, rather die fighting than to live by the grace of the slaughterer. Let us defend ourselves to the death. Vilna, in the ghetto, January 1, 1942.' "

No one spoke for a while. Then Dr. Kohn asked, "But what good can it do? You say they'll be killed anyway."

"They?" Uncle Moses asked. *"We, Kohn, we."*

"Bare hands against tanks and artillery?" Kohn asked.

Kovel turned to Anelevitz. "Do you have any guns?"

"None yet. But we're teaching the Zionist youth to obey orders, to work with broomsticks pretending they're guns, to organize on military lines."

"We'll be soldiers first, then get guns," Eva said.

"That sounds like Jews," Uncle Moses said. "Not a gun among us, but soldiers."

Dr. Kohn was shaking his head. "The Germans can be bribed. I know it. The Warsaw ghetto is valuable to them. They know the war is finished. The Americans are in the war. They're losing Africa. The Russians will hold Moscow—"

"And we will all be dead while all that is happening," Kovel said.

"They need our factories, our workrooms," Kohn

went on. "Uniforms, leather goods. We Jews are skilled craftsmen."

Kovel got up. "I cannot seem to make you understand that the murder of Jews is central to their plan. They care less about losing territory here and there, an invasion, a two-front war, than they do about killing Jews. That is their primary aim."

"Oh, rubbish," Kohn said. "Even Hitler is not that insane."

The argument went on for a while. Kohn was outvoted. My father and my uncle took their stand with the resistance.

My mother had been eavesdropping from the small adjoining room. At the conclusion of the discussion, she entered, ladylike and elegant in her old robe, apologizing for her undone hair, and gave my father the money that had been sewn into her coat.

"Ah," my father said. "For the children . . ."

"No, Josef. To buy guns."

In January, 1942, Muller finally lived up to his word. He had Karl transferred to the artist's studio at Buchenwald, a favored place to work, since it was indoors, warm, and the artists were a rather privileged group.

What kept them privileged was the vanity of the SS who enjoyed having their portraits painted, and even more, having their alleged family trees—intricate genealogical diagrams—created in glowing colors.

In the studio Karl had made the friendship of a small frail artist from Karlsruhe named Otto Felsher. Felsher had been a successful portraitist on the outside, and hence was something of a favorite of the guards, although he, like Karl, had been beaten and starved before they decided to make use of his skills.

The truth was, although they were now better treated, Karl and Felsher detested the work assigned to them.

"And how is the Muller family tree coming, Weiss?" Felsher would ask.

"Lies on top of lies. What whores they make of us."

"It's how we survive."

Karl looked at the intricate, multi-colored family tree he was designing for Muller. "The bastard has me painting in Charlemagne and Frederick the Great."

Felsher laughed. "They're jealous because we go back to Abraham."

"So we do. For all the good it seems to have done us."

Sergeant Muller came by daily to look at the work in progress. "Beautiful, Weiss, beautiful. Don't forget the two Crusaders."

"Here they are," my brother said.

Muller beamed. "Weiss, you and I may get to be friends when this is over. Who knows? With America in the war, I may need a Jew to say nice things about me."

"Don't count on me, Muller."

The SS man took a letter from inside his tunic. "After all I've done for you? Your wife was here yesterday. The monthly letter from the fair Inga."

"I don't want it."

"Of course you do, Weiss."

"You made her pay the usual price, didn't you?"

Muller shrugged. "It came postage due. She had to pay, yes. She can afford it."

"Get away from me. I don't want to hear from her again. Tell her—no more letters, none from her, or from me."

Muller shoved the letter at him, jamming it into the pocket of his striped prison suit. "She won't be coming here any more, so it doesn't matter. You're being transferred. You and Felsher. We've had a request for a couple of high-class artists."

"Transferred?"

"Oh, you have reputations. The Buchenwald studio is famous. They want you, and some others of our skilled workers, at a new camp in Czechoslovakia. Theresienstadt. The Paradise Ghetto. Reserved for the most deserving Jews. A vacation resort."

Muller winked, sighed, as if an old friendship were ending. "I shall miss playing mailman for you, Weiss.

But I think I will have to arrange more frequent leaves to Berlin."

Karl had grown tough, stringy, in the camps, even on the dreadful diet, the appalling conditions. A certain recklessness—absent in him as a youth—had crept into his character.

As Muller walked away, my brother started after him.

"Don't, Weiss," Felsher said. "It isn't worth it."

"The bastard. He used my wife, the way a man uses a saw, or a paint brush . . ."

"To hell with him."

Karl crumpled the letter and threw it to the floor. He sat, silent, at his drafting table, staring at the fake family tree. Felsher retrieved the letter from the floor and gave it to him.

"Listen, kid," the older man said. "Nothing's the way it should be any more. Go on, read it. Be tolerant."

Karl nodded. There were tears in his eyes. He opened the letter (for which Inga had paid Muller's usual price) and read it.

My beloved Karl, dearest husband,
I miss you so much. More each day. At least we can communicate now, and that is good, but it makes me yearn for you even more. We must keep hope alive. I have been to several government offices, but they say your case cannot be reopened. I took a somewhat better job, as a secretary to the head of a small factory making farm equipment. It is odd. We have been at war several years, yet the private factories and corporations do not seem to be suffering. Our wages are ample; there is sufficient food; apart from the men at the front, the civilian population lives rather well. People seem a bit disturbed by America entering the war, but the hope is Russia will collapse before they can help; and England will surrender. My boss, incidentally, knows I have a husband in prison, but he is willing to overlook it—apparently I'm listed somewhere as a "race defiler"—since he says I'm the hardest working and least-complaining secretary he's ever

had. (Don't worry, darling, he's fat and old and a devout Lutheran.) I wish I had more news of your family. Not a word from Rudi. He's vanished. Miraculously, an old letter came out of Warsaw a week ago from your mother. They both seem fine, both are working. Life is not easy, but it is bearable, your mother said. Darling, we must never give up hope. I have had to do things to get these letters to you, and I hope you will understand. . . .

Karl gently folded the letter and put it back in his shirt.

He and Felsher said nothing for a while. Then the older man said, "I have heard of this Theresienstadt, Weiss. It's supposed to be a model camp, a real city for Jews. Maybe we're lucky. Maybe they'll even let your wife come to see you. Me, I have no family, so one place is the same as another."

Karl glared at the genealogical chart he had been painting for Muller with its Charlemagne and Crusaders. He picked up a pot of red paint and hurled it at the painting. Then he bent his head to the table and began to cry.

Erik Dorf's Diary

Berlin
January 1942

A few prefatory remarks before I get into the matter of this entry, namely the Gross-Wannsee Conference of January 20.

Heydrich, some months ago, let drop some information of great importance. Some time in the summer of 1941, when our Einsatzgruppen were cleansing Russia, Reichsführer Himmler summoned a man named Rudolph Hoess, commandant of a relatively obscure camp in Auschwitz, Poland, to his office, and told him: *"The Führer has given the order for a final solution of the Jewish question."*

Himmler reemphasized this a month or so later, in a speech to Blobel, Ohlendorf and the others (I was not present) in which he assured them they bore no "personal responsibility for the execution of the order, that the responsibility was the Führer's alone."

I mention this speech, because I have had a strange feeling, call it an intuition, that if something goes amiss—God forbid, if we lose the war, or our diplomacy fails to split the Allies and they fight on and these camps are discovered, if bodies are dug up—certain rewriters of history will seek to place the blame on *us*. By us, I mean the determined, devoted men of the SS, the Himmlers and Heydrichs, and yes, the Dorfs.

The Führer will be depicted as "just another German politician," unaware of the horrors.

Yet the curious thing is, that while cunningly never using the exact words such as "murder" or "extermination," the Führer has made most clear in speech and writings exactly what he wants to do to the Jews. I even get the crazy feeling that the denial of the earth to the Jews is his *foremost aim,* and transcends the subjugation of the Slavs, the punishing of France, the world rule by Germany. A rather silly notion, I admit, but the emphasis placed on our work, the privileges we get, and the ease with which Himmler has his way lead me to this peculiar conclusion.

Surely Hitler is not aware of every Jew we shoot or hang; he may not even know the precise statistics on the reduction of Russian ghettoes. But he knows, he knows. He has said many times that nothing happens *without his knowledge.* Yet I am certain that in years to come, lesser figures will be painted as the chief engineers of this awesome work, and certain scholars will try to remove him from it.

Hitler's closest aides also know what is going on. A few weeks before the invasion of Russia, last year, Goering wrote to Heydrich and assigned to him the job of "carrying out a solution of the Jewish problem as advantageous as possible." I don't think this meant settling them on farms and in villages. Goering wants, a full report on "an overall plan concerning the organizational, factual and material measures necessary for the accomplishment of the desired solution of the Jewish question." ·

(Another aside: For years, many influential Jews have regarded Goering as a possible mediator for them, a fellow who is "soft" on anti-Semitic measures, and will keep Himmler and the other racial intransigents from carrying out these policies. How surprised they would have been to have read his communiqués to Heydrich!)

Of course there has never been any doubt in anyone's mind what a "final solution" means—although we rarely talk about it. Only fools like Hans Frank go around babbling about how they will annihilate Jews the way they would lice. But we have effectively reduced his areas of responsibility in Poland, so that he is now nothing more than a figurehead, a creature of the SS. We've taken over; we will fulfill the Führer's desires, as quietly and efficiently as possible.

In any event, the events described above, and other interesting developments, such as the building of certain secret camps at Chelmno and Belzec in Poland, where unique new systems for solving the Jewish problem were being tested, led to the meeting at Gross-Wannsee on January 20.

Besides Heydrich and myself, there were thirteen men present at the meeting. It was held in the offices of the RSHA—the Reich Security Main Office—which Heydrich heads, and which deals directly with Jewish matters, in the Berlin suburb of Gross-Wannsee.

What interested me, as the men assembled and made small talk, was that not only top police and SS officials of Germany were present, but also five *civilian* Undersecretaries. It was quite clear what Heydrich had in mind. No branch of the German government, civilian, police or military, was to be kept in the dark about our plans. (I wondered as I looked at these civilian chaps what excuses they were already preparing in their crafty brains, should questions be asked at some later date.)

Eichmann was present. We are fairly good friends by now. My strained relations with some of the Einsatzgruppen chiefs—notably that boor Blobel, and the sneak Artur Nebe—make me more than willing to seek out Eichmann's support, since I have always found him rational, gracious and of an open mind.

"Ah, Dorf," he said, after asking about Marta and the children. "New developments in the wind. The Auschwitz business."

"So I hear."

"I was there recently. Himmler's given Hoess a green light. I'm trying to coordinate train schedules and so on with Hoess."

"Why Auschwitz?"

"Oh, it's got a fine rail setup. Lots of space for ensuring isolation. Lots of Jews around it. Poland is our real problem. All these new places—Chelmno, Belzec, Sobibor—they'll all be in Poland." He bent to me and whispered. "The Führer doesn't want the holy soil of Germany contaminated with Jewish blood, you know."

"Understandable."

I was surprised by my cool reaction to this information. The SS, including the RSHA, being the coiled, tangled nest of competitors that it is, Himmler sometimes goes around Heydrich, or keeps him in the dark, and although I knew of these new camps, I was not absolutely certain what is taking place there. My primary area of responsibility has remained the Russian campaign.

Hans Frank saw me entering the conference room and grabbed my arm, steering me away from Eichmann. "New camps, I heard that. Don't look so dumb, Dorf. Try sniffing a little gas, get a taste of it."

I shoved his hand away, and heard him mutter to one of his aides: "What a meeting—Heydrich, a part-Jew, and Dorf, a Berlin shyster."

The conference got underway.

Heydrich made clear to everyone present—especially the civilians, who included such eminences as the Undersecretaries for Foreign Affairs and the Interior

Ministry—that he, Reinhard Heydrich, was the Führer's chosen instrument for "the final solution of the Jewish question."

"All areas?" someone asked.

"All."

"Ah . . . that is to say, in Germany, and all conquered areas?"

Heydrich's response was that *all* the Jews of Europe, which he estimated at eleven million—he included English and Irish Jews—were to come under our eventual jurisdiction, and would suffer the same fate.

He never defined in so many words what this "final solution" was, though not a man present at the meeting misunderstood him. We knew.

"Emigration has been a failure," my boss went on. "No one wants these Jews, not America, nor England, nor anyone else. Besides, the logistics of getting them, especially the Eastern European Jews, out of their diseased villages and cities are too much for us, or for anyone else. So there will be a stepped-up evacuation of the Jews to the east—largely Poland."

On a chart, Heydrich showed how all European Jews —French, Dutch, English, Italian—would be sent "east."

"What happens then?" asked Hans Frank. "After you've dumped them on me?"

Heydrich ignored him. "The Jews will form labor units. Natural decline through disease, hunger, the attrition of hard work for which Jews are unsuited, will take its toll. There will be, of course, a hard core of Jewish survivors, the tenacious and strong ones."

"And what happens to them?" Eichmann asked.

"They will be treated accordingly."

People smiled, shifted in their seats. Two of the civilian ministers, like proper schoolboys caught smoking with the village ruffians, snickered, nudged one another.

"Could the general expand on that?" asked Gauleiter Meyer.

"Well, first let it be understood that these surviving Jews will represent a direct threat to Germany. They can rebuild Jewish life. Natural selection will make them strong. So—they will have to be dealt with accordingly."

"Goddammit, there are over three million Jews in Poland now," Frank roared. "Gluttons, parasites, full of disease, leaving their shit all over Poland. Well, I can tell you, as I told my division chiefs, we can't shoot or poison three million kikes, but we shall find some way to exterminate them."

"May I remind the governor-general to be careful of his language?" I said.

Frank pounded the table. "Dammit. You are talking annihilation. I'm sick of these fucking code words, these substitutes for the real thing."

Heydrich eyed him coldly, and if I were Frank, I would have feared that icy stare.

Eichmann, ever the diplomat, tried to divert the discussion. He asked whether the Einsatzgruppen would be expanded, to which Heydrich responded in the affirmative. And would new methods be considered? asked Eichmann.

"The use of gas is being considered," Heydrich said.

A high-ranking civilian official—I forget who—acted surprised. Heydrich told him tests were being made under laboratory conditions. Behinds shifted, noses were rubbed. Men stared at the lofty ceiling.

Dr. Luther, representing the Foreign Office, pointed out that the clergy had protested some years back when the "useless" were subjected to mercy killings by gas. I made some offhand comment to the effect that that should not deter us. Luther turned on me and cited protests from the Vatican, and the Protestant churches, how the Führer himself had backed down.

"Well?" Heydrich asked.

The other civilian was equally distraught. "It can happen again. The mass shooting of people in a war, that's one thing. There are always excuses that reasonable men, churchmen included, will accept. But gas! On women, children, the old! We can't get the churches angry at us again. Heydrich, this bloody business is getting out of hand."

"Calm yourself," Heydrich said. "These are Jews we will be dealing with."

Luther was furious. "Yes! Controlling the banks, the press, the stock exchanges, the Communist apparatus in Russia! Whispering in Roosevelt's ear!"

Heydrich leaned forward. "Take my word for it, doctor. No one will lift a finger to protect Jews."

Eichmann nodded his agreement.

It seemed a good point at which to support my chief. "Besides, we'll be on firm legal ground. We will be executing—no matter what the means—enemies of the state, spies, terrorists. Such acts are permissible in a war."

Luther, having been silenced on this subject, then raised some minor points. In some countries, notably Norway and Denmark, it was doubtful that the civilian population will co-operate in the program. The Italians aren't very cooperative either. They shrug, make excuses. Mussolini hasn't got his heart in it. And even Franco—of course, he's neutral—has been hiding Jews, letting them sneak into Spain. Wherever the SS has met strong resistance from local Christian populations, they have suddenly become less than vigorous in handling the Jewish problem. Of course in the long run, Luther said placatingly, there should be no real difficulties in the Balkans and Eastern Europe, where feelings against Jews are rather strong.

Some other civilians were obviously upset; yet they remained silent. No one else seemed to have anything left to say. Frank finally blurted out that Heydrich's theory of "working" Jews till they dropped was nonsense. Most of the Jews in Poland were so starved and diseased as to be beyond productive work.

"That is why new camps are being built," Eichmann said gently.

"Yes, and I know what for!" Frank bellowed.

He is the same weakling I faced down in Warsaw a year and a half ago. On the one hand, he still muses over the beauty of the law, the abstract notion of justice. On the other, he is determined to prove himself as tough as any of us.

"Remember what the Führer once told a group of lawyers, and you'll feel better," Heydrich said and smiled.

"I don't recall," Frank grumbled.

Heydrich turned to me. "Dorf?"

I knew the quotation. " 'Here I stand with my bayonets and there you stand with your law, and we'll see which prevails.' "

It was a good note on which to end the meeting at Gross-Wannsee.

Later, a select few of us sat in Heydrich's private office, watched the flames flicker in a huge logfire, drank French cognac and smoked.

Eichmann, Heydrich and I sang old songs and proposed toasts, first standing on the floor, then on chairs, then on a table, rising higher and higher with our glasses. Heydrich said it was an old North German custom.

The chief dozed at the fireplace, and Eichmann and I discussed the decisions made that day.

"Momentous, truly momentous," Eichmann said. "The world really doesn't understand our aims."

"Maybe they don't want to," I said.

"Oh, we've done a superb job of camouflage. No one believes us, and many don't want to believe. Not even the Jews."

I leaned forward. "Tell me, Eichmann, as an old friend, do you ever have second thoughts? Ever?"

"Of course not." He didn't even hesitate. "We're obeying the Führer's will. We're soldiers. Soldiers obey."

"But the way the Führer himself never appears at these meetings . . . the way his orders to Himmler and Heydrich seem to, well, waltz around the heart of the matter."

"Means nothing. He's said it over and over. He'd hang every Jew in Munich, he said in 1922, then start on the other cities. Remember, Dorf, our only law, our only constitution, is the will of our Führer."

He was right, of course. "I suppose he'll know about this new program."

Eichmann drained his cognac. "The details won't interest him. He's running a two-front war. But he'll want the job done. And he'll approve. You know what he said years ago—'Nothing happens in my movement without my knowledge and approval.' "

I rather admire Eichmann. He has a clear if relatively untrained mind, and he has a way of putting things in order, like a good office manager. He has told me over and over that he bears no malice toward Jews. Indeed, from a historic viewpoint Eichmann finds them fascinating—the founders of the world's great religions, eminent in science, art, all forms of scholarship. He boasted again about his time in Palestine as an agent, his familiarity with Hebrew. ("A difficult tongue, Dorf," he said, "an absolutely staggering grammatical system.")

With his usual charm, Eichmann then changed the subject to my wife and children, whom he remembered from that lovely day when he hosted us in Vienna. His own family was thriving, he said, in spite of annoying wartime shortages, occasional acts of sabotage.

I felt mellow, fulfilled, and I said, "No question, Eichmann, it is for our wonderful families, our wives and children, we perform these hard jobs. They give us courage and determination."

He agreed.

"We owe something to the next generation of Germans. The decisions we made today—terrible as they may seem—are an absolute necessity to preserve the purity of our race, the survival of Western civilization."

Later generations may not have the strength or will to finish the task. Or the opportunity. I think of my home, my family, and I know we are doing the right thing.

In the office, we drank, silently, and Heydrich slept, weary from his long, tiring day.

Rudi Weiss' Story

More wandering. We had been told, after our escape from Babi Yar, that there were bands of partisans wandering in the forests of the Ukraine. We wanted to join one.

Of Babi Yar, we heard little. The Ukrainian farmers—not all of them as brutal and cowardly as their compatriots who joined in the massacre in the ravine—shrugged their shoulders when we asked about it.

But it was no secret. One old farm woman, her toothless gums working away, informed Helena that 140 carloads of clothing had been distributed to the poor Christians of Kiev and the countryside around it. "From the Jews," she kept saying, "from the Jews."

One cold morning, Helena began to shiver. She was sleeping in my arms in a ruined peasant hut, abandoned by a farmer gone to God knew where, perhaps drafted into the Red Army, perhaps a prisoner. It was cold and damp. I had stolen some blankets and we slept together, trying to absorb warmth from each other's bodies.

"I'm cold," she said. Her poor teeth chattered.

"Come closer."

"It won't help, Rudi. I'll never be warm again."

I rubbed her hands and wrists, but she would not be cheered, or warmed. "I can't run any more," she wept. "I'm cold. I'm hungry."

"You think we should have stayed in Prague."

"I don't know . . . I don't know. At least we could get food there. I had my apartment, friends . . ."

"Your friends are all in concentration camps."

"I am a burden to you," she said. "I cry too much."

I looked at our few crude utensils on the table—metal cup, metal plate, spoons. Then I picked up the cup and hurled it against the fireplace. "Dammit. Dammit."

She sat up in bed, weeping loudly now. "Rudi, it is hopeless."

I grabbed her, lifted her from the straw mattress. "No. No. You gave me those lectures about that Zionist homeland you and your parents want to build in Palestine, out in some desert surrounded by Arabs. You think you'll get that by sitting back and crying? By giving in to anyone who threatens you? That guy with the whiskers who talked about it—what's his name—"

My ignorance made her laugh. "Oh, Rudi, you are crazy. His name was Herzl."

"Well, that dream of his won't mean anything unless Jews learn to fight. You think you'll get that land without killing people? Or a lot of Jews getting killed?"

She shivered. "I'm sorry. I can't think when I'm cold. I can't be worried about Herzl when I'm freezing."

Outside the hut I dug in the frozen earth and found some turnips that had not been harvested the previous fall. They were frozen, half rotten, but perhaps I could cut out some edible parts. A small orange cat followed me back into the house.

"Close your eyes," I said to Helena. "I have a present."

She did. I put the kitten in her lap.

"Pure-bred Ukrainian Siamese Persian. All for you."

"Oh, Rudi . . . it's as weak and hungry as we are."

"Learn something from him. He's a cat. He gets by." I gave her a slice of turnip. "Try some. Full of vitamins."

She gagged on it, began to retch.

"Make believe its a fresh breakfast roll. Hot strudel. Stollen. Mmmm. And the fresh coffee. Cream and sugar?"

I made her laugh. In feigned anger she threw the turnip at me.

Chewing on mine, I began to reflect. "Here we are, a proper Berlin family. Mama, Papa, and Cat. But we'll never live in Berlin, Helena."

"Nor Prague. We'll go to Eretz Israel."

She walked in back of me, put her arms around my neck. "It doesn't matter," she said. "Wherever you are, I'll be happy."

"And I will, too."

"And our children."

I petted the starved cat. "They'll never believe the stories we'll tell them. Running away from Prague, into Hungary, Russia."

Helena laughed. "They'd better! They'd better believe every word."

I took her in my arms. "I can see my son, Helena. Some little squirt with your Czech eyes and your terrible Czech accent, making fun of me. 'Papa, you're full of knockwurst!'"

She laughed again, but it was only to hide her misery. Poor, frail girl. We'd run off at my urging. Often she had misgivings. Her life in Prague had been pleasant enough until the Germans came. It was hard for her to break away. I felt guilty at what I'd talked her into. But I was convinced it was the only way.

I stared at her now, stroking the cat. A small, vulnerable girl, with a heart-shaped face, intense eyes, dark-brown hair. And I raged within to think of the way the Nazis murdered people like Helena—without hesitation, restraint, second thoughts. What in God's name had created such monsters?

It seemed to me at that moment that the peril hanging over us, the horrors we had seen at Babi Yar and elsewhere, made it all the more vital that we love each other, never hurt each other, always be truthful and gentle with each other. Helena understood that also. I could see it in her eyes, sense it in her sighs, and small cries, and reluctance to let go of me, when we made love in barns, deserted homes, fields.

The cat jumped from the table, meowed, stretched and walked to the open door of the hut, as if attracted by something.

I heard noises outside. Soft footsteps, a sound of bodies brushing against foliage. A life in the wild had tuned my ears for these noises. Partisans? But which kind? We had been turned away by one band of Ukrainian guerrillas. *No Jews,* they had told us. And added we were lucky they didn't shoot us on the spot.

Someone kicked the door open, waited.

I took the knife from my belt and backed against the wall of the hut, motioning Helena to get behind me.

"Who is in there?" a man's voice asked.

But he waited. He did not enter. I whispered to Helena, "Get under the bed."

"It's no use, Rudi . . . let's give up."

The man's voice came again: "Come out. Hands over your heads. There are fifty of us here, all armed."

The man who had spoken entered the doorway. He had on rough wintry clothing, odds and ends, not quite a military uniform, but suggesting one. He had a fur hat, an old Red Army coat, felt boots. Around his shoulders were two bandoliers. He pointed a Red Army rifle at me.

"Rudi, it's no use," Helena whimpered. "Put down the knife."

"She's right. Drop it. Out, both of you. Clasp your hands on your heads."

We did so. He stood aside to let us pass. I thought of jumping for him, but there were others outside, at least two whom I could see, a man and a woman in the same quasi-military collection of rags, old clothing, felt boots. But oddly, they were unarmed.

The man with the rifle spoke in Russian to Helena. He seemed to be in his early fifties, grizzled, with a lined face.

The three stood facing us in the dead garden of the vanished farmer.

"One lousy gun," I said to Helena. "I should have jumped him and taken it from him."

"Will you try it now?" he asked.

"No, but I may later. Where are your fifty armed partisans?"

"They'll be here when I need them."

There was a moment of quiet, as we studied each other, and then the realization dawned that all five of us were Jews!

"Who are you?" the older man asked. "Don't lie."
He stared at Helena. "Would you prefer that I speak
Yiddish?"

"We are Jews," she said. "Running away. He's a German Jew and I am from Prague."

The young woman opened the collar of her tunic and
revealed a Star of David on her neck. "Shalom," she
said quietly.

"Shalom," said Helena.

I still hesitated to move toward them, so suspicious
had I become. But Helena did not hesitate. She fell
into the girl's arms, weeping for joy. The older man
lowered his rifle and extended his hand. I shook it,
and then we too embraced, and the younger man
hugged me, and unashamedly kissed me.

"I can't believe it," I said. "Jews with guns."

"Very few guns," the young woman laughed. Her
name was Nadya. She was very dark, with strong,
intelligent eyes. "Those fifty armed partisans are part
of Uncle Sasha's imagination."

The older man was Uncle Sasha. He told us, as we
began to walk through the woods, that he was the commander of the partisan brigade in the Zhitomir area.
All the people in the brigade were Jews. The Ukrainian
partisans had their own units, and would permit no
Jews to join them.

I told him how Helena and I had been turned away
by just such a band.

The young man—he was called Yuri—nodded. "You
are lucky you were not killed by them. It is inconceivable to us. The Germans are enslaving them, killing
their young men, burning their homes, stealing their
crops, and you would think they would make common cause with the Jews of the Ukraine. But no. They
still find time to hate us, to reject us. It fills a man with
despair."

"To hell with them," Uncle Sasha said. He paused
before we entered a thickly wooded area of tall trees,
a kind of semi-cultivated forest, perhaps an abandoned
tree nursery. "Careful, now. Single file. You, the Ger-

man, follow me. You look as though you won't mind getting into a fight."

"I'd be happier with a gun."

"We plan to get some very soon. Come along."

We walked through the damp, cold forest. Once I looked over my shoulder at Helena. She was smiling. At long last, a glimmer of hope.

Sometime in March 1942, my brother Karl and his fellow artist, Otto Felsher, were sent with a shipment of Buchenwald Jews to the new camp at Theresienstadt.

The camp was thirty miles or so from Prague, and had once been a garrison town in the time of the Empress Maria Theresa, later an ordinary Czech village. But the Czechs had been moved out, the buildings enclosed and isolated, and it was now a prison, but a very special kind.

It was, in effect, a "showcase" camp—a false front to deceive the outside world. While Jews starved and died there, and later were merely kept for a brief time before transport to their doom, the Germans spread the word that it was a "Paradise Ghetto," an "old folks' home", a "special camp" for VIPs, Jewish heroes of the First World War, educated and refined Jews from Germany and Czechoslovakia.

Doing research for this story, I learned that Rabbi Leo Baeck of Berlin, the leading Jewish clergyman in Germany, was a prisoner there. So were several Jewish generals. And a Jew who had been on the board of I. G. Farben.

Several hundred people from Buchenwald were herded off the trains and marched into the main square of the camp. (I visited it after the war, and I could not help but be impressed—from the outside at least —with how attractive it was. Baroque buildings, heavy doors, clean streets. But it was all a fraud.)

The commandant welcomed the new visitors. He was an SS colonel, an Austrian, and he stressed, over and over, that this was a city given to them by the

Führer, a city for the Jews, and it was up to them to keep it clean and neat, to obey the laws, to cooperate with the authorities. Theresienstadt would disprove all those lies people were spreading about the terrible things Germany was doing to Jews.

If they disobeyed his orders, he added, if they told lies, smuggled, stole, made the city filthy as was the habit of Jews, then they would suffer the fate of common criminals. And he directed their attention to a gallows just beyond a side gate, near a small inner fortress, from which were hanging the bodies of three young men.

The group was then disbanded, and told that their own community leaders would supply them with quarters and job assignments.

An attractive middle-aged woman named Maria Kalova, who survived the holocaust and from whom I received much of the information concerning Karl's years in Theresienstadt, then approached my brother and Felsher.

"Weiss? Karl Weiss?" she asked.

"Yes." He laughed, turning to Felsher. "I can't believe it. A committee of welcome for a prisoner. Did you expect my friend Felsher also?"

"Indeed we did. Word gets around. I'm Maria Kalova. I work in the art studio. You two are assigned there. In fact, one of the SS officers heard about your work and requested you."

Felsher made a sour face. "More bloody genealogical tables. Proving these thieves and liars are all descendants of Frederick Barbarossa."

"Be grateful," she said. "It is no hotel here, but one manages to get by."

She walked them through the camp. To Karl's astonishment, there was a neatly kept main square, and a series of stores. Stores in a concentration camp! And a bank, a theater, a cafe.

He asked the woman Maria Kalova about them.

"They are all fakes, false fronts. Truly, this is the Potemkin Village of all time. The bank circulates useless currency. The bakery never has bread. In the luggage store you can buy back your own valise. Perhaps a cup of warm ersatz coffee once a week in the cafe."

"What is it?" asked Karl. "A game?"

"No, it is much more than a game to the Nazis," Maria said. "When you go to the barracks you will find them filled with old, dying people. We are barely sustained with the food they give us. Punishments are severe for the slightest infraction. You see that small fort there? That's the Kleine Festung. The SS torturers do their work there. This is really not much different from Buchenwald except in its external appearance."

"I don't get it," Felsher said.

"Theresienstadt is their passport to respectability," Maria said. "Periodically the International Red Cross, or some neutral—the Swedes, for example—will demand an inspection of a concentration camp. They are brought here. And so they are shown the bank, the cinema, the bakery, the shops—and they are asked for their approval. What are those Jews complaining about? The Führer has given them this beautiful city."

"And they get away with it? The inspectors believe them?" Karl felt he was losing his mind.

"Maybe they want to believe," Felsher said.

The artists' studio at Theresienstadt was large, airy and light. Karl understood at once that the people employed there were an elite, looked upon with favor by their SS masters.

He soon learned why. They were all part of the Nazi scheme to present the camp to the world as a model city, to distract the world from the true facts of life in the camps—the Auschwitzes and Treblinkas that were soon to go into business as the great factories of death.

On the wall were colorful posters with legends like SAVE FOOD! CLEANLINESS ABOVE ALL! and the eternal WORK WILL MAKE YOU FREE! The art work was superb. It should have been. Some of the very best Czech and German artists were imprisoned in Theresienstadt, as well as many musicians, including several orchestra conductors, composers and performers.

Several men were at work at easels, painting scenes of what can only be called "happy ghetto life in Theresienstadt." Karl, who had seen children in the streets of Buchenwald, and even Theresienstadt, fighting over crusts of bread, winced.

A husky man came forward from his drawing board and introduced himself to Karl and Felsher. His name was Emil Frey, and he was the director of the studio. He had been a rather well-known artist and teacher of art in Prague.

"You're pleased to be finished with Buchenwald, I gather," he said.

"This looks like an improvement," Karl said.

Frey said, "We're the lucky ones. You, Weiss, and you, Felsher, keep your noses clean, and you might survive also."

"Does anyone ever escape?" Karl asked.

"This is no ordinary prison," Frey said. "It's guarded and guarded again—walls, barbed wire, dogs, SS, Czech police. The last thing the Nazis want is for the world to know they are lying about Theresienstadt—and all the camps."

As Emil Frey spoke, Karl began to stroll around the various easels and drawing boards, studying the works in progress and the finished, idealized paintings. There were tributes to German womanhood, the Führer in knightly armor, charming drawings of "camp life"— musicales, theater performances, playgrounds.

Maria and Frey fell silent as Karl made his tour of the studio. Felsher trailed Karl, shaking his head.

He stopped at the edge of Frey's drafting table and looked at him intensely. "These paintings are a collection of lies."

Frey again was silent. Then he said to Maria, "Stand watch at the windows. We must begin the education of our two apprentices."

As soon as Maria was at the large window, Frey removed a board from his table and extracted a roll of drawings. He unfolded them and held the corners down.

"We are a rather eclectic group here," he said to Karl and Felsher. "What you see displayed is one style, perhaps romantic, but we also deal in realism, social commentary if you will."

The first picture was a pen-and-ink drawing—bleak, terrifying, entitled "Condemned." Three bodies dangled from a gallows. SS men stood about leering. The second was called "Last Voyage"—a pencil drawing of a wagonload of coffins, each marked with a Star of David.

"Yours?" Karl asked.

"All of us."

Maria called from the window. "Commandant," she said. "And an inspecting party."

Frey rolled up the drawings and returned them to the space beneath the loose board in his table.

Seconds later the SS commandant, an Austrian named Rahm, and two civilians entered. The civilians, as nearly as Maria remembers, were from the International Red Cross—Swiss, perhaps.

Rahm, the SS chief, asked cheerfully, "And how are my artists today?"

Everyone came to attention. Frey answered for all. "Quite well, Herr Commandant. All of us busy."

Rahm beamed at his guests. "These gentlemen are from the Red Cross. They have heard about our extensive art program, our creative painters, and wanted to visit the studio. Quite an atelier, eh, gentlemen? Hardly a torture chamber, as the Jewish press keeps insisting in America. Frey, show our visitors those portraits of children."

Karl and Felsher watched as Frey displayed some pastel drawings. The children looked like angels, not the starved, dirty, bread-grubbing kids Karl had seen outside.

"Charming," one of the Swiss said. "Truly charming."

Helena and I were now in what the Russian partisans, especially the Jews, called "a family camp."

Members of entire communities had fled to the forests —the old, the young, infants and people who were natural leaders like Uncle Sasha.

They lived in a true community—sharing, keeping family units intact as much as possible, looking after the sick and the old and trying to organize some kind of resistance against the Germans.

Uncle Sasha's camp was one of the most famous. It varied in numbers from 100 to 150 people. They lived in temporary huts, tents, any kind of dwelling that could be hastily built and torn down. They were forever on the move, to keep out of the reach both of the Germans and of the Christian partisan bands, who would kill stray Jews without a moment's hesitation. (Helena and I had been lucky in our encounter.)

The atmosphere in the family camp always seemed to me dreamlike, enshrouded in mists. People talked quietly, if at all. There was none of the noisy chatter, the gossiping, the arguing so characteristic of Jewish communities. These people had been witnesses to dreadful crimes against their families and friends; they had no time for argument among themselves, for trivia.

Only some of the children seemed to have escaped this change of character. They played ball, pulled practical jokes on one another, raced around the fireplaces and huts in the timeless way in which the young behave.

Helena and I became friendly with the young couple, Yuri and Nadya, who had been with Uncle Sasha the day they found us. They had run a photography shop in a Ukrainian village, had seen all of their relatives shot to death, had refused (as we did) to respond to a call to report to a "work camp" and had run off to the forests.

One night we ate our simple meal of groats and potatoes (food had to be bought at great risk from Ukrainian farmers, who might at any time inform on us) and we watched some men praying beyond the huts. One of the partisans was a rabbi named Samuel, a youngish man with a long, sorrowing face.

I noticed that Uncle Sasha did not join them. He sat with one of his men, poring over a scrawled map of the area, planning some kind of raid. We now had three rifles, all stolen from local gendarmes, but we needed a good deal more before we could attack the Germans.

"Who is he?" I asked.

"Sasha?" Yuri asked. "He's a doctor."

"You're joking. Where's his office?" I was assailed with memories of my father—the house on Groningstrasse, the waiting room, the smell of medical alcohol as my father washed his hands. And the way he took a pulse so gently, or taped my sprained ankles, as expertly as any team trainer. And his heavy tread on the stairs, his voice, ever gentle and considerate.

"He can still take out an appendix. And with a kitchen knife. Delivered two babies since we've been here."

"And the rabbi?"

"Samuel Mishkin. From the same village as Sasha. He wants to fight with us when we go out."

"That's my idea of a rabbi," I said. "He might get me back into the synagogue someday." Karl and I had not been in one since we were bar-mitzvah'd.

More men joined the rabbi in evening prayer. They bobbed and jerked their heads. Their eyes were closed. The shawls covered their heads and they seemed lost in some other world.

One of the boys, by mistake, tossed the ball into the midst of the prayers.

The rabbi picked it up and threw it away. "Get away," he said sternly. "This is a *shul*."

"It don't look like one," the kid said.

"I'll take care of you later," the rabbi said. "Where Jews gather to pray is a House of God. Now, go."

Helena and I both laughed.

"Like when I was a kid," I said. "I was always getting chased away for playing ball on Saturday."

The camp—misty, smoke-filled—made me think again of my home. I asked Yuri. "How did you people get here?"

"Most of us came from Koretz with Uncle Sasha. He led us out. The Germans shot his wife and his two daughters. They killed more than two thousand Jews in one afternoon. Made them dig their own graves, undressed them, shot them. A bullet in the neck. My parents were killed. My brothers. Most of Nadya's family. One of Uncle Sasha's patients, he was a Ukrainian, a lawyer, a good guy, he warned us in advance. He hid a bunch of us in his cellar until the roundup was finished. Then he sneaked us out. His name was Lakov, and someday I'll see that people remember him, if I live."

Nadya picked up the story. "Other Jews joined us. From Berdichev, Zhitomir. All the ghettoes were being wiped out. The Germans were killing all the Jews."

"But why? Why?" Helena asked.

"They don't need reasons," I said. "Any excuse works for them, because they have the guns and we don't."

Yuri shifted his legs, threw a twig into the fire. "This is our fifth camp. We have to keep wandering. They know we're out here, and every now and then the SS sends patrols into the forests. They don't want a single Jew left alive in Russia."

"When will you fight back?" I asked.

"When we have enough guns," he answered.

Nadya shook her head. "It is not easy. Uncle Sasha says we cannot desert the old people, the children, the sick. That is why he calls this a family camp. We must survive as a community, he says, a *yishuv*."

I looked at the partisan leader. He was sitting alone now, smoking one of those flimsy Russian cigarettes, staring into the flames. He had a tough, lined face, but underneath it there was gentleness and compassion, and again I saw my father.

"Why doesn't he pray with the others?" I asked.

Nadya responded: "He ripped his prayer shawl after his family was murdered. He tells all who come here, no more accepting death, no more marching peacefully to death. We will die anyway, so we must die fighting."

"But," Helena said, "you are just a handful of people. Thousands have been killed, tens of thousands who did nothing."

"Be tolerant," Nadya said. "People were overwhelmed. They never believed it would happen. And who had guns, who knew how to organize a resistance? Before they knew it, they were arrested, marched off, killed."

Uncle Sasha got up from his seat near the fire and walked toward us. He seemed tired all the time, driving himself to another day of wandering, keeping the "family" together.

"Weiss, you can start guard duty," he said to me. "You know how to shoot?"

I pointed to the old bolt-action rifle he shoved at me. "Will that thing fire?"

"If it doesn't use it as a club."

"That I can do."

He smiled. "You look as though you've been in a few fights."

"I have, And I won most of them."

We started walking to the edge of the camp, where the sentries were posted, twenty-four hours a day. He looked at me from the corner of one eye. "What are you smiling about?"

"I was thinking . . . my father is a doctor."

"Where?"

"He was in Berlin for many years. Then he was deported. He lives in Warsaw, the last I heard." We paused. Helena was standing nearby. "Funny. He once wanted me to go to medical school."

Uncle Sasha laughed. "Couldn't look at blood?"

"No. Just a rotten student."

I felt a warmth toward him, something vital that had been missing in my life since the day my father had been deported, since I had run away from Germany.

Helena came forward. "May I walk his post with him?"

"I guess so," Uncle Sasha said.

A boy of about fourteen, carrying another of those ancient rifles, approached.

"Vanya will show you your post. Stay awake. And no talking. You are soldiers."

We started to follow Vanya into the woods. On an impulse, I turned and spoke to Uncle Sasha. "That fellow Samuel, the rabbi," I said.

"What about him?"

"Will he perform a wedding?"

"Why not? And you can even owe him his fee. He's married several people here already. But save the romance for when you're not on guard duty."

Helena kissed me. She was shivering slightly. We held hands. I slung the rifle over my shoulder.

We were married by Rabbi Mishkin two days later. The women of the camp made a wreath for Helena's hair out of evergreen leaves, and a veil from an old lace shawl that one of the women had brought from her village.

One of the partisans was a fiddler and he played strange, wild tunes, dancing around us, now acting the fool, now making his violin wail as if crying. My mother would surely have sniffed at his performance.

We stood under a canopy—the Yiddish word for it is *chupa,* I learned, with much joking about my "goyishness"—and were married, joined as man and wife by the partisan rabbi.

"Some Jew," Uncle Sasha said, teasing me, as the service was about to begin. "The yarmulka doesn't even look like one on his head. He wears it as if it were a Boy Scout cap."

Mercifully, it was a short ceremony. In deference to my ignorance, much of the service was conducted in Yiddish, close enough to German so that I understood it. Years ago, I had lost all my knowledge of the Hebrew Karl and I had briefly studied in *cheder.* Those strange vowels and impossible verbs had rattled around in my head, no competition for soccer scores, bicycling races, prize fights.

But I was respectful and happy, and when Helena and I exchanged rings—cheap copper bands, fashioned by a jeweler who was a member of Sasha's band—and

I kissed her gently, I felt fulfilled, part of an old tradition. An odd thought rattled through my head as the rabbi recited the service. *If they want to kill us so desperately, then surely we are worthwhile, valid, of importance to the world.* . . .

"Beloved, come the bride to meet," the rabbi intoned, "The Princess Sabbath let us greet . . ."

There was a reading from the Bible, none of which I understood, but which Sasha later translated for me. *In distress I called upon the Lord and He answered me with great deliverance* . . .

Finally, I was told to smash with my boot a kitchen glass set on the earth. (A good wine glass should have been used; but there was none in camp.)

I did so, shattering the glass.

People cheered, shouted, and the fiddler struck up a gay tune.

"Kiss the bride, kiss the bride!" all shouted.

"I suspect they've kissed a few times before," Uncle Sasha said, winking at us.

Helena and I kissed. Her eyes were rimmed with tears.

"May your years be blessed with happiness, and fulfillment, and children," the rabbi said. "And above all undying love for each other and for the Lord our God. In the faith of Abraham, Isaac and Jacob, you are man and wife."

Sasha dug me in the ribs. "New responsibilities now, Rudi. House, insurance, a burial society. Save your money."

We laughed. *Money!* We lived like wandering ghosts, worse than gypsies. Perhaps it explains why I have adapted so well to life on the kibbutz. In my years of wandering I learned how little a man needs to get by.

People began to dance, holding arms, forming circles, kicking, singing. Sasha hugged me. "We will outlive these bastards who want to kill us," he said. "And soon we will have our revenge. You and Helena and the other young ones will live in peace again, I swear it."

Nadya took Helena's arm. "We're sorry there's no roast goose for the wedding feast—not even a herring."

"It's all right," she said. "We are happy."

I was a bit embarrassed—I never liked being the center of attention unless it was on a soccer field—when they joined arms and danced around us.

Ten minutes later the wedding celebration ended.

Avram, one of the sentries, came racing into the camp. A Ukrainian farmer, one who had treated us decently and had traded with Uncle Sasha, had seen Nazi patrols along the road.

"Break camp," Sasha ordered. "Tents down, fires out. We are moving out again."

Helena and I gathered up our meager possessions —the tin cup and plate, the knife and fork, our blankets. "It wasn't much of a honeymoon," I said to her.

"You owe me one, Rudi."

I took her in my arms. "And much more."

Yuri grabbed us both, ordered us to help dismantle the tents and pack them.

So ended my wedding day. Soon we were marching, into the night, deeper into the forests.

Erik Dorf's Diary

Minsk
February 1942

From the beginning of this damned incident, Heydrich and I had misgivings about it. (I don't mean our overall operation; I mean this specific incident involving Reichsführer Himmler.)

I've gotten two stories on how it came about.

One is that Himmler asked Colonel Artur Nebe, the commander of Einsatzgruppe B—the action team that is responsible for the Moscow area—to arrange a sample "liquidation," so that he might himself see how the job was done.

The other story is that it was Nebe's idea. Trying to curry favor with the boss.

In any case, neither Heydrich nor I liked the notion. We discussed it *sotto voce,* as we walked across a frozen field outside the Russian city of Minsk. Since this was just a "demonstration," Nebe's men had rounded up about a hundred Jews, all male except for two.

"Nebe is an idiot," Heydrich whispered to me. "I know our esteemed Reichsführer better than he does. He's full of theories, and he's good at measuring Jewish skulls, but he doesn't like to get close to blood."

"Neither do I, sir," I said.

"But you have gotten used to it," the chief said.

I did not answer. But I suppose I have. In view of the great goal, the wartime necessity of isolating and diminishing Jewish influence, we must have the courage to face up to onerous tasks.

The hundred or so Jews were assembled alongside a deep ditch. They were naked. Nebe explained to Himmler that his men had already shot 45,000 Jews in the Minsk area.

Colonel Paul Blobel, who was walking with me, muttered, "Piker. We got rid of thirty-three thousand in two days at Babi Yar."

The party halted perhaps twenty yards from where the Jews were standing, and a curious thing happened. Himmler's eyes came to rest on a young Jew, quite tall, well formed, with blue eyes and blond hair.

To our amazement, the Reichsführer walked up to the youth and asked if he were a Jew, refusing to believe that such a Nordic-looking fellow could be one.

"Yes," the man said. "I am a Jew."

"Are both of your parents Jews?"

Heydrich and I exchanged looks—critical, dismayed.

"Yes."

"Do you have any ancestors who were not Jews?" .

"No."

"Then I cannot help you."

Heydrich whispered to me, "At least he did not deny his heritage. That took a bit of courage."

I wondered if subconsciously Heydrich was thinking about the rumors of his own Jewish blood.

"Whenever you are ready, Reichsführer," Nebe said.

"Yes . . . yes . . ."

The soldiers opened up with their machine pistols and the Jews fell in heaps into the ditch. We observed Himmler. He was trembling, sweating, wringing his hands. Incredible. This man who passes out orders daily on the mass murder of millions could not bear to see a hundred shot!

Through some strange coincidence, the two women in the group were not dead. They were merely wounded, and their naked arms kept reaching up, imploring.

"Kill them!" screamed Himmler. "Don't torture them like that! Sergeant, kill them! Kill them!"

At once the women were dispatched with pistol shots in the neck.

Himmler stumbled about as if he were going to faint.

"First time . . . you realize . . ." He was choking.

"Miserable fucking chicken farmer," Blobel said to me. "We kill Yids by the hundreds of thousands, and he gets sick when he sees a handful go to their Jewish God."

Nebe then made things worse by telling the Reichsführer that this was a mere hundred, and that the good German soldiers who had to shoot thousands daily were being affected by it. Of course, they obeyed and they understood their duty to the Reich and to Hitler, but some of these men would be "finished" for life. (I disagree, but I said nothing; it is amazing how much cognac and cigarettes and loot from dead Jews can keep our enlisted men going—that and the assurance that as long as they are shooting Jews, they will not be shot at by the Red Army.)

Himmler, moved to his very soul, then made a brief speech to the assembled officers.

"I have never been prouder of German soldiers," said the Reichsführer. There was a heavy smell of gunpowder in the air. A work party of Jews was shoveling dirt over the dead.

"The men are appreciative, Reichsführer," Heydrich said.

Himmler's eyes were glazed, lost behind his prissy pince-nez. "Your consciences can be clear. I take full responsibility before God and the Führer for all your acts. We must take a lesson from nature. There is combat everywhere. Primitive man understood that a bedbug was bad, a horse good. You may argue that bedbugs, rats and Jews have a right to live, and I might agree. But a man has a right to defend himself against vermin."

His voice, that schoolmasterish, low voice, dwindled. In the privacy of this diary, I am forced to note that he is, with his pinched face, sparse hair, paunch, and sissified voice, hardly the ideal of the Aryan hero. How much more of an ideal is Reinhard Heydrich! No wonder they detest and distrust each other.

Himmler's eyes took us all in. "Heydrich, Nebe, Blobel . . . all my good officers. This shooting is not the answer. We must look for more efficient ways of getting this business done."

Later, Himmler was taken on a tour of an insane asylum. He told Nebe to finish off the inmates, but in an efficient, clean manner, something more "humane" than shooting. Nebe suggested dynamite.

That afternoon, I ran into Colonel Nebe and Colonel Blobel again at the Einsatzgruppe headquarters in Minsk. Heydrich had been upset over the day's events, and I made known his—and my—annoyance with Nebe, accusing him of botching the entire affair. I failed to use his title when I addressed him, and it bothered him.

"I am Colonel Nebe to you, Major Dorf."

"You're lucky you are not a sergeant after that mess today. Why didn't you talk the Reichsführer out of his lunatic notion to observe a shooting? And couldn't you find gunners who could get rid of them all in one volley?"

He and Blobel were taken aback by my assault.

"Damn you, Dorf, don't go barking at me," Nebe said.

"Your operation was a disgrace," I said.

Blobel, boots on Nebe's desk, whiskey glass in hand, glowered at me. "Shut up, Dorf. Some of us are sick of your goddamn interference."

"Are you? Well, for your information, Blobel, Heydrich is not happy with the results of Babi Yar. We are told that so many bodies are buried there that the gases are erupting the earth. We want those bodies dug up and burned. Burned so that no trace is left."

"What? All those bodies? Who the hell are you—"

I cut him short. These men, deep in their hearts, are cowards.

"Get your fat ass back to the Ukraine, Blobel, and do as you are told."

Nebe nervously paced the floor. Outside the window I could see his men, aided by Lithuanian "volunteers," parading more Jews to the countryside. "Major Dorf, you have no right to talk to us in this insulting manner."

"Sure he does," Blobel said. "He's Heydrich's pet, his favorite shyster. You and that half-Jew think you can—"

"That is a lie. Anyone who spreads such lies will have to answer for them."

"Go to hell," Blobel said. He shook the dregs from his bottle. "I need a drink."

They got up. I was not invited. But Nebe was still trying to placate me. A weak man. "Listen, Major. I think I have some good ideas on what Himmler has in mind. I mentioned dynamiting large numbers of undesirables to him. But there are other ways. Injections. Gas. It's been tried in a few places, you know."

"To hell with him, Nebe," Blobel said. As they walked out, I could hear Blobel, in a voice intentionally loud, saying to his fellow officer, "We've got to do something about that scheming little bastard."

Berlin
May 1942

Exhausted from this past tour of the occupied territories, I'm back in Berlin. At last a chance to hold Marta in my arms, kiss her beloved fair face, stroke her hair, join our bodies in that sweetest of unions.

I can't wait to see the children. Peter is in training with his Jungvolk unit, the preparatory organization for the Hitler Jugend. He says he wants to join the SS when he is old enough, a combat unit, such as a Panzer division. I told him the war will long have ended by then, with Germany victorious. Little Laura is getting top grades in school. Her teachers adore her—so pretty, so vivacious, so obedient.

My work is mounting, my areas of responsibility broadening each day. Heydrich says I am a glutton for work. I get more done in a day than any of his other aides do in a week. Major "Heart-of-the-Matter," he calls me.

We discussed alternative methods this morning, May 21, in his office.

Two months ago, the new camp at Belzec began using carbon monoxide gas, but the results are not too good. Heydrich wants a full report. And at Chelmno, near Lodz, an ingenious method is being tried—huge mobile vans, in which the exhaust is passed into the sealed body of the truck. There is some question about the efficiency of this method also.

We enjoyed a good laugh about Blobel. I must have scared the pants off him. He went back to Babi Yar and dug up a great many bodies, burning them to nothingness on giant pyres of railroad ties soaked with gasoline. Amazing, what with wartime shortages, and the army demanding every drop of motor fuel, that Blobel was able to get the stuff. But the army jumps when we give orders. And I may have underestimated Blobel. His method of disposing of corpses is remarkable, so that, as Himmler has decreed, "even the ashes disappear."

As I was about to leave, Heydrich called me back and handed me a single sheet of paper. "What do you make of this, Dorf?"

I read it, and as I did, it was an effort to keep my composure.

"Aloud," Heydrich said.

" 'Major Erik Dorf of your staff was in the early thirties a member of a Communist youth group at the University of Berlin. His father was a Communist Party member who took his own life in a scandal involving money. Dorf's mother's family may contain a Jew in the background. All these matters are worth an investigation.' "

"Well?"

"It's not signed," I said.

"They never are. What about it, Erik?"

"Lies. As we say in court, in its parts, and in the whole. My father was briefly a Socialist. Nothing serious. He and his brother. They got over it. Oh, excuse me. One part is true. He did take his life, but there was no scandal. He was wiped out in the depression. My mother's family is free of taint."

"You're certain?"

"The usual check was made on me in 1935. My God, General, why after seven years of faithful service a thing like this has to surface . . ."

"Oh, I agree. Unfortunately, Himmler got one of these also. I'm afraid he wants another report on you. Family records and so on."

"Didn't you reassure him about me?"

"You know how it is in the service. Himmler and I have had our rivalries. I'm afraid you got caught in the middle."

"Do you have any idea who sent out this poison?"

"It could be any of a dozen. A way of striking at me."

I was stunned. "But you're second in command. Everyone knows you run the SS and the SD, and the Jewish Resettlement program."

"That's why they're wary of me. You see, Erik, I know a great deal about all of them—top to bottom. I know what a collection of thugs and scum many of them are. Useful to us, but not really to the taste of men like us. We're intellectuals, Erik—armed intellectuals, if you will. But most of them—a bloody rogues' gallery."

There were photographs on the wall of some of our leaders, and Heydrich ticked them off as he walked by them. "Goering, drug addict and bribe taker. You should see him in his Roman toga, perfumed, toenails painted, rouge on his cheeks. Rosenberg—a Jewish mistress. Goebbels—scandals on top of scandals. Himmler? Something fishy on his wife's side. And then we come to dignitaries like Streicher and Kaltenbrunner who aren't much better than common criminals. That's why the Führer needs a few brains around him, Erik. People like us."

"I trust I'll never become a member of your rogues' gallery," I said.

He returned to his desk, smiled, dropped the paper with the false charges. "Why should you?" And as I trembled inwardly, he added, "Assuming this letter is —as you claim—a pack of lies."

I am disturbed. As much by the campaign of slander that has been launched against me as by Heydrich's revelations about our leaders.

How much of it is true? And how much intended to frighten me, to show me how wide-ranging his powers are? I cannot resolve the matter in my mind. I tell myself that all men of greatness have failings. For example, in SS circles, it is firmly believed that Roosevelt is a syphilitic. Hence his confinement to a wheelchair. The world knows Churchill is a drunkard.

But it is strange to me that Heydrich would talk so freely, with such mockery, of our chiefs. They hold the power of life and death over millions.

Is there a vague, faint possibility that there is something out of kilter in some of our leaders, and the kind of wars they wage, the government they have created? But, look how we have won support from every level of German life—church, business, corporations, labor unions, educators! The German people, the heirs of Goethe and Beethoven, would not countenance criminals as their prophets and kings. Heydrich exaggerated, perhaps to scare me a little. Or was the secret part-Jew in him at work?

Chelmno, Poland
June 1942

Today, June 17, I rode with Colonel Artur Nebe behind one of those experimental vans. It was quite an experience. Indeed, so profound was it that I forgot my unease over the campaign of slander against me.

Nebe and I rode in a chauffeured staff car, along a secondary dirt road. Some distance ahead of us, a huge van labored to make the grade. It was a drab-green vehicle, totally enclosed, windowless, bearing the sign GHETTO AUTOBUS.

"He's laboring," Nebe said. "Close to forty inside. Too many."

"How long does the process take?"

"Oh, it varies. Ten, twelve minutes. Longer when the truck is so heavily loaded. The gas pressure can be irregular, and sometimes it can take a long time to finish them off."

"And this is your more efficient method?"

"We're trying, Dorf, we're trying."

I don't care for it. It seems a makeshift way of disposing of our problem. Vans and trucks all over Poland and Russia, grunting and groaning their way around the countryside? Instead of letting the carbon monoxide escape into the atmosphere, it can be circulated inside an enclosed space and used to "resettle" Jews. There are permanent installations using carbon monoxide from diesel engines at several camps, but they are also in the more or less experimental stage. Almost all the Jews of Lublin, for example, were given this special treatment with engine-exhaust gases at the Belzec camp. Other such centers are now ready to begin to operate—Treblinka, Auschwitz, Sobibor. But as yet we have found no perfect method, one that combines speed, efficiency, disposal and, if I may be candid, a certain humane element, so as to end suffering quickly.

"The design of those trucks will have to be changed," I said.

"They weren't built for this sort of thing," Nebe said.

Again, the van labored, nearly halted, as the driver shifted into a lower gear.

"What is it like inside?" I asked.

"Oh, a great deal of clawing and scratching goes on. Sometimes you can hear them pounding on the sides."

I cocked an ear, listened.

"Not now. The truck motor is too loud."

After another five minutes along the dirt road—the grade had lessened, so the driver was able to make better time along a level stretch—the van veered off into a field, then into a grove of scrub trees. A familiar stench assailed my nose: rotting bodies. Flies swarmed around us.

Nebe looked at his watch. "Not bad. A half-hour from the Chelmno camp. They should certainly all be finished."

I was shaking my head. "It isn't what we have in mind. We'll be burning out truck engines all over Poland. Far too expensive, laborious."

Nebe agreed with me. "Yes, new methods are needed. Colonel Blobel, Colonel Ohlendorf and I discuss the matter frequently."

"Do you? What else do you discuss in these meetings?"

"Many things."

"Do you ever compose anonymous letters to Himmler and Heydrich about some of your colleagues?"

"I don't know what you're talking about, Major."

"Don't you?"

He did not want to finish the conversation. Instead he motioned for me to follow him to the van, where the driver and another SS man, assisted by some Polish workmen, were pulling naked bodies from the rear of the van. We covered our faces with handkerchiefs. The stench of feces and blood was overwhelming. The bodies were grotesque, stained brown and red, eyes popping, mouths twisted, as if they had died in agony.

Suddenly, I could see the sergeant yanking at a small form, pulling it away from a corpse. Then he pulled and tugged at another. These were children, perhaps six or seven years old. One of them was a male child with the odd shaved head and curling earlocks I had seen among Orthodox Jews of the East. They were alive, mumbling, crawling.

The sergeant quickly killed each one with a shot in the base of their necks.

He came up to Colonel Nebe and saluted. "All dead, sir, except for the two children. Sometimes the mothers protect them."

We walked back to the staff car.

"Bad, bad business," I said.

"Yes, one can be touched by it, even if they are Jews. Some of the men break down."

I looked at Nebe with contempt. He had ordered the massacre of hundreds of thousands. Surely these were the hugest crocodile tears ever shed by anyone. Hard and cold, like my masters, I suppressed any sense of pity. It has become relatively easy for me to dismiss the humanity of those we rid the world of. One can accomplish miracles with the will.

"That isn't what I meant," I said. "It's utterly inefficient and wasteful."

Rudi Weiss' Story

At Theresienstadt, Karl had now been drawn into the circle of artists who were working secretly, at great risk to themselves and their families, to leave a truthful record of the camp.

He joined Frey, Felsher and the other artists with vigor and all his artistic skills. He no longer heard from Inga, and he pretended not to care.

Maria Kalova, one of the artists, remembered him looking angrily as another "inspection team" toured the camp and agreed that Jews really had no cause for complaint.

"Another Red Cross inspection," Maria said.

Karl laughed bitterly. "They have fooled the world. Or else the world doesn't give a damn. What confounds me is that no one seems to ask what right they have to put us in prisons at all. The assumption seems to be that it's all right for Jews to be jailed and treated like dogs, provided they aren't murdered."

Frey walked to the studio window. "I am not so sure we are not being murdered. And I don't mean the deaths here from disease and hunger, the reprisal hangings."

"What do you mean?" Karl asked.

"Systematic murder. Large groups of people. One of the Czech police told me something about trains being sent to Poland . . . stories about new camps."

They returned to their drawing boards.

Karl was working on a large poster. Happy faces. People at work. It read: WORK, OBEY, BE THANKFUL. Suddenly he tossed his brush down, held his head in his hands.

Maria tried to comfort him. "I don't blame you. We all feel that way sometimes."

"Why did they take over the way they did? Doesn't anyone ever say no to them?" He looked up. "Did I ever tell you about my kid brother, Rudi?"

"No. Just about your parents, and your little sister." She hesitated. "And about Inga."

"That Rudi. He ran away. Braver than any of us, or maybe a little crazy. He's dead by now, or maybe he's killed some of them. Four years my junior, but he used to defend me in street fights. I think about him a lot."

"It sounds as if you had a marvelous family. I wish I knew them."

"I'll never see them again. And Inga, damn her. I never want to see her again."

She touched his hand. She was a woman in her late forties, still attractive, with a warm heart. Her husband had been a leader of the Jewish community in Bratislava. He had been taken out and shot on the first day of the German occupation. (She now lives in Ramat Gan, near Tel Aviv, and is the director of an art school; we have become friends.)

"Karl, you mustn't condemn her simply because she is a German, a Christian."

"That's not why. She brought me letters when I was in Buchenwald, accepted my letters. There was this SS sergeant she'd known before the war—a family friend. He was our mailman."

"That is no crime."

"He had a price for his services. She obliged him."

"She did it for you, Karl. So she could hear from you, write to you. From what you tell me, that was her only reason."

Karl sighed, leaned back. "The hell of it is, Maria, she was always stronger than I was. I wanted her to be stronger. And then . . . to give in to that bastard Muller . . ."

"You are not as weak as you think you are," Maria Kalova said. "You are a superb artist."

"A hack. A dauber. I was a disappointment to my parents, especially Papa. Rudi and me both. We never lived up to what they expected."

"I am sure they loved you very much. Just as Inga still loves you."

"She should have said no to Muller."

"You must not hate her for it. When you see her again, and I know you will, you must tell her she is forgiven."

Karl could not be comforted. "You heard what Frey said. We'll all die. There will be no happy reunions."

"You must be more hopeful."

Karl lifted the poster he was finishing. Under it was a charcoal sketch, one of the secret drawings the artists were creating, pictorial histories of the appalling conditions in the camps, the bestial inhumanity of the Germans.

It was called "Ghetto Faces," and it was a mass of starved, hollow-eyed children, holding out their dinner plates, begging for more food. It is a haunted, terrifying picture. I saw it at Theresienstadt when I went there after the war.

"Be careful, Weiss," Frey said.

"Let them catch me."

"It won't be just you," he said. "Several of us are involved. When you joined us, you agreed to keep that stuff hidden, work only at night."

He stared at the faces he had drawn. Maria swears she remembers him asking, of no one in particular: "Rudi . . . where are you, brother?"

By July 1942, we had enough guns to begin raids against our enemy. Or rather, our enemies. Much of the Ukraine was patrolled by local militia. They wore the same uniforms as the SS, with a special insignia, and they entered energetically into the murder and torture of Jews, and anyone else the Nazis felt were threats to their rule of the Soviet Union.

On a sticky humid night, I crouched in a thicket at the side of a road leading to the nearest town, along with Uncle Sasha, Yuri and four others of our band. Our faces were blackened. Each of us had an old bolt-action rifle.

"Scared?" Sasha asked.

"Yes," I said. "Never been more scared."

"Don't get caught. Remember what I told you?"

"They'll torture me, make me tell them where you are."

"That's right. Kill yourself if you have to."

I did not want to get caught; I did not want to kill myself; and for all my bragging to Helena, my insistence that I wanted to get back at them, I was terrified, wondering if I could kill someone. There was hate in me, a great deal of it. But I found there was a lot less courage than I had imagined there would be. In those moments of waiting I felt less contemptuous of those Jews I had seen surrendering quietly, meekly following orders, standing naked, unprotesting, in the ditches.

"How long?" I asked.

Sasha put a finger to his lips. "Ssssh. I hear them."

We heard it also. Boots on the road. A man singing. Voices.

"Germans?" I asked.

"Ukrainian militia," Sasha said.

"Do we want them?"

"We want their guns and their bullets and their boots, boy. Besides, they've killed Jews since the first Germans came here. You know, the bastards have a whole army—an *army*—fighting for the Nazis?"

I felt my hands tremble around the stock and trigger of my gun. So little ammunition did we have that we could not even have target practice. We pretended, shooting empty guns against paper targets. And I was painfully hungry. We ate very little in the family camp.

Six men in SS uniforms came down the road. They obviously were not in the least expectant of any danger, for they walked in close formation, one man singing, others chatting. Their rifles were slung over their shoulders. One seemed drunk and was being helped by a comrade.

"Fire!" Sasha cried.

I needed a moment to react. It did not seem fair to me. We were killing them the way they killed Jews. Too many soccer matches, handshakes, notions of sportsmanship and such schoolboy ideals, Sasha said later.

We blasted them with our rifles. Three men fell at once. One screamed and began hopping about on one foot. Another ran for cover and began firing a machine pistol at the bushes where we were hidden. The last started to run.

Yuri crawled out. He and Sasha began to circle the

man firing with the Schmeisser. Sasha screamed at me, "Get the one who's running!"

I could see him loping down the road, back to the town. He ran clumsily, weighted down by his gun, his pack. Bullets sprayed and painted yellow streaks in the night. Luckily, the man with the machine pistol —he must have been the squad leader—was preoccupied with his attackers. He could have shot me down in an instant as I ran to the fleeing man.

I knew I would catch him. I could always run. When I was a yard behind him—he was breathing heavily, pumping—I smashed at his back with the stock of my rifle. He went down. He whimpered. I dragged him to his feet and stared at him. A kid. Maybe sixteen. He had fat pink cheeks, stupid eyes, and long hair the color of cornflowers. I dragged him back to the hedgerow. The shooting had stopped. All the other Ukrainians were dead. Yuri and the others were stripping the bodies of guns, ammunition belts, boots and anything else of use.

I disarmed my captive and shoved him toward Sasha. He fell to the ground and reached for my boots. He was sobbing in Ukrainian, but I understood not a word he said.

"Take him in the bushes and shoot him," Sasha said.

"Shoot . . . ?"

"I said kill him."

"Why? He's a kid. Can't we send him back?"

Sasha grabbed the rifle from me. "If you don't, I will. That little shit has killed Jews as if they were flies. You let him live, he'll go back to the village and bring the SS. Shoot him."

He was right. We were in a war of annihilation. I dragged the young boy into the woods, shoved him around and muttered something about tying him up. Then I leveled the rifle at his skull and blew the back of his head off.

My hands shook. I began to cry.

Sasha paid no attention to me when I came out of the hedgerow. He was shouting orders at the raiding party, telling them to hurry. "Enough, enough. We don't want their underwear. Just boots, belts, guns. Let's move off."

We ran off the road into the woods, keeping far apart. We walked swiftly. Camp was at least two hours away.

I walked alone, through the dark woods, straggling, stumbling, keeping an eye on Yuri, who was ahead of me. Never had I killed anyone. Oh, I had bragged a great deal, told Helena over and over how much I wanted revenge. But the sight of that stupid boy's terrorized eyes, the knowledge that he was finished, would never see a sunrise, or a girl's face, or swim in a clear lake again—all these rattled me, made me wonder if I were the bloodthirsty avenger I'd imagined myself to be.

I knew something about myself. Killing was indecent, depraved. I would not get used to it. One killed to survive, to keep one's loved ones alive. No good attached to ending the lives of others. That Ukrainian kid had parents, a family, hopes. Like the millions of us now dying for no reason.

I consoled myself. They were notorious murderers, paid killers, merciless in their hunting down and shooting of Jews. There should have been triumph, exaltation in my heart. But I was no warrior King David, exulting in the slaying of thousands. I was miserable, and cold, and drained. Worse, I began to wonder if there was any point to our resistance, to Sasha's "family camp," his hardheaded determination to evade, strike, kill. But there had to be, I decided. We were all marked for death by the Nazis, and the death Sasha had chosen was better than the one they had planned for every Jew in Europe.

Back in the camp, exhausted, I rested on the cot in the hut I shared with Helena and another couple, and stared at the sagging boards in the roof.

"He was a kid, maybe sixteen," I said again.

"Rudi, don't talk about it any more."

"Yuri says he was the kind who kills Jews for pay, for a loaf of bread."

"Please, please, Rudi . . . no more."

"I never killed anyone before."

"You had to."

"The back of his head. It sort of floated away. Look. His blood on my tunic."

She got a damp rag and began to rub the dark stain. "He would have killed you. He's killed hundreds."

"Yes. I should be happy. Dancing. But we're not like them. We can't do it and be happy. They probably get drunk, and dance and screw after they kill Jews."

We said nothing. Outside, I could hear Sasha, tireless, driven, taking inventory of our haul from the raid. The big prize was the machine pistols. Now we could go after some Germans.

"My baby, my baby," Helena said. "Why are we made to live this way?"

"I don't understand it. My parents didn't either, and they're probably dead by now. Maybe Sasha knows. Maybe he's the only one who understands. Kill or get killed."

"We want to live, Rudi, that's all. You've said it yourself."

"It's not enough. Where will we go? Who'll want us?"

"Oh, Rudi . . . to Palestine. Eretz Israel. Mr. and Mrs. Weiss."

"Me? Picking oranges?"

"I'll make you do it. I'm your wife. Kiss me."

"Yes, you are."

We held each other. She kissed me over and over, eyes, nose, ears, my neck. "Orange groves and cedar trees. And farming villages. And the blue sea."

"I almost believe you. Not altogether, but almost."

"You must believe me."

I sat up. She had, for the moment, made me forget about the boy I had killed. There was laughter outside the hut: Jews with guns. I wanted to be part of them again. Odd, how brief had been my doubts, my fears.

"You saved my life in Prague," I said. "I owe you a trip to this great Zionist homeland you keep talking about."

"Not a trip. Our life. Where they can't jail us, or beat us, or kill us. Or even call us bad names."

I looked into her dark, slightly slanted eyes. "My small, dark Czechoslovakian wife. Do you remember the first time we made love in Prague? In that cold apartment?"

"Don't embarrass me, Rudi. You make me feel like . . . like a street woman."

"It was beautiful. The best thing I ever did in my life."

"For me too, Rudi."

"Each time we're together, the wonder of it drives me wild. Two people being close like that. Not just the bodies, Helena, but as if we became one person, I don't know—God, or nature, or something, deciding that's the way it should be. The way a flower must bloom at some time."

"I know, dearest," she said. "That's why we won't die. We'll never die."

Erik Dorf's Diary

Berlin
June 1942

Heydrich died today. June 4, 1942.

My patron, hero, idol. The most brilliant man I've ever known. I am shattered, inconsolable.

Six days ago a bomb was thrown under his car by Czech terrorists as he was driving in Prague.

I offered to fly down at once to be at his bedside, but Himmler dissuaded me. The office had to be kept running. Heydrich's spine was severed, and he died in extreme agony. A rumor is going around that on his deathbed he expressed deep contrition for his deeds.

Himmler has wasted no time in punishing the guilty. Over 1,300 people have been summarily executed in Prague and Brno to avenge our fallen leader. And a village called Lidice has been razed, all of its inhabitants have been killed or imprisoned. Goebbels (never a close associate of my late chief) had 152 Jewish hostages in Berlin shot. The resettlement program for Jews henceforth will be known as "Operation Reinhard" in his memory.

So shattered have I been by this event, that I have been unable to keep my memoirs for several days. They have named no successor to Heydrich (who could fill his shoes?), and with the enemies I have made in various branches of the service, always secure in Heydrich's patronage, I am now worried about my future.

On the day on which Heydrich was attacked— May 29—Marta and I had a painful scene. Things have become strained at home. She is devoted, loving . . . but she has always felt that I am not ambitious enough. And I must confess my sexual appetites, my attentions to her, have diminished. A psychologist perhaps could explain it. But I have seen so many naked bodies—disgusting, wasted, dirty, doomed Jewish bodies—alive one minute, dead and bloodied the next, that in some strange way I am revolted by the very thought of the body, *anyone's*. Is life perhaps more important in the abstract, in our minds and our souls? Were not the venerable saints and hermits who ignored their bodies nearer to some great truth?

And so, on that warm May night before I got the news, I was sitting up in bed, smoking, unable to sleep, thinking of those heaped corpses, the way the Jews fell on one another in Minsk, Zhitomir, Babi Yar, a hundred places.

Marta awakened. "Erik? Is anything wrong?"

"No, darling. I'm sorry my smoking bothered you."

"You don't sleep well. Not since that last trip to the east."

"There is nothing wrong with me. Just a little tired.

It's you, sweetheart, who must preserve your health. For the children."

"I'm fine." She rested her head on my chest. An arm embraced my loins. I felt revulsion, but I did not move.

"You mustn't hide it. Marta, ever since that day in the doctor's office—what, seven years ago—I knew you were ill. You've always minimized your illness, and I admire you for it. You're braver than your husband with his black uniform and Luger."

"How can you say that? With all the dangerous jobs you've had? All the important things you've done for Heydrich?"

I took her arm from me, sat on the edge of the bed, lit another cigarette. "Marta, I'm afraid the war is lost. Maybe it was lost the day the Americans came in. Their industry, their armies will be the end of us. They will supply the Russians, and the Russians will show us no mercy."

"No. I don't believe it."

"I've heard the bigshots. They're talking of deals already—playing the west against the Soviets. But it won't work."

"We are going to win."

"Darling," I said, "think that, if it will make you feel better. But I see what is happening."

"Erik, you must never talk this way." She is made of forged steel.

"Listen to me, Marta." I put the cigarette out and turned to face her. Then I stopped talking.

A week ago, I had seen some of Nebe's men shove a young Jewess into the gassing van. She was blond, fair, more beautiful than my wife. She had refused to undress. They had torn the clothes from her body, then kicked her in the buttocks as if she were an animal, and driven her with their rubber truncheons into the death wagon. For a second, I saw this woman's face instead of my wife's.

"Listen to me," I went on. "Some day people may tell monstrous lies about us. What we did in Poland, Russia. Lies, all of them."

"I will not listen to them."

"They will try to force you to listen. When they do, you must tell the children that I was always a good and honorable servant of the Reich, that I do nothing more than obey orders like a combat soldier . . . orders from the very top."

"I won't let anyone lie about you."

Nebe . . . Ohlendorf . . . Eichmann . . . Blobel. Their faces loomed in front of me. Sure of themselves. No apologies, no doubts. They took orders, carried them out. Someone jokingly asked Colonel Biberstein, our former cleric, whether he sometimes said prayers for the Jews about to be shot, and he responded, his eyes merry: "One does not cast pearls before swine."

I wanted to tell her about my comrades, but I could only choke out some disjointed phrases about Hans Frank boasting of the millions he would take care of, of Hoess, dutifully obeying orders, building this processing factory at Auschwitz.

"You must be dutiful also. That is how you get ahead."

"Yes, yes. Hoess, incredible fellow. Spent eight years in jail for murder. In the party's interest, of course. He was framed by Jews. He adores his wife and his children, a naturalist, loves animals. An ideal German. And yet what he's doing now—"

"Stop! I don't want to hear about them. You're better than the lot. You're educated, refined, intelligent. Better even than the ones at the top!"

Abruptly, I began to shiver, and I asked her to hold me. We nestled together in bed for a few minutes. She seemed to be excited sexually, but I could not respond.

"Oh, Erik, my child, you are trembling."

"Hold me, Marta."

"You must never doubt yourself. Never doubt what you are doing."

How much does she know about my work? Some of our wives know all—Hoess' lives right at Auschwitz. Others remain good ignorant German *Hausfraus*—

church, kitchen, children—and ask no questions.

At that point the phone rang. It was Heydrich's office with the news that he had been severely wounded in an assassination attempt and was in a Prague hospital. I was needed at headquarters at once.

I expected Marta to weep, or scream, but instead she grabbed my shoulders and said, "Be aggressive, be bold. This is your chance."

As I dressed, I said nothing. I refused to believe that Heydrich would die. Not that creative, vibrant man.

"You can succeed him!" Marta cried.

Hitler calls Heydrich's death "a lost battle." But there are suspicions that Reichsführer Himmler is secretly relieved. Himmler gave the eulogy at the funeral and was full of praise. He called him noble, valiant, honorable, a master, an educator. He followed the coffin, right behind Heydrich's widow, and held Heydrich's sons by the hands. Later, Himmler supposedly told someone he "felt a bit funny holding two mongrels by the hand"—a reference to the rumors of Heydrich's Jewish blood.

And now I have no protector, no patron. It was believed in many circles that once the war was over, and at a time when Hitler was ready to step down, Heydrich would have been a logical successor—so superior in intellect and imagination was he to the others. Now all that is over; and I am afraid all is over for Germany also.

Rudi Weiss' Story

Slowly, the Jewish Fighting Organization was being formed in Warsaw.

My Uncle Moses was now in the thick of it. He was one of the older men, in his early fifties, never very daring, quietly humorous, but he threw his lot in with the younger people, the Zionists and political activists. My father, telling my mother little, also gave his support to the resistance fighters.

Earlier in this account I mentioned a boy named Aaron Feldman, a student of my mother's in the ghetto school. This boy, about thirteen, wiry, small, fearless, had been an expert smuggler, and he too now joined the resistance. His knowledge of tunnels, alleys, holes in the wall, the timetables and characters of various guards—ghetto police, Polish police, SS—proved invaluable.

A prime need of the resistance was guns. And so contact was made with Polish resistance groups outside the wall to see if they could be of help.

Uncle Moses volunteered to follow young Feldman into the "Aryan" side to buy the first guns, contact having already been made through messages. (If you were caught outside the wall, punishment was immediate death by firing squad.)

Moses carried a package of drugs—his excuse would be that he was on an errand of mercy, delivering pharmaceuticals to gravely ill friends. It would not have saved him, but it was better than no excuse.

My father tried to dissuade him. "You're too old for this."

"Too old for almost anything else," Moses said. "If I'm lost, the only loss will be to modern pharmacy."

"Move out," Zalman said.

And so Moses followed the boy into the night.

They climbed stairways, came out on rooftops, descended down ladders, hid behind trash bins. At one point, they halted while the daily death cart rumbled by—a flatbed loaded with a dozen skeletal corpses. Food was running out. People looked after themselves. Who could blame them? The Germans had imprisoned half a million people in an area of Warsaw intended for 25,000. They lived nine and ten to a room, caught typhus and cholera from one another, waited for death.

Aaron knew just when to avoid a policeman walking

his beat, where the next hiding place—cellar, abandoned hut, pile of rubbish—could be found.

Finally, he asked Moses to help him remove a large paving stone on a side street, then another. There was barely room for them to squeeze through. They replaced the stones. Moses struck a light and saw they were in a tunnel. They walked for about ten minutes and Moses realized they were passing under the infamous wall, into the Christian district of Poland. Once the boy seemed to lose his way, seemed confused, and Moses (he told Eva later) had visions of them suffocating in the tunnel, or wandering until they starved. But Aaron suddenly stopped and pointed to a rusted metal cover.

"Up," the boy said. "It goes up. Push."

The two of them shoved at the metal cover and it slowly lifted from the roof of the tunnel. It was obvious to Moses that the boy had used this passageway many times.

With a clatter that terrified the old man, the lid was shoved aside, and the two lifted themselves onto a cobbled side street. They were outside the ghetto walls.

"The other side," Moses said. "I guess you have been here many times."

But the boy was not listening. With a sixth sense I understand from my years on the run, he grabbed Moses' sleeve and dragged him into a hallway. They hid in the darkness. A second later an SS patrol car rode by slowly, the soldiers shining lights into doorways, alleys, stores. Then it moved on.

"How did you know they were coming?" Moses asked.

"I can smell them."

My uncle could not tell whether Aaron was joking or not.

More back streets, alleys, hidden passageways. And finally to an apartment building. Aaron led my uncle into the hallway, down a flight of steps, and to a door opening on a basement apartment.

He knocked four times.

The door opened and a young Pole, whom my uncle remembered as being active in patriotic groups, opened the door for them. His name was Anton. There was another, older man in the room, whose name Eva could not recall.

"You are Anton," Uncle Moses said.

"Yes. I don't want to know who you are. But I know him." He indicated the flop-eared boy in the oversized coat. "I've seen him around."

"Yes, he knows his way," Moses said. "Well. Here is the money." He gave Anton a thick envelope.

Anton counted it. Then he took a wooden box from the older man and set it on the table.

Moses lifted the lid. Inside was a single revolver, an old-looking firearm.

"I was told you would have a dozen," my uncle said.

"One gun. It's the best we could do."

"I gave you money for twelve."

"We'll owe you the others," Anton said.

"That is not fair. Give me the rest of the money back. We had an agreement."

"We still have one. You don't want the gun, leave it here. My word is good. When we have more guns, you'll get them."

Moses knew he had no choice. He threw his arms up. "Why don't you help us more? We have the same enemy. The Germans have made no secret of their plans for you. You will be their slaves, just a notch higher than the Jews. I know you have not exactly liked us in the past. But surely now . . ."

Anton said nothing.

Aaron tugged at Moses' sleeve, as if to say, "There's nothing to be gained here, let's go."

"We will help you fight Germans," Moses pleaded. "If we get together, we can drive them off, help the Allies."

Anton looked at him with what seemed almost pity. "But Jews don't fight," the Pole said. "You know it's true. You know how to make money, to run businesses, you pray a lot. But you don't fight."

"We will now," Aaron said. "You'll see."

The Pole patted him on the head—the first sign of humanity Moses observed in him.

The older Pole spoke up. "Get out, both of you. The longer you stay, the more danger for us."

They returned to the ghetto as they had come, in peril every minute. But Aaron knew the secret ways, and they came to resistance headquarters with their single gun.

A few days later, Mordechai Anelevitz assembled a group of resistance people in his secret headquarters. The most important people there were the Zionist youths—boys and girls in their late teens.

The older people—Uncle Moses, my father, Zalman, Eva—sat against the wall and watched. Anelevitz himself was a dedicated Zionist and had been a leader of a group called Hashomer Hatzair for many years. But now he was not interested in anyone's politics. He wanted to train soldiers, fighters.

With a single gun.

He stood in front of the young people and showed them the workings of the gun. Trigger. Barrel. Chamber.

He then looked at the young boys and girls. "Who wants to be first?"

A boy came forward. He was no more than sixteen.

"It could be Rudi," Eva remembers my father saying.

On the distant wall was a paper cutout of a German soldier—coal-scuttle helmet, tunic, a large swastika.

Anelevitz turned the boy toward the target and slapped the revolver in his hand. "Sight along the barrel. There is a small sight that should rest right between the V. The top of the sight should touch the target."

The boy extended his arm.

"Take one deep breath and hold it," Anelevitz said. "Then, do not jerk the trigger, but squeeze it slowly, as if you were unaware when it will go off."

The boy followed instructions. Everyone watched

him. He pulled the trigger, and of course there was nothing but a loud *click*. They did not have a single round of ammunition.

But everyone cheered and laughed.

Uncle Moses said to my father, "That is a Jewish army for you. One gun, no bullets, and a lot of opinions."

"It is a beginning," my father said.

Erik Dorf's Diary

Auschwitz
October 1942

Since Heydrich's death, I am somewhat in suspension. Himmler, fearful of creating another rival, has named no successor, and is trying to run everything himself—the transports, the work camps, the new installations.

Today, I was at Auschwitz, the former Polish town of Osweicim. It will be the main arena for the final solution. It is near a rail junction, on a main line. Forests surround it. Many Jewish ghettoes are nearby. And there is a whole complex of war factories around it—I. G. Farben, Siemens, others.

Rudolf Hoess, the commandant, listened attentively as Himmler unrolled a huge diagrammatic map and explained his desires to Hoess.

"Auschwitz will be doubled in size. And these new systems should be expanded at once."

The systems are ingenious—a waiting area, large tiled rooms for the actual act, conveyor belts to take the bodies to the furnaces. Of course, they were in operation already, but on a small scale.

"Where will the labor come from?" Hoess asked.

"You will get more laborers than you can handle. A selection process must be instituted. Jews who appear capable of work can be spared for labor details —cleanup, sanitation and so on. Any useless ones, the old, the sick, the cripples, the children, can be sent immediately from the railroad siding to the delousing plant."

This is another of our euphemisms. Delousing means something else entirely.

"I shall have to fight with I. G. Farben for workers," Hoess said.

"They will do as they are told. This work takes priority over any manufacturing process."

"Even of war materiel?" he asked.

"Yes. Eichmann regularly takes trains from the army for transports, and the army does not object."

"Hoess," the Reichsführer said. "We are moving toward a grand destiny, something fate, or God, or history has ordained us for. I'm told your family wanted you to study for the priesthood, so this should be something you can understand."

"I won't disappoint you. From my childhood, Reichsführer, I have been taught to obey."

They talked about Heydrich's death, the tragic loss to the party. All agreed that an efficient, productive operation of an expanded Auschwitz, together with the centers at Chelmno, Belzec, Treblinka and Sobibor, would be fitting memorials to that great man.

Himmler suddenly looked up from the vast map, the diagrams on the table. His small nose quivered, like a rabbit's, and his scholarly pince-nez jiggled.

"The stink," he said. "From the chimneys. Hoess, see if something can be done about it. After all, as noble as our work is, we want it played down. It is for our own knowledge alone."

I was tempted to laugh. How does one annihilate eleven million people—as Hitler and Himmler have ordered—and keep it secret?

Rudi Weiss' Story

Once more, Inga lost track of Karl. She knew he was in Theresienstadt, the so-called "Paradise Ghetto" in Prague, but she had no way of reaching him.

She refused to communicate with Muller, or to see him when he came to Berlin. He bragged that he was instrumental in having Karl sent to Czechoslovakia, to what he called "a vacation resort" for Jews; but he had no way of getting mail to him now. Inga would no longer give her body to Muller, whom she detested.

But on his visits to Berlin, he invariably came to her apartment, pleaded with her, vowed his love for her, and when she tried to leave, followed her to the street.

One day, as she was entering St. Hedwig's Cathedral—she was not an observant Christian, but she felt the need to talk to Father Lichtenberg—Muller accosted her.

"I told you not to follow me," she said.

"I'm trying to help you. Praying won't do you any good."

She hated him. But Inga was determined and resourceful. "What will? Can you get Karl out of that other camp?"

"No. I won't lie to you." He seized her hand. "I love you. I am entitled to your love."

"Let go of me."

"You can divorce him. He's an enemy of the Reich. He'll be worth nothing when they let him out of Theresienstadt—if they ever do. You are a Christian, an Aryan, you can get rid of him now. Listen to me. Since those times in my barracks . . . I can't stop thinking of you. I do love you."

She yanked free. "Get away from me. Don't come near me again."

"You used to beg me to get letters to him. Now I am begging you."

Inga said, "I hate you. I hate all of you. You're incapable of love. All you know is brutality, how to inflict pain. You glory in it. And the worst of it is, we have let you take us over, willingly. A whole nation, my nation, finding joy in hurting people, in causing pain and death. Muller, I am as evil as you are."

"No, no. This is a war. Sure it's cruel. People get

hurt. I had nothing against Karl. I have nothing personal against Jews."

"Leave me alone. Go away."

She walked into the cathedral. Muller watched her, but did not follow. He waited.

As I have said, Inga was not a regular communicant. She and Karl practiced no religion. But she had remembered Father Lichtenberg's sermons of two years ago, and she wondered if he could give her some advice.

In the rear room she found the old sacristan she remembered from some years back. He was lighting candles. It was dusk.

"Yes, miss?" he asked.

"Is Father Lichtenberg here?"

"Oh, no, miss. The father is gone."

"Gone?"

"Yes. They took him away."

"They?"

He whispered. "Gestapo. They warned him to stop talking about the Jews all the time. It was none of his business. They searched his room and found sermons he was going to give about the Jews, saying how they shouldn't be hurt."

"Where did they take him?"

"Place called Dachau."

"Oh, dear God. That good man."

The sacristan turned his back, as if the matter were closed, and kept lighting candles, muttering as he did. "I warned him myself, but he kept saying someone had to talk about it. But why him? Other priests and ministers were smarter. Kept their mouths shut. Why, I hear up in Bremen, they're dedicating churches in the Führer's name. And it's no secret we're all praying for the army to beat the Bolsheviks. So why not forget this Jewish business?"

Inga paused in front of an altar, kneeled, crossed herself. On it, on either side of a crucifix, were two photographs—one of Father Bernard Lichtenberg and the other of Pope Pius XII.

Muller had not left. "Can I walk you home?" he asked. "Maybe after your prayers you will feel more charitable toward me."

As Inga told me later, the idea struck her suddenly, like a flash of summer lightning. If the brave priest could suffer the fate of the Jews, so would she.

"You can do more than walk me home," she said.

"Good. If this is what church does for someone, I may become a believer myself."

"That isn't what I mean."

"Inga, my darling, you know how I feel. I would do anything for you."

She stopped. "Denounce me. Turn me in to the Gestapo. You have a thousand excuses—defaming the Führer, aiding Jews, spreading lies about the war effort."

"You'll be imprisoned."

"That's what I want. I want to be sent to Theresienstadt. I understand they have a section for Christian prisoners there, that they are not all Jews."

Muller stopped, as if stunned by a brick. He could not comprehend the deep impression that Father Lichtenberg's fate had made on her. The notion had struck her almost at once. Some Christians would have to make a stand, demonstrate their support of the Jews. She thought of that kind, gray, intelligent priest, consigned to a concentration camp, for nothing more than living his faith as he saw it, for speaking words of mercy. She would do the same.

Her life had become unbearable without Karl. She was truly alone now. There was no communication with her family. She had become mechanized, indifferent—apartment, job, shopping, sleep. A life without love—even in a prison barracks—would be preferable to the life she now led.

"Lichtenberg was an old fool," Muller said. "You're trying to be as foolish. I warn you, Inga, the best of those camps, like Theresienstadt, is no beer garden. They get sick and starve and die there. You'll be marked as worse than a Jew."

"I don't care. I have made my mind up."

"You'll give up your freedom for Karl Weiss?"

"Yes."

Muller tried once to reach for her waist, but when she drew away, he stopped. He said nothing. Only stared at her, then nodded slowly.

Erik Dorf's Diary

Hamburg
January 1943

Under orders from my new chief, Ernest Kaltenbrunner, who has been appointed Heydrich's successor, I have been sent here on a most important mission.

Hoess is building Auschwitz with great speed, expanding it into the largest facility of its kind in the world. I don't mean the usual barracks, the factories, the workrooms, and kitchens. I mean the centers for special handling. (I might as well call them what they are—*factories for mass killing.*)

Hoess has erected, in addition to the makeshift early chambers, with their limited capacities, two vast complexes, containing anterooms, the actual chambers for the gassing and the ovens for final disposal. The famous Erfurt construction firm, Topf, specialists in the building of ovens, are putting up the crematoria. The biggest private corporations and engineering firms are aiding Hoess in his work, and, I might add, are making handsome profits.

I've seen diagrams and plans. The most impressive is the underground chamber, or *Leichenkeller,* complete with an electric elevator for hauling the dead to the furnaces.

Hoess is also anxious to keep observers—Poles, locals, anyone not connected with the work—away from these units. Therefore he has had an attractive landscaped "green belt" of tall trees built around them.

But there remains a very real impediment to the implementation of the final solution.

It concerns the agent. Carbon monoxide is proving inefficient. It takes too long. The bodies are badly mangled, making the shaving of heads and extraction of gold difficult.

Hence, I was sent to the Hamburg firm of Tesch & Stabenow to look into something more efficient. There have been experiments on a limited basis with an agent called Zyklon B, which is largely hydrogen cyanide and is simple to use.

Mr. Bruno Tesch took me into his small laboratory, explaining as we entered that his firm is largely a retailer and distributor, and that a vast cartel called Degesch, formed of several private firms, actually manufactures the material, and developed its use for large-scale fumigation against rats, lice and other vermin.

We walked among the crucibles, retorts and Bunsen burners. among the white-coated chemists. Tesch told me that Zyklon B has a prussic-acid base. He held up a can about the size of a large tomato tin, explaining that it had to be kept tightly sealed, not only because of its lethal nature, but because it vaporized the instant it struck the air.

Pointblank I asked him if it had been tested on humans. Tesch claimed no such knowledge, remarking that I would know better. He was only a businessman. I persisted, using information I'd gotten at the SS Hygiene Section. Had not people died in terrible agony in tests? Again, he denied such knowledge. All he could do was recommend it as clean, quick, lethal, and usable without machinery, such as a diesel engine to produce carbon monoxide.

I asked him why he mentioned carbon monoxide, and he said he'd heard rumors. Nothing confirmed, mind you, just rumors. I tossed the can a few times. It was as innocent as a tin of cocoa.

Then I placed an order with him. Shipping documents were to specify it was for "disinfecting only." The shipment was to go to our "Hygiene Section" in Berlin. He understood.

At a gray slate table he paused and showed me a glass Petri dish, covered with a glass lid. Would I care to see how it worked? I said I would. Was there no danger? No, Tesch replied, it was a single crystal. It would dissipate. Besides, he'd opened the window.

Tesch lifted the glass cover. From the tiny blue grain, wisps of gray smoke rose, infusing the air with a harsh acrid odor. I pressed a handkerchief to my nose.

                                            Berlin
                                    January 1943

Hoess came to our headquarters today, complaining that it was wrong to take him off the job, with all the work we had burdened him with. But he was pleased with my report on Zyklon B.

He showed me photographs of the interior of a typical chamber—shower heads (false ones), faucets, pipes, tile walls. Outside, signs reading BATH HOUSE —DELOUSING.

He explained the differences between the four chambers, the two underground units, with their intricate machinery, and the two aboveground chambers. There were apertures on the roofs or the side through which the cyanide pellets could be introduced.

I reminded him that a peephole at each chamber might be a good idea. How else could he determine what was taking place? He agreed.

He had made plans for moving his huge diesel engines about, and in fact, thousands were already being "resettled" with the carbon monoxide system. I told him he would not need them at all any more. They were cumbersome and inefficient, and we had found a better way.

Hoess, ever obedient, nodded. "You'd better order a stockpile. Auschwitz, Sobibor, Chelmno, Maidanek, Treblinka—they'll be going full blast."

I made a note. A steady supply will be a problem. Tesch informed me that Zyklon B had a life—even canned—of only three months. It is unthinkable to stockpile useless material. Therefore a continuous flow of the agent will be necessary, a system whereby the centers will be able to maintain a supply of fresh, usable gas.

As I was mentally trying to solve this problem—perhaps a central supply depot at SS Hygiene Headquarters could do the job—Ernst Kaltenbrunner entered my office.

He is a huge man, almost seven feet tall, with a scarred face, not from any dueling incident or combat, but from an automobile accident. Why Himmler selected him to succeed an intellectual, creative man like Heydrich I do not know. True, Kaltenbrunner was a lawyer, but he has no fineness in him, no subtlety. He is a man I fear.

"Dorf. Hoess." He glanced at the photographs Hoess brought with him.

"General," I said, "Major Hoess and I have been reviewing the special handling problems."

"Special handling!" Kaltenbrunner laughed. "By God, Dorf, I was warned when I got this job that I'd have a master of language on my staff. You mean killing centers, don't you?"

"Of course, sir."

"Hoess," he said. "Will you excuse us a minute?"

Hoess saluted, picked up his photos and diagrams and left.

Kaltenbrunner had brought a rather odd item into my office. He was hardly the sensitive type, yet it looked like an artist's portfolio.

He smiled at me—the smile of a polar bear, a shark. "By now you've learned I'm a different sort than that violin-playing half-breed you worked for."

I told him he was being unfair to Heydrich's memory.

"Oh, screw him. He's dead. Jesus, those deathbed rantings of his. Forgiveness for what he'd done to the Jews. He was a kike himself."

"He was in agony. His spine was severed. Delirium."

"Don't bother defending him. Worry about yourself."

What is the truth about Heydrich? He was more of an enigma than I will ever know. Is it true, as some said, he lived only to "kill the Jew in himself"? Who knows the truth? It does not matter any more. We are knee-deep in blood. Any pause, any faltering, will imply—as Heydrich's alleged deathbed mutterings did —that we doubt the rightness of our mission.

As much as I am terrified of Kaltenbrunner, I need him. I am part of the cause, the great campaign to change Europe, the holy crusade. Flattery got me far with Heydrich; I tried more of the same on this hideous giant.

"Why should I worry? The job is getting done, thanks to your superb work. The ghettoes are being reduced. The new camps are ready to start functioning on a larger scale."

"Stop babbling." He pointed a finger the size of a bratwurst at me. "Black marks against you, Dorf. I've seen the letters in your file. Father maybe a Red."

"I was investigated and cleared."

"Blobel, Nebe, some of the others complain about you. Schemer, informer."

I said nothing. What good does it do to fight liars? They are in trouble themselves. The Einsatzgruppen are giving way to a far more thorough, speedy program.

Kaltenbrunner dropped the subject. Then he opened the portfolio on his desk and with his giant hands began to spread five large pen-and-ink drawings on the table.

"What the hell do you make of these?" he asked.

I studied the drawings. They were obviously originals. They were unsigned. And they were done by professionals, men with talent.

They bore titles, and were evidently depictions of life inside one of our camps. The style was frightening, satiric, rather like George Grosz at his worst, pictures full of bitterness and anger, distortions of the human condition.

I read the titles as I studied each work. " 'Waiting

for the End.' Old people. What's this one? 'Routine Punishment.' " It was a drawing of a gallows with four Jews dangling from the crossbeam. SS guards, shown as fat, apelike creatures, stood around grinning.

There was one called "The Master Race"—more piggish humanoids. Another, "Ghetto Children," kids with starved, haunted eyes. And one entitled "Roll Call"—a rather terrifying sea of people standing as if under a great cloud, while SS guards checked their ranks.

"One of our agents found them in Prague," Kaltenbrunner said. "All we need is for the Red Cross to see this kind of crap."

I could appreciate his concern. We are going to enormous expense and effort to sell the world the notion of Theresienstadt as a lovely vacation home, a resort for Jews. Recently, one of our best documentary film makers shot a movie there called "The Führer Gives a City to the Jews." It was superb—happy, smiling Jewish women in the dress shops, Jewish orchestras, a bakery where one could almost smell the fresh rye bread, athletic contests, all in a most attractive setting. It is designed to get the few remaining Jews in Germany—wealthy hostages, VIPs, decorated war veterans—to volunteer for Theresienstadt. More important, it is designed to show to those who have been protesting our alleged ill treatment of Jews.

But this kind of horror propaganda, these dreadful drawings, if put in circulation, can destroy all our efforts in this direction.

"Dorf, get down to Czechoslovakia and get in touch with Eichmann," said Kaltenbrunner. "Between the two of you, you should be able to find out who drew this shit."

"I assure you, sir, I'll find out."

"You goddam well better." His ogrelike figure bent over the desk, angrily looking at the pictures. "If these bastards did five, maybe they've done fifty. Maybe they want to smuggle this stuff out in batches, and undo all our work."

"May I take these?" I asked.

"Yes. And find out who drew them, Dorf. If you don't I'll start reading your file again."

I saluted, tried to hide my fear.

As I left, he began to dress down Hoess for not moving fast enough at Auschwitz.

Rudi Weiss' Story

Karl was now a full-fledged member of the "artist' cabal" at Theresienstadt.

Each night, with drawn blinds, he and Felsher and Frey and a few others worked at producing a damning record, in pen-and-ink, charcoal, water colors, of what life was like in that pesthole. They knew about the lying film the Nazis had made; they would counteract the lies with their art. (Most of the people who appeared in that film, "The Führer Gives a City to the Jews," were eventually gassed in Auschwitz.)

Frey was the head of the team. One night, as they were at work, Frey began checking one of the folios. He noticed something awry and turned to Felsher. "Those sketches we did last week? You know . . . Karl's of the children. The one called "The Master Race"? I can't seem to locate them."

Felsher looked about nervously. He knew that the pictures, if discovered by the SS, could produce disastrous results. "I . . . I sold them," he said.

The others stopped working and looked up.

"You sold them?" Frey asked.

"Yes . . . yes. One of the Czech policemen wanted some. He's a decent guy, he likes us. I only sold five of them."

Frey was upset. "Felsher, we agreed that those pictures must stay hidden in the camp. If the Nazis get hold of them, we're finished. Besides, some of them were mine, some were Weiss'."

Poor Felsher! Maria Kalova recalls that he looked as if he wanted to cry. "Look, Frey, I needed cigarettes, a jar of marmalade. I . . . I won't do it again. I'll share the cigarettes."

"To hell with the cigarettes," Frey said.

Maria came forward. "You've put us in great danger," she said.

Karl spoke. "What's the difference? We play this game thinking our pictures will ever make a difference. Don't feel guilty, Felsher."

But Frey was worried. "I pray the Gestapo doesn't get its hands on them. All of you pray."

Felsher was frightened. He kept muttering, "Is it a crime to want a pack of cigarettes?"

They returned to their tables, their easels.

"Poor guy," Karl said. "I sometimes wonder whether all this secret work is worth it."

"So do I," Maria sighed.

Karl was drawing a picture entitled "Transport East." More and more, old, sick so-called "unproductives" were being sent to some unknown destination in Poland. Rest homes, they were told; places where they could get better medical care. The sketch showed a line of stooped, defeated Jews, all marked with the yellow star, boarding a train.

"What is this all about?" Karl asked. "Why are they sending them away?"

Maria looked at her own drawing. "I'm not sure. But there are stories . . . of course, no one believes them."

There was a sound of footsteps outside. Normally the guards and the ghetto police left the studio alone at night. It was assumed the artists loved their work so much that they worked overtime.

Everyone began to hide their work—in the tables, in drawers.

"Go on, Weiss, see who it is," Frey said.

Karl walked to the door, opened it—and was face to face with his wife, Inga.

"Inga . . ."

"Karl, my darling."

They did not embrace at once, so dumfounded was

Karl. She was carrying a valise. Her hair was bound in a scarf. She had just arrived with a small shipment of Christian "enemies of the state." There was a special section of Theresienstadt reserved for non-Jews; among these prisoners were numerous Czech clergymen who had protested Nazi measures.

For a moment she stood in the dim light, staring at his gaunt face. She had to make the first gesture of love. She came to him and embraced him. They kissed. But he was like an automaton, a robot, barely responding. He seemed almost fearful of her.

"How . . . how did you get here?"

"Getting *into* a camp is no problem. I decided I could not let you be without me. If I could not free you, I would come to you."

He tried to talk, found his mouth dry.

"Oh, my darling. You're pale and thin. Your hair is gray. But you are as handsome as ever."

Embarrassed, Karl led her into the main studio. "I'm all right. You can see. I have a job, an easy one. Friends."

He introduced the others. "Frey, Felsher, Maria Kalova."

Maria came forward and hugged Inga. "Karl has spoken of you a great deal. He has never forgotten you."

Inga smiled. "I'm happy to meet all of you."

Frey tried to be cheerful. "I don't know what you know about this place. But it is better than other camps, if you keep busy. And we're all pretty busy here."

"That's right," Felsher said. "We're still around."

Frey gave Karl the key to the storeroom. A cot was kept there, where the ghetto police sometimes stole a snooze while on duty. "Here," he said. "You must want to talk to her."

"There might even be some tea left," Maria said. "Go, have a happy reunion."

As soon as they were in the small dark room, Inga seized him and kissed him passionately. She had hungered for him. It was as if she wanted to erase the stain of Muller's defilement with her love for Karl. He resisted at first—not so much resisted, as remained cold, apart. Then as her mouth kept probing his, her face nestling closer, her hands stroking his lean back, he responded.

"Oh, my darling Inga," he sobbed. "I never thought I would see you again. They burn your hopes out. They make you hate yourself, hate life . . ."

"I told you not to despair, Karl."

"Yes, I remember your letters to Buchenwald. Always full of hope, kind words." He broke away from her and faced the wall. "And I remember who brought them."

"Muller told you," she said.

"He bragged about it."

"I knew he would. I could not help it."

Karl turned, crying gently. "Inga . . . why?"

"To reach you. To keep us together."

"You chose a strange way. When I think of that pig, that beast, with you . . . joined . . . with you, Inga . . ."

"Karl, you must believe me. I tried not to. There was never any love for him. I hated him. I felt like a whore when I was with him. I hate him even more now."

"God, I would have preferred not hearing from you."

"Would you?"

"Others have been brave enough to remain alone— no letters, no family. And they've survived. Old Felsher doesn't have a soul in the world. Maria Kalova's husband was shot by the Gestapo the day they entered her city."

"I felt you were not like other people. You needed my love, if only in a letter."

"You mean I am weaker than other people. Yes, there's truth to that. The poor Karl, the frail artist, who couldn't survive without word from his wife."

"Karl . . . we must put that in the past." She touched his lips. "Remember when you used to call me your Saskia? Rembrandt's wife? We'll make the best of it. And we'll be free. I know it."

"No. They'll get rid of us long before they surrender. There's a story going around that a whole damned German army was captured at Stalingrad. But they'll keep fighting to the end, and when they start really losing, they'll blame us, and get rid of us."

"We won't give in! Not so long as I am here!"

"And what have you got? A third-rate artist. I've got a lump of clay where my heart should be. You think these camps make people better? No. The artists out there are an exception. We have a kind of . . . camaraderie. But most of the prisoners would kill each other for a piece of bread. I damned near did once . . . long ago."

She sat at the edge of the cot, indicated that he sit next to her. Like a dutiful child, Karl obeyed.

"Remember when your father left for Poland," Inga said. "How he kissed your mother, and told the children to be brave, and then he said she must remember her Latin—*Amor vincit omnia*. Love conquers all."

"All the love in the world can't get the best of their guns, and clubs and jails. And worst of all, their diabolical cunning."

"I know what you have suffered, Karl. I know. But we are with each other again. I can help you."

He got up from the cot, rested his head in his arms against the wall. "You should not have come. Let me make the best of what's left to me. You and that bastard Muller . . ."

"I beg of you not to talk about him any more. Please, Karl. You say that these camps often bring out the worst in people. They kill for a piece of bread. You and I will be different."

"How different were you when you—"

He was about to start the accusations about Muller again, but he stopped. Seated on the narrow cot, her back straight, her hands folded, she was as beautiful in her strong serene way as the day he had seen her in the art school, a prim, efficient secretary, Karl had battled my parents interminably over marrying her.

For the first time in his life he had shown determination, refused to bend to Mama's will. (Anna and I had cheered him on. We told him we would back him to the hilt.)

Now he recalled how he had had to fight for her love. And how good she had been for him. They had been tireless museum-goers, never missed an art-show opening, took courses when they could afford them. They had long talked about a trip to Italy. Karl's dearest possession was a book on Renaissance art Inga had given him on his twenty-second birthday. Perhaps all these memories flooded over him.

The sin, (if sin it was), that she had committed with Muller had to be seen as an effort to reach out to him, to give him the support of her letters, to let him know she still cared. He was beginning to understand now.

"Karl, I know we will be free someday," she said. "You've suffered far more than I have. I want to share your suffering. I want to be hungry and cold and despised. We will share the bad things, just as we shared so much that was good. Do you remember the holiday we had in Vienna? When I could not get you to leave the rooms full of Rembrandts?"

He was smiling. The memories revived him and softened his feelings toward her. They had shared a great deal. They had so many times experienced that communion, that elevation of the spirit in the presence of a great work. Once, in Amsterdam, Karl told me, he and Inga had had to sit, and think, and be silent, just holding hands, in the presence of "The Night-Watch."

"You are my husband and I love you," she said. "Come sit with me. I will never leave you."

Karl fell to his knees in front of her, buried his head in her lap. In the darkness, they were man and wife again.

But as Karl knew, and as Frey had feared, life in Theresienstadt was a great lie. Inga was required to live in the Christian women's barracks. Karl remained in his quarters, packed in, four people to each narrow bunk, several hundred in a building intended to hold forty.

One day there was a commotion in the streets.

Frey looked from the large window and saw an SS squad, with rifles at port arms, running at doubletime through the street. They were headed right for the studio.

The door burst open and the squad flew into the room. Everyone was ordered to stand against the wall. No one dared speak.

Maria recalls several of the artists looking at Felsher —as if to say, "You have given us away; those sketches have been found."

Tables were smashed, wallboards ripped apart, easels turned over. The stockroom was searched from top to bottom, the file drawers where Frey kept paints, brushes, and other supplies were yanked out and thrown about.

One soldier went through Karl's desk, checked every portfolio, threw all the posters to the floor. The sergeant stood in the middle of the floor, smacking a machine pistol against his side, shouting, "Find them, find them, goddammit."

What the SS could not know was that all the incriminating drawings had been removed the previous day. They were safe, protected. Still in the camp, but hidden elsewhere.

Erik Dorf's Diary

Theresienstadt
April 1943

Eichmann, to my surprise, was rather casual about the affair of the "horror propaganda" pictures. I know why though. He is in Kaltenbrunner's good graces because of his transport system—Auschwitz is going full blast—and if any blame devolves from the matter of the secret paintings, the ax will fall on me. There are no secrets from Eichmann; he knows I have been given the prime responsibility for finding the guilty artists and the remaining works of art.

Rahm, the Theresienstadt commandant, was present, as we looked at the sketches I had brought from Berlin.

"Do you have any idea who did these?" Eichmann asked him.

"It could have been any one of a dozen. We pamper those bastards, give them privileges—and look how they repay us. I'd like to hang the whole bunch."

"Calm down, Major," Eichmann said.

He then studied the drawings with a connoisseur's eye. Eichmann has that wonderful cool quality. In the midst of consigning thousands to die, he can still appreciate a landscape, a fine bit of ceramic.

Rahm and I wondered why Berlin was in such an angry sweat over five paintings. And Eichmann seemed rather indifferent himself. "Actually these are not bad," he said. "A kind of Georg Grosz decadence, but whoever did them has talent."

"Berlin demands the identity of every artist involved," I said. "And they want every such secret work—painting, drawing, whatever. And also the conspirators who smuggled them out. We can't let the outside world see these. Theresienstadt cannot be defamed by these disgusting pictures."

Rahm shook his bull-like head. "Such a fuss over some lousy paintings."

"The Jews have to be kept quiet, believing," I explained. "We must proceed with the final solution in a swift and orderly manner. There have been some minor rebellions in the eastern camps."

Eichmann rapped the desk with his crop. "Bring them in," he said.

Rahm left us.

Eichmann winked at me. "It sounds as if you're under a bit of pressure, Major."

"Pressure?"

"How well do you know your Old Testament? 'Now

there rose up a new King over Egypt who knew not Joseph.' Kaltenbrunner's our new king, eh, Dorf?"

I knew what he meant, but I said nothing. My career had been a direct rise so long as Heydrich lived. And now . . .

"But you are right about no impediments to the resettlement plan," Eichmann said. "Have you any idea the pressures I'm under? We're liquidating the last of the Polish ghettoes. Warsaw is the only tough nut remaining. All the Jews remaining in Vienna, Luxembourg, Prague and Macedonia are going directly to Treblinka to meet their Jewish God. We are giving the Führer his Jew-free Europe, Dorf."

"More credit to you, Eichmann."

Rahm and an SS corporal returned with three prisoners. They were unremarkable-looking men. Unlike the inmates of other camps who wear the striped suits, these men were in civilian dress—work shirts and trousers (marked front and back, of course, with the yellow star)—and seemed a bit healthier than the usual prisoner. They were all artists and were all under suspicion.

Eichmann introduced himself, told them who I was. His manner was polite but authoritative. "In turn, please, your names, home cities and any other pertinent data."

"Otto Felsher, Karlsruhe," said the smallest and oldest of the trio.

"Emil Frey, Prague."

"That big bastard is the ringleader," Rahm said. "Give me an hour with him and we'll find out."

"Karl Weiss, Berlin."

He was tall and thin, stooped, with a sad yet handsome face. A dark pensive man.

"Good." Eichmann said. "Now please, each of you come forward and tell me which of you is responsible for these horror pictures."

Rahm jabbed Frey in the back. "Move!"

The three men walked to the large desk. (The office is quite ornate, beautifully furnished; the furni-

ture came from some of the best Jewish homes in
Prague.)

I arranged the drawings on the desk—"Waiting for
the End," "The Master Race," "Ghetto Children,"
the others.

"Well?" asked Eichmann.

To my amazement, Frey, the big man who was
alleged to be the leader, pointed to two pictures.
"These are mine," he said.

Felsher indicated one. "Mine."

Weiss touched the last two. "I did these."

"Splendid," Eichmann said. "Now we are getting
somewhere. Sit down, all of you."

The men did so. Eichmann offered them cigarettes,
smiled at them. They were obviously frightened to
death—they knew what went on in the Kleine Festung
—and seemed more than willing to co-operate.

"Now to the heart of the matter," Eichmann said.
"Major Dorf has come from Berlin to find out how
many more of these atrocious pictures exist, where
they are hidden, and who are your contacts on the outside who are helping you smuggle them out. Surely
there are more than these five, and surely your intention is to flood the world with them and tell lies
about us. Frey?"

"There are no other pictures."

"Weiss?"

This man, who looked vaguely familiar to me,
lowered his head. "There are none. These were the
only such drawings we made." I saw at once he was
terrified; the answers would come from him.

"Felsher?" Eichmann asked.

"They . . . they . . ."

"Please go on," I said. "Tell us."

"They . . . are the only pictures done in that manner. The commandant knows our work. Posters, portraits."

Rahm cracked the back of his hand against Felsher's
face. "You lying, sneaky kike. Talk."

"No . . . no . . . others."

Eichmann motioned to Rahm not to hit him again, and like a schoolteacher, paced in front of the three. He stopped in front of Weiss and asked, "You—what is the function of art?"

Oh, how he enjoyed the role—man of culture, critic, collector.

"The function of art?" asked Weiss. "Berenson said the function of art was to enhance life."

A glow suffused Eichmann's face. "Superb! Marvelous! To enhance life!" He indicated the drawings. "You call these life-enhancing? This garbage, this filth? How could you distort reality like this and dare to call it art?"

"It is the truth," Weiss said. He said it in a soft, persuasive voice—and I had a sudden recollection of the Jewish physician I had known years ago. But Weiss is a common name; there were thousands in Berlin.

"Then tell me why the Red Cross has inspected this camp a dozen times and never found such conditions."

"They were deceived," Weiss said.

Rahm now smashed *him* across the face. A thin stream of blood trickled from the man's nose.

I got up. "Weiss, be reasonable. I am a Berliner, like you. And we Berliners are practical people. You won't be punished. You people have privileges here. Just tell us who your contacts are on the outside. How you intend to get this stuff out."

"We have no contacts."

"Then tell us where the other pictures are hidden."

"There are none."

Rahm was muttering to Eichmann. "Give me an hour with these lying bastards and we'll know. With all due respect, Colonel, they don't appreciate your art lectures."

"Weiss? You two?" I asked. "Care to change your mind?"

They said nothing. Frey, the big man, looked firmly at the other two.

I tried a new tack. "Weiss, the commandant tells

me you have a lovely Aryan wife, who arrived here recently."

He straightened up, turned white.

"I am sure she would want you to tell the truth," I said.

"I am telling the truth."

"Felsher?" I asked. Here surely was the weak link.

"I . . . I . . ."

To my amazement, my fellow Berliner, Weiss, grabbed his arm. "There's nothing to tell."

"Let him answer!" Rahm shouted.

"No . . . nothing," Felsher said.

Whispering, I suggested to Eichmann that I talk to Weiss. Many Jews, despite their attempts at bravery, can often be argued into agreement, submission, merely by *talk*—perhaps part of their heritage of Talmudical discussion.

I took Weiss to the corner of the room. "Is it possible we've met?" I asked.

"I doubt it."

"Listen, Weiss. Forget about those Austrians and Czechs. This is Berliner to Berliner."

"Berliners have kept me in prison four years. Berliners sent my parents to Warsaw."

"Well, maybe something can be done to make amends. Tell us where the paintings are. Perhaps I can work something out."

"Freedom?"

"I can look into it. Otherwise, you'll be turned over to Rahm's people. Your wife won't want to look at you when they are finished with you."

For a moment the old ghetto fear shaded his face; the fear of pain and torment and humiliation, which we have perfected, which we have made a national policy. (Heydrich, my mentor, understood this—the total modern state, the use of technology, the refusal to shrink from using any and all means to keep control, to bend wills, to force issues.)

But then he seemed to recover his courage, and he said, just as stubbornly as before, "There are no more pictures."

I shook my head and walked back to Eichmann, who was now seated at the desk. "Useless." I said.

Eichmann gave Rahm the order to take them away. They were marched out. The older man, Felsher, was weeping softly.

"You look as pale as they do," Eichmann said.

"Do I?"

"Don't let it upset you. Rahm's guards will get the information. You can go back to Berlin a hero—with a collection of ghetto art under your arm."

Rudi Weiss' Story

In April 1943, Karl and two other artists were interrogated by Eichmann and some other SS bigshots. None of them would talk. My brother, who shrank from street fights, ran from kids calling him dirty names, was defying these murdering sadists.

Inga recalls Karl and two other men, Emil Frey and Otto Felsher, being marched from the commandant's office, shoved on a truck, and taken to the Kleine Festung—the isolation and punishment barracks.

She and Maria Kalova and some other women hurled themselves at the rear of the truck and tried to drag the men off. They were beaten back by kapos. An SS corporal fired shots over their heads.

Inga screamed that he had done nothing, that they must let him go, but the truck took off. Karl smiled at her and made a "thumbs up" signal. But all expected the worst. Few people ever came out of the Kleine Festung alive. A Hussite clergyman, a Czech suspected of contacting the resistance, had been tortured to death there a few weeks back.

The three men were put in separate but adjoining cells—iron doors with slots for food, one tiny high window, thick stone walls.

They were able to call to one another.

"What will they do to us?" Felsher cried.

"Beat us, I imagine," Frey said. "Felsher, remember our agreement."

"It . . . it was my fault. I had no right to sell the pictures."

"You can make up for it now," Karl said. "Just keep your mouth shut."

"But I can't stand pain, Weiss."

"Neither can I," Karl said. "But we'll learn to."

"I'm past sixty," Felsher wept. "Weak kidneys. I'm no hero."

Later, Inga told me, Karl realized his own surprising courage stemmed from his need to prop up Felsher; without Felsher to reassure, to encourage, he might have cracked.

"They won't kill us," Frey said.

"Yes, and they tell me that after a while, you don't even notice it," Karl added.

Felsher would not stop sobbing.

Karl rattled the iron door to get his attention. "Listen, Felsher, have you ever been to Italy?"

"No."

"Frey?"

"No, Weiss, but it's been a dream of mine for years."

"Well, let's make an agreement. When this is over all three of us will go there. Venice, Florence, Rome, Siena. I've always wanted to see Michelangelo's David—not a photo or a copy, but the huge, real white thing, all by itself."

Frey continued the game. "You've got a deal, Weiss. The three of us and our wives. Italy! Yes, an artist's tour. We mustn't forget Arezzo. I am a Piero della Francesca man myself. There, Weiss, is the greatest figure of the high Renaissance."

My brother laughed. Felsher had stopped sobbing. "Well, I have a prejudice for Pinturicchio," Karl said.

"Bah," Frey said. "An illustrator. Not in the same class with Piero."

Felsher was beaten first.

The guards stood him against the wall, with his back

to them, and slowly, methodically beat him with rubber clubs, starting at the back of his head, working their way down his back, buttocks, legs, feet.

He screamed, of course, and my brother and Felsher kept shouting at him not to say anything.

"To hell with them!" Karl shouted. "We've given in too long! Felsher, tell them to go to hell!"

At length his screams diminished. He must have fainted.

Karl was next.

The two SS men entered his cell. "Well, Jewboy? Want to go back to the commandant's office and talk? You saw what we did to the old man."

"It's easier than getting hit," the other said.

"I have nothing to tell you."

They repeated the punishment with Karl. He was stripped, made to face the wall, as if having a chest X-ray taken—chin and chest against the stone, legs back, arms on hips.

They beat him for fifteen minutes, hard, punishing short blows against his head, back, kidneys, legs, genitals, feet. He screamed also. Frey shouted at him to be silent; not to surrender. And he was silent about the pictures. There were several hundred paintings and drawings—what the Nazis called "horror propaganda"—hidden about the camp. The artists were determined that they would not be found.

Frey was shouting, trying to make himself heard over Karl's screams. "Florence!" he shouted. "Listen to me, Weiss! Venice, Perugia! We'll spend a whole day in the Ufizzi Gallery! A day in the Bargello!"

Finally, Karl collapsed and slid to the floor. His back was a bloody mass of bruises.

"Talk?" a guard asked.

"No."

"You will next time. Stand him up."

They beat him again; he collapsed again.

They then did the same to Emil Frey, and he too refused to divulge any information about the works.

When the guards returned to Felsher's cell, on the

assumption that a second beating would loosen his tongue, they found he was dead.

Apparently there was now a pause, as the SS men returned to Rahm's office to report on Felsher's death.

Inga and the other women, waiting outside the office, held back by the kapos, shrieked at the SS guards not to hurt the men again. No one learned immediately that Felsher had been beaten to death.

A guard grinned at Inga. "They'll talk now. Talk or Auschwitz."

In the Kleine Festung, Karl and Frey, soaked with blood, bruised so badly they could not move, heard the guards returning.

"They won't kill us," Frey whispered. "The idea of those drawings is driving them insane. They have to have them. The bastards have an unnatural fear of being found out. In their corrupted souls, Weiss, they know they are evil, and that they will be punished someday. So they will have to keep us alive."

"I can't hold out," Karl muttered.

"I'm not sure I can. We'll make it a contest, Weiss. Whoever can hold out the longest . . . he gets a free gondola ride in Venice."

And so the beatings resumed. Every hour the guards returned. At the end of the day Karl and Frey were senseless, inanimate lumps of flesh, deformed, misshapen, their bodies screaming with pain, their faces twisted like gargoyles. But they had not talked.

But while this was going on, Inga and Maria Kalova had buried the last of the paintings. They were stored in waterproof metal containers, wrapped in waterproof paper. Then they were hidden in a dozen places—the vegetable garden, flower beds, an abandoned gravel pit. They would never be found until after the war, Inga was certain.

As the women tossed earth on the last of the works of the "Artists of Terezin," Inga began to cry.

"Oh, Maria," she said. "Does it mean anything? For them to suffer so over these pictures? Why don't we just give them to the SS."

"Karl believes in the pictures, Inga. They are the truths that the world will have to know."

"I suppose so. But I tell you, I want to rush into the commandant's office and say, 'Here they are, give me my husband.' "

"He and Frey would prefer this. I know."

"I hope so. Oh, I hope so."

For four days Frey and my brother were beaten.

On the last day, Karl, through cracked lips, called hoarsely to Frey. "They broke my hands. All the fingers. Bones cracked."

"Mine too," Frey said.

"So we can't paint again."

"They'll be finished with us soon. They know we won't talk. They'll get bored with the damned paintings and get on to something else."

"Or kill us. Sometimes I wish they would."

"No, no, Weiss. Hang on."

"Frey? You hear me? I was a coward when I was a kid. Coward all my life. Cried the first day my mother took me to school. Maybe I'm making up for it."

"You are, Weiss, you are."

They talked again of Italy, discussed itineraries, and decided that Ravenna would be an obligatory stop. And Frey was right. The beatings finally ended. But they were kept in isolation, and never allowed to return to the studio.

Erik Dorf's Diary

Theresienstadt
April 1943

This ridiculous business with a handful of Jewish artists has ended, thank God. None of them will talk. Perhaps they are telling the truth. Perhaps there are no other drawings, and perhaps they have no contact with the outside.

Be that as it may, I have failed.

Eichmann keeps teasing me about having to confront the "big bear"—Kaltenbrunner—when I return to Berlin. It is a prospect that does not please me, and he knows it. To be done in, to be frustrated by three miserable Jewish daubers?

But he will have other things on his mind, and that may save my neck. The new camps are more than filling their schedules. I am told Hoess has perfected a system where 2,500 people can be handled at once; burning and burying of the ashes follows immediately.

The most recent offensive in Russia has failed. The Allies have all of North Africa, have invaded Sicily, and are dropping hints about the invasion of Europe.

Meanwhile, we obey orders, do our duty to Führer and Fatherland and proceed with the final solution.

Do I truly believe in it, or not? I must. I cannot stop now, cannot have second thoughts or repent, or cast doubts on our work.

But I am not pleased with this return trip to Berlin. Even my relationships with Marta are suffering because of the tension under which I am forced to work.

Still, I am always happy to see the children. They are good, and loyal, and always cheerful. I wish I could tell them we were winning the war.

IV

THE
SAVING
REMNANT

Rudi Weiss' Story

I must now backtrack on my account of my parents' fate in Warsaw and relate their involvement in the mass deportation of Jews from that city (as from all Polish ghettoes) to the death camps.

In the summer of 1942, the first orders were passed down from the SS commandant Hoefle to the Judenrat. Six thousand Jews a day were to be supplied for the transports to the east.

My father, Uncle Moses, and Dr. Kohn were among the officials notified of this action.

"But what do we tell these people?" asked my father.

"The truth," Hoefle said. "They are going to a family camp in Russia. A work camp. Fresh air. Better food. Parents and children will be kept together. It is better than staying in this pesthole that you have let Warsaw become."

My Uncle Moses said, "People may resist."

Hoefle snickered. "You people haven't resisted yet. You don't know what it is to fight. And you realize, since the murder of Heydrich we can't be as generous and gentle as we have been."

My father did some calculating. "But at the rate of six thousand people a day, the ghetto will be emptied."

"Nonsense," Hoefle said. "We want to drain off the excess, make life easier for all of you."

"How will selections be made?" asked Dr. Kohn.

"That's your worry, not mine. But I want six thousand, and there will be an accurate head count, a list of every single name. If people fail to show up, they'll be grabbed off the streets at random." He smiled. "We might even start with a few of you."

And so the trains began to leave Warsaw. It was

amazing how quickly the ghetto began to empty. In a month's time. 180,000 people had been sent "east." But life was no easier. The Germans had stopped all trade with the outside; food was scarcer, deaths from disease and starvation increased.

One night in September, Uncle Moses waited in the railyards, hiding in a tool shed.

A train returning from the "East" clanked in, stopped. Zalman, the union leader, rolled from under a freight car, sneaked along the siding, and found Moses.

"Well?" Moses asked.

Zalman took a moment to catch his breath. "Those trains are not going to Russia."

"Where, then?"

"Place called Treblinka. It's three hours away. I checked the numbers on the wagons. Same trains that left yesterday are back today."

"Treblinka? A work camp?"

Zalman shook his head. "A death factory. Polish Christians are sent to a work camp. The Jews go to this big building. The SS tell them it's for delousing."

"God in Heaven. What we suspected."

"Fake signs everywhere, as if they were going to register the Jews for work after the delousing—hatmakers, tanners, ironworkers. They tell them, when you get your bath you'll get your job assignment. But they never come out. They go in, and they are gassed."

"You . . . saw this . . ."

Zalman nodded. "Got it from a kapo. He didn't know who I was. Undress them, keep them waiting, herd them in. Women and children, old people, all of them. All of the Warsaw ghetto will end up there."

Moses took his arm. "You and Anelevitz and Eva, you were right all along. You knew. You understood."

Zalman tugged at his cap. "Come on. We have to tell the resistance."

Some time later in Anelevitz' headquarters on Lesano Street, they discussed Zalman's report. Few of them in the Jewish Fighting Organization—Kovel, Zalman, Eva, Lowy, all the young people—had ever believed the Nazis' lies. But the bulk of the ghetto dwellers, with an infinite capacity for self-deception, the ever-present hope that "things would get better," yet put their faith in "family camps" and "resettlement."

They listened hopefully to the BBC shortwave broadcasts, for some hint that the world knew of their fate and would make it public.

The announcer talked about gains in North Africa on the Libyan front, and of 140 sorties flown by Allied planes over the channel.

"Word from Polish resistance forces states that the Nazis are engaging in atrocities against Polish civilians, singling out priests, teachers and anyone who might form a Polish leadership," the BBC announcer said. "Shooting of Polish civilians is an everyday occurrence, for minor infractions."

It was true, of course. But not a word had been uttered about the fate of the Jews in Poland.

"They've known about Treblinka for weeks," Uncle Moses said. "And not a word from them. They've been liquidating the Warsaw ghetto since July—and nothing. What is wrong with the BBC?"

"Now you know why we are Zionists," Anelevitz said. "We do it for ourselves, for no one else will."

"Maybe they can't believe the reports," my father said.

Eva added, "Or refuse to believe them."

"We got word out through the Swedes," Zalman said. "The Jews of Poland are being systematically destroyed. 'Broadcast it!' we begged. You know their response. 'Not all of your radiograms lend themselves to publication.' What the hell does that mean?"

Anelevitz turned off the radio. "It means they choose not to believe. Or they think we are lying. The crime is so enormous, they won't believe it. That's what the Germans are counting on."

Kovel nodded. "There's only one answer. More guns. The ghetto is being reduced every day. If only a few hundred of us fight, it will mean something."

It was decided that my Uncle Moses and the boy Aaron would make another trip, several if necessary, outside the wall, to try to get help from the Polish resistance.

My father—my mother also was present at this meeting, Eva recalls—then got the idea of setting up a clinic at the rail station, the so-called Umschlagplatz. He would attempt to take people off the transports, younger, stronger people who might be useful to the resistance, who would join the fight.

"It may help," Zalman said gloomily. "But the only response is guns."

Someone called. A roundup was taking place.

Several of the resistance fighters went to an upper room, and from the cracks in a boarded-up window they watched SS guards marching off the people destined for Treblinka. At one point two young men broke away; one actually fought with the SS guard before he was shot dead. The other was dragged out of a building and also shot.

"At least they are not going so willingly," Anelevitz said.

"But why don't they all fight?" Zalman asked. "There are hundreds of thousands of us, a handful of guards. We will die anyway."

My mother put her hand to her mouth. "Oh, Josef. The boy with the briefcase. He is one of my students. He is thirteen years old."

"You don't have to look, Berta," my father said.

"Why not?" asked Kovel—not cruelly.

And so they were marched out to their doom—six thousand Jews a day from the Warsaw ghetto, to the death camps. Only now and then did they resist— sporadic, wild acts of defiance. For the most part, they left quietly, telling themselves that they were going to a "better place."

My father's attempt to set up a clinic near the rail station, and rescue a handful of Jews from the gas

chambers, can be looked on in retrospect as a foolhardy, trivial attempt to counteract the enormous
crime.

My wife Tamar, a realist, a true sabra, tends to
scoff at my accounts of it. "Nothing important," she
says. "The world has had enough symbolic gestures
from Jews. Mass action is all that matters. Power.
Strength. Policies."

In any case, during the deportations to Treblinka,
one summer morning, a vacant store near the rail station reopened. The windows were draped with clean
white cloth. A Red Mogen David hung over the door,
on which was written "Railroad Branch, Ghetto Hospital."

Max Lowy and his wife were among the first people
saved by my father.

Lowy was important to the resistance—he was a
skilled printer, crucial to the underground press. When
my father saw him sitting disconsolately on his bag-
gage, awaiting, with a mass of other Jews, the train
to the "east," he went into action.

In his white coat, stethoscope around his neck, clip-
board in hand, my father approached the Lowys.

"Hey, doc, what are you doing?" the printer asked.

"Stick your tongue out," Papa said. "Let me feel
your pulse. You're too ill to travel. Your wife too.
Get into the clinic."

"What? The SS will notice."

"Never mind. You know what will happen to you if
you get on that train. Go on, it's all right."

"But . . ."

"Act sick. Hold your head. You're incubating typhus."

Lowy caught on. "You don't have to tell me twice.
Come on, Chana."

In that manner, my father rescued a family of three,
some strong young men—potential soldiers in the fighting organization—and a few others.

As he was herding the last of the people into the
clinic, a kapo named Honigstein followed him. Inside,

my mother, in a nurse's uniform, was making people lie on cots, thrusting thermometers into their mouths. Uncle Moses was running a modest dispensary.

The kapo entered a few paces behind Papa.

"What the hell is going on?" he asked.

My father ignored him. "Aspirin for those two," he said. "That man in the corner may have cholera. He must be isolated."

"What is this?" Honigstein asked.

My father did not even look up. "Rail-station clinic. To make sure the transports aren't infected."

"If this shipment is short, you're in trouble, Dr. Weiss. And me too."

"This has been fully authorized. Get out of my clinic. We have orders not to let people who might spread contagion get on the trains."

The kapo left, but my mother, standing at the window, saw that he was talking to an SS man. "Oh, dear God . . . he's telling him," she said.

"Papa said, "Lowy. You and your wife leave by the rear door."

Moses passed out aspirin and water to the other family. The two young men remained on cots, simulating illness.

The kapo returned with the SS man.

"He says it's a special clinic," the kapo said.

The SS man was a dull-eyed clod, and he seemed fooled. He looked at the people on the cots, my mother in white uniform, Moses moving about like an orderly.

"This woman has typhus, and her children may have it also," Papa said. "I have orders not to allow infected persons on the trains."

He made it sound logical. The SS man scratched his face, waited. All knew that if the ruse was discovered, my parents and Moses would be the next to leave for Treblinka.

"Nurse," my father said. "Cover that woman. And the children may have to go to the hospital." He turned to Moses. "Can we get some disinfectant soap?"

"I'll try."

The charade seemed to work. Outside, the loudspeaker was ordering the Jews to begin boarding the
trains. People were being told to stay together, so that
they could be assigned living quarters at the "family
camps."

The SS man and the kapo, anxious to push the loading along, departed. Everyone was relieved for a moment.

My parents and Uncle Moses watched the Jews of
Warsaw climbing aboard the trains to their death.

"And so they leave," Papa said. "Six thousand today, six thousand tomorrow."

"Josef," Moses asked, "Does it mean anything . . .
the five or six we spare?"

"I have to think so," my father said.

Erik Dorf's Diary

Auschwitz
May 1943

In a sense I am being punished.

My failure to crack the artist-conspirators at Theresienstadt has not helped my reputation with Kaltenbrunner. He was furious at the way the Jewish artists
defied us. But he has bigger problems at the moment—
the annihilation of the Jews, a pressing matter indeed, now that the Russians are on the offensive.

Erratic, paranoid, he in no way fills Heydrich's
boots, yet he has taken over all his posts—the Security
Office, the Gestapo, and the RSHA, which is largely
concerned with the Jewish problem.

Kaltenbrunner senses my fear of him. He has assigned me to the death centers, as a kind of roving
reporter, to brief him on the progress of Maidanek,
Sobibor, Belzec, and most of all Auschwitz, which is
becoming the heart of our efforts.

Hoess, the commandant, proved a thoughtful host
for me, and for a certain Professor Pfannenstiel, an

expert on hygiene from the University of Marburg. The commandant explained that not only is each of the several camps at Auschwitz surrounded by barbed wire, but that each block *within* the camp, an area holding about four thousand inmates, is surrounded on all sides by barbed wire. The exterior barbed wire is a double fence, strung on concrete, the space between patrolled by dogs and armed guards.

"Himmler is afraid of an Allied air attack," Hoess told us. "He fears some of them may escape."

I questioned him about some reports of deliberate sadism on the parts of guards. (Unfortunately, our lower ranks do not always attract the finest kind of German soldier.) Hoess conceded that the famous Sergeant Moll, whose job it is to dump the Zyklon B crystals into the chamber, once took "target practice" against a party of Jewish women. The women were naked, quite beautiful, it was reported, and not all died immediately of their wounds. He was reprimanded.

A woman guard named Irma Grese, obviously a deviate of some kind, is said to have cut open the breasts of Jewish women with her whip. These women were then operated on without anesthesia by a physician, while Miss Grese watched. Hoess claimed he would look into it, but such activities, he explained, were known as "making sport."

As for medical experiments, Hoess shrugged. This was not his department. He had orders from above, he claimed, to let them proceed. My old friend (and nemesis) Artur Nebe has supplied gypsies for seawater experiments, in which they were forced to drink salt water, and died in excruciating pain.

I knew about the selecting process, and did not care to see it. The Jews arrive from all over Europe, in filth-strewn, crammed cars. A triage is made at the rail siding. Those fit to work are sent to the barracks; the aged, infirm, children, mothers with young and any potential troublemakers are marched at once to one of Hoess' four installations.

On this lovely May morning, I stood with Pfannenstiel on the roof of one of the chambers. To one side, in a parklike setting, an orchestra of women prisoners in blue uniforms played airs from *Die Fledermaus*.

A lawn and hedges have been cultivated on the roof of the building. Some distance away are the famous plantings of trees I had been told about, where the Jews are made to stand while awaiting their turn.

Hoess and Pfannenstiel indulged in some technical discussion of disposal problems. They discussed the furnaces connected with the larger and newer crematoria, where bodies are burned immediately, as opposed to the outdoor system at the older units, where bodies have to be dragged out by the Sonderkommandos—special squads composed of Jewish prisoners who eventually are gassed themselves—and burned in the open.

"Human fat is a remarkable fuel," Hoess was saying. "We use dippers to draw it off and start new fires. Of course, in the ovens, everything is consumed at once."

The chimneys behind us were working, and I had to cover my face. The odor was quite strong. Polish residents for miles around could smell it. Apparently our technology has as yet perfected no way to stifle the stench of burning flesh.

I now saw the first files of Jews approaching. They were made to run from the barracks area to the small forest. Women tried to hide their breasts, their pudenda. I saw one woman, still wearing underpants, pleading with a guard to let her keep them on. Furious, he slapped her face, then yanked them from her legs, ripping them apart.

Voices drifted up to me. "Don't carry on, don't worry," a guard was saying in Polish. "It's only a delousing operation. Once you're out and free of lice, you'll get your job assignments."

I stared for a while at a woman holding a child in her arms. Two old people supporting one another. A beautiful young girl with soulful eyes. Suddenly she began to scream at a guard, "I am twenty-two! I am twenty-two!" He silenced her with a blow with a rub-

ber club. I wondered why such a lovely woman had
not been pulled out for service in the camp brothel. It
is no secret that such an institution is maintained—
several, in fact, both for officers and for enlisted men
and rankers. But the women are largely Poles and Russians. Himmler is strict about "race defilement,"
hence, I suppose, even a Jewish Venus cannot be
spared from the fires.

Pfannenstiel wandered off to study the door, to look
through the peephole—the chamber was not in operation—and Hoess took me aside. "So Kaltenbrunner
got rid of you."

"That's not true."

"I'm told he wants you to get a bellyful of this. I
hear your stomach isn't too strong, too much desk
work in Berlin."

"It is quite strong enough, Hoess."

"Yes, I imagine it is. You helped us get Zyklon B."

The professor returned, and Hoess took us into the
vast chamber. He pointed out the shower heads, the
pipes, the faucets, the tile walls.

"We're managing twelve thousand a day here, when
they're all going," he said.

Pfannenstiel was impressed. "Incredible. At Treblinka I'm told you processed a mere eighty thousand
in half a year."

"That lousy carbon monoxide," said Hoess. "Bad
stuff. Slow. Sometimes we had riots. The Jews suspected what was in store for them and raised hell.
Here, we get it over fast, and they stay fooled right to
the end."

"Or want to stay fooled," I said.

"What's the difference, as long as the job gets done
quickly and efficiently."

He showed us the conveyor belt, the ovens with the
gas jets burning inside. There was a charred, sickening
odor.

"We run forty-six ovens like this," Hoess said. "In
addition to the outdoor burning pits. So you can see
it's a big operation."

"How many can this one take?" I asked.

Hoess thought a second. "Top, about twenty-five hundred. Not counting small children. We cram them in pretty well. You'll see. That is, if you want to see."

"Where are these people from?" I asked, as we walked back into the chamber. I noticed the gutters along the wall, for drainage of blood and other fluids, I imagined, and for easy cleaning. There was a huge electric fan at one end, which, Hoess, explained, was used to clean the gas out when an operation ended. The Sonderkommandos had to rush in, and using canes and crooked sticks with which they dragged the dead by the chin, load them on to the conveyor.

"They are directly off the trains," Hoess said. "This morning's transport. From all over Europe—France, Holland, Poland, Germany. The Führer is getting his wish."

"And the ones who are spared?" I asked.

"They'll go eventually. They're a bit tougher to fool once they've been assigned to work in the camp. They know by then, but they go anyway. Life isn't exactly paradise in the barracks, so I suppose this comes as a sort of relief to them."

Hoess pointed to an aperture on the roof. "That's where the crystals are thrown in. A better system than the old diesels."

Hoess began to complain about his problems in stockpiling Zyklon B. It deteriorates, and a special distribution system has been organized to keep him supplied. He heard about the intricate holding company set up to manufacture, sell and ship the stuff, and he is a bit piqued. He knows huge profits are being made on the sale of Zyklon B and he feels he should have a share. The party bigshots, the industrial moneymen, are reaping profits from the sale of the gas, while he and others like him do the work that creates the demand.

"We're about ready," Hoess said.

He led the professor and me to a high point, from which we could see the Jews being herded from the cover of the trees to the open steel door of the big chamber. The music continued in back of us—lilting, gay, as if we were spending a spring morning in the park.

"How wonderfully compliant they are," Pfannenstiel said. "Almost a religious rite. You know, I am no theologian, but I have discussed this with churchmen and they feel that in a way, the Jews are being sacrificed so that Europe may be saved from Bolshevism. That is to say, they should feel . . . well, Christlike, holy . . . for providing this service."

Hoess glared at him. "Nonsense. I'm a serious Christian with a Christian wife and children, and what you say is garbage. They are vermin. They corrupt everything. I get my orders and obey them, and there is no theology involved."

He went on to explain how the Sonderkommandos extract gold teeth from the dead, glass eyes, artificial limbs, shave the women's hair, before loading the bodies onto the moving belt. They work swiftly, so the next batch can be processed. Twelve thousand a day is a miracle, and Hoess deserves credit.

Below, a sergeant was shoving a group of hesitant older people: "Move, move. Five minutes, and you'll be out, all nice and clean. Then a warm bed, coffee and cake. Move."

To my amazement, when the chamber appeared absolutely crammed, the guards began passing small, screaming children over the heads and arms of the people already in. It was as if every last cubic meter of space had to be used.

"It's important that they all go in," Hoess said. "We don't want any of them getting back to the camp with stories that will upset the others."

The steel door slammed shut. The walls were very thick, and it was almost impossible to hear any sounds from inside the chamber. The music had gotten louder.

On the roof of this chamber were some odd mushroom like contraptions, and a sergeant of the SS was now removing the cap. I had noticed a German army ambulance parked below. Now, a soldier bearing a can —that familiar can like the one I saw in Hamburg not long ago—climbed up the side of the chamber. He tossed it to the man at the "mushroom."

Hoess nodded at the man. I learned later that this was the famous Sergeant Moll.

Moll twisted the lid off the can and held it away from his face. Then he emptied the bluish crystals into the "stem" of the mushroom, saying as he did, "Okay, give them something to chew."

We waited a moment—Pfannenstiel, Hoess and myself.

Then a murmuring noise, like a wind rising, a low-pitched howling, seemed to issue from the chamber. Hoess left us to look through the viewing hole. He invited us to go along. Pfannenstiel had already seen what it was like inside. I made some excuse.

"Yes," the professor said. "It takes about twelve minutes. They claw and scratch and try to get to the door, but it is hopeless. There is often a great deal of blood and feces on the bodies. I would suggest, Major Dorf, you not look, when they open the door. It takes a bit of getting used to."

He kneeled and put his ear to the roof of the chamber, and smiled. "Fantastic. Absolutely fantastic. It sounds like the wailing one hears in a synagogue."

Berlin
May 1943

In an effort to curry favor with Kaltenbrunner, I arranged a screening for him of some of the operations at Auschwitz.

He seemed pleased with the photographs I had projected in his office, where once Heydrich sat. I told him of Hoess' excellent administration—assigning the healthy to I. G. Farben, Krupp, and Siemens, where they are worked to death, dispatching the useless to the chambers.

At one point Kaltenbrunner quoted Himmler, after looking at a photograph of the bodies jammed together like a scene from Dante's *Inferno* at the door of the chamber. "The boss has said that what people call anti-Semitism is really delousing. Getting rid of lice is not a question of ideology, it's a matter of cleanliness."

The reasons we have for killing Jews are manifold. For Himmler it is "delousing," for Heydrich it was a multi-level political tool, and for the Führer it is the be-all and end-all of his world view. So be it. I obey. Thoughts of the naked children being passed over the heads of their parents, and into the chambers, flit through my mind. But to Kaltenbrunner I say nothing. What is there to say once one accepts the need for the program?

When the screening had ended, Kaltenbrunner's hideous face was actually smiling at me. "Dorf, you've taken to your new assignment with your usual dedication," he said.

"Thank you, General."

"You can go now."

I paused. "I meant to talk to you about this new job. It keeps me in motion all the time—Poland, Russia. I had hoped for a permanent assignment to Berlin. To make your job easier."

"No, no, Dorf. I want you in Poland. I want you close to the camps. There are reports the Jews are getting fractious, rebellious."

Again, I hesitated. I feared him. "It's the problem of my wife, General. I hate to bring it up."

"Ah. A little cheating while Papa is away?"

"Not at all, sir. Mrs. Dorf is ill. She's had a weak heart for some years. These prolonged absences of mine are having an adverse effect on her. Food shortages, the bombings . . ."

"Take her to our hospital. A vacation. Nothing is too good for the wives of SS officers."

"That's kind of you, sir. But she needs me . . . here."

Kaltenbrunner swung his huge legs around, got up. He towered over me. "You astonish me, Dorf. Our armies are being bled white at Stalingrad. The whole

Russian front is blazing. The Allies are working their way up Italy. And you complain about a sick wife."

Once more I appealed, and once more Kaltenbrunner rebuffed me. He referred to the rumors about me—my alleged left-wing connections, enemies I'd made. I tried to defend myself, but he had no further need for me. Briefly I felt like Hamlet, comparing his dead father to Claudius—*like Hyperion to a satyr*. So was my fallen chief to this brute, this dull-headed glandular savage.

Tonight there was more than the usual tension between Marta and me. Since Heydrich's death (it's already a year ago), she has sensed in me a fear, an uncertainty, a loss of the surefootedness I enjoyed while he lived.

I have begun to drink a bit. I'm no drunkard, but a few glasses of cognac at night help to relax me. Tonight Laura was asleep. Peter was off at a training camp. (There are rumors that fifteen-year-olds will be organized into "wolf pack" defense battalions if the Russians ever breach our lines defending Germany.)

Suddenly Marta opened a manila folder and began to read aloud. I knew at once what she had—copies of letters I had written to camp commandants. I made no effort to stop her, kept drinking, and listened.

Her voice was mocking, edged with a sneer. " 'All corpses buried at Babi Yar must be dug up and burned. Not a trace is to remain. Blobel, your work was sloppy and left vast areas untreated. This is highest priority.' "

"You had no right to look at those."

"I like this," she went on. "To Hoess. 'I am not satisfied with the system for taking the burned remains to the mill for grinding into ashes. Can we not develop a furnace that destroys everything? And how long can the Sola River absorb these tons and tons of ashes?' "

"Stop."

"Or this," Marta went on. " 'Better control must

be exercised over the medical experiment programs. I realize the Reichsführer's fascination with twins, but I am told some non-Jewish sets of twins have been used by the doctors. This is bad policy. I also would like a full report on the sterilization-by-injection experiments, as well as the program to sterilize Jews by X-ray. Why all this fuss over a sterilization program, when their eventual fate is known to all by now?' "

She slapped the letters down.

"Those were not for your eyes, my dear," I said wearily.

"Oh, I've suspected for a long time. All that talk about executing spies and saboteurs, controlling disease behind enemy lines."

I was too exhausted, mentally and physically, to talk to her. Finally I said, "And now you are disgusted with me."

"No. I want to help you."

I had no idea what she meant. I assembled the carbons of the letters and replaced them in the folder, making a mental note not to keep such documents in the apartment any more.

"What did Kaltenbrünner tell you today?" she asked.

"I go back to Poland tomorrow."

"You didn't stand up for yourself? After all you have done for them, Erik?"

I poured another cognac. "It doesn't matter where —Poland, Russia, here. The walls will soon tumble."

She sat next to me on the sofa. We have acquired, through Eichmann's generosity, a marvelous collection of fine furniture from his warehouses in Prague. They go well with the old Bechstein.

"It does matter," Marta said. "Kaltenbrunner must sense this . . . this . . . air of defeat in you when you speak to him. No wonder your career is at a dead end. You are lucky Heydrich promoted you before he died. These letters . . . the tone in them . . . it sounds as if you are revolted by your work, ashamed of it."

"Perhaps I am at times."

Her voice rose. She grabbed my wrist. "You can't be! You must go on! If you—if we—stop now, the world will assume we are guilty. But if we go on, and explain what we are doing, we'll succeed!"

I leaped from the sofa, spilling cognac over the Turkish rug. "Good God, Marta, how I misread you! Gentle Marta!" I began to laugh. "And I thought you were furious with me because I am up to my neck in the blood of Jewish children!"

"Don't say it! *Don't!*"

"And all that outraged you is that I'm not prouder, not more energetic in my labors!"

She was shrieking at me. "You must be! Do what you are told, to the very end! That will convince people that what you are doing is *right!* Obey, obey, like Hoess, like Eichmann. But every time you look doubtful, or question something—like these experiments—you help dig our graves!"

I laughed again, collapsed on the sofa.

"And don't laugh at me!"

"I'm not. I'm amused by my own stupidity. Of course. I must enter my work with more eagerness, more enterprise."

For some moments she stared at me. Then she turned down the overhead light. The only illumination in the room was from a fine cloisonné lamp, courtesy of Eichmann. Marta kneeled in front of me, rested her golden head in my lap, put her arms around my waist.

Her voice was ghostly. "Erik . . . sometimes I am afraid we will be punished."

"Punished?"

"All of us."

"You've done nothing at all. And I have been a good soldier. *Un bon soldat,* as Eichmann would say."

"Those letters. The ovens. The pyres. The experiments. A river full of ashes." She looked up at me. Her eyes were dry. Her lips looked drained of blood. "That's why they must all die. So no one knows. So no one is left to tell. So that no one can tell lies about you. Do you understand?"

I stared at her, drew her close. But our bodies were cold, and we could not make each other warm.

Rudi Weiss' Story

All through the latter part of 1942, the ghetto was drained of Jews—to Treblinka, Auschwitz, other death camps. And still the people went in silence, with only minimal acts of resistance.

Dr. Kohn, the most cooperative of the council, had taken his own life with a cyanide pill. He did so after Hoefle, the SS commandant, had increased the daily quota from six thousand to seven thousand.

As yet, no resistance could be mounted against the Germans. There were simply not enough guns, virtually no ammunition.

But my father continued his little deception at the rail station clinic, saving a dozen people now, a half-dozen later, convincing the authorities that his "branch" of the hospital had been authorized.

One day, he and my mother looked from the draped window. The Nazis had a new trick. People were offered a loaf of bread and a tin of marmalade as an inducement to board the trains. They stood dumbly, weary, confused, waiting to board—clutching their precious bread and jam, hopeful to the end.

That day, Zalman had been ordered to the train. My Uncle Moses boldly plucked him out of the crowd, explained to a kapo that the man was terribly ill, and walked him into the clinic.

"Go to the sink," my father ordered. "Vomit. Jam your finger down your throat."

Zalman looked worried. "They were eyeing us. Hoefle's out there."

"I'll handle them," my father said.

Moses, standing watch at the window, now saw Hoefle and a man named Karp, the ghetto police chief, approaching.

"They're coming," Moses said.

"Berta, leave by the rear door," Papa said. "Go to

320

the school. Better hide with someone. Zalman, go with her."

The two left. Almost the instant my mother and Zalman had departed, Hoefle and Karp entered. The latter was a tool of the Nazis, a converted Jew who had earned the hatred of everyone in the ghetto.

Karp barked, "Everyone on their feet!"

Papa protested. "These people are ill."

"Shut up, Weiss. On your feet in front of Major Hoefle."

The half-dozen people in the small room got to their feet.

"What in hell is going on here?" asked Hoefle. He and his officers rarely set foot in the ghetto. They governed through underlings—noncoms, Ukrainian militia, ghetto cops.

"A branch clinic of the hospital, sir," my father said.

"They don't look sick to me," Karp said. "Where's the written authorization for all this?"

"It exists," my father said. He struggled to control himself. "I can't help it if your office is inefficient."

The ghetto police chief and the SS officer wandered around the clinic—picking up the bottles on Uncle Moses' tiny dispensary table, inspecting under beds.

"What kind of racket are you running here, Weiss?" Karp asked.

"I am *Dr*. Weiss, Karp."

Hoefle smiled at this: Jew against Jew.

Karp stopped at a cot on which a young woman reclined. She was a cousin of Eva Lubin, a woman who had said she would fight in the resistance.

"What's wrong with you?" Hoefle asked her.

"Fever."

Hoefle—he was a vicious killer, formerly an Einsatzgruppe officer—gently put a hand to her forehead. He looked at Karp, said nothing, and the two of them left.

My father and Uncle Moses watched them depart. They knew now they could expect the worst. But they were determined to keep up the pretense; perhaps some miracle would result in their being bypassed. My father again tried to convince Karp that it would be a mistake to let diseased people ride the trains. But Karp would not let my father into his office.

Hoefle lost no time in striking.

It was learned later—through an informant in Karp's police force—that the clinic was to be burned, and everyone in any way connected with it sent out on the next transport.

The first blow fell on my mother.

She was rehearsing the children in Jewish folk songs, village airs that she had gotten them to sing for her (quite a change for that grand lady, so proud of her Mozart and Beethoven), when Karp and an aide entered the classroom.

Her presence was so dignified, so calm, that he was subdued, apologetic. "Excuse me, Mrs. Weiss," he said. "You must come with me."

"May we rehearse the song once more? It's for the children's musicale."

"I'm afraid not."

"May I see Dr. Weiss?"

"Your husband will be at the station."

At once she understood what was about to happen. Calmly (so one of her students told me) she got her coat, her pocketbook, and said goodbye to the children.

"You coming back, teacher?" asked Aaron Feldman.

"Of course. In my absence, Sarah, will you take the class?"

The oldest girl nodded, and went to the front of the room.

"If I am gone for some time," my mother said, "you are not to neglect your lessons. You will be better people for being educated, for knowing Shakespeare, and the Pythagorean theorem. Goodbye, children."

They bid her goodbye. They had seen people leave for the rail station a thousand times; they knew about the transports.

At the station, the usual mob of seven thousand were being assembled, registered, grouped. My mother looked at the small clinic and saw that it had been destroyed. She glared at Karp.

"I'm under orders, Mrs. Weiss."

Lowy and his wife were also on the transport. My father had rescued them once. But now, the printer had been swept up in the newest roundup of victims. Mrs. Lowy was bawling uncontrollably.

"Cut it out," Lowy said. "How bad can it be? Be glad to get out of this hole."

Soon, my father, carrying two valises, appeared. He was allowed to take some of his medical supplies. He wore the dusty, battered Homburg he had worn making calls in Berlin, the same dark topcoat.

He and my mother embraced.

Lowy and his wife greeted him. "Sorry, doc. You tried. I guess we're just destined to get shipped out together all the time."

"Yes," my father said. "Fellow passengers again, Lowy."

The people on the shipment were a cross-section of the ghetto—the poor, the starving, middle-class Jews, and even relative aristocrats like my parents.

My father tried to joke. "You know, Berta, I almost feel as if Lowy is an old classmate."

The Umschlagplatz was a dreary, depressing place —a yard about thirty by fifty meters. Around it ran a high brick wall and the rear of an abandoned building. Those scheduled for transport were herded through a wire fence. Inside, they sat on bags and valises, bartering for food, trying to cook, making last-ditch efforts to be released.

My parents remained there twelve hours with the Lowys and hundreds of others before the trains arrived. It was a terrifying time. At one point, two young men tried to escape. They sneaked into the abandoned building and tried to cross from its roof to the adjoining house. The SS guards shot them down. Older people began to moan; children wept. There were no toilets. People relieved themselves in corners of the vast yard.

"I wish they'd get on with it," Lowy said. "The family camp has got to be better than this."

"Yes," my mother said. "I believe we were ready for a change. Isn't that so, Josef?"

And yet all had been told the truth of the transports by my Uncle Moses: *they were going to their death.* Still, they tried to joke, to make light of the fate that awaited them. The guards were soon doubled—ghetto cops, Latvians, SS. This meant the train was due any moment.

My father asked Lowy, "So the resistance is losing the master printer. How will they manage?"

"I've trained Eva. If she keeps at it, she'll make a good pressman."

My father nodded. The resistance. He would no longer be part of it. "What about my brother?" he asked Lowy.

"Hiding with Zalman. It won't be easy. The Germans are sweeping out whole blocks. Anyone hiding—shot on the spot."

At about five in the afternoon the train appeared. Again, the loudspeaker blared its orders—people were to proceed in orderly fashion into the cars, fill them, observe sanitary rules. There was a single bucket in each car for that purpose.

So they moved to the train. My mother and father went arm in arm. A young mother, holding a child, pleaded with my father for medicine. He said he would help her once they were aboard.

Karp, one of the most hated of all people in Warsaw, came abreast of my parents. "I'm sorry, Dr. Weiss."

My father made a last appeal. "Karp, get my wife off the transport," he said. "She's a teacher, an interpreter. She speaks better German than your masters. Make an appeal for her."

"No chance, doctor."

At the edge of the surging crowd, a young man had

lost his mind, was struggling to escape through the wire gate. He was being methodically clubbed to the ground.

"Josef," Mama said. "You cannot get rid of me that easily."

He smiled. "Oh, I was just saying goodbye to our friend Chief Karp."

"Don't blame me," Karp said. "They'll get around to me one of these days."

"If we don't first," Lowy said.

They moved up the planks into the cattle cars. People ran for places near the openings in the slats. Breathing, moving, would be difficult. Lowy's wife became hysterical.

"Stop bawling," Lowy said. "What did you expect? The Paris Express?"

"I can't help it. I'm frightened."

"So are we all, Mrs. Lowy," my father said. "But we must look at things bravely."

More shots rang out in the Umschlagplatz. They had killed the crazed young man.

My parents entered the cattle car. My father found a place, set his valise down as a seat for the two of them. "There," he said. "First-class reservations. I must talk to the conductor about the deplorable condition of these cars."

She took his arm. "Josef, as long as we have each other, they cannot destroy us."

"Of course, my darling."

They were not aware of it, but their train was to be routed to Auschwitz, rather than Treblinka. The latter camp, more primitive, with smaller facilities, was jammed to capacity.

By January 1943, our partisan band, under Uncle Sasha's leadership, had raided the Ukrainian collaborators three times. We had guns and ammunition, and had killed several dozen of them. The time had come to attack the Germans.

On a snowy New Year's Eve, we gathered in a woods outside the town of Bechak, where an SS garrison had newly arrived. Samuel, the rabbi who had married us, conducted a brief service, as the soft, silent snow fell, covering our fur hats and heavy coats. Most of us wore boots stolen from the Ukrainians. We were all thin and hungry. Food was hard to come by in the winter, and we were forced to be on the move all the time.

"Hear, oh Israel, the Lord our God, the Lord is one," Samuel intoned softly.

I had forgotten how to pray. Bar-mitzvah, high holidays, those had been the extent of my religious training. We attended (when we did) a reformed synagogue, with much of the service in German. I noticed that Uncle Sasha did not join in the prayers.

He and I stood to one side, protecting our rifles, waiting.

"What about you, Weiss? A prayer or two?"

"I don't know how."

"I know how, but I won't. Not after my family was murdered." He looked up at the wintry sky. The snow came down in powdery clouds, almost caressing us. "Give us a quote, rabbi, something that will help Jews going into battle."

Samuel finished his praying, smiled at Uncle Sasha and said:

" 'And David said unto his men—gird ye on every man his sword.' Amen."

There were seven of us in the party—all men. Sometimes the women went on raids. But against a German garrison, Uncle Sasha had decided that only men should fight. The rabbi left us to return to our camp.

Soon we saw the lights of the village of Bechak. It seemed far away, on a different planet. The party came to a halt. I suddenly became the center of attention. They removed my fur hat and put a German helmet on my head. I took off the loose tunic I wore. Under it was a German army overcoat, belts, ammunition case. I carried a Mauser rifle.

Sasha stared at me. "You'd fool me."

"I almost fool myself."

"Ready? Start walking. We'll be a hundred meters behind you, one group on your right, one on your left."

"I'll remember."

"Remember something else," Sasha said. "Kill fast."

I walked alone, keeping to the countryside, plodding through the snow. Cold, frightened, I thought of my brother—doomed to rot in prison forever, it seemed. Of Anna, dead under circumstances that filled me with suspicion. Of my parents, living in the hell of Warsaw. (I was unaware that they had been sent to Auschwitz, or what their fate was.) And of my grandparents, dead by their own hands, unable to face the horror.

Soon I was in the town. It looked beautiful, like a painting, in the snow. A dog howled at me. The streets were empty. In all occupied towns, curfew was strictly observed.

We had scouted the town earlier. Yuri, disguised as a tinker, had wandered through the village a week earlier. The Germans had set up their headquarters in the town hall. They were an SS unit, probably sent to round up any remaining Jews. Their appetite for killing us was insatiable. We were not sure how many were there—perhaps a company, perhaps only a platoon. In any case, the enlisted men's barracks were at the edge of the town, in an old mill. But the officers were quartered in the town hall.

I entered by a side street. My boots crunched in the snow. There were two sentries on duty outside the hall. It was brightly lit. I could hear singing from inside. Of course. A New Year's celebration. The Germans had Russian and Ukrainian whores and girl friends.

The sentries passed one another in front of the hall. Then one moved on, vanished from view. I hurried out of the side street and walked briskly up to the remaining soldier.

"Hell of a way to make a man spend New Year's," I said.

"Hey . . . who are you?" he asked.

"Battalion messenger. The goddam phone is out again. I have a message for the captain."

I'd come upon him so brazenly that he did not even

ask me for the password. He was very young and small. And I sounded like, and looked like, an ordinary German soldier.

"What captain?" he asked.

"How the hell do I know? Wait, here it is."

I dug a paper from my coat pocket and gave it to him. The sentry walked toward the reflected light from the town hall and squinted at the paper. I got behind him.

"Looks like Captain Van Kalt. Isn't that what it says?"

"There ain't no such captain. What the hell—"

I whipped a leather cord around his neck, dug my knee into his back and wrestled him to the ground. All the anger that had boiled inside me these years found itself in my arms, my hands. He struggled awhile, then stopped. I yanked the leather thong a few more times to make sure. Then I took his rifle. I dragged the body to the side of the stone steps and pressed myself against the building.

In seconds, the other sentry turned the corner. I played no games with him. Instead I leaped from the brick wall and smashed at his neck with the rifle butt. His helmet flew off, and before he could shout, I'd batted him again. His head exploded.

Uncle Sasha and the others came racing out of the shadows.

"Yuri and your men, the back door," Sasha said. "The rest of us, in the front. Go in firing, but for God's sake don't hit one another."

We plunged into the main room of the hall, without warning, without a word.

There were a dozen German officers in the room, and perhaps an equal number of women. A young lieutenant was playing the piano.

They all seemed weary, sated. It was not a very happy New Year's party; and we did not make it any happier.

Uncle Sasha fired the first bursts and killed three men near the door. Yuri shot the man at the piano, and he fell noisily on the keyboard. The women shrieked. Some—men and women—fell to the floor. A captain rose, holding his hands high.

Uncle Sasha grabbed him by the collar. "The gun room."

"All right. Don't kill us."

"Fast. Yuri, guard the others. Everyone else with me."

The captain—he had been slightly wounded in the arm—unlocked the gun rack. We festooned ourselves with machine pistols, rifles, handguns. Each of us took as much ammunition as we could carry. There was a medicine chest, and we took that also.

"Can you manage that, Weiss?" Sasha asked me. He was pointing to a light machine gun.

"I'll try." I picked it up, balanced it on my shoulders and followed them into the main room.

Inside, Yuri had started to bind the hands of the remaining Germans. But Sasha was in a hurry. "There's a faster way," he said.

He led us through the door. Then he ordered us to hurl grenades into the headquarters. We did. The explosions lit up the whole village; we knew that the soldiers at the main barracks would be on our tail any minute.

We began to run.

I felt the bullet slam into my shoulder. My back turned wet, warm. I got to my feet, but had to drop the machine gun. Yuri and another man helped me. When we got back to the camp, I was in a dead faint.

I next remember Uncle Sasha cutting my clothing away. I was on my side. The disinfectant clogged my nose, burned my back.

Then I heard a snipping, and the pain in my shoulder became unbearable. I howled. And on top of my howling, I could hear Helena screaming.

"Stop! Stop! You're hurting him!"

She ran to the opposite side of the cot and began to kiss me, but she kept shrieking.

Uncle Sasha's voice boomed over her screams. "Quiet! Get away from him, or I'll throw you out, wife or no!"

"You'll kill him with your damned stupid raids!" Helena yelled.

"How is it, Weiss?" he asked.

"It hurts like hell."

"I've almost got the bullet out. We can't spare the morphine for this kind of thing. Hang on, you'll be all right."

The snipping and clicking of Sasha's medical instruments bothered me almost as much as the pain. Until he began to probe deeply, stabbing at nerves. The disinfectant, some kind of potent Red Army concoction, helped. My mind was so distracted by its harsh odor that I gritted my teeth and grunted, determined I would not scream.

My father, examining my bruises once after a rough game played in the mud, decided I had a high threshold for pain; I could take a great deal. "It's common among athletes," Papa said, smiling. And almost added —"and those who are less intelligent and sensitive." But I'm sure he didn't mean that. It was simply that I was *expected* to be the family roughneck, and I obliged. Just as now, with a bit of male bravado, in front of my wife, I would not yell, howl, or complain.

Helena wept, sat down on the edge of the cot and kissed the back of my neck.

"Worse pain once," I chattered. "Worse . . . broke my ankle . . . didn't play a whole year."

Sasha growled at her. "Get out of my way, dammit."

"No."

"Then it'll take longer and he'll suffer more."

Yuri, standing to one side, staring at my blood staining the blankets, tried to calm everyone. "It was worth it. One man wounded. And what a haul—rifles, machine guns, ammo. We must have killed eight of them."

Helena jumped from the cot. "I don't give a damn about your haul!"

"Ah, hell, it's still bleeding," Sasha said. "Hand me one of those bandage packs."

He worked on me for another fifteen minutes. Helena refused to leave the cot, stroking my head, kissing me. Finally, Sasha held up the misshapen slug. He had swathed my back in bandages.

"There it is, Weiss," he said. "From a Mauser. Something to show your grandchildren."

Yuri laughed. "Have it gold-plated."

Helena grabbed it from Uncle Sasha's hand and hurled it against the wall. "Stop! Stop! I hate all of you! I can't stand this damned joking, as if it were some kind of game! Sure it's a game—but one we can never win! He's almost bleeding to death and you make jokes about the bullet that almost killed him! I'm sick of this camp, and this useless war and the way you think you're accomplishing something. So you kill a German here, a Ukrainian there—what of it? One day we'll all be dead . . . one winter more will kill us all . . .

Her voice became a choked, heaving sob. She fell on her knees and began beating the icy logs of the hut, screaming all the time that we were all doomed, that we might as well give ourselves up to the Germans.

"I don't want any more . . . I don't want any more . . ." she kept sobbing. "No more . . . no more . . ."

Uncle Sasha assembled his medical kit and nodded at Yuri, as if to say, "This is between man and wife." They started for the door. I turned painfully on my elbow.

"You did that almost as good as my father," I said. "Nobody could tape the way he could."

Sasha smiled at me. "Sorry I never met him. Maybe someday. I'll see if we have anything to help you sleep. You may have to settle for the last of the cognac."

They left. Helena crouched in a corner, wiping her tears away.

"Come to me," I said.

She got up, came to the cot, and sat beside me again. Even in bulky winter clothing, felt boots, she was beautiful. Her hair had been cut short. Her face had seen no makeup for years. And still she shone, a woman to be stared at, desired, loved.

"Oh, Rudi . . . you could have died. And for what?"

I held her hand. "To show them we are not cowards. That they can't keep killing us and get away with it."

"But they are killing millions, we know it. And so few fight, so few escape."

"All the more reason for us to fight them."

We said nothing for a while. She rested her head on my chest, and I stroked her cropped hair, kissed her ear. Each move sent a jolt of pain through my shoulder and arm, but at least the bleeding seemed to have stopped.

"Tell me again how much you love me," I said.

"More than ever." Then she began to cry again. "But they'll come looking for us. They'll know where we are. Someone will tell, someone will be tortured. Then we will all be—"

"You once said we'd never die."

"I don't believe it any more," my wife said.

"We'll live, you'll see. You'll meet my parents, Karl, Inga. And they'll all love you as much as I do. They'll joke about a Czech in the family, but it'll just be a joke."

She smiled at last, stroked my forehead. I was afraid then, afraid of dying, and so was she. We loved each other too much. The enemy would make sure that our love would be killed. But we dared not tell each other how afraid we were. It was wrong of me to talk about my family, and happy reunions. It made it harder to deceive ourselves.

Finally, she looked up. "Rudi, I have something to ask of you."

"Anything."

"The next time you go out to fight with Sasha and the men, I want to go along."

"Oh, no."

"Some of the women do. Nadya does."

"Not my wife."

"But I must. I must be with you all the time."

Her eyes were solemn, shadowed. It had been four years that we had been together, and it was a lifetime. We had suffered much, seen horrors, survived, fought, and learned to be passionate, tender, under-

standing. And most of all to read each other's minds.
We could hide nothing from each other, nothing. I
knew what she meant. There was a good chance the
Nazis would catch us someday. They and their local
allies were determined to wipe us out. It was reported
that a Waffen SS battalion, had been brought into the
area, to find us and crush us.

Our luck might run out someday. Helena was telling
me—I knew it, I saw it in her face—that she wanted
to die with me.

"I'll talk to Sasha about it," I said.

Sasha came in with the cognac. He patted Helena's
head. "Visiting hours are over. Patient has to get his
sleep."

For reasons that I still do not understand, my brother Karl was permitted to live for several months in the
isolation of the Kleine Festung.

In that curious, unpredictable way in which the
Nazi bureaucracy worked, both he and Frey were
beaten from time to time, and Frey died after a few
weeks. But Karl stayed alive—barely—in a dark cell.
He was almost a skeleton, his eyes unaccustomed to
light, his voice reduced to a croak. And his hands,
the hands of an artist, were two deformed lumps of
flesh and bone.

One day the guard came and unlocked his cell.

"Let's go, Weiss."

"Don't beat me again," he begged. "I'll die this
time."

"No more beatings. You're luckier than your friends
Frey and Felsher."

"You killed them."

"They wouldn't talk."

"I won't either."

The guard shrugged. "Who cares any more? They're
sending you to Auschwitz. Lovely place, nicer than
here. A family camp. They treat the Jews better there
than the Germans get treated in Berlin."

Some truly lunatic business followed. Karl was
marched into the office of Commandant Rahm and

made to sign a "confession" admitting certain crimes against the Reich. Rahm said that when the war ended, he, Karl Weiss, artist of Berlin, Jew, would have to stand trial for "serious crimes against the German people." Karl signed. What did it matter? He was already one of the walking dead—what long-term inmates called a "Mussulman."

Then he was told he had a half-hour to see his wife before being put aboard the transport for the "east." Theresienstadt was now in the process of being emptied. Every day trains left for some destination in Poland. It was Auschwitz, of course, and everyone was assured it was a "family camp," that there they would be joined—parents, children, old folks—and be given fruitful work, good food, a decent home to live in.

When Karl staggered into the studio for the last time, Inga let out a cry. His striped uniform hung loosely on his frame. He was bearded, hollow-eyed, bent over like an aged cripple. Spittle kept forming in the corners of his mouth.

She hugged him. Maria Kalova and a few of the artists who had not been involved in the conspiracy came forward.

"Oh, they have let you free, Karl," Inga said. She and Maria led him to a chair, found some tea for him. He tried to hide his hands when they offered him the metal cup.

"Oh, my beloved Karl," she cried. "What they have done to you . . . your hands."

The others were ashamed to look on. They moved away. Maria went to her drafting table. The SS kept them at work turning out "morale" posters, warnings to behave, promises of wonderful days to come.

"I am still alive," Karl said. His voice was lost, distant. "I never told them. Are the paintings safe?"

"Yes," she whispered. "Maria and I hid them."

He nodded. "I'll never paint again. They made sure of that."

Inga grasped his broken hands and began to kiss them.

"You can't make them well again. The way my mother used to kiss my bruises when I was a little boy. It didn't work then." He looked at his hands. "They say one gets used to it. But you never do."

"Don't talk about it." On her knees, she put her face against his hands.

"In the Kleine Festung, to keep from going crazy when they beat us, Frey and Felsher and I kept shouting that we would go to Italy. Florence, Venice. Frey insisted on Arezzo, too."

"We'll go there, dearest Karl, I promise."

He shivered, hunched over, rested his head on her yellow hair. "We will never see Italy as man and wife. My brief moments of courage are over." He sat up. "They're sending me to Auschwitz. They're finished with me. I suppose I'm not even worth killing, the way they murdered Frey and Felsher."

"You won't leave," she said. "If they send you, I'll go also."

He shook his head.

Maria Kalova left her table and walked over to them. She looked at them for a moment, then said: "You can't, Inga. You must tell Karl."

"Tell me . . . ?"

"At least, here in Theresienstadt, you have a chance, Inga," Maria went on. "You can work, they will spare you, but . . ."

"What are you talking about?" asked Karl.

Inga looked up at him. "Karl. Your child is in me."

"Child . . . ?"

"Ours."

He began to tremble again, shoved the teacup away, held her at arm's length. His arms were like thin pipes. "No. You mustn't have it."

"But I will. That is why Maria says I must stay here. Children have been born here. At least there is a clinic, and they will look after me."

"I've seen the children born here," he said. "They're cursed for the rest of their lives. Their eyes show it."

"It need not be that way."

Maria stepped forward. "The women will protect Inga, as long as they can. We'll be good to the child."

"No," my brother said. "If you love me, end its life before it opens its eyes in this damned place."

"No, I won't. I want your blessing. I want you to sanctify its life. Oh, Karl, I sometimes think I am more of a Jew than you, or Rudi . . ."

"I want no child born here."

"The rabbis say each life makes God's name holy. Please, Karl."

"They did not see Theresienstadt."

Maria said, "Karl, she is right. You must let Inga have her baby."

He lowered his head to his hands. "All right. It doesn't matter. It's a child I'll never know."

Inga said, "But you will. I promise you."

A kapo entered, stopped in the doorway. He was rounding up people for the transport. He said nothing.

Karl looked at him, got slowly to his feet. He whispered to Inga, "When the child is old enough, show him the paintings. So he will understand."

They kissed for the last time.

"Goodbye, my beloved wife," he said. "Perhaps all will go well. Perhaps they are telling us the truth. I've been saved at Buchenwald and at Theresienstadt because I could paint. Perhaps it will happen again." Then he looked at his clawlike hands and laughed bitterly.

She would not let him go, kept kissing him.

Finally, Maria had to separate them, as the kapo, slapping the truncheon against his leg, entered the studio.

"You must let him go, Inga," Maria said.

"Goodbye, Karl. Goodbye, my love."

They watched as he was shoved into a line of confused, frightened people—the once privileged inmates of the "Paradise Ghetto"—destined for the death camp. The guards ordered them to march off.

My parents were in Auschwitz. But Uncle Moses, now an active member of the Jewish Fighting Organization, had escaped the roundups. There could not have been more than fifty thousand Jews left in the ghetto, from a peak population of almost half a million. And those that remained were ill, hungry and terrified.

On January 9, Himmler visited the ghetto to see with his own eyes the pitiful remnants of European Jewry. He ordered a final total liquidation. Every last Jew was to be sent to Treblinka or Auschwitz.

The Jewish Fighting Organization, numbering about six hundred activists, but supported by perhaps a thousand other "irregulars," decided to make a stand when the next roundup occurred. It was becoming harder and harder for the Germans to deceive the Jews. All the promises of family camps, the bread-and-marmalade, were now known to be lies.

On a day in mid-January, my Uncle Moses and Aaron Feldman, pretending to be peddlers, shoved a pushcart toward a section of the wall that had been evacuated.

A ghetto policeman warned them that there would be a curfew in ten minutes.

Uncle Moses tipped his hat. "Yes, sir," he said. "We're just getting our merchandise home. Pots and pans, you know." Then he whispered to Aaron, "Don't worry. He was bribed."

As dusk fell on the wintry, deserted city, the man and the boy approached the wall.

Aaron leaped onto the cart, and with the aid of a grappling hook and a rope, scaled the wall. He kneeled on the top and whistled softly.

Two men from the Polish resistance—one was the man named Anton—ran from a doorway. They tossed a wooden crate to Aaron, who in turn dropped it to the cart below. The procedure was repeated with a second crate.

Then Aaron slid down the rope. Uncle Moses put the crates under the dirty canvas covering his "wares" and they started back to the resistance headquarters.

"You're late," the ghetto policeman said.

"My apologies," Uncle Moses said. And as he walked by, he bribed him a second time.

In these final months of the ghetto, whole neighborhoods had been emptied—the inhabitants either wiped out, or shipped to their death. It was in secret apartments in these areas that the so-called "illegals" now lived, the resisters, the fighters, the ones determined not to be led away praying and weeping.

To an apartment on the upper floor of what appeared to be an uninhabited building, Uncle Moses and Aaron carried the crates they had gotten from the Poles. It was a piddling contribution. No section of the resistance, the various Zionist groups, the Bundists, the left, had been able to make a dent on the Christian Poles. Some sympathy, yes. But little in the way of arms.

Eva Lubin and some others were present as they opened the crates. There were five new revolvers in one, and ammunition for them. There were also grenades.

"How do we start an uprising with these?" Moses asked.

"It's a beginning," Eva said. "Let's start loading them."

They began inserting bullets into the revolvers.

"If we can kill a few," Eva said hopefully. "Then get their machine guns, their rifles. To add to our small arsenal. We might make an impression."

"I'm not sure they'll oblige us," Moses said. "The word is they are going to bring in Waffen SS and Lithuanian auxiliaries. A building-by-building sweep. We may be too late with this."

Moses picked up two guns, twirled them. "I'm not a very convincing cowboy. I wasn't meant for this sort of thing. Jews and guns don't seem to go together."

There was a signal-type rap at the door—two short raps, a pause, then three more. Moses nodded at Aaron to unbolt the door.

Zalman entered, out of breath, covered with dust. He had crawled through mounds of rubble to reach them.

"The SS has blocked the street," Zalman said.

"The roundup?" Moses asked.

"Yes. Von Sammern's announced it. The last of the Jews are to come out."

"But why here?" Uncle Moses asked. "This is a deserted neighborhood. It's supposed to be empty."

"They may have followed you and the kid."

Moses took command. "Pack everything. Everyone take a gun. Grenades in pockets. Hide the crates. We'll leave by the rooftops."

As they obeyed his orders, they heard German voices below, boots kicking against doors, orders being shouted.

"Jews out!"

"All Jews out!"

"Come quietly, we mean no harm!"

Aaron ran from the room and peered down the stairway. Far below, on the ground floor, he could see three soldiers kicking in doors. Thus far they had found no one. The building, except for the apartment in which the fighters were hiding, had long been deserted.

Aaron and the others could hear the voices.

"What the hell are we looking for in this dump?"

"Someone said the Yids are supposed to have stolen guns."

Moses ordered everyone to stay in the apartment. He sent Eva and Zalman and Aaron into closets and the adjacent room. He himself wedged behind the door.

They could hear the Germans outside the door.

"Go on, you're always bragging what a hot shit you are."

"Bust it in, they're only fucking Jews."

"Think I'm afraid? Afraid of Jews?"

Boots, rifles, heavy bodies slammed against the bolted door. It splintered, gave way. The Germans entered the room.

Moses came from the corner and shot the first man in the face from a distance of no more than a meter. He fell, his face a crimson splotch.

The other two, before they could aim their rifles, were hit by a hail of bullets from Eva and Zalman.

One, less badly wounded, dragged the other out to the stairs.

Zalman took the machine pistol from the dead soldier's hands. Aaron ran into the hall, threw a grenade down the stairwell. The soldiers lurched, stumbled, rolled in gray-green heaps to the ground level.

The Jews looked at one another in amazement.

"They ran," Moses said wonderingly. "My God, they ran. At last I've seen it. They bleed and die and they are frightened—like us."

Aaron flew down the steps and yanked the arms and ammunition belts from the other two soldiers, then raced back up the stairs.

In the room, Zalman made a decision. "All of us out. They'll be back in force. Across the roofs. I'll go first."

Heavily armed now, they fled down the corridor, and climbed the metal ladder to the rooftop door.

All over the city now, sporadic fighting had broken out. Anelevitz himself had led an attack on a party of Germans escorting Jews to the Umschlagplatz. With five grenades, five pistols and a few Molotov cocktails, they had won a partial victory, liberated some Jews.

Still, the Germans managed to deport 6,500 Jews during this January battle. But it was far less than they had anticipated.

All over the ruined city, new leaflets from Lowy's old press began to appear, to encourage the Jews to fight.

The German occupying forces have begun the second stage of extermination!

Don't go to your death without a fight!

Stand up for yourselves!

Get hold of an ax, an iron bar, a knife—anything—and bolt the door of your houses!

Dare them to try and take them!

If you refuse to fight you will die!

Fight! And fight on!

After the firefight at Moses' apartment, and several other battles throughout the city, some of the resistance fighters assembled at another apartment. There they learned that many of their comrades were dead.

The Germans had been fought off at the Toebbens workshop in the center of the city, but at a high cost in Jewish losses.

In the second flat, Moses' group was met by others. They distributed the machine pistols and the rifles they had gotten in the first battle.

Aaron, at the window, saw a truck of SS soldiers enter the street. The truck emptied, but this time the Germans were cautious, hugging the sides of the buildings, wary of fire.

Zalman demonstrated the machine pistols to the others. "Don't aim it like a rifle," he said. "Just spray shots."

"I want one," Aaron said.

Moses patted his head. "Wait till you grow up."

Moses was at the window. He saw the SS men spreading down the street. He smacked a hand in his fist. "By God, the time has come to fight them on our ground."

As he spoke, four Germans entered the building.

"In the hallway," Moses commanded. "Fire when I give the order."

They ran into the corridor, hid in broom closets, behind the stairs—Moses, Zalman, Eva, Aaron, others.

This time the Germans were unable to kick a door in.

They were blasted with guns and grenades from above, and could not return the fire. They staggered back, bleeding and dying, to the street, piled into their trucks and left.

"I can't believe it," Zalman said. "They're going . . . going . . ."

"They die like anyone else," Moses said.

There was no doubt about it. The Germans, in that battle of January 1943, were giving up the fight—for a while. They had never counted on Jews firing back.

Later, as the resistance leaders gathered at the headquarters on Mila Street, stories came back to them of the courage—often doomed—of the Jews, who were denying the Nazis their attempt to clean out the ghetto.

Apparently a young woman named Emilia Landau was the heroine who started the resistance. When the

SS invaded the carpentry shop where she worked, she threw the first grenade, killing several SS men. But in the firefight that followed, she was killed.

At the headquarters of Kibbutz Dror, another battle took place—here the Germans were forced to retreat.

And around the Umschlagplatz itself, where my father had once so pathetically tried to save handfuls of doomed people, a score of running battles took place.

Some supplies now came in from a few sympathetic Poles outside the walls. The majority refused to help. There was even a group of Fascist Poles who warned their brethren not to aid the Jews, because the fighting was a ruse—the Jews would join with the Germans to crush the Polish resistance. (Their Fascism did not help them; the Germans intended to stamp them out also and make slaves of those who survived.)

Among the supplies sent in were land mines, grenade launchers, a mortar, and one machine gun.

"At last," Zalman said.

"Yes," Uncle Moses said bitterly. "All paid for. Cash on the line."

Eva asked, "Is there any hope they will join us?"

Anelevitz shook his head. "It is unlikely. They do not want to spill Polish blood in our behalf. We have learned by now. Only we can save ourselves."

"Save?" asked Moses.

"Yes," the young Zionist said. "Even if it means we die. We are still saved."

My uncle cocked his head, gingerly looked at the flat land mine, packed in waterproofing grease. "What does the Talmud tell us about assembling land mines?" he asked. No one laughed.

Anelevitz pointed to the calendar. "Remember the day, January 21, 1943. In the ghetto, we are at war."

On arriving at Auschwitz, my parents were spared the immediate trip to the gas chambers.

The selection was done at the railroad siding, by an SS officer in immaculate uniform. Those deemed unfit for work were sent to their deaths at once. My parents,

in comparative good health—all these things were relative in the camps—were marched to separate barracks.

Papa was assigned for a while to the camp infirmary, a dismal mockery of a place, some more of
that grim German humor. He did the best he could to
treat the ill and injured. It mattered little. The first
sign of weakness, of uselessness to the masters, and
people were marked for a trip to the "delousing" area.
Virtually no medicine was available. It suited the Nazis
to let people die in the barracks area. It took a load off
the four gassing complexes, the forty-six ovens.

My mother worked in one of the kitchens with Chana
Lowy.

Although men and women prisoners were kept in
separate parts of the camp, my father, as a physician,
was able to slip away now and then and visit her.

One day he came with what all felt was remarkable
news. One of the medical orderlies who had done
some work in the SS barracks had heard the Germans
talking in low, saddened voices. *An entire German
army was said to have surrendered at Stalingrad*. Not
a division, mind you, but an *army*.

Papa tried to cheer my mother up. She was sitting
on the edge of the bunk she shared with Lowy's wife,
and sewing. Life in the camps was a nightmare of
filth, lice, hunger, foul water, thin soup and moldy
bread. She, who had presided over elegant dinners and
played Mozart on the Bechstein . . .

Over her bunk she had placed photographs of Karl
and Inga in their wedding clothes, and one of Anna
and me. I know the photo. I'm wearing a striped
soccer shirt, holding the ball under my arm. Anna's
just kicked my shins because I teased her. But you
can't see it in the photo.

"If they catch you here you'll be punished, Josef,"
my mother said.

"It's all right. Lowy forged a pass for me. Besides,
I'll say I'm making a call."

"Josef, you've become a daredevil."

He kissed her cheek. "And how are you?"

"I'm fine. There's a rumor that a group of us in this

barracks, all who are strong enough, and that would include me and Mrs. Lowy, will be taken to work at the I. G. Farben factory tomorrow. That's surely good news."

"Perhaps they need a concert pianist."

"Or perhaps you could hire me as a nurse."

They both knew the rules at Auschwitz: those with no jobs, no skills, not needed to run the camp, or supply labor for the factories, for the giant corporations that kept the German army moving, did not last long.

"At least you are safe in your hospital job," she said.

He did not tell her that orders had come down to cut the infirmary staff by a half. Seniority would prevail; as a newer member he would probably lose his post.

Chana Lowy leaned over from the top bunk. "Max says there's road work to be had. Some German engineer, he's looking for people to build roads."

Lowy worked in the camp laundry, but it was not a safe place. The weakest, least likely to survive labored there, and it was often no more than a way station to the chambers.

"Road work?" asked my father. "That sounds good. Outdoor work."

"Oh, Josef, you?" my mother laughed. And they hugged each other again.

They heard a woman kapo outside, hurrying new prisoners to the barracks.

"You must go, Josef."

He held her in his arms. "They have consigned us to hell, Berta, but we must defy them. I insist we try to live, to sustain ourselves. I think a great deal of the boys, and of Inga."

"I too. I cannot forget them."

"Something tells me Karl and Rudi are alive. If one of us should die, the other must find them. And love them, stay with them. There must be a family Weiss again, Berta. Grandchildren, a home. Do you understand?"

"Of course I do."

"Not just because we are one family, and united to

each other, but because we are Jews. If they wanted so terribly to destroy us, then surely we are people of value, of worth. Perhaps we even have something to teach the world." He blinked, shook his head. "My goodness, I sound like a lecturer, a rabbi."

There was a commotion at the door to the barracks. A woman kapo entered, dragging a slender young girl with her. The girl could not have been more than seventeen. Once she slumped to the floor, and the kapo yanked her to her feet by her hair.

The kapo spied my father. "You. Against rules. Out."

"I'm leaving. Medical visit. I'm Dr. Weiss."

"Don't let me see you here again."

My father left.

The woman kapo shoved the girl into the crowded, fetid room. At once, the girl, making moaning noises, sank to the floor on all fours.

"Find her a place, any place," the kapo said. "She's crazy."

My mother got from her bunk. "What did you do to her? No. Don't strike her again. I'll look after her."

"I didn't do anything. She got off the train yesterday like this. She was all right until they sent her parents for delousing."

"And why can she not see them?"

"Who knows? Maybe it was an extra-long delousing shower. Or they went to a different part of the camp."

The women prisoners were silent, somber. They knew what the showers meant.

"See she don't mess herself," the kapo said. She left.

The girl was thin, very pretty, with long dark-brown hair and dark skin. My mother knelt beside her and stroked her back. "It's all right, my child. We won't hurt you here. Are you hungry?"

The girl would not talk, but she rose and embraced my mother. On the breast of her ragged cloth coat, next to the yellow star, someone had pinned a tag: SOFIA ALATRI, MILANO, ITALIA.

Chana Lowy joined my mother and they helped get the girl to her feet, and to one of the wooden berths.

"Are you hungry, my child?" my mother asked.

Mrs. Lowy suggested they might find some bread in the next barracks; one of the women, a former prostitute, was a notorious trader and usually had some extra food.

But the girl would not speak. She buried her head on my mother's chest and continued to moan.

"Do you want some water?" asked my mother. She even tried talking Italian to her; through her musical training she spoke fairly good Italian.

But Sofia Alatri seemed beyond help. And so my mother decided that affection, just the warmth of another human body, was all she could offer. It is odd, as I write this, from information I received from a woman who was in Auschwitz in that very barracks, how clearly I can see the scene. My mother had that talent for endowing any place she was with dignity and charm. She behaved elegantly and politely, and thus hoped to change the world.

"It's hard to remember that we are more than names on a tag," my mother said. "Or a blue number tattooed on one's arm. We're all people, yes, and we still are, dear Sofia. People with names, homes, loved ones. They cannot take that from us."

"But they have," Chana Lowy said. "That's how they'll finally do away with us. No names, nothing. So we're not anything any more."

My mother began to brush the girl's hair, and Sofia stopped moaning. The touch of a human hand, the sense of love, and warmth, perhaps.

"Poor child," my mother said. "You make me think of my daughter Anna. How can people be so cruel? How can they do such things to innocents?"

"It's an old story," Chana Lowy said. "When you have nothing else to do, pick on Jews. We were in their way, that's all."

My mother put her arm around Sofia. "You can talk to me. I am your friend."

The girl covered her face. Still, silence.

My mother took the photos down from the boards

over the bunk. "Look. My children. They are such good young people. Like you, my dear."

Sofia said nothing. But she looked dumbly at the old wrinkled photos.

"My Karl. And his wife Inga. That's Rudi in the striped shirt. He's twenty-four now. You would like him. So handsome. And that's Anna next to him. She would . . . would be . . . a bit older than you."

"They've scared her wits out of her," Mrs. Lowy said. "You know, I'm as frightened as she is, but I try not to show it."

"It's nothing to be ashamed of," my mother said.

"Well, maybe work tomorrow. I mean, real work, in the factories, where they need us."

Sofia began to shiver. My mother put a blanket over her shoulders. One small stove, usually cold, was all that any barracks had.

"You're cold, Sofia, come sit closer. Tell me about your family. Your mother and father. Oh, I know about Italian Jews, they are very fine people. Sephardim, scholars. Tell me about Milano."

Chana Lowy shook her head. "Nothing. They've killed her mind. Maybe she's better off not remembering. Maybe that's what's wrong with Jews, they remember too much."

Mama held the girl's chin up and looked into her eyes. "So beautiful. Like my Anna. Come, I'll sing to you."

Sweetly, softly, my mother sang the *Lorelei,* rocking the girl back and forth in her arms.

For a few moments there was no sound in the barracks, except for my mother's singing. Some of the women joined, humming softly. Some wept, with memories of the lives they had once known—homes, families, meals together, children going to school, weddings, all the happy fragments that make for a good life.

Then there was silence.

Two women kapos and an SS guard carrying a machine pistol stood in the doorway.

The first kapo spoke. "Everyone in this barracks fall out."

"Why?" a woman asked. "We've had our medical inspection."

"You have work for us?" Chana Lowy asked.

"No questions," the SS man said. "Just fall out."

"Nothing to be afraid of," the kapo said.

But they all knew. Those that did not know, pretended not to. The deception would take place to the very end—and the self-deception.

"Hurry along, ladies," the SS man said. He was a squat, pockmarked man, one woman recalled, unfit for front-line duty. "Form a double file outside, fast."

"It must be for the jobs," Chana Lowy insisted.

My mother combed her hair. She would go to the end neat, clean, as proper as she could make herself appear. "I am afraid not, Mrs. Lowy. We must do as they tell us, and do it with dignity."

The Italian girl would not get up when the others rose. The woman kapo lunged at her with the truncheon.

"Stop!" my mother cried. "Don't touch her."

"She's crazy."

"She will come with me. Do not hit her."

My mother, Berta Weiss of Berlin, musician and housewife, daughter of a hero of the First World War, then lifted Sofia from the bunk and held her close to her. She kissed her cheek.

"You will walk with me, Sofia," she said.

Outside, the older women were helped along by the younger. They knew. I am told this was a common occurrence. When the transports were light, when Hoess' chambers and ovens were slack, entire blocks of barracks would, without warning, be emptied. No excuses saved anyone; no privileges mattered. It was a matter of getting the job done, of filling quotas. The goal was twelve thousand a day, and the Führer and Himmler would have their twelve thousand.

They were marched across the barracks area, under guard, out of a gate, and toward the famous rows of trees Hoess had planted. Ahead of them loomed the concrete chamber, with its long flat roof. It was wintertime. The famous women's orchestra was not serenading guards and victims that day.

In the freezing cold, they were ordered to undress. Clothing was piled neatly. Valuables taken for "safekeeping." They were advised that the fumigating, the delousing, would take about five minutes. Their property would be returned as they left.

"You'll be better fit for work," the SS men told them.

And they stared at the naked women.

"Help her, she's crazy," the woman kapo said, pointing to Sofia, who had again fallen to the ground. My mother and Chana helped her undress. She seemed pitiful, defenseless. The Reich was doing away with its mortal enemies.

"You'll feel better afterward," a guard shouted.

Apparently, the undressing of the women was an event, a diversion, for many of the SS men. They gathered in groups, grinning, nudging one another. Their bestiality had no limits. No one has yet explained it to me.

My mother turned to one of the women kapos—a Jew like herself, and one who with the Sonderkommandos later dragged the corpses out and to the ovens—and said, "I am Berta Weiss of Berlin, and this is Chana Lowy, my friend. Please tell our husbands what happened."

The woman nodded. Kapos and *Sonderkommandos,* too, when the time came, would be committed to the chambers.

It was cold, damp, and it almost seemed that some of the women welcomed death. Or they preferred to believe to the end that the Germans were not lying.

"They say it's good for the lungs," an old woman said to my mother.

"Breathe deeply," the guard said. "Hold the children high, so they can breathe it in. It's good for you. No colds, no coughs."

Chana Lowy began to weep.

"Be brave, Chana," my mother said. She was holding Sofia erect, talking softly to her.

"Less than five minutes, you'll be out," the guard said.

A young red-haired girl broke from the ranks of people being marched from the trees to the opened metal door. They caught her. She screamed, howled, begged, refused to join the line of march. An SS officer appeared. He ordered her dragged behind the trees. Two shots were heard. There was no more screaming.

"Move, move," the guards shouted. "It's only a shower room."

My mother paused at the door, turned her head toward the camp, and said, "Goodbye, Josef. I love you."

The camp records reveal it was a slow day. Only seven thousand were gassed. The bodies were consumed by the gas ovens and the ashes thrown into the Sola River that flowed near the camp.

My father and Lowy missed selection for the chambers that same day, through a stroke of luck.

Lowy had mentioned that a road-working detail was being set up, and that it meant a good long assignment. By a freakish coincidence, both he and my father were pulled out of their jobs—where people were being randomly selected for death—and assigned to the road team.

Outdoor work usually meant an extra ration of food. It was also rather unusual for Jews to last on this kind of work any length of time. They were held in contempt as laborers by the Germans. Poles or Russian war prisoners were preferred.

But the day after my mother was murdered—my father had no knowledge of it—Lowy and Dr. Josef Weiss found themselves spreading hot tar over a road on the outskirts of the barracks area. It was vital work, providing a new link between one of the factories making armaments and a railhead. Eichmann and his transports of Jews had so clogged the railway lines in and out of Auschwitz that war materiel destined for the front was often sidelined, or was delayed.

The work was arduous at the road-building site. But it was work that would last. Moreover, the man in charge, a German civil engineer named Kurt Dorf, had achieved something of a reputation among the Jews. He was alleged to have saved hundreds of Jews by selecting them for work, by insisting they were good laborers, and somehow keeping them out of the clutches of Hoess' insatiable underlings.

Dorf was a tall, weathered man, soft-voiced, slow-moving. (I have since met him, and, of course, knew about his testimony at Nuremberg. He and I have corresponded quite often, and as will be seen at the end of this narrative, he let me see Erik Dorf's diaries and other papers.)

The fumes of the hot tar, the backbreaking work, made my father dizzy that first day, and he staggered.

"You okay, doc?" asked Lowy.

"Yes, yes, I'm fine."

"Maybe you should go to the hospital."

"You must be joking, Lowy. That's where they damned near selected me for special treatment. Thank God this engineer grabbed me. I've learned a lesson. You do work they need, you survive."

"Maybe," Lowy said cynically.

They looked up at Kurt Dorf—tall, pipe-smoking, in his civilian coat, reading a set of blueprints.

"That guy Dorf," Lowy said. "He isn't like the rest."

"Because he's spared our life?"

"Sure. He's hid maybe five hundred of us on his jobs. I heard the SS guys wanted to get rid of him."

My father bent to his work on the hot tar. "Strange. Where are the others like him? Only thirty-three percent of the Germans voted for Hitler in 1933. What happened to the other two-thirds?"

"They got to love him. Or the Nazis scared everyone. Jail, murder, torture. They showed the world how. Listen, I was in the printers' union with lots of Christian guys, friends, Socialists. Where are they? They joined the parade."

My father all but fell. He walked away from the roadbed, rested on one knee. The fumes were affecting him.

Kurt Dorf saw him and walked down from the construction shack in which he had his office.

"Are you ill?" he asked my father.

"No, no, just a bit tired. I'll get back to work."

Kurt Dorf halted him. "What is your name?"

"Weiss. Josef Weiss."

Lowy piped up, from the road: *"Dr.* Weiss."

"Medical doctor?" the engineer asked.

"Yes. I used to be in general practice in Berlin. I had my own clinic."

Kurt Dorf looked at my father for a moment. A small supply truck had driven up. Supplies were being unloaded. "Why don't you work on the truck the rest of the day?" he said. "It's not as arduous."

My father nodded, started to walk away. Then he turned. "We are grateful to you. We know what you are doing."

Dorf was embarrassed by this. A party of SS, led by an officer, had appeared and were waiting for him at the construction shack. Blueprints rolled under his arm, he turned and walked toward them.

Erik Dorf's Diary

Auschwitz
February 1943

Pleasant surprise at Auschwitz today, on my weekly visit. Well, pleasant up to a point.

I found my Uncle Kurt at work on a new roadbuilding project. This place is so vast and complex, so much work is being accomplished here for the war effort, that it is possible not to know about a relative or a friend who may be employed here. Kurt was at the Buna artificial rubber plant for some time, redesigning buildings, and now he is working on the road to I. G. Farben.

We shook hands, a bit coolly at first, then embraced with a good deal more warmth. I wanted to enjoy the privacy of the reunion, so I dismissed my aides.

"So," he said. "Uncle and nephew reunited. How are you, Erik?"

"Well enough. Let's see. When did we last see each other? Christmas two years ago in Berlin, correct?"

"With Marta and the children. *Silent Night* around that beautiful piano." He smiled. "Good to see you, Erik."

"And I'm delighted to see you. Reminder that I have a family."

Kurt then invited me inside his tiny office in the wooden shack. He said he had some real coffee—not ersatz—and we would celebrate our meeting with a cup.

We were silent awhile, sipping the hot coffee, looking out of the large glass window (the shack was on a height) at the city that had grown out of Auschwitz. Distantly, the four high chimneys smoked.

"Your roads have been a great help to us," I said. "Not only for the transport of war goods, but for prevention of contagion, simplifying disposal procedures."

He looked at me strangely. "I understand there is a great deal of disease in this camp."

"Oh, yes. The Jews are a filthy people."

"I imagine there is also infection among those who run it?"

"Some."

"Not of the body so much as of the spirit. Of the soul, perhaps."

I sensed where the discussion was moving. Kurt had always had a bit of the moralist in him. Never a party member, he could not understand our goals, our long-range policies.

"You've gotten even more righteously indignant, Uncle. What we do, we do out of necessity."

He got up. "You need not lie to me. I am of your blood. Save your lies and deceits for those thousands and thousands of innocent Jews you are murdering in this place. Yes, and Russians and Poles, and anyone else you deem an enemy."

I said nothing, crossed my legs.

He walked away, suddenly spun about. "Why in God's name must you strip them naked before they die? In the name of all that is decent, can't you leave them with a shred of dignity before you murder them? I've seen your SS louts grinning at Jewish women, those poor souls trying to cover themselves. I never really believed in Satan, or that there was pure evil in the world, until I came here."

"It took you a long time," I said quietly. "You were at Babi Yar."

"Maybe I wanted to believe your lies. Like so many of our countrymen."

"Uncle, you are defending criminals, spies, saboteurs. These Jews are spreaders of contagion, both physical and political. We are sanitizing Europe, eventually the world. More people agree with us than you imagine." I spoke calmly, rationally, trying to make clear to him my commitment to my duties.

Kurt looked at me with icy blue eyes; the harsh eyes of my father when he had caught me in a lie. "I heard a remarkable story the other day," he said. "In January, the Jews in the Warsaw ghetto revolted. They actually killed German soldiers, forced the SS to retreat. Think of it, Erik, those unarmed, despised, terrorized people, fighting back against the lords of the earth. It almost restores one's confidence in Divine Providence."

"Almost. But not altogether."

I had heard about the rebellion in Warsaw in January. It is rumored that the Jews are still arming, preparing to resist our efforts to dislodge the last fifty thousand remaining there. It is of no consequence. In the end we will prevail. But I felt I owed my father's brother something. Engineer though he was, road builder, he could find himself in deep trouble expressing such sentiments.

I looked out the window at his road gang. "I am told

you have been using several hundred Jews as laborers. Extra rations, privileges. There are Poles available."

"What of it?"

"Jews are marked for special handling. They are to be worked until they are useless and then marked for special handling."

"Say what you mean, Erik, say the word. Murder."

I ignored him. "I shall find you some Red Army prisoners. Strong backs and dull minds. They can replace your Jews. If we let the Jews survive, they will destroy Germany someday."

"I want you to leave my workers alone."

"You curry favor with enemies of the Reich, is that it? The children of these Jews . . . the children we send . . ."

To my astonishment, he ran at me and grabbed my collar, almost tearing the insignia off. I am not a physical man, I never have been. I detest violence, fighting. My Uncle Kurt is tall and well muscled. Years of outdoor work have made him powerful. I felt the strength in his hands. He shook me as if I were a puppy.

"I should strangle you with my own hands, you bloody murdering bastard. As a favor to my dead brother. How many dead will satisfy you, Major Dorf? A million? Two million? How many bodies will you burn over there before you are secure? Dammit, Erik, show me some sign of humanity before this ends, show me that there is something decent left in you!"

"Take your hands off me."

He hurled me against the wooden wall. I did not resist him. I was armed, of course, but it was unthinkable to draw my weapon. Besides, his anger had subsided into a kind of sick disgust.

Straightening my uniform, trying to ascertain whether any of my men had witnessed the embarrassing scene, I tried to tell my uncle precisely what Marta, with her womanly intuition, had said to me recently. Persuasively, I told him that if we were to stop killing Jews now it would be an admission of guilt. When one is convinced of one's rightness, one cannot halt a course of action simply because it is distasteful, or because others misinterpret it. Therein lies real courage: doing what is often sickening and apparently brutal, but is necessitated by a great goal, a far-reaching plan.

"What we do is a moral act," I said, "a historical imperative."

He came at me again, and I thought this time he would surely kill me.

But he stopped short, and whispered, "I understand too well. I understand all of you too well. Get out."

His anger, his irrationality, concerned me. But as long as he does the job for Hoess, builds roads, modernizes factories, he is useful. Besides, he apparently keeps his traitorous views to himself—except for me.

Rudi Weiss' Story

The day after my mother was gassed to death, my father learned of it. In the evening, after he and Lowy had finished their work at the road-building site, they had, with forged passes, made their way to the women's sector.

There they found an empty barracks. A woman kapo, one of those who had marched my mother off to her death, told him that all the women in that block had gone to the gas chambers.

The men broke down and wept. There was little they could say to each other, no words of comfort.

Someone told me that my father went in and sat on my mother's bunk for a long time. He went through her valise, touched her meager belongings, and took from it a folder of piano music—her old, yellowed, fraying music, from our home on Groningstrasse. Mozart, Beethoven, Schubert, Vivaldi.

"Goddam them," Lowy wept. "Why doesn't anyone ever say no to them? Why don't the Allies bomb the railroads here, the ovens, the gas rooms?"

My father had neither answer nor solace for him.

On Sunday, April 18, 1943, the Jewish Fighting Organization, in which my Uncle Moses, once a timid druggist, was now a key member, learned that the Germans were preparing a mass attack on the remaining Jews. It was to start at two in the morning of the following day.

Anelevitz called his subcommanders together. Weapons were given out. Key points in the ghetto were manned. It would be a fight to the death. Of actual armed combatants, of which my Uncle Moses was one, there were about five hundred.

What they did not know was that Von Stroop, the SS general in charge of the operation, had *seven thousand* men ready to destroy them—Waffen SS, regular army including artillery, tanks and planes, two battalions of German police, Polish police, key members of the SD, and a battalion of Ukrainian, Latvian and Lithuanian auxiliaries.

The armed Jews were sent out in small groups to three main areas of the ghetto—the central area near Nalewki and Zemenhof Streets, and the factory area near Leszno Street.

Inside an apartment on a high floor, Uncle Moses and Zalman sat at a window, waiting. The room was dark, but the family who owned the apartment, incredibly, were preparing for Passover. A woman was setting the table with candelabra, matzohs, the haggadah.

In Uncle Moses' detachment, besides Zalman, who sat with him at the window, were Eva Lubin and Aaron. Aaron slept at the rear of the room, atop an ammunition case. In the areas I have mentioned, similar small parties of armed Jews waited. The streets were deserted.

Zalman yawned. "Passover, Weiss. April 19, 1943."

"I'm afraid you and I shall have no seder," Uncle Moses said.

"We could have attended one last night. The SS invited us. Didn't you hear the sound truck they sent through?"

"Oh, indeed," Moses said. "Did anyone go?"

"Not even Elijah the Prophet."

"A pity. I might have gone if I didn't have this job. You know, Zalman, when I was a kid, I never got to ask the four questions. Maybe last night General von Stroop would have given me the honor."

"Perhaps. Before shooting you."

Eva recalls my uncle suddenly reminiscing about his brother and sister-in-law, my parents. A bachelor, he had no family left. He missed them, wanted them.

"Yes," Zalman said. "We could use a doctor now."

"To treat the wounded?"

Zalman nodded.

"My inclination will be to shoot them if they cannot be rescued. We know what kind of people we are fighting."

They talked about new rumors—a platoon of Jewish police, who were supposed to take part in the attack, had been executed by firing squad; Himmler had come to Warsaw to witness the end of the ghetto.

"I wish there were more than a handful of us," Moses said.

"These people," Zalman said, not without sympathy, "these people, our people, they were not trained to shoot guns."

"Was I?"

Both men peered into the dark street. Zionist banners hung from many buildings—the blue-and-white star, the blue bars. There were also Polish flags and appeals to the Poles to join the fight. To the end, there was hope that they would.

Moses spoke. "Tomorrow is Hitler's birthday. The SS has promised us as his birthday present. Warsaw will be cleaned out to celebrate the Führer's anniversary."

"Candles on his cake," Eva said.

Moses sighed. "I never thought I would be resigned to dying. But I am. That fellow Anelevitz taught me a lot. The world will know we did not all march off, docile, dumb, accepting."

A light went on in the rear room.

"Put it out," Eva ordered the woman.

"I'm cleaning up for Passover."

"Clean up in the dark," Eva said.

"Passover," Zalman said. "Still they observe. I'm not critical of them, Weiss, just speechless. Maybe we needed less tradition, fewer prayers—and more guns."

An old man in the rear of the room was praying—shawl, skull cap, opened prayer book. He bent and swayed in holy ecstasy.

"Be tolerant, Zalman. This was their life. They knew nothing else, and it kept them together for a long time. Maybe it will keep us together when this hell ends."

From the street below, there were drum beats, martial music. The gate to the ghetto had swung open and a detachment of ghetto police, unarmed, walked into the empty streets. Behind them were the foreign auxiliaries. They carried rifles, machine pistols.

A sound truck now appeared and stopped in the midst of the square. From its speaker, a friendly voice issued forth:

"A happy Passover to our Jewish friends! Put down your guns! Come out in peace! We shall arrange a seder for you! Forget this foolish battle, for you are being led by traitors who only seek your death, while they escape!"

Uncle Moses, who had practiced shooting in the basements, raised his rifle and blew the loudspeaker apart with one shot. It dangled on broken wires.

The truck went into reverse. On orders barked from SS noncoms, the ghetto police and the auxiliaries formed battle lines. They were not leaving.

The drums began to beat again. They marched farther into the street. It had been agreed upon earlier by Anelevitz and the other commanders to save ammunition for the Germans.

"First our miserable police," Zalman said.

"Let them pass," Moses said.

Eva wriggled to another window and leveled her gun. Aaron slipped off the ammunition chest and moved forward, bringing boxes of bullets with him, extra guns.

"Lithuania, Latvia, the Ukraine," Moses said. "The old familiar faces."

"Hold fire," Zalman whispered.

"Someday I shall look a Latvian in the eye and say, 'Brother, I spared your life in the Warsaw ghetto.'"

Incredibly, they kept marching in. Now there was a battalion of Waffen SS in the square. They set up desks, field telephones, a kitchen. It was a major military operation.

"Now!" Zalman shouted.

There were massed volleys from a dozen windows around the square. The Germans, singing loudly, marching smartly to the corner of Nalewki and Gensia Streets, were cut down. Their formation broke. Dead and wounded were left in the street.

From attics, balconies, and upper windows, like the one in which Moses, Zalman, Eva and Aaron crouched, a concentrated hail of fire sent the Nazi column into a confused retreat.

They could hear the German officers shouting below:

"Where the hell are they?"

"Back!"

"Take cover!"

Uncle Moses leveled his rifle again, and said, "There's a God in Heaven after all. I'd begun to have my doubts."

"A man could die with a happy heart seeing this," Zalman said. "Look at them pull back."

"For the first time in my life," Moses said, as he jammed a fresh clip into his weapon, "I feel the blood of King David in me. Believe me, it's better than just filling prescriptions."

"Don't go overboard, Weiss," Zalman said.

Several times the Germans tried to regroup, to come back for their dead and wounded, and each time they were stopped by a wall of fire. Sometimes, Jewish groups, armed with pistols, would descend to street level and fight it out with the Nazis, building to building.

This first armed encounter lasted roughly two hours, from six to eight in the morning, and incredibly, there were no casualties among the Jewish fighters. They had caught the SS completely by surprise.

Von Stroop, the German general, who refused to

enter the ghetto and debase himself by battling Jews, later admitted in his report that "The Jewish resistance was unexpected, unusually strong and a great surprise. At our first penetration into the ghetto, the Jews and the Polish bandits succeeded, with arms in hand, in repulsing our attacking forces, including the tanks and Panzers." It was all true, except the reference to "Polish bandits"—all the fighters were Jews.

But of course the Nazis returned, and in greater force—as always shoving their Ukrainian and Baltic lackeys in front of them—but now taking cover behind tanks, no longer marching in the middle of the street, no longer singing martial airs and assuming the Jews would surrender at the sight of a German soldier.

In the apartment, at dusk, Moses and his group could hear the family reading the Passover service.

" 'When Moses was grown he one day came on an Egyptian smiting a Hebrew, and he smote the Egyptian. Moses fled from the face of Pharoah and dwelt in the land of Midian . . .' "

When a young boy at the table asked, "Why is this night different from all other nights?" Zalman and Moses could not help smiling. Yes, it was different. Unlike any Passover in the history of the Jewish people.

" 'And it is written,' " the old man in the rear room read, in Hebrew, " 'we cried unto the Lord the God of our Fathers and the Lord heard our voice and saw our affliction and our toil and our oppression . . .' "

For a moment they all listened. Then Moses said, "Let's join with him."

And they all recited together:

" 'And the Lord brought us out of Egypt with a mighty hand, and with an outstretched arm, and with great terror and with signs and wonders.' "

Soon their position became untenable. Tanks and artillery entered the ghetto. Mortars began to lob shells to the upper floors and the roofs, from which the firing originated.

Moses ordered the family to end their seder. God would understand. They had to get out. A mortar shell had exploded on the roof. The woman took the sacred books, the matzoh, the plates, the wine cups. The others followed her.

A second mortar shell exploded against the side of the building. Zalman suffered a wound in his left arm from a chunk of masonry.

"We can't hold here," Moses said. "They have too much power below us. Everyone grab weapons, ammunition, and down to the tunnels."

Ten minutes later, following Aaron, who knew the tunnels the way the rats knew them, they emerged into another apartment.

This apartment overlooked Mila and Zamenhofa Streets, and the buildings around it had excellent firing positions. There was at least one machine gun, and a number of hidden soldiers, armed with Molotov cocktails, grenades, and automatic rifles.

Moses and his party had the joy of seeing the first German tank that rumbled into the intersection turned into an inferno by the Molotov cocktails. The crew was burned alive. Two other tanks pulled back. Germans took cover behind them, waiting, wondering.

"They're pulling out again," Moses said.

"It's the crossfire," Zalman said. He was still firing, using one arm, as Eva bandaged his wound.

Someone unfurled another Zionist flag and hung it from the window.

"Good," Moses said. "Let the bastards see it. Let them know who we are."

Another German retreat was underway.

"How does it feel, Zalman?" Moses asked.

"My arm's fine."

"No. Watching these sons-of-bitches run."

"Better than anything. Weiss, we have smitten the Philistines hip and thigh."

The fighting went on for twenty days. Von Stroop, weary of his underlings failures, took personal command. For two days, with my uncle and his friends, in the thick of it, the resistance held the position in Muranowski Square. Here, Von Stroop first brought in anti-aircraft artillery, with the aim of reducing every point of resistance, building by building.

I must note that in this battle, a party of six Polish Christians, led by a man named Iwanski, entered the ghetto and joined in the fight against the Germans. They brought a new supply of arms. Four of them died fighting side by side with the Jews. These are the kind of people for whom some special memorial is needed; some tribute.

On April 23, the Jews were still fighting from scattered bunkers around the city. Himmler, furious that the world knew about the Jews' resistance, sent Von Stroop an angry telegram:

"The round-ups in the Warsaw ghetto must be carried out with relentless determination and in as ruthless a manner as possible. The tougher the attack, the better. Recent events show just how dangerous these Jews really are."

I am no psychologist, but my wife has studied a great deal of it. She says Himmler was a coward deep down, afraid of the weak, fearful of humiliation, exposure. After ordering the murder of millions of unarmed, helpless innocents, he now quailed before several hundred armed Jews.

On the very day Himmler sent the message to his generals, Anelevitz addressed a statement to contacts in the "Aryan" sector, in a last hope that they would enter the battle.

"The Jews in the ghetto are defending themselves at last and their vengeance has taken a positive form. I bear witness to the superb and heroic battle being fought by the Jewish insurgents. . . ."

Slowly, the bunkers were being reduced. Night fighting became the general rule. The Germans hesitated to enter during the day. Instead they bombed from the air, lobbed artillery shells in, started huge fires. A systematic siege of the ghetto began. The resistance knew that its days were numbered. The Germans were engaged in a military campaign.

In one of the more disgusting aspects of the entire

battle, Polish civilians stood around the gate outside the ghetto and *cheered and applauded* as Jewish men and women, burning, roasted alive in the buildings, leaped to their death.

"Another one!" they would shriek.

"And another!"

But the courageous Iwanski, the Polish army officer, came back *again* to fight with the Jews. His brother was killed and his son seriously wounded. Few knew about him. If many Poles abandoned us, laughed as we died, there was at least an Iwanski to uphold some honor.

By May 8, the resistance had dwindled to a handful of bunkers, from which firing could be heard. Tunnels had been explored for secret escape routes. There were few left. The Germans had also explored the underground passages and blocked many of them.

In the bunker at 18 Mila Street, Anelevitz spoke to his commanders by telephone. He begged them to hold on, to wait for aid from the outside. New appeals were being made to the Poles. Surrender was out of the question.

On Max Lowy's old printing press—Lowy had long been deported to Auschwitz with my father—a final appeal was run off.

Their guns empty of ammunition, Moses, Zalman and others rested against the damp walls of the bunker.

"How many days, Zalman?"

"We started on April 19. It's the ninth of May. Twenty days, and they haven't beaten us yet."

My uncle said, "We never gave Hitler his birthday present."

"We did. But not the one he wanted."

Anelevitz took the fresh sheet of paper from Eva Lubin's ink-stained hands, and began to read:

" 'Thousands of our women and children are being burned alive in the houses. People enveloped in flames leap like torches from windows. But we fight on. It is a struggle for your and our freedom. We will avenge Auschwitz, Treblinka, Belzec and Maidanek. Long live freedom. Death to the murderous and criminal occupants. Long live the life and death struggle against the German barbarian.' "

A young ghetto fighter, dressed in a captured German uniform, stepped forward. Anelevitz gave him the leaflets. "See if you can get through with these. Good luck."

Eva looked sadly at the printing press. "The last of our paper," she said.

But the SS had scouted the area. Every possible exit from the bunker, every sewer, cellar door, aperture was being guarded.

The young man carrying the leaflets emerged from a rubble-covered cellar door, and was shot dead by two SS men.

Inside the bunker the others waited.

"I have never been a very brave man," Uncle Moses said.

"Nor I," Zalman added.

Eva smiled at them. "You are brave enough."

"But I learned something," Moses said. "We all have to die, so why not make it worthwhile?"

As they talked in low voices, waiting, listening to the occasional bursts of fire in the street above, Aaron, breathless, came running back. He had led the young man in Nazi uniform to the exit. "They shot him," Aaron said. "They know."

Above them, they could hear voices now, the rumble of a truck, orders being shouted.

Suddenly an acrid, choking odor began to seep into the bunker.

"Some kind of gas," Moses said. "Everyone cover your faces . . . use wet cloth."

Eva recalls mothers huddling with their children. There was a lot of weeping now. An old man began to pray.

Anelevitz stood up. "It's over," he said calmly.

Zalman came to his side. "The pills?"

"Not enough for everyone."

"Maybe some want to leave, take their chances outside."

Anelevitz nodded. "They are free to do so."

People were coughing. In addition, artillery shells were pounding the heavy walls above the bunker. The long narrow room shivered. The end was close.

Uncle Moses walked to a group of people. "Whoever wishes to leave . . . I will take them."

"And I will take others," Eva Lubin said.

Aaron and some others chose to follow Moses to one escape route. Eva would look for another—an old, disused sewer that led beyond the walls.

Moses embraced Zalman and Anelevitz. "Goodbye, my friends."

Zalman shook my uncle's hand. "Goodbye, Weiss. We really didn't get to know each other too well."

"Next time, Zalman."

"Of course."

Someone began to sing the songs of the ghetto. Then they sang *Hatikvah,* the Zionist hymn.

A column formed behind Moses, another behind Eva.

"I have the right name," my uncle said, "but I am afraid I can lead you to no promised land. Stay in line. Aaron, you bring up the rear. Let us proceed with dignity and courage."

He walked off. Eva went the other way.

The SS were waiting for them. Perhaps you have seen that famous photograph—the haggard, unarmed Jews, rising from a hole in the rubble, as those grinning soldiers watch, rifles leveled at them.

In the bunker below, Anelevitz and many others chose to take their own lives, like the heroes of Masada.

"You will not be harmed," a German lieutenant said. "This is only for a search and then registration. All of you face the wall, hands high."

They turned, Moses, Aaron, all his friends of the resistance.

"Come, children," Uncle Moses said. "Let us all hold

hands and pray. Will someone start it, please? I'm a bit rusty."

He took Aaron Feldman's hand on one side, an old woman's on the other. The old bearded man who had presided at the seder twenty days ago began the Shema.

"Shema Isroel Adonai Elohenu, Adonai Ehud . . ."

They kept praying, reaffirming their faith, until the guns opened fire. All died.

Eva Lubin's party had better luck. For thirty hours they wandered through the sewers of Warsaw. One morning, they heard an explosion above, saw daylight, and emerged on the outskirts of the city.

Contact had been made with a group of Jewish partisans. A truck was waiting. The handful who had survived the Warsaw ghetto rebellion were driven to the forests. In the city itself the resistance had ended.

Erik Dorf's Diary

Auschwitz
August 1943

More and more, I find myself away from Berlin.

Never have I seen our officials—especially Kaltenbrunner and Eichmann—more determined to get the job done. Why? I wonder. It is only a matter of time before the war is lost. Mussolini was arrested the other day. Sicily has been invaded. Our last offensive in Russia failed. There is even a chilling report that a Red Army guerrilla force, quite large, has penetrated the Carpathian front—five hundred miles beyond our own lines.

Today found me at Auschwitz, checking with Hoess to see if the supply of Zyklon B is sufficient, if Eichmann's transports are on time.

The load on Auschwitz and the other annihilation camps—odd, how I have steeled myself to the use of that word—will be heavier. Himmler, now that Warsaw has been liquidated, has ordered the immediate destruction of all Polish ghettoes. That means one thing: more work for us.

I must note here the fact that some Europeans do not agree with our plans. The Bulgarians, for example, a Slavic people for whom I have no regard at all, have defied us and dispersed and hidden their Jews. And the Italians continue to be difficult, refusing to cooperate, sending Jews into convents and monasteries and the Italian countryside. It disturbs me that whenever our units are defied in this manner, they more or less acquiesce, and turn to other business.

In any event, on this hot afternoon, I dined in the officers' mess at Auschwitz. Eichmann and Hoess were present. They were, as always, cool, dedicated, full of new plans. The river is becoming clogged with ashes. They are now dumping the product of the ovens in a field some distance from the camp.

From the corner of my eye I saw my Uncle Kurt enter the dining room. He avoided my eye, took a seat by himself and sat in silence, puffing on his pipe. Since the scene at his office, where he dared to lay violent hands on me, we have exchanged no words.

I was halfway through a letter from Marta when I started.

"Something wrong?" asked Eichmann.

"Good God," I said. "Our street was bombed."

Eichmann commented that the English and Americans were utter barbarians, without any respect for human life, the culture of cities. Churchill was a savage, unloosing his warplanes on innocent civilians, Hoess added.

Marta, in her letter, assured me that she and the children were safe in the shelter during the raid. There was some damage to the apartment. Our beautiful piano was scarred with falling plaster.

There was another bit of news in Marta's letter. Father Lichtenberg, the troublesome priest who refused my advice regarding his sermons about Jews, died in

Dachau. The circumstances are unknown. I feel a bit sorry for him. He simply did not understand the need to run with the tide, to accept the inevitable. I mentioned Lichtenberg's death to Eichmann and Hoess. They were not interested. And why should they be? What is one more death—priest or layman, German or Pole? The important thing is to rid Europe of Jews; we all knew it; we all understand the urgency of our mission. This campaign of extermination is *central and vital* to everything the Führer has taught us. It is the fulcrum, the lever, the nucleus of our movement. It is not merely a means, or an end, but both the *means and the end* to a racially pure Europe, ruled by Nordic aristocrats.

Eichmann threw down his knife and fork. He refused to eat his cutlet. "You know, Hoess, the stink from those chimneys is awful. Gets worse every day. How can a man enjoy his lunch in this place?"

Hoess' appetite was not affected. He drank his Czech beer, downed his schnitzel. "Can't be helped, Eichmann. We're still processing twelve thousand a day, top production at any camp. I hear Theresienstadt is also marked for liquidation. Romania, Hungary, they'll all be delivering us their Jews soon. Forty-six ovens won't be enough."

"We've all got our problems, Hoess. I'm still fighting the army for trains. The bastards insist they need the rolling stock for their armies in Russia. What comes first? I asked them—Russia or getting rid of Jews? They had no answer. They know what the chief's orders are."

It occurred to me that as Eichmann's and Hoess' voices rose, my Uncle Kurt was hearing it all. He had not been eating, merely smoking, sipping his coffee, his somber face, taking it all in.

Suddenly he got up, slapped down some marks and walked past us. As he did, he looked at me with a revulsion and hatred I did not think him capable of. Then he left.

Again, I saw in Kurt's eyes that same reproach,

that same anger I had seen in my father's face when I was a boy. Do grownups realize the hurt they inflict on children with their disapproval?

I felt a need to teach my uncle a lesson, to squelch that moral superiority he shows me, that self-appointed conscience he has become. So I asked Hoess what the policy on using Jews as laborers was. He replied that it was the same as always, but more "urgent." That is, not only were they to be worked until they were fit for "special handling," but that whenever possible they were to be replaced with Poles and Russians—even if they gave evidence of being strong enough to work.

"I'm told there are several hundred Jews still working on the roads," I said, "and I have seen lots of Christians available to replace them."

"Then they should be replaced. I can't keep track of everything, Dorf."

He reiterated. Every Jew now in Auschwitz, and every one who would come here, was marked for special handling. Skills, strength, privilege no longer counted. I made a mental note to send Hoess a written memorandum on Uncle Kurt's Jews.

Rudi Weiss' Story

The blow fell on my father sometime in August 1943. I have not been able to pinpoint the date.

At some day in mid-month, he and his friend Max Lowy, who had been with him in Berlin and Warsaw, and all of their detail were summarily marched from their jobs to the gas chambers.

Papa and Lowy, and a third man—one who survived and told me—were working a grading machine. The third man had heard news from a newcomer—the Warsaw ghetto had risen. Many Germans were killed. They had used tanks and planes and artillery to subdue the Jewish fighters. They both asked him if any of their friends had been involved; but he knew very little. The resistance was wiped out, but the Germans had needed seven thousand men to do it.

As they talked, they saw an SS sergeant approach Kurt Dorf and give him a sheet of orders. An argument ensued, but Dorf, a civilian, had only limited authority. They heard the sergeant say, quite clearly, "The detail will be replaced."

A half-dozen SS men now appeared.

The Jews working for Kurt Dorf were ordered into a column of twos. They were told they were being taken for delousing, fumigation. A new outbreak of typhus was feared.

There was a pause. Then the men assembled. Some began to weep. One man fell to his knees and embraced the SS sergeant's boots.

"He should not," my father said. "Let's at least go with pride."

Lowy gulped. "I guess it's over, doc."

"Yes, you and I have had a long journey."

"Not exactly a vacation, doc."

They were marched off, toward the concrete buildings, the distant chimneys.

"You've been a good friend, Lowy," my father said. "And I might add, an excellent patient. You always paid your bills on time, and you did little complaining."

Lowy blinked back tears. He looked at the guards. "Doc . . . why don't we just jump on them? We'll die anyway. Take a few with us. What's wrong with us?"

"We were trained all our lives not to."

They walked across the hot, dusty compound, on the road they had helped build. They turned once. The engineer was standing alone, arms folded, watching them.

"Give me your hand, Lowy," Papa said.

"I feel like a kid. First day off to school."

My father tried to joke to ease the terror. "Lowy, did you ever have your gall bladder looked after? I've been warning you about it for years, ever since you first came to my office on Groningstrasse."

"I may have it done this fall."

They kept marching. Men stumbled. They knew.

"A hell of a way for a man to die," Lowy said.

Someone behind them called out, "Maybe it's what they say—just a delousing."

Lowy nodded. "Yeah. Delousing." He looked at his gnarled hands, a printer's hands. "Dammit. There's black ink under my nails, doc. Well, maybe the pamphlets helped."

"I'm sure they did," Papa said.

They were gassed several hours later, with two thousand others.

In September, Uncle Sasha had gotten word of a trainload of Luftwaffe pilots that was due to pass over a railroad not far from our newest camp. He decided to attempt to blow up the lines and ambush them.

We had conducted a dozen raids by now, against the Ukrainian militia and the Germans, and we felt this would be our best haul so far. We had lost men, but the family camp had remained intact under his firm leadership. We had more guns than ever, more food. It was amazing how the local farmers, seeing us armed and defiant, learned to respect us.

Helena insisted on going along. She had been on several raids—against my will—but I was especially worried about her on this one. It was too dangerous. The trains were always heavily armed with machine guns mounted fore and aft.

Sasha sent me out to tie the dynamite to the railroad ties. It was a terribly hot day. I was soaked through my khaki shirt. In the trees and bushes at the side of the railroad, a dozen partisans, including Helena, Yuri and Nadya, waited.

I had learned a great deal about explosives. None of these things are hard to learn. What is difficult is getting up the courage to put them into practice. (In Israel, Tamar says, Jews became soldiers overnight. Armed and trained, they made the world forget that they had been frightened ghetto dwellers.)

Distantly we heard a train whistle.

"Hurry," Sasha said.

"There's time," I shouted back. I made sure the dynamite sticks were secure, that the caps were in position. The pounding of the heavy wheels would set them off. As soon as the explosion took place, we would rake the rail cars with automatic fire and grenades. It would be our biggest action to date.

I made my last knots, then walked into the cover of the foliage, unlimbering my machine pistol.

Helena stood next to me. She looked small, unprotected. But she too carried a machine pistol, and had grenades draped around her neck.

"Some necklace," I said.

"I'm proud of it."

I kissed her cheek. She was frightened. We all were. But we had learned not to show it. We would never plead for mercy. We would die before giving in.

Uncle Sasha had an ear cocked in the direction from which the train was due. He looked concerned.

"What's wrong?" I asked.

"I think they're stopping."

We all listened. Beyond a curve in the tracks, there came a sound of *chug-chug-chug*—an engine locomotive slowing down. Then the sound ended, and the engine seemed to sigh.

We waited. Seldom had I seen Sasha so upset. He nodded at me. "Rudi, sneak out to the edge and see what's happening."

I crawled on my belly, holding the machine pistol in my cradled arms, and reached the shoulder of the rail line. A few more yards and I could see the locomotive. It had stopped.

On the roof of the first car was a machine gun with a crew. They were standing, looking about. The train was a good fifty yards from the explosive charges I had set. Something had aroused their suspicions. Maybe it was just a security measure—they knew there were partisans in the area.

Then I saw a half-dozen soldiers come out of the train, all in combat gear. They began to walk slowly down the track, while the train remained stationary.

I crawled back to Sasha and the others.

"They're sending men out," I whispered.

Sasha frowned. "They've been tipped. Let's clear out, as fast as we can."

"We can take them," I said. "Ambush them. Let them come."

"No. Only when we have an advantage. They'll kill us with those heavy machine guns. Everyone move off."

We started through the woods.

Evidently the Germans suspected something, for we could hear orders being barked out, men running along the gravel shoulder. The train also edged up, but did not reach the explosives.

Then, without warning, the machine gun opened fire.

Twigs and branches split and cracked around us.

"Scatter!" Uncle Sasha shouted.

I grabbed Helena's arm and we raced through the forest. Branches cracked at our face, clutched at our clothing. I wanted to turn and fire, to try to stop them, for I could hear them behind us—boots pounding, shouts in German, cracks of their rifles, louder bursts from the mounted gun.

And suddenly Helena was hit. She fell without a word, still holding my hand.

I stopped and kneeled over her. Her face was calm, pale. There was no agony on it. The bullets had entered her back and killed her instantly. She lay there, looking tinier than ever, more beautiful, and I buried my face on her breast.

Why they did not shoot me down also, I do not know. A rifle butt smashed against my head and I was unconscious.

Some of our band had escaped. Four, including Yuri and Helena, were killed. Two other young men and I—again for reasons that elude me—were marched to a collecting point for Red Army prisoners.

The usual rule on partisans was to shoot them on

sight. But perhaps they planned to torture us and get information on the entire partisan movement.

We were not fed, given just enough water to keep us from dying of thirst, and then, unexpectedly, with a great rush of action and orders, we were herded aboard a cattle car.

I huddled in a corner, and I felt I was being transported to my death. Perhaps I had cheated death long enough. I thought of Helena dying silently under the fusillade of bullets. She had wanted to come on a raid so that we could die together. Now she was gone; I lived. I felt guilty, miserable, unworthy. I should have argued her out of her foolish desire. I wept for a long time as I squatted in the rattling, noisy wagon. The trip was interminable. One of the men said we were going to Poland. He had seen road signs.

That made me certain that we were to be killed. Perhaps worked as slave laborers for a while.

Finally the train was unloaded at a town called Sobibor. We were walked for a mile or so to a concentration camp—barbed wire hung on concrete pillars, floodlights, a high fence, dogs, sentries. A bleak, dreadful place. Chimneys smoked in the distance. A death camp.

Eventually, I was assigned to a barracks, where I climbed into a bunk and fell into a long, nightmarish sleep. I dreamed of my boyhood in Berlin, the games I'd played—and it was a time of terror and defeat in my mind. When I awakened, I expected Helena to be at my side, as she had been for years. I may have even called her name. But I cried no more. A great hole had grown inside me, eaten at my emotions, my heart. She was dead. Our cause was a lost one. I would never see Sasha or my partisan friends again.

The barracks was crowded, hot, malodorous. Surprisingly, it was very quiet. Some men were speaking softly in Russian, and I caught a word here and there. I pretended to be sleeping, turned, and saw five or six rugged-looking men in tattered army uniforms sitting on a bunk. They were looking at a drawing on top of a box.

One man stood between them and me, evidently appointed to keep an eye on me.

"Mine field," I heard him say. "Here. Here."

I had learned a good deal of Russian in my days with the partisans and from Helena. Again, I listened.

"Barbed wire, double strands," the man was saying. "We might need wire cutters."

Another man asked, "What about the SS barracks? The guns on the water tower?"

"We'll have to knock them out," the other man said.

I soon gathered that the man in charge was a Red Army captain. His name was Barski. The man who spoke to him, his lieutenant, was named Vanya.

This Vanya suddenly said, "Captain Barski, we don't have a single gun."

"We will get them."

I raised myself on one elbow. The bunk creaked. The man watching me said something to the others.

Vanya said, "The bastard, he's awake and he's been listening."

He came over to the bunk and pulled me down. I struggled. We almost came to blows. Others separated us.

"Keep your hands off me," I said in bad Russian.

Vanya tried to punch me in the stomach. I parried the blow and went for him again. He and some others shoved me to a lower berth.

"What did you just hear?" Captain Barski asked.

"I didn't understand it. I'm a German Jew. My Russian isn't that good."

Barski switched to Yiddish—close enough to German so that we could talk. "Go on, what do you think we were talking about?"

"It sounds like you're going to break out."

Vanya shook his head. "He's a goddam spy, Barski," he said. "The SS planted him here. German Jew, hell."

Barski tapped my shoulder. "What's your name, kid?"

"Weiss. Rudi Weiss."

"What the hell are you doing here in Sobibor?"

"Sobibor? I don't know. I was on a train with a bunch of other prisoners. I was a partisan in the Ukraine."

They looked at one another. Barski sat down opposite me. "Listen to me, Weiss, if that's your name. If you're a spy, we'll have to kill you. This is a death camp. There's a gas chamber here, furnaces. We're getting out. If the Germans put you here to spy on us, I'll strangle you myself."

So I told them my story—running away from Berlin years ago, wandering across Europe, Czechoslovakia, the Ukraine. When I got to the part about joining Uncle Sasha, Barski's eyes brightened.

"What did he do before he became a partisan?" the Red Army captain asked.

"He was a doctor. In a village called Koretz."

He asked me more questions—who were some other members of the band, was there a rabbi with them. My answers appeared to satisfy him. I told him of some of the actions I had fought in—the attack on the SS headquarters, other assaults.

When I'd finished, he looked at the others. "I believe him," Barski said. "It sounds crazy, a guy from Berlin, a German Jew fighting down here, but crazier things have happened."

"I say kill him," Vanya said.

But Barski was convinced. He shook his head. "Listen, Weiss, you know what happens in this camp? They gas two thousand a day. The SS men sleep on pillows stuffed with the hair from the Jewish women they murder. They have their fun knocking out the brains of Jewish children. There's a field outside, three feet deep —ashes of the Jews."

I nodded. "I believe it. I believe anything about them. Just get me a gun. I'll fight with you."

Erik Dorf's Diary

The Reichsführer called a meeting of about a hundred officers involved in the final solution.

We met in the lobby of a hotel, here in Posen. A lot of my old colleagues were present—friends and enemies. Among the group, Blobel, Ohlendorf, Eichmann, Hoess.

In the old days I would be right at Heydrich's side, notebook in hand. Alas, Kaltenbrunner didn't want me that close to him. The ogre sat to one side of Himmler, listening. I sat somewhat at the rear of the room. More and more, I find a need for large doses of cognac to get through the day. I also find my mind less able to concentrate on important matters. Long noted for my detail work, I know I am becoming forgetful, sloppy.

Blobel was bragging about his work at Babi Yar. All the bodies (so he claimed) had been dug up and burned. Vast pyres of railroad ties soaked with gasoline had been used to, as someone put it, "burn the evidence."

But why? I wonder to myself. Why bother?

Blobel reported that over 100,000 corpses had been disposed of. Then Eichman did some boasting about his trains. Hoess talked, modestly and quietly, about the functioning of Auschwitz.

Himmler kept asking if these things were being done "secretly." He seemed more concerned than ever that the outside world not know of our work of the past few years. And yet, when one officer suggested we halt the exterminations so that Jewish labor could be used, he was silenced at once—by Reichsführer Himmler himself.

It was stuffy and hot in the hotel lobby. Most of us

were weary. We wondered why Himmler had called
us together.

Someone else—possibly Globocnik—requested a
dozen Iron Crosses for his men, for their heroic work
in ridding eastern Europe of Jews, Himmler liked the
notion. He had already given out numerous decora-
tions for officers involved in the crushing of the Warsaw rebellion.

More business was discussed. Blobel, sitting with
Ohlendorf not far from me, nudged the latter in the
ribs and said, loud enough for me to hear, "Silence
from the Great Dorf."

"Maybe he's turned yellow," Ohlendorf said. But he
nodded at me. A very polite, educated fellow. He freely speaks about his killing of ninety thousand Jews
in the Odessa area.

Suddenly—out of the blue—Himmler asked, "May I
ask that all of you submit suggestions on the eventual
dismantling of the camps?"

"Dismantling?" asked Blobel.

"Yes," the Reichsführer said. "Our job is all but done.
I . . . I am not suggesting Germany will be defeated,
of course. But the evidence, the remains will lead to
misunderstandings."

"I don't think so, sir," I said. My voice was emboldened by the half-bottle of brandy I'd consumed.

"Dorf? Ah, our resident semanticist." Himmler smiled
at me.

"Perhaps we should let the camps and the furnaces
stand," I said, "as a fitting memorial to our great
work." The alcohol loosened my tongue. "Perhaps we
should tell the world how we achieved—"

Blobel grabbed my arm. "Shut up, Dorf."

They all looked away from me. It was odd. I noticed that a small recording machine was on the table
and was operating.

Himmler ignored my interruption, and began to
speak again. "I must talk to you frankly about a very
grave matter. Among ourselves it should be mentioned
quite frankly and yet we will never talk of it publicly.

I mean the evacuation of the Jews, the extermination of the Jewish race."

Obviously it had been on his mind a long time.

"It is one of the things it is easy to talk about," Himmler rambled on. His tiny eyes seemed to vanish behind the pince-nez. "The Jewish race is being exterminated, and it is quite clear it is in our program, elimination of the Jews. And we are doing it, exterminating them."

In a way, it was refreshing. After all the wordplay, the euphemisms, the code words (many of which I created), it was almost exhilarating, cleansing, to hear our leader come out with it. And still the recording apparatus spun.

He went on to be critical of those Germans who knew "a good Jew" or who would ask that a Jew be spared. "Not one of those who talk this way has witnessed it," he said, "not one of them has been through it. Most of you know what it means when a hundred corpses are lying side by side, or five hundred, or a thousand. To have stuck it out and at the same time to have remained decent men, that is what has made us hard. This is a page of glory in our history which has never been written and is never to be written."

What his speech meant to him personally, or to us, I am not sure. I am certain that the annihilation process will be speeded up. But his insistence on secrecy, on the possibility of a plan for dismantling the death camps, bothers me.

I stumbled to my feet and asked to be heard. There was such total silence in the room, from these officers who had murdered—four million souls? five?—that I was able to command their attention.

"Permit me to say, Reichsführer," I said, "that if our work is truly that noble, we should advertise it to the world."

"Quiet, you damn fool," Blobel growled.

"I believe the major misunderstands me," Himmler said.

"If I may, sir," I went on. "The Führer has pointed out many times that we are performing a service for western civilization, for Christianity. We are defending the west against Bolshevism. As for Jews, even our great religious figure Luther saw them as menaces."

"Oh, I quite agree, Major," the Reichsführer said. "But others will not see our aims as clearly. And the Jews will lie about us."

"Let them," I said. "Let them. Those who are left. But I say we should flood the world with film, photographs, affidavits, lists of the dead, testimony. Let us build working models of Hoess' Auschwitz, let us tell the world every last detail about our heroic deeds. And let us insist to all that what we did to the Jews was a moral and racial necessity! Surely the western Allies will appreciate that."

I seemed to have transfixed them. I could see the sweaty, hot faces staring at me in that dismal hotel lobby.

"Yes," I went on, "let us maintain that we have committed no crime, but have merely followed the imperatives of European history. Eminent philosophers and churchmen can be called upon to support our case. I'm a lawyer, you know. I understand these things.

"No shame, gentlemen, no deceptions, no apologies for dead Jews, or excuses about spies, or disease or sabotage. We must make clear to the world that we stand between civilization and the Jewish plot to destroy our world, to pollute the race, to dominate us. We, *we alone,* have been men enough to accept their challenge. Why hide it? Why keep it a secret? Why invent excuses?"

I noticed their cold stares. Himmler was frozen.

"We have to convince the world—friend and foe alike—that the Jews forced this war on themselves . . . that we, we alone . . . we stood . . . we stand between the survival of . . . of . . ."

My voice dwindled into silence. They sat, all of them, looking at me as if I were a diseased dog.

Finally Himmler broke the silence. "Major Dorf has a point, I suspect. The details of our future attitudes toward our work can be the subject of another meeting. What is important is that we feel in our hearts that we have fulfilled this task with love for our own people, and that we have not in the process been damaged in our inner souls."

I got up to speak again, but Blobel and Ohlendorf this time grabbed me, each by an arm, and led me to the corridor, thence up the stairs of the dingy hotel to my room. There were Polish whores, some of them quite beautiful, available for all of us, but I wanted only my cognac bottle.

"You fucking idiot," Blobel said.

I could hear Himmler's prim, small voice, still addressing his men. "We have remained decent, loving men, and for that we may be proud . . ."

Rudi Weiss' Story

Vanya, the prisoner who had not trusted me, soon became my friend. He managed to get me work in the cobbler's shop, where, it was agreed, the revolt would begin. As yet we had not a single gun.

Before we were marched off to work that morning, I remember Barski telling us, in the dark barracks, "Do it in such a way that they don't make a sound."

A half-dozen of us carried small hatchets jammed into our belts.

We opened the shoemaker's workshop. Vanya began to replace heels.

I kneeled in a corner and began to polish the black boots of the SS officers.

About an hour after we had opened, a young SS lieutenant came in. He carried a Luger in a holster in his belt.

"My boots ready?" he asked Vanya.

"Yes sir. You can try them on, if you wish."

The officer sat on one of those low stools one finds in boot shops and waited. He saw me, kneeling, polishing. "Who's that?"

"New prisoner, sir."

There was a fleeting moment of suspicion on his

face. Then he decided he had nothing to fear. I was gaunt, bruised, dressed in prison rags.

Vanya yanked at the officer's boots, as he sat on the lower part of the stool. He got the new boot on. I got up with the pair I had been polishing and carried them to the shelf behind the stool.

I placed them on the shelf over the name of their owner. Something must have warned the lieutenant.

He spun around, and as he did, I smashed his skull with the hatchet. It was odd. He did not have time to reach for his gun, or make a sound. I hit him so hard that his brains spattered Vanya, who was several feet away.

Vanya yanked the Luger from his belt. We dragged the body into a closet, cleaned up the blood and brains.

About ten minutes later an SS captain entered. He, too, was looking for a new pair of boots. I did not even give him a chance to say good morning. From behind the door, I leaped at him and killed him with one blow of the hatchet. He wavered, staggered, seemed reluctant to die. I hit him a second time.

This time I took his pistol. We dragged him into the closet also.

Coinciding with these actions, other men in Barski's unit killed Germans in the tailoring shop, the cabinet-maker's, and the barber shop. We were very lucky. The soldiers had dribbled in, alone or in pairs, and were cut down before they could sound a warning.

Finally, Barski and a small party, armed now with handguns, raced into the weapons room, killed a half-dozen guards, and unlocked the gun rack. We met them there and loaded up with guns and ammunition.

By now almost a hundred prisoners had gathered in the barracks area.

Barski distributed guns to the men. For the women, there were hatchets, broom-handles, shovels. We would kill any way we could.

An alarm had been sounded somewhere.

The Klaxon drew guards from their quarters—we could see the Germans and their Ukrainian auxiliaries running out, armed, confused, shouting commands.

We took cover behind the barracks.

Barski assigned me to command a group of about twelve men, some armed, some willing to fight and die with shovels and rakes in their hands.

A squad of SS enlisted men came charging down the main street in the barracks area, and I gave the command to fire. We killed them all—seven or eight. The other units held back, not so ready to take us on.

It was Barski's plan to assault the camp arsenal before we fled, arming our entire party, and turning us into what amounted to a small army.

Several units raced forward, holding close to the sides of buildings, trying to reach the arsenal. But as we approached, a machine gun on top of the camp water tower opened up, and scores of us were cut down.

Barski stopped the squad leaders behind the camp mess hall.

"Useless," he said. "We've got to forget about the arsenal. To the gate."

By now we had been joined by a mob—almost six hundred Jews, eager for freedom, willing to face the German guns, to race for the gates unarmed rather than submit to Sobibor's gas chambers.

I followed Barski. Vanya led another group. From behind the cover of water barrels and sheds, we opened fire on the guards at the central gate and killed them all.

A mad rush followed. All six hundred Jews raced for the exit. Some threw stones at the guards, tried to blind them with sand.

I could hear Barski screaming at them not to run to their left—the land there was laced with mines, and there was a double strand of barbed wire to cut through. It was a dreadful sight. The land mines began to explode; dozens were blown apart.

Barski led us to a passageway behind the officers' barracks, where we knew the earth had not been mined. Shots began to crack around us from the barracks. But Barski was right. The field was not only free of mines, but the barbed wire was thin, and we climbed over it.

Bullets kept cracking around us. Men fell. Women stumbled. I thought of Helena dying in the forest. And I kept running. A hundred meters . . . two hundred meters . . .

In the evening, we stopped beside a stream.

There was just a handful of us in our party. But we hoped others had made it safely out of the death camp.

A girl named Luba, a Red Army auxiliary, staggered into our midst at dusk. She was covered with blood, wounded in the arm and hand. She sat down and wept for a long time before she could tell her story.

Yes, six hundred Jews had fled to the gates. Four hundred, most of them without guns, actually made it to the woods and meadows outside the camp. But more than half of these were killed by landmines, pursuing SS and police, aircraft. Several thousand Fascists were sent in pursuit of the escapees from Sobibor. And, we learned later, Polish Fascist groups in the forest finished off those who escaped the SS. An old story to me.

There were about sixty of us with Barski. We were better armed, trained, tougher. We would try to reach a Soviet partisan brigade.

Years later I learned that we had killed ten SS men and thirty-eight Ukrainians. Another forty Ukrainian guards fled rather than be called to account by the Germans. And two days after our breakout, Himmler ordered Sobibor destroyed. We had made the bastard uneasy, thrown a scare into the great murderer.

Barski said that he and his comrades would head east and try to find a Red Army unit. There was a report that the Russians were about to recapture Kiev. Barski wanted to be part of the action.

Kiev. I thought of Helena and how we had stolen bread, hidden from the Germans. How Hans Helms had betrayed us and then been killed. And how we had run away from the procession of doomed Jews, and from afar seen the massacre at Babi Yar.

The hole in my insides began to eat at me, like an acid, a slow fire. I wanted her to be with me again, sharing crude meals, sleeping with me in haylofts, barns. But I would never see her again. I doubted now that I could love again, ever give myself to a woman.

Barski invited me to join them, but I said I wanted to travel alone. He warned me that I'd be in danger of capture, that by heading west I was moving toward German lines. I said I didn't care. If I died, I died, and besides they hadn't gotten me yet.

"Good luck, kid," he said. And he embraced me.

"Can I keep a gun?" I asked.

"Sure. You've earned it."

I walked off, following the stream, seeing Helena's face in every tree, every leaf.

My brother Karl did not survive another winter. He had been transported to Auschwitz with a trainload of other Theresienstadt prisoners, marked for gassing.

Somehow—perhaps the word had gotten out that he was a gifted artist, and might be used—he was spared immediate death.

That he lived as long as he did was probably due to the kindness of a man named Hirsch Weinberg, who told me of Karl's last days. This was the same Weinberg who had been a tailor with Karl at Buchenwald, five years earlier, after the arrests that followed *Kristallnacht*.

One day Weinberg noticed this tall, gaunt man, hiding his hands under his tunic. He studied the face and recognized him.

"I know you," Weinburg said. "Weiss . . . the artist . . ."

They were in the same barracks, and Weinberg looked after him, tried to find work for him, sneaked bits of bread to him.

"Weiss, don't you remember anything?" Weinberg asked. "The day we had the fight over the bread? When they hung us on the trees?"

Karl nodded. He even smiled.

"Sure, you remember," the tailor went on. "You had a Christian wife. Used to smuggle letters in to you."

Karl nodded.

Weinberg brought him up to date. A lot of news had seeped into the camp. The Red Army had entered White Russia. Although Jews from all over Europe were still being sent to Auschwitz, something was in the wind. There had been a lull in extermination selections. Hoess was said to be in trouble with his bosses.

Oh, there was all kinds of good news. Italy had declared war on the Germans; Smolensk was in Russian hands; the Allied invasion was imminent . . .

Karl's voice was lost, weak. "My father . . . here . . . mother . . ."

It fell to Weinberg to have to tell him that both my parents had been gassed a year before. They were among the two million victims who had fed the furnaces. Weinberg had met my father once; he had liked him, as had everyone.

Karl could not cry. He listened, nodded, asked for water.

(How strange. I, too, had difficulty crying for a long time after Helena died. What happened to us? Did the evil of our persecutors, their lack of humanity, infect us?)

Then Weinberg saw Karl's hands. "My God. What they did to them!"

He studied the gnarled, broken claws, stroked them.

"Punished," Karl said. "For drawings."

"Listen, Weiss, we've come this far. Hang on. We'll be free someday."

"Paper," Karl said. "Pencil . . . charcoal . . ."

Weinberg went looking through the barracks and found a large piece of gray cardboard, and a chunk of charcoal from the stove. He propped Karl up in bed and gave them to him.

Karl's ruined hand could barely clutch the charcoal. He smiled when he succeeded, asked Weinberg to hold the cardboard steady.

Then he proceeded to draw, in great sweeping lines.

I have seen the picture. Inga has it. I'm not sure what it means. A swamp, darkening sky, clouds, and from the murky waters, a hand rising, reaching toward the sky.

He kept drawing, thanked Weinberg, and asked him to save his last picture.

Karl died some weeks later—typhus, cholera, no one knows. Perhaps he starved to death. Or simply lost the will to live.

His body was hauled away and burned, and his ashes mingled with those of our parents, and millions of others.

Erik Dorf's Diary

Auschwitz
November 1944

I have become a wandering emissary of the Third Reich—reporting endlessly on the final solution, keeping statistics, checking with Eichmann, Hoess, all the others involved in this staggering labor.

Last July, the Russians overran the Lublin concentration camp. The secret was out—as if it could ever have been kept. The horror pictures—so-called—have been shown to the world. We, of course, deny them, and claim that they are actually *Russian* atrocities perpetrated on the Poles.

But the fact that the world is slowly learning of our vast "resettlement" plans has not deterred Eichmann. He is arranging—even now, as the death-camp details are being revealed—for the mass deportation of Romania's Jews. All through this fall of 1944, Eichmann, with my support, has kept the transports rolling, from Holland, Belgium, France. Survivors of the Krakow ghetto were dispatched to Auschwitz. Only last month, Eichmann sent 35,000 Jews from Budapest to various camps, all of these people marked for "resettlement."

In Lublin, the Russians are hanging our staff men

at the Maidanek camp. Yet Eichmann, Hoess, and many others, myself included, persist.

Himmler has sent orders out that the Auschwitz crematoria be *destroyed*. Gassings are all but stopped at Auschwitz. Instead we are desperately moving the inmates west, shifting them from camp to camp, a step ahead of the Russians.

All sorts of lunatic, irrational things are happening, as if no one is in charge, or knows precisely how to act in the face of our imminent defeat. Today orders came to ship only "Hungarian Jews" from Bergen-Belsen to Switzerland—orders from who? why?—and tomorrow I may receive a cable ordering that everyone in Auschwitz be marched west, to places like Gross-Rosen and Sachsenhausen.

Does Himmler really think he can hide our work?

Does he (and Kaltenbrunner and my other superiors) honestly think they can change the nature of our efforts by shifting several thousand starving ghosts?

Yet we keep them wandering all over Poland, Germany, Czechoslovakia, tens of thousands of these Jews, in rags, dying by the roadside, collapsing of starvation and disease. Would it not make more sense to take them out of their misery by the simple expedient of Zyklon B? Could we not then say that our measures were of a humane nature? That human endurance, the will to live, having been terminated in these Jews—and others—it is only decent to let them die as quickly and painlessly as possible? But no. My chiefs keep up this pretense that the camps never existed, that no deaths occurred there, that there were no such things as gas chambers and ovens. I sometimes feel I almost believe it myself.

Of course my personal life has suffered. I see Marta rarely, and we do not converse much, let alone share a bed. Peter is in uniform now, training with the so-called "wolf packs" who are supposed to fight to the death to save Berlin. He is a tall, handsome lad; yet, when I saw him last, I had little to say to him. Laura wept a great deal. She was hungry most of the time, and in the selfish way children have, blamed Marta and me for everything. The Bechstein is still in our apartment—damaged but playable. Marta thought of giving Laura lessons; nothing came of it.

So today I am at Auschwitz again, trying to carry out Himmler's orders—dismantle, destroy, burn, obliterate the evidence. What a farce! But I am going through the motions.

And yet, there are times when I wonder if these efforts are as futile as they seem. For so many years, despite rumors and even direct reports, the world refused to believe that we were doing what we were. We were good at deception. And we found willing believers. Our Aesopian language worked well. Of course. The Jews. Problems. Have to be resettled, you understand.

How astonishing, the way the world turned away, took our word, trusted us!

As early as 1942, the Swedish government had word of the killing centers. Through a report from one of their diplomats, via a talkative SS officer. But the Stockholm government *did not let this information out*. And even the BBC, and other voices of our enemies, were cautious about uttering a word about the fate of the Jews. So perhaps I am being unduly harsh in my judgment of our SS leaders; properly handled we might well convince a vast area of public opinion that we never harmed a hair on a Jew's head, executed only criminals, permitted the Jews to live peaceful lives in little cities of their own. Perhaps.

Not long ago, as Russian guns boomed at the I. G. Farben calcium mines outside the camp, and Soviet planes bombed us, I was on the phone with some flunky in Berlin, who kept screaming at me that the camp must be destroyed, all records burned, every last inmate evacuated, or killed, or whatever. It is all of a senselessness that defies belief.

But I have obeyed orders a long time, and I keep shouting at Josef Kramer, who has replaced Hoess, to keep at the job of blowing up the crematoria, dismantling the gas chambers.

Today Kramer laughed. He was stuffing papers into

a briefcase, packing a valise—like a salesman off on a hurried trip.

"They're all out of their fucking minds," Kramer said. "Hide this place? Shit, it's all on paper, all recorded. Eichmann's already told Himmler we've killed six million—four million in the camps, and the rest by the Einsatzgruppen. It's in writing, in memos, all over the place. What the hell will it mean to blow up a few buildings?"

"No more gassing!" I shouted. There was a plan to get rid of the last of the Sonderkommandos. "No more—"

"So Berlin can say *we* did it, they didn't know a thing that was going on. Like that asshole Hans Frank. When the Russians captured him, he said he never had a thing to do with it, never killed a Jew. It was us, the SS, the RSHA."

I began—I don't know why—to pull open the Auschwitz files and throw folders into the blazing fireplace. I ripped papers apart, heaped them high in the flames, while Kramer mocked me.

"You'd be better off burning more Jews, Dorf."

"No. No. Berlin says move everyone west. Himmler is convinced the allies will understand. Britain and America will be sympathetic to us. It's the Russians we have to avoid. Himmler wants to negotiate with the Americans. He—"

Kurt Dorf suddenly entered the room. My uncle saw me dashing about, pulling open desk drawers, ripping file cabinets apart, stuffing the fireplace with the documentation of Auschwitz.

My uncle watched me for a few seconds. "It's useless, Erik. Katowice has been evacuated. The Volksturm is melting away. The Red Army will be here in a day or two."

"And you will cheer their arrival?"

He did not answer, merely shook his head. "I understand, Erik, that there are seven tons of human hair, neatly bagged and labeled, in the warehouse. Should not someone be assigned to burn it?"

I paid no attention, but kept burning papers. Himmler may be smarter than any of us. We can play the Russians off against the allies—explain our motives —the Führer was right, we are saving the West, saving civilization. We didn't want this war—the Jews forced it on us, and we had to make them pay.

Kramer was on another phone. I must say that although he was planning a fast departure, he was following some of my orders. He was telling his subordinates to march out the 58,000 remaining prisoners—in freezing weather—and keep them marching west.

Kurt stopped me, grabbing my arms. He is much older, but stronger. "Dear nephew," he said, "didn't you once tell me that we should make our glorious deeds public? That we should boast to the world how we had solved the Jewish problem? Why this change of heart? Amazing how an artillery barrage can change a man's mind."

I tried to tear away, but he shoved me against one of the filing cabinets I had been trying to empty. "You sneaking liar. You bloody coward. Do you honestly think you can now hide the murder of six million people?"

Kramer shouted from his phone, "I don't fear anyone, Russians, Americans, any of them. I did a job. I obeyed orders. I am a soldier."

"So am I," I said.

Kurt shoved me away. "You know, you may just manage to cheat the hangman with that kind of logic. But I hope to God you don't."

Kramer came to my defense. "Oh, who the hell are you to lecture us? You built roads and factories with slave labor, Jews included."

"Yes, you are right," Kurt said. "I watched, and knew, and said or did nothing. And when I did it was much too late. I prolonged the lives of a few, when I should have talked, fled, let people know."

I slumped into a chair. Where to? What next for me? All my despair, disgust and hatred was directed at my uncle. "I should have had you shot long ago," I said.

Now the artillery barrage is louder. The bursts are more frequent. Distantly I hear them, the Soviet bombers.

Alt-Aussee, Austria
May 1945

Here, in a hidden valley of Austria's Salzkammergut, many of us, in civilian clothing, are in hiding.

We try to avoid one another. Blobel is around, an embarrassment to all with his drunken blabbering. Eichmann has been seen at various places, but in the past few days has mysteriously vanished. Kaltenbrunner holds court at an old castle; he is convinced nothing will happen to us. Yet why do we hide like this?

A word about Kaltenbrunner. It is rumored that he has been desperately trying to contact the International Red Cross and prove that he acted humanely and decently to Jews. Indeed, that his main concern toward the end was to liberate the Jews of Theresienstadt.

And there are two even more astonishing stories making the rounds.

On April 19, in a farmhouse outside of Berlin, Himmler is alleged to have met with a certain Dr. Norbert Masur, a Swedish Jew and an official of the World Jewish Congress, Himmler himself requested the meeting, which was conducted in secrecy. Indeed, the Reichsführer had to excuse himself from Hitler's birthday party to keep the appointment. (This was eleven days before the Führer took his life.)

My understanding is that Himmler was polite, cordial and rational with this Dr. Masur. He explained that the camps were all like Theresienstadt—nice little communities run by the Jews. He and his dear friend Heydrich had wanted these camps to function as proper Jewish communities all along, but were sabotaged by the Jews themselves.

As Masur questioned him about death camps, gassings, ovens, and so on, the chief calmly explained that this was "horror propaganda," circulated by ungrateful Jews and the Russians. A burning American tank had caught fire at Buchenwald, some prisoners died, and the world press distributed photos claiming prisoners were burned by the guards. Lies, lies.

He also told Masur that the Jews were notorious spies and saboteurs and spreaders of disease, especially in Eastern Europe, and hence there was no choice but to lock them up in camps. How, Masur asked, could they commit espionage and sabotage if they were all in camps or walled-in ghettoes? Himmler did not concede the point; Jews were clever and resourceful and would find ways.

We've discussed this interview and find it hard to believe. Himmler has, of course, vanished. He, like us, is wandering, hiding, in civilian clothing. Evidently nothing came of his talk with Dr. Masur.

No less extraordinary is the report that Eichmann, before he wandered into Alt-Aussee and then wandered out again, invited one M. Dunand of the Red Cross to Prague, and at a rather formal dinner, backed him into a corner and explained that the Jews in Theresienstadt were better off than the poor Germans in Berlin and elsewhere.

One thing I am certain of. There will be no contrition on my part, no begging for mercy, no attempts to explain away our deeds.

I won't be a Heydrich, asking forgiveness on his deathbed; or a Himmler, currying favor with an important Jew; or an Eichmann, making excuses to the Red Cross.

Should I be captured, I will be as courageous as the Führer, and tell my captors that I am an honorable German officer, who obeyed orders, followed my conscience, and believed deeply in the acts I was ordered to commit—because I had nothing else to believe.

There's still hope for us. We will be able to make a logical case for Auschwitz. As a lawyer, I know that any action can be defended.

I admired Himmler far more when he spoke to us

at Posen, and said that true bravery was in seeing hundreds of thousands of dead, and not flinching, being true to ourselves. Now he babbles on about "Autonomous Jewish cities." A pity.

My thoughts often turn to Marta. She was, in a sense, the engine behind my career. When I faltered, she buoyed me up. When I had doubts, she dispelled them. We should have loved each other more. We have not slept together these last few years.

I'm drinking a great deal more than is good for me. I long, perhaps for just a day, to be with Marta and the children. Perhaps in a park, a visit to the zoo. They will say a great many terrible things about us. But they can never besmirch our basic decency, our love of family, homeland, the Führer.

[Here the Dorf diaries end.]

Rudi Weiss' Story

I have selected two letters, from among hundreds I received in the course of tracking down the fate of my family, to include in this narrative.

The first is from a man named Arthur Cassidy, a former captain in United States Army Intelligence, now an associate professor of Germanic languages at Fordham University, in New York City.

March 15, 1950
Department of Languages
Fordham University,
Bronx, N.Y.

Mr. Rudi Weiss
Kibbutz Agam
Israel

Dear Mr. Weiss:

First, let me say how much I admire your ingenuity in finding me. Although it was only five years

ago that I interviewed the late Major Erik Dorf,
the army has a way of losing track of these things,
especially after someone returns to civilian life.

Yes, I was the intelligence officer who conducted
the interview with him. Dorf was picked up for routine questioning in the town of Alt-Aussee, which
was a hideout for SS officers, much in the way that
Hot Springs, Arkansas, in our country is said to be
a "cooling off" place for Mafia criminals.

I did not participate in his arrest, but I understand he had no identification on him, was in civilian clothing, and at first denied any complicity
in the death camps, or the SS. What trapped him
were the pages of a diary, sewn into his jacket lining.
He later admitted that the bulk of this diary,
kept over a long period of years, was in a metal
box in Berlin, in his apartment.

This was not an unusual circumstance among
these men. Frank, the governor of Poland, kept
thirty-eight volumes of detailed notes on his activities, tried to hide them, and wept like a child when
he learned they had been discovered.

Dorf was a man in his early thirties, slender, well
built, nice-looking. He did seem a bit haggard and
nervous at first, but as soon as he discovered I was
fluent in German, he relaxed, smiled and was altogether charming and approachable. Hardly one's notion of a man involved in mass murder.

He was one of scores of war criminals I interviewed, and I of course kept records of these conver-
sations. They probably exist in some file somewhere,
and had Dorf ever come to trial you probably would
be able to track down my interview. But I will do
my best to reconstruct the trend of our conversation.

We had a file on Major Erik Dorf, and his name
was on numerous letters and memoranda concerning
the Jews, especially when he was an aide to Reinhard Heydrich. So we knew he was no mere by-
stander.

Dorf kept insisting to me that he was nothing

more than a glorified clerk, or courier. He claimed he
knew nothing of any so-called atrocities and mass killings, but that, of course, as a fellow officer I would
understand that spies and saboteurs and criminals
were often put to death.

I then confronted him with several dozen photographs of the death camps, and asked him to tell
me about them. You have seen these photos, I am
certain, and you know what they look like—bodies
stacked like cordwood, the mountains of ashes, the
naked people lined up outside the chambers, the mass
hangings. He professed no "direct" knowledge of
them. He kept insisting that the dead were probably
guerrillas, bandits, people who were marked for
death by reason of their activities, not their racial ori-
gin.

Dorf said—several times, I recall—that he bore
no personal malice against Jews, and in fact had
once patronized a Jewish physician in Berlin, and had
rather admired the man.

I then asked him if he was aware that when
the last Sonderkommandos began cleaning up
Auschwitz, they discovered that one of the open
burning pits was coated with *eighteen inches of human fat*. He shook his head. All sorts of queer stories
come up, he seemed to be saying.

His manner remained affable, cordial, that of
an educated man— he stressed to me that he had a
law degree—and he kept insisting he merely trans-
mitted orders and that "others" made policy regarding the Jews and other minorities.

Finally, while showing him photographs of a
group of dead Jewish children, evidently shot by
the Einsatzgruppen and piled into a mass grave, I
informed him we had testimony from twenty-four
people, Germans and non-Germans, who had seen
him present and acting in an official capacity at the
gas chambers, at the ovens, at mass shootings. One
witness even claimed to have seen Dorf himself kill a
Jewish woman in the Ukraine, after being chal-
lenged by Colonel Paul Blobel. (I should say the

late Blobel, since he was executed some years ago.)

At this point Dorf's cool manner seemed to leave him. He started a lengthy explanation about how the Jews had to be destroyed since they were Christendom's old enemies, the agents of Bolshevism, Europe's deadliest enemies, a virus, and so on.

"The children, Major," I said. "Why did you murder the children?"

He replied that regrettable as it may have been, if the children had been allowed to live, they would have formed the nucleus for a new attack on Germany. The Führer had explained it all. (If you are familiar with some of the testimony at Nuremberg, you'll recall that Otto Ohlendorf, also a charming, intelligent, educated fellow, freely admitted that he ordered the annihilation of ninety thousand Jews in the Crimea and used the same reasoning.)

I informed Major Dorf that if I had my way I would gladly put a bullet in his head that moment, giving him as much chance as he gave the Jews. He turned white. But I quickly added that we were a democracy and did not do things in that manner. However, his confession and any information he could give us about his labors for the SS and the RSHA would be useful, and might serve him well when he came to trial, which I saw as inevitable.

I gave him another batch of photos to look over, and also some copies of his correspondence with people like Rudolf Hoess, Artur Nebe, Josef Kramer and other functionaries of the final solution. Then I made the mistake of going to the door and calling for a stenographer. (I had been making brief notes up to now, but I wanted a full transcript.)

Somehow, even though he had been searched, Dorf had managed to hide—or had had sneaked to him—a cyanide capsule. He bit it, the instant I reached the door. He was dead by the time his body hit the floor. Like so many of his kind, he preferred this way out to facing up to the monstrous crimes he had committed. And yet—what a damned charming young man he was!

I am truly sorry about the fate of your family. If I can help you in any other way in your research, let me know.

Cordially,
Arthur Cassidy

A second letter bears on this story of my family, and I present it here. It is from Kurt Dorf, the uncle of Major Erik Dorf. I had less trouble finding him. He was a witness for the prosecution at Nuremberg. His name is memorialized in the Yad Vashem, as one of Europe's "Righteous Christians."

Bremen, Germany
July 10, 1950

My Dear Mr. Weiss:

Your informants are correct. I am the uncle of the late Major Erik Dorf of Berlin. I don't know what I can add to your search for the fate of your late family. To say I am sorry, that I offer my condolences would be senseless. How does one apologize for a crime unprecedented?

You know of my testimony at Nuremberg. I have been vilified and condemned for it, and my work as a professional engineer curtailed. It is my hope to emigrate to the United States within the next six months. Some Jewish friends are arranging it.

Erik Dorf committed suicide on May 16, 1945, during an interrogation by U.S. Army intelligence. This was precisely a week before his chief, Himmler, committed suicide, in the identical manner, after being arrested by British authorities in Lüneburg.

On learning of my nephew's death, on my next trip to Berlin, I called on his widow and children. Frau Dorf showed me an unsigned letter from "a comrade" saying that Erik Dorf had died a hero's death in defense of the Reich. I could not let the matter stand, and I told them the truth—that Erik Dorf was a criminal, a mass murderer, a participant in the most appalling crime in human history. I regret to say that neither Marta Dorf nor her children accepted this, and I was told to leave—indeed, called a "traitor" by Peter Dorf, the Major's fifteen-year-old son.

As for your father, I did know him at Auschwitz. He and a man named Lowy were members of my road-building team. You have read my testimony and you know that I made repeated efforts to save Jews from the gassings by selecting certain men and more or less sequestering them from the SS. I regret that I could not protect your father longer than I did. I suspect my nephew, with whom I had been at odds for some time, had something to do with his consignment to the chambers.

Your father appeared to me a man of great kindness and dignity and I am numb with shame and guilt that I was part of the nation that destroyed such people. That is why I have chosen to speak out and be heard. For what little consolation it is, he went to his death with courage and even, as I recall, a touch of humor. In my hazed mind, I seem to recall him joking the prisoner named Lowy as they were marched off.

No, I did not know your mother or your brother. They both seem to have been wonderful people, and again I am left with that dread, drained, defeated feeling as I look back on the destruction we visited on so many people in those nightmare years.

In my own defense—weak as it is—I still had four hundred Jews working for me, saved from the chambers, at the time Auschwitz was liberated.

Please feel free to write to me again if I can be of help. That I am numbered among the "Righteous Christians" of Europe is an honor I am not certain I merit. But I accept it humbly. Perhaps someday we will meet in Israel.

Most truly yours,
Kurt Dorf

On May 11, 1945, I rode into Theresienstadt with a Czech brigade. Many of the soldiers were Jews. There was even a man from Helena's street in Prague, who had known her, and known her parents. He told me they were long dead; he didn't know the details. In turn, I told him very little about Helena. Yes, we had been married. My silence told him something about me—an odd duck, this Berliner, ex-partisan.

I still did not cry. I tried not to think of her. I had loved her too much, too intensely. In danger all the time, we had clung to one another. We had lived several lifetimes in our years together. Now she was gone. I was isolated, cold. I had trouble listening to people talk. They wore me out with their stories. There had been too much suffering, too much misery. I found that I wanted to sit alone, lapse into silences, make no attachments.

On my way back to Czechoslovakia, I wandered through Auschwitz and learned from some survivors that both my parents and my brother had died there. Of course there was no trace of them.

Later, at a camp called Gross-Rosen, I ran into this man Hirsch Weinberg, the tailor who had known Karl in Buchenwald and had seen him again when he was dying in Auschwitz. Weinberg told me about the last picture Karl ever drew. That strange, crude thing— the hand reaching out of a swamp. Weinberg told me he also had reason to believe that my sister-in-law Inga was still in the camp.

I came into Theresienstadt on a sunny spring morning. It was amazing. The town had just been liberated, Jews were still dying of hunger and disease—and the original Czech inhabitants who had been expelled by the Nazis to create the camp were moving back in, as if nothing at all had happened.

The Red Cross was there, taking care of the ill, feeding people.

And so was an organization called the Jewish Agency for Palestine, which had set up an office and appeared to be registering former prisoners. I walked down the street—it was an attractive place, despite the hideous things done to people there—and wondered if I would find Inga.

In my mind I kept keeping a list of the dead. I tried to blot it out, but the names and circumstances kept recurring, and soon I was feeling guilty that I had been lucky enough, tough enough, cunning enough, to be alive, when all of my family had been lost.

My grandparents, the Palitzes, suicides in Berlin . . .

My parents, gassed in Auschwitz . . .

My sister Anna, killed, God knows where, and for unknown reasons . . .

My brother Karl, dead of starvation in Auschwitz . . .

My Uncle Moses, shot to death in the Warsaw ghetto . . .

It was hard to believe that I was now twenty-seven years old, and that I had spent the last six years of my life as a wanderer. And I wondered why I had come there. Even more, where I would go.

In a muddy field outside the building marked with the Jewish Agency sign, some young boys were kicking a soccer ball. I glanced at them. I thought of the hundreds of games I'd played in, and the professional career people said I'd have, and the day they kicked me off the semi-pro team. It seemed to be another life I'd lived. On another planet, centuries before.

A stocky man in a khaki uniform came out of the Jewish Agency building and stared at me a moment. He was talking to another man, smaller, older. Were they looking at me?

I moved on. I saw the fake shops, the false bank, all the trappings of a city, with which the Nazis had foisted upon the world the notion that the Jews were living in a community of their own. This, while twelve thousand a day were gassed at Auschwitz alone, not to mention Treblinka, Chelmno, Sobibor.

But at some time one must close one's mind, or at least redirect it. But how? Where did I belong? Who wanted me?

I saw Inga.

She was carrying a small boy, perhaps ten months old. He wore a coat two sizes too big for him. He was a pink little boy with Karl's somber eyes.

"Rudi," she said. "I hoped you would come."

We kissed each other.

"And kiss your nephew," she said. "He is Karl's son. I have named him Josef, for your father. People say he looks like Karl."

I kissed the baby's cheek. He smelled of sour milk, like most babies. "He looks more like Churchill," I said.

"Oh, you are the same Rudi," she said, smiling. "Come, sit down and talk to me."

But what could we say? She knew of Karl's death, of my parents' death, of Uncle Moses in the Warsaw ghetto. And she told me the truth about Anna. She had learned about Hadamar and the "mercy killings," and she blamed herself for taking Anna there at the advice of the doctor.

"I remember the day you left Berlin," she said. "Alone, you against the world."

"I was lucky."

The baby whimpered. I tickled his cheek. "Smile, Churchill. I'm your uncle."

She told me about Karl and the artists, how the Germans tortured him, how he refused to tell them about the hidden paintings, or inform on the other artists. He was courageous to the end.

"And they'll get away with it," I said. "Because no one will believe a crime that big. People will say, 'Impossible, they could not kill that many, torture that many, be so cruel.' People will say that there are limits, that human beings stop at some point. But they didn't stop."

Inga said, "You can hate me if you wish. I am one of them."

"No. I don't hate you. I'm a blank, empty. No hate, no love, no hopes. I'll just keep going. Like one of the Mussulmen, the walking dead in the camps."

"No, Rudi. Not you. Never."

I told her about Helena, and how much we had loved each other. God knows what they did with her body. I would not go back to look for it. Probably buried in some pit, burned by the Germans.

"But you had each other for a while," Inga said, "and you loved each other."

"Yes. I know." I sighed, stared at her. "Where are you going?"

"Back to Germany. But I won't stay. I won't raise Karl's son there. Perhaps America. And you?"

"I don't know. I'll wander."

"Alone? With no money?"

"I got by for a long time."

She asked me to come to the studio, where Karl had worked, where he had done the secret pictures that had so enraged the Germans, and that had led to his death.

We got up. There was a lot of activity in the camp —outdoor kitchens, first-aid units, people moving belongings on carts, Czech army people, the few Jews who were left, the Czech Christians moving in.

We walked the cobbled streets. I pinched my nephew's cheek.

In the studio, I met Maria Kalova, who had worked in the studio with Karl.

She and Inga spread dozens of drawings and sketches on the tables. Karl and other men had created them. They were the truthful story of the horrors of the camp—hangings, beatings, starvation, degradation. They were the artists' answer to the Nazis.

"Your brother was a talented man, and a good one," Maria Kalova said. "All of the paintings will go to a museum in Prague, so the world can see them."

"They killed him for these?" I asked.

Inga began to cry. "Rudi, if you could have seen him, with his hands smashed, those beautiful hands . . ."

And of course there was his last picture. The hand rising from the swamp, reaching for the sky.

I looked at the drawings, and I saw Karl and myself, as kids, playing in the street in front of Groningstrasse. Sometimes we played cowboys and Red Indians. Karl always hated to make believe he was firing a gun.

But I could not cry. I only said stupidly, "Poor Karl. Skinny, afraid. But he wasn't afraid of them. Braver than I was. I had a gun most of the time."

And then I had a flashing mental image of my father in his white coat, the stethoscope in his pocket. His kind, tired face at the window. He is rapping to us, signaling to us to come in for dinner. It is early fall in Berlin. Leaves are falling. Karl and I wrestle each other playfully, race for the steps to the house. I always win.

I looked at the baby, wondering what kind of life he would have. Within me, old memories stirred. A loving mother. A kind father. Brother, sister—a family who shared things, laughed, got angry, found beauty in music, joy in sport, all of us quietly admiring our harassed father, that physician always with his thoughts on an ill person, a patient lost. And all of us a bit fearful of our mother, so dignified, lovely, intelligent.

All destroyed. Burned, the ashes scattered to the winds. And how many millions of other families they had destroyed, without a sign of pity, without reason, in a monstrous outburst of murder and hate that I still did not understand. I saw it coming. I saw the irrational hate in their eyes early, and I ran. But I still cannot comprehend what motivated them.

"He looks like good boy," I said. And choked back the first emotion I had felt in months.

"He is, Rudi."

Inga was weeping, holding my hand. "God blessed me letting me be part of your family. I am filled with guilt and shame that I am still alive. I have no right to be."

I shook my head. "Maybe we loved each other too much. Maybe that's what ruined us."

"No, Rudi. You must never believe that, or even say it."

I said goodbye to Maria Kalova. Inga, holding her son, walked with me to the square. "Where will you go?" she asked.

"I have no idea. I'm nobody. No family, no country, no papers."

"Come to Berlin with me and little Josef. Until you decide."

"No. I'll never go back there."

She kissed me. "Goodbye, little brother."

The coldness was still in me. I barely felt her kiss. "Goodbye, Inga," I said. And I pointed to my nephew. "Teach him not to be afraid."

And I walked away. There were some friends I'd made in the Czech brigade I wanted to talk to. Men who had known Helena's family; maybe they had some advice.

Once-more I passed the field where the boys were kicking the soccer ball. They were strange-looking kids, very dark, shaved heads, skinny. Their clothes were ragged. Yet a few of them knew how to play well, move the ball, head it.

I stopped to watch. As I did, the stocky man I had seen earlier came out of the doorway. He was smoking a cigar.

"Some of those kids aren't bad," I said to him. "Who are they?"

"Greek Jews. Their families were massacred in Salonika. A parting gift from the Germans."

A look of anger, the old desire to *kill* someone in revenge, must have changed my expression. All I could think of was—where are the bastards who killed their parents? Why are they not shot? Why does the world let them get away with this?

"You're Rudi Weiss," the man said.

"How do you know?"

"There are no secrets in a liberated camp. Not among the Jews, anyway." He extended a strong hand. "My name's Levin. I'm with the Jewish Agency for Palestine. I'm an American."

"So?"

"I know a few things about you."

"Like what?"

"Oh, you were a partisan for a long time. They say you broke out of Sobibor."

"What else do you know?"

"Forgive me, Weiss. Your parents and your brother

died in Auschwitz. Your wife was killed in the Ukraine."

"You know a lot."

I was vaguely annoyed with Levin. I wanted to be left alone, to make my own way, to bury the past. I started to walk away.

"Hold it, Weiss," Levin said.

"What for?"

"You want a job?"

I smiled. "If you know so much about me, you must know I never finished high school."

"For this job I think you're qualified."

He took my arm and led me closer to the wet field, around which the Greek children were kicking the ball.

"See those kids?" Levin asked. "They need a shepherd."

"Shepherd?"

"Someone to sneak them into Palestine. There are forty of them—no parents. Someone's got to take them. You interested?"

"I don't speak Greek. Or Hebrew. I'm not sure I'm much of a Jew."

Levin smiled. "You'll do."

I remembered Helena with her dreams of Zion, the warm sea, the farms in the hills and the desert.

"It won't be as dangerous as the partisans, Weiss, but it won't be a Purim party either. No guns, but plenty of action. How about it?"

I thought no more, and responded, "Why not?"

Then I dropped my knapsack and ran to the soccer field.

"We'll get you a passport," Levin called.

Two kids had collided, and one went down. He got up swinging. I separated them. "You want to play soccer, stop fighting," I said. "Give me the ball."

I started babying the ball down the field, using all the old moves, nudging it between players, passing off, heading it, directing the attack.

They raced around me, laughing, shouting in a language I could not understand.

Someone had placed two empty oil drums at the

edge of the field to mark the goal. I nudged the ball to one side, feinted, and then kicked it through the space.

When I retrieved the ball and came back to the shaven-headed kids, they already knew my name. They clung to my legs, grabbed my hand, and one of them kissed me.

ABOUT THE AUTHOR

GERALD GREEN has published seventeen previous books, including *The Last Angry Man, The Lotus Eaters, To Brooklyn With Love* and *Tourist*. He has also written the teleplay for *Holocaust*.

Here are the Books that Explore the Jewish Heritage-Past and Present.

Fiction

☐ **Exodus** Leon Uris	11090	$2.25
☐ **The Heart Is Half A Prophet** Ruth Goldstein	10701	$1.95
☐ **Last of the Just** Andre Schwarz-Bart	10469	$1.95
☐ **Mila 18** Leon Uris	11937	$2.50
☐ **The Wall** John Hersey	2569	$2.25
☐ **Holocaust** Gerald Green	11877	$2.25

Non-Fiction

☐ **Questions & Answers About Arabs and Jews** Ira Hirschmann	11199	$1.95
☐ **A Bag of Marbles** Joseph Joffo	6407	$1.75
☐ **The New Bantam-Meggido Hebrew & English Dictionary** Levenston & Sivan	2094	$1.95
☐ **The Essential Talmud** A. Steinsaltz	10199	$2.95
☐ **A Kabbalah for the Modern World** Gonzalez-Wippler	6410	$1.95
☐ **Treasury of Jewish Quotations** Leo Rosten	10877	$2.95
☐ **The War Against The Jews** Dawidowicz	2504	$2.50
☐ **Battleground: Fact and Fantasy in Palestine** Samuel Katz	11778	$1.95

Buy them at your local bookstore or use this handy coupon for ordering: